"Funny . . . tender . . . Sandy's coming-of-age winds up being about more than just finding Mr. Right (beginning with the realization that there is no such creature). It's about accepting the sometimes monstrous flaws in the people we love, about forgiveness, and about what it means to move on."
—Karen Karbo, *The New York Times Book Review*

"A hilarious debut novel . . . It's a smarter, meatier *Bridget Jones's Diary* that you'll read in one sitting."
—*Glamour*

"*Me Times Three* is a guilty pleasure, like reading *People* magazine at the checkout counter of your grocery story. It oozes personality, juicy revelations, food lust, and bitchy wit."
—*The Gazette* (Montreal)

"*Me Times Three* is witty and wise, an irresistible dissection of love in the city."
—Joan Didion

"A funny and moving coming-of-age story that is an important recollection of a specific time in this city. It's a very real tale about trying to be somebody—about who you are, who you pretend to be, and who you really want to be. It doesn't matter how old you are, if you're single, it's the truth. I loved it."
—Sarah Jessica Parker

"Alex Witchel is a very smart and witting writer. *Me Times Three* is a fresh and insightful romantic novel with a great heart. Ms. Witchel, with her keen observation and irony, redefines the world of single career women in Manhattan and finds compassion, dignity, and great humor. This is a novel of elegant skill and comic depth."
—Wendy Wasserstein

"Smart, witty, and fast-paced."
—*Library Journal*

"Expertly mixing humor and tragedy, Witchel's debut novel is much more than its premise, and ends up being an absorbing, compelling read."
—*Booklist*

Me
Times Three

A   N   O   V   E   L

Alex Witchel

A Touchstone Book
Published by Simon & Schuster
NEW YORK LONDON TORONTO SYDNEY SINGAPORE

TOUCHSTONE
Rockefeller Center
1230 Avenue of the Americas
New York, NY 10020

First Touchstone trade paperback edition 2003
Published by arrangement with Alfred A. Knopf, a division of Random House, Inc.

TOUCHSTONE and colophon are registered trademarks of Simon & Schuster, Inc.

For information about special discounts for bulk purchases, please contact Simon & Schuster Special Sales: 1-800-456-6798 or business@simonandschuster.com

Designed by Virginia Tan
Manufactured in the United States of America

1 3 5 7 9 10 8 6 4 2

Library of Congress Cataloging-in-Publication Data is available.

ISBN 0-7432-4085-5

For John,
>whom I miss

For Frank,
>whom I cherish

Acknowledgments

First and foremost, I must thank my editor, Peter Gethers. Virtually every smart suggestion that ended up in these pages is his. He is, you should excuse the expression, a prince.

As for Knights in Shining Armor, I have three: John Breglio, whose constant and generous support is invaluable to me; John Montorio, formerly of the *New York Times*, whose patience and understanding were crucial in helping me finish the book; and Bob Bookman, the closest thing to a sorcerer I've seen in real life.

I thank Kathy Robbins and Rick Kot for shepherding me through the unglamorous parts; Benjamin Dreyer for his expert, painstaking care; Jon Fine for his humor and guidance; and Kathleen Fridella, Jeffrey Scales, and Abby Weintraub for making the insides and outsides of the book so much better.

I am also grateful to Barbara Denner, Cynthia LaBorde, Phoebe Kahanov, Suzanne Goodson, Ron Albrecht, Evelyn Witchel, and Sam and Barbara Witchel for all the help they are to me, always.

And as for my husband, Frank Rich, he is still the true gift of my life.

Me Times Three

Prologue

Looking back, I wonder about that day of the party at the Met. What article was I editing? What did I eat for lunch? I can't remember.

In the years since, I've tried to imagine what would have happened had I stayed home that night. Nothing, for a while. A few weeks, a month, maybe, before the inevitable occurred. It couldn't stay a secret forever.

But when I woke up that April morning in 1988, none of that mattered. I was twenty-six and my future was written in gold: I would marry Bucky Ross, my prom date, the love of my life. I wouldn't have a maid of honor like everyone else. I would have my own best man, Paul Romano, my closest friend. I would work at *Jolie!* magazine as an editor until I got pregnant and moved to a Tudor mansion in the suburbs, where I would write children's books in a studio over the garage and never miss a car pool. Bucky would grow more and more powerful at the agency. Paul would visit, and our kids would love him. He would take us to all the movies he produced, and when he won Oscars we would stay up late and cheer.

Actually, the day after Bucky proposed, I was so excited that I finally opened the green velvet book with gold leaf trim that he had given me to write my stories in. On the first fresh white page I wrote:

#1   A Classic Is Always in Style
by Sandra Berlin

The poor Prince! It felt as if he had been searching forever to find his bride. Where could she be? He had looked high and low in the Emerald City but couldn't find anyone who fit his glass slipper.

When he finally arrived at the very last house on the left along the Yellow Brick Road, he dutifully asked for the resident maiden, got down on his knee, and pulled out the slipper. But she, a veteran bookworm with incipient bunions, was too smart for such tricks.

"I don't wear glass," she sniffed, which surprised the Prince, who spent most of his time playing tennis and knew nothing about retail.

"But I thought this was the way to get a princess," he said, puzzled. "Isn't the glass slipper what everyone in the Emerald City talks about?"

"No, that's the ruby slippers," she corrected him.

He looked up at her, helpless. "Well, would you marry me if I brought some of those?" he asked.

She shook her head. "Ruby is out," she proclaimed. "What I would prefer are black peau de soie pumps. A classic is always in style. I will also require an unlimited clothing allowance for the premieres of Paul's movies, and, naturally, a car and driver."

"Certainly," the Prince promised, and he rushed back to the Royal Shoemaker, who made him the pumps, posthaste. The shoes fit like magic, so the Prince swept the maiden up onto his white horse while all the Munchkins waved and serenaded them. And the other fair maidens, who had cut off their toes to fit the glass slipper, glued them back on and raced out for some black peau de soie pumps of their own—even Dorothy, because she knew that if she went back to Kansas wearing red shoes, Auntie Em would kick her behind right out of the house.

"My darling," the Prince said to his bride, "I bless the day I found you. Everyone follows your advice and lives happily ever after. I will love you and your pumps forever."

And he did.

The End

So, it wasn't exactly original. Even though I wanted it to be true.

This is the story of what happened instead.

1

I knew nothing about art.

That wasn't a bad thing, necessarily, except that it was 1988 and art was a spoil of war for the Wall Street and Madison Avenue guys in Armani who made up the bulk of our eligible dates. Their staggering bonuses had already purchased new duplexes with marble bathrooms and climate-controlled wine closets, where they could properly store their requisite cases of Château Margaux. One guy I knew liked to make a ceremony of opening a prize bottle, then chugging it as his friends cheered him on. You could just imagine what he'd be like in bed.

More important than owning wine, however, was owning art, preferably a major piece by a hot SoHo star—though it would be useless, of course, unless it matched the custom-made couch. Those details were left up to the decorator—that's what the guys were paying her for, after all. She would buy all the right things and then tell her clients what they were, so they could tell everyone else at cocktail parties. It didn't take me long to realize that knowing nothing didn't look half bad when set upon a landscape of cash.

Besides a lack of cash, my immediate problem was that after two years of hard labor at *Jolie!* magazine—fetching coffee and telling the publisher that the senior editors were in meetings when they were really at the Plaza, in bed with the guys from ad sales—I had become the leading candidate for the position of Arts and Entertainment Editor.

These days it seems that *Jolie!* has been around forever, but it only began in 1986, *the* new thing, fresh from Paris. Apparently, pictures of models jumping in the air wearing five-dollar T-shirts and three-thousand-dollar organza skirts were just what the world had been waiting for, and *Jolie!*'s instant success sent editors at the other women's magazines into a competitive frenzy.

We were off base in one way, though, and that was the reason why someone who knew nothing about art was being considered for the position of Arts and Entertainment Editor. Unlike other fashion magazines, *Jolie!* had a policy that kept movie stars off the cover—we used models only. This was because Jean-Louis, our art director and aesthetic heir of Roman Polanski, decreed most female stars over twenty-one to be "old and ugly." Banned from cover consideration, none of the big names would come near us, which meant that the editor with the fancy title would spend many miserable hours on the phone each day listening to desperate publicists pitch star wannabes for a measly three paragraphs and a head shot.

To be fair, I hadn't really spent my entire time at *Jolie!* fetching coffee, though it often felt that way. During my second year I was promoted to assistant editor (on the same day that *Les Misérables* opened on Broadway, which I tried not to take personally). This new job meant that someone else scraped the curried chicken salad out of the seams of the conference table after the lunchtime story meetings while I started dealing with writers and "the words." This was a fearsome concept at a fashion magazine where the pictures ruled, so I learned fast that the fewer words there were the better everyone liked them, and when Susie Schein reviewed the results—most of the time, at least—she approved.

Me Times Three

The words at *Jolie!* were supervised by Susie, the number two editor and my boss. Just as I had worked all my life to please my parents and my teachers, I now worked to please Susie Schein—which was a little like trying to cuddle up to Mrs. Danvers in *Rebecca*. Unlike most of *Jolie!*'s staff, who seemed to view life as an endless Mardi Gras, dressing in everything from pastel Chanel suits to tiny black rubber dresses, Susie wore gray pants, a white buttoned-down shirt, and no makeup. Every day. Her contacts never fit properly, so she almost always squinted. And rarely smiled.

She was pushing fifty, I knew, and had been married once. I also knew that more than one person had seen her at clubs making out with Norma Wilder, an editor at a downtown art magazine. Susie never mentioned Norma Wilder, probably because she was a world-class denier about anything having to do with pleasure. Bagel, no butter. Chicken, no skin. Susie Schein was one grim broad.

It was she, for example, who instituted the policy of signing in and out each day. I tried explaining that the reason I was coming in past nine each morning was that I needed to stay until eight most nights, since Hollywood was three hours behind us and no one in the movie business returned calls until they got back from lunch, but Susie was unmoved. She herself worked twelve-hour days, though she seemed to occupy most of those hours filling her date book with appointments she almost always canceled.

Be it a cocktail or a comma, Susie had a problem with commitment. She would read a piece I had edited and remark distractedly, "Oh, yes, very good," and then two hours later, after canceling a lunch so that she could read the piece again (while eating only half of a hastily delivered portion of tuna packed in water, so that at five o'clock she could fall on the remains like a starved wolf), she would come back to me and say ruefully, "Well, you know, maybe this *could* use some work." By the time the writer and I had gone back through all of Susie's "maybe"s, we didn't even remember the original assignment.

Unfortunately, I had little skill at hiding my irritation every time she wavered. Since the first grade, when I got a "Needs Improvement" in the "Following Directions" category of my report card, this criticism had remained a sore point with me. I would try to be conscientious about doing my job correctly, and so would the writers, but the first round of Susie's directions bore no resemblance to the third round, or the fifth. Sometimes I would catch Susie looking at me during one of our editing sessions, studying whatever my face was saying as if she were trying to remind herself why she had hired me in the first place and considering whether I should be allowed to stay.

Then, as if to test me, she would mention some other writer whose work I should know, a genius among women everywhere whom I had invariably never heard of, an expert on rape in Haiti, say, which, of course, was exactly the kind of article you wanted to read in a fashion magazine. If Susie had been a man I could have turned my inexperience to my benefit, playing just dumb enough so that she could, for the sheer rush of hearing herself talk, explain why that writer was so important. But being a woman meant the opposite of sympathy. "If I've worked hard enough and long enough to know all this," she implied, "then you should too, and now." The only thing that kept me calm at those moments was knowing that the possibility of Susie making a lasting decision about my future at *Jolie!* (or about anything else) was not on the agenda in my natural lifetime.

I eventually grew accustomed to the fact that I seemed to truly bother her. If it wasn't my editing, it was my smoking, which she loathed. And if it wasn't my smoking, it was the way I dressed, in clear violation of her "few good pieces" philosophy, which was that even though her inevitable gray-and-white getup might resemble a prison matron's, it was made of the finest materials and cost a fortune. I, however, was of the "many not-so-good pieces" persuasion, so that I wouldn't die of boredom.

Despite her prevailing dismay at finding me on her staff, there were some occasions when Susie did seem to like me. Or, more to the point: After two years of trial and error, I had learned some tricks about dealing with her. Mainly concerning story ideas.

"A writer in Texas called to say that there's an old Hispanic woman there called Pastor Brico who runs a church out of a parking lot near her house," I announced one day, stepping into Susie's office.

She glanced up from her ink-smeared, indecipherable date book and squinted, waiting for the payoff.

"When she's not running the church, she's a psychic, and people line up for hours in the parking lot to see her. She also does readings by phone."

Susie snapped to attention. She was obsessed with psychics. She always had a call in to yet another one, desperately waiting for word that her life was about to begin. "She does? Is she expensive?"

"Well," I went on, glorying in the rare spotlight, "I understand that after a reading, she asks for a donation to her church, and most people send one because they're afraid she's going to put a hex on them otherwise."

"Do the piece," Susie ordered. "And get me her number."

A few hours later she summoned me to her office. She was so animated, there was even a hint of pink on her forehead.

"She told me she saw an arm," Susie said breathlessly. "My mother's been having trouble with her arm and needs an operation, and it's been on my mind. The pastor picked up on it immediately!"

"Wow, that's incredible," I said, though secretly I was disappointed. I had been hoping that Pastor Brico would encourage Susie with visions of a career change—shouldn't someone get down to Haiti and help that expert? But Susie was an immediate convert, and for at least a month I could do no wrong.

The two of us soldiered along in this delightful pas de deux until the day the one other hardworking assistant editor, who had been there as long as I had, quit after it was revealed that she'd been routinely vomiting her lunch in the ladies' room on the floor above ours. The women up there, less than enchanted, had asked her to stop, and when she tried the floor beneath ours, they had already been warned. The assistant editor was then reprimanded by the publisher, to which she replied, "Fuck this, I'm getting married anyway," and left with all the stocking samples she could carry. A bunch of the remaining staff, including two of the three assistant editors with whom I shared an office, gathered in the fashion closet to pick over those she'd left behind. The majority opinion was that she should not have said "Fuck this," because in a business like publishing you should never burn your bridges. What if the marriage didn't last? The stockings, everyone knew, mattered not at all.

A few days after the big blowup, Susie Schein called me in to say that Miss Belladonna, the editor in chief, wanted to have lunch with me. This was an especially big deal, and I knew that Susie must have engineered it, so I tried being extra-friendly and helpful, but she didn't seem to notice.

Miss Belladonna, whose first name was Giulia, although I never heard it said aloud, was the absolute opposite of Susie Schein. The first time I saw her, she was just in from Paris and wearing a hat that must have been four feet across. Her mouth was fire-engine red, her skin was as white as the orchids on her desk, and even though she wasn't as skinny (and certainly not as young) as the models, they seemed humbled, somehow, in her presence. She spoke her expert Italian and French in a throaty voice burnished by Bordeaux and Gitanes, and whenever any of the male executives from the business side barged into her office, she would cross her legs so that her stockings gleamed and they promptly forgot what it was they had come for.

Although Miss Belladonna's real job was to gallop the world with people like Valentino and Azzedine Alaia in Milan or Paris or down the Nile in the name of *Jolie!*, she always returned to New York to approve each issue, and it was usually just in the nick of time. As Susie reached the pinnacle of her holier-than-thou behavior, holding the sign-in sheet up to the light to see if anyone had faked her times, Miss Belladonna would appear, snapping her crimson-tipped fingers, and Susie would heel like some sad dog whose hiding place had just been discovered. Together they would go to face The Wall, as it was known, the surface on which the following month's issue was being laid out in preparation for closing. The bad news was that facing The Wall meant that some-one was going to have to make a decision. Which photographer's spread would be bumped, if not enough advertising pages had been sold? Which writer's masterpiece would be cut in half (again), to save space?

And even though Miss Belladonna acted as if she knew every-thing, she still didn't want to be the one to make Jean-Louis mad, or Evan, the British publisher, madder, so she would wheel around to Susie Schein and demand, "Well, *you* tell me why we should do this." Susie would get even paler, if such a thing were possible, and while she dithered six o'clock would arrive, and no one on the staff was even *allowed* to sign out. My office mates, Coco Church, Pascal Reich, Pimm Sanford, and I would stay until midnight while no decisions were made except to feed us elaborate platters of smoked turkey and grapes.

The four of us were jammed into an office the size of a large dressing room, though the window did look out onto Fifth Avenue. Pascal Reich was the only male on the staff—well, the only straight male on the staff except for Jean-Louis—and he had taken a job at *Jolie!* to subsidize his work on the Great American

Novel. After a childhood spent at Swiss boarding schools, his fluency in French, Italian, and German had gotten him hired, and he was the one who dealt with the European writers. His family's fortunes had appparently changed since his childhood, hence the searing inconvenience of having to get up every day and go to work, which seemed, for the most part, to consist of him hollering long-distance at odd hours.

Coco was one of those girls who had grown up in New York City, gone to private school, and seen it all. She was the kind of attractive that didn't appeal to other women but drew men like magnets—big brown eyes and perfect skin. Her blond permed hair was unkempt, and she was overweight, fashion-magazine standards aside. Still, she had a radiant smile and lots of energy and she was always sleeping with someone new or going somewhere fabulous for the weekend, dressing up in leather bikinis, happily spanking her dates. She also spoke perfect French and cooked with foie gras. Next to her I felt as if I'd spent my life in a convent.

Which is why I was grateful for Pimm. She was a city girl, too, but shy and plain, with Coke-bottle glasses and a bookish air. No one would ever guess she had grown up on Park Avenue. Her father was an investment banker, and her mother was a hippie-turned-photographer who always carried a camera, just in case anyone forgot. Pimm was a kind person who clucked sympathetically at any tale of woe, laying down her fact-checking materials so often to lend an ear that she invariably had to stay late just to catch up. But after too many nights of being ordered to stay there with her, Coco repeatedly called the guy who sold her Ecstasy and pleaded with him to wait before going out clubbing, and Pascal began a campaign to print up T-shirts that said: "*Jolie!* magazine. We never close."

Despite all of Miss Belladonna's waffling at The Wall and her rather forbidding elegance and laser-sharp eye for any style disaster (the fake leather bag I bought at Baker's Shoes for fifteen dollars comes to mind), I had always preferred her to Susie. She had a certain "Let's get on with it" quality I admired. Both she and I knew that *someone* had to deal with those Hollywood phone calls, so my strategy for our lunch meeting was to stress my areas of expertise; then, when she brought up art, I would just nod knowingly. Nodding knowingly is a vastly underrated means of communication, though one highly valued among magazine editors who are expected to know a lot about everything, which they don't. But they do know whom they can call to find out. Nodding knowingly buys time.

On the art front, the important thing was that I did know who the good writers were, since there were only a handful and I had filched their numbers from a senior editor's Rolodex one night after she went home. I could talk to them well enough, though "A picture is a picture is a picture" had been my motto since bolting Art History 101. How many fat and happy girls can you watch lolling on a hillside when you're not one of them? In my own defense, I should say that at least I've never been one of those people who stand in front of a virtually blank canvas and say, "Well, I could have done that, too." Mainly because it would never occur to me to leave anything empty. I've always been the kind of person who fills things up.

On that particular Thursday afternoon, the day before lunch with Miss Belladonna, I put in a few calls to those writers to ask some nonchalant questions about what they thought of certain exhibitions around town, so that the following day, after the Perrier was poured, I could oh-so-casually mention that the Whoever showing at the Wherever was absolutely Whatever, especially his use of color and the unexpected direction of the line. And I would wait for Miss Belladonna to nod knowingly at my staggering expertise, at which point my future, or at least my immediate future, would be secured.

. . .

Anyone might have wondered why I was devoting quite so much effort to getting this promotion—not only because my raise would be all of two thousand dollars, but because my engagement to Bucky and the Tudor mansion was shiny new.

John Buckingham Ross, known as Buck to the boys and Bucky to me, had been my prom date at Green Hills High and my boyfriend since we were seventeen. He was a football player, a baseball player, and, to top it off, a direct descendant of Betsy Ross. Of course, in his family, with its three sons and gangs of cousins who were also all boys, that meant lots of jokes about who was going to sew the buttons on their shirts. But the Rosses were very proud of their ancestor, and if she wasn't quite a Founding Father, a Founding Seamstress was close enough in my mind to qualify her—and Bucky—as American royalty.

I, on the other hand, came from a long line of Polish Jewish horse thieves who, once in America, took to reinventing themselves. Their original name was something with a "kowski" attached to it, but my paternal grandfather had a secret fantasy about being a German Jew, which, if you had to be a Jew at all, was the preferred brand. German Jews liked to affect a superiority to other Jews, which always seemed to me like lawyers considering themselves more beloved than dentists. As soon as he arrived, therefore, my "kowski" grandfather renamed himself Berlin, so that he could assure his new countrymen: "Yes, my family came from there." Of course, he couldn't say that to anyone who was from Berlin, because the Berlin Jews knew exactly who they were, and that my grandfather was not one of them.

His story seemed to change in its details every time he told it. Some days his hallucinations were so geographically vivid that our family even hailed from Alsace-Lorraine, *excusez-moi*. But the gist of it was usually about how the Kowskis, as I came to call them, sailed down (or was it up?) the river one day and found themselves in horse-thief territory that has since become Russia, or Belorussia—anywhere but Poland. Neither my brother, Jerry, nor I gave these genealogical fantasies a second thought until the day he found our father's passport in his top dresser drawer, and the birthplace really read "Poland." We were shocked; in one second, we had been transformed from supreme German beings with cunning French accents into the punch line of the "One Mexican guy, one American guy," jokes.

None of which really mattered to me, though, because I had found my own ancestral ladder to the top. Sandra Berlin would become Sandra Ross, and I would waste no time propagating little heirs to the American flag, maybe even some girls whose expert needlework would stun my new family. My genes were handy for this, at least on my mother's side, for my maternal grandmother had been a milliner. Although Mom sewed well too, she had neither the time nor the interest. She was a psychology professor, and when she wasn't teaching she was happiest in the lab, where the cages were filled with hungry little rodents who were conditioned to behave in all sorts of peculiar ways before pushing the levers that would reward them with pellets of food. Mom found her rodents so absorbing, in fact, that she often left our dinner waiting when she went to her office in the morning: a frozen block of string beans in a pot and a chicken on a timer in the oven. When we heard the beep, we were conditioned to begin eating whether she was home yet or not.

My father was also an academic, a history professor who was traditionally chattier about Trotsky than anything having to do with his family. Luckily, he also played the stock market with enough skill to keep us ensconced in the swanky New York City suburb of Green Hills, with its superior public schools, though in that particular financial food chain we were nearer the rodents than the royalty.

From time to time I did try to question my father about his

family's extremely confused nationality. On this subject, however, all of his historical outlines and time lines counted for nothing, and he never gave an answer that made any more sense than the original lie.

It was not the original lie, however, that concerned Bucky's family; the type of Jew I was or wasn't scarcely mattered to them. What mattered was that I was any type of Jew at all. When Bucky and I were dating in high school, his parents thought they could wait it out. "Oh, look, there's that Jewish girl cheering from the sidelines. No matter." Or: "Oh, well, he's taking that Jewish girl to the prom. No matter. They'll go to separate colleges and never see each other again."

To their unending dismay, I wound up going to Smith and Bucky to Amherst, so we saw each other all the time. When we went home for vacations, Mrs. Ross would make an elaborate show of looking up at her youngest son adoringly, wrapping her arms around his waist, and saying, in her most wheedling tone, "I'm still your best date, aren't I, Bucky?" Every Christmas Eve after Midnight Mass at the Presbyterian church, when he would leave to take me home, his mother would trill to him, always within my earshot, "Hurry home, dear, so you can kiss the Baby Jesus good night," referring to the not one but two crèches displayed under the not one but two Christmas trees in the Rosses' front hall and living room.

The Rosses had another chance to be heartened when we graduated from college and, from all indications, I appeared to lose my mind.

For years I had planned to go to law school, but the night before my boards I started to sob in my mother's bathroom. While she sat in her makeup chair and I lay on the floor, we talked for hours until I admitted to her that I didn't want to be a lawyer after all. I wasn't sure why, but it just didn't feel right. And I still didn't understand what "tortious" meant, even after looking it up three times.

Part of my hesitation came from the fact that, the previous summer, I had worked for Joseph Papp, the head of the New York Shakespeare Festival. Actually, that's an exaggeration: I did work at the Festival offices, pasting articles about the theater into scrapbooks and answering phones and watching the staff run in the opposite direction whenever Mr. Papp was angry, which seemed to be daily. A few of my co-workers, when they weren't hiding, were filled with advice to avoid law school (too dull) and recommended their own alma mater, the Yale School of Drama, instead. It had a program called Theater Administration, which trained producers and managers, and some of its graduates had even gone to Hollywood. Management, to hear them tell it, seemed little more than an opportunity to run other people's lives and get paid for it. What could be bad?

Actually, I had always wanted to be some sort of writer, but my father reminded me regularly that I would never be able to support myself as one. Years later, when I came home triumphant, having just been hired by *Jolie!*, he snorted dismissively at its fashion roots and instantly dubbed it a "pseudo-job." Hell hath no fury like a pseudo-German career academic at a community college.

Rather than brave the marketplace straight from Smith, I thought a master's degree in some kind of management, even if it was in the theater, couldn't hurt. And I would have three more years to figure out what to do next. Once I arrived in New Haven, though, it didn't take me long to realize that under the heading of "management" fell tasks like doing the actors' laundry. The Yale Repertory Theatre is a real, live professional playhouse with real, live professional actors, and students pay tuition for the privilege of servicing drama with a capital D. Whenever a T-shirt accidentally shrank or the jeans weren't quite dry, the actors would call Equity and complain and the students would get yelled at. We, in turn, would yell at the woman at the laundry to whom we had slipped a few bucks to supervise the spin cycle while we went out for coffee.

I remember when one of those actors asked Paul Romano to do his laundry. Or, more to the point, ordered him. Paul was my best friend, and he came from Los Angeles. He was drop-dead gorgeous and sported an impeccable tan whenever possible, carrying himself with the inimitable ease of a child of privilege. His shirts were crisp, yet open at the neck, pants pleated, but never creased. His smile was ready, his expression game. He could have wandered in from the drawing room of a Philip Barry play.

And here he was faced with this actor, a short, pockmarked creature who hadn't been hired in New York for at least five years, waving his dirty sheets around, threatening not to go on, right before curtain. Paul laughed in his face, and before the night was over the creature was on his knees in Paul's apartment giving what Paul later described as "only passable head."

Paul was the first openly gay man I had ever known. Having grown up in Green Hills, where I was assiduously trained to regard any male as a potential enemy on a stealth mission to get me pregnant and ruin my future, I appreciated the novelty of the situation. We met the first day of school, on line at the bank. He was dressed all in white, with a gold watch that sparkled, and we chatted while the line barely moved. When we were only two or three people away from the front, he threw up his hands, disgusted, and turned to go.

"But we're almost there," I protested.

"I hate waiting," he announced, even though he had already waited at least an hour. He stalked out as if he were starring in a movie with a grand exit scene and someone had just yelled "Action." When I ran into him again later that day, he seemed to have forgotten the entire incident. He was only delighted to see me and in immediate need of a hamburger. We were off.

"You know, you're very good at starting things," I would tell him later on. "But you never seem to finish them. You have no staying power. Maybe it's the rich-kid thing."

"Well, Sandra," he responded dryly, "you have *nothing* but staying power. You don't just finish things, you wrestle them to the ground." He smiled dazzlingly, to take off the edge. "We're a perfect team."

He was definitely a dish, if a touch pretty for my taste, and aside from my initial disappointment the first few times we had dinner together and he didn't kiss me good night, his sexuality was a nonissue for me. No one was better company. He danced like a dream, and would sit uncomplaining in the dress department of any major department store for hours (I would return the favor in the men's department, for even longer). He lit my cigarette with his monogrammed gold lighter and laughed at my jokes—most of them, anyway.

Paul was a whirlwind. He had to see every movie, every play, eat in every restaurant, drink every martini. On one of our first trips together into New York, we were strolling down Fifth Avenue when he took my elbow and guided me to the front door of Buccellati, the posh jeweler.

"What are you doing?" I asked, but all he said was "Come with me."

A middle-aged man in a dark suit appeared and almost succeeded in hiding his disdain for my denim skirt and Frye boots, left over way too long from college.

"We're looking for a bracelet," Paul announced grandly, and we sat in front of a table while Paul kept the salesman hopping up and down, bringing more and more samples and fumbling with the clasp on each one. I was too scared to laugh and finally just started to pretend that I was Paul's co-star in this particular movie. He was the good-looking playboy, flicking open his gold lighter and leaning back in his chair, puffing languidly on his cigarette. All he needed was an ascot. The salesman narrated the bracelets' respective pedigrees, and after I switched arms, he and I noticed my Timex simultaneously. To his credit, I was the only one who winced.

"How about this one?" Paul asked, lifting a gold-and-diamond scrolled chain from its blue silk pillow. "This would go perfectly with your earrings, darling," he said brightly. "Do try it on."

"Mmm, smashing," I murmured as the bracelet was looped around my wrist, but I could sense that while the salesman was willing to play along with the good-looking playboy, Miss Frye Boots was not allotted any dialogue. I took it off, quickly, myself.

After Paul loftily informed the salesman that we would think about it and he and I were back on the street, I tried to catch my breath. "What was that all about?" I yelled, half laughing, half shaking. "How could you just lie like that? Those bracelets were four thousand dollars *each*! You weren't going to buy one."

"So what?" He shrugged and walked on. "They have nothing to do in there most days anyway. Why shouldn't we have some fun?" He turned and looked at me. "It was fun trying them on, wasn't it?"

I stopped. "Well, yes, now that you mention it, I guess it was."

"You can't let people with money intimidate you, Sandra."

"I don't," I insisted. But he was right. I did.

Paul didn't. He grew up in Bel Air, the ritziest of the ritzy Los Angeles neighborhoods, and his grandfather had made a fortune importing Genoa salami, building an international company that Paul's father now ran. Before Paul came to Yale, he'd spent his spare time picking up extra money—and extra guys—as a model for Calvin Klein. He went to Hollywood parties with valet parking, and one night he met Diane Keaton poolside, where they laughingly compared their front teeth, and how they both overlapped slightly. Paul was like one of those guys in the liquor ads—money, looks, the world by the balls.

But he also had humor. And brains. And a huge heart. He cried as easily as my grandmother—at the opera, or seeing a man on a street corner without a coat. After I'd had a fight with Bucky once, early on at Yale, Paul called and I cried and told him I didn't want to go out that night. Minutes later he rang my bell, flowers in hand, and waited for me to get dressed so that we could go to a show at the Yale Cabaret.

"Why are you doing this?" I snuffled, pulling on my jacket halfheartedly.

"Because, Sandy, you can't lock yourself away over a fight that doesn't mean anything," he said sensibly. "We just got here. We haven't explored half of what there is to see. Come on now."

He bundled me into the elevator, and because it wasn't quite time yet for the show, we walked up and down Chapel Street, where the Rep was, window-shopping while Paul gave a running commentary on the podunk stores and their contents, comparing them to Fifth Avenue and making me laugh out loud.

Weeks later, near midnight on a Saturday after we had finished working a show, we walked out the theater's back door and found it snowing, the sky suffused with a dark lavender light. We held hands in the parking lot, our faces tipped upward. We stood there a long time, silent, just smiling at each other and watching.

But most of the time we bantered, characters in what became *our* movie, delighting ourselves with witty quips or shocking each other with bald comments. I informed him that I was sure I gave a better blowjob than the wimps I saw him with. "Oh yeah?" he challenged. We discussed techniques. That was the beauty of Paul, really. Anything went with him. The freedom! The lack of rules, of even a pretense of propriety!

"Do I look fat?" I asked him once, for the thousandth time, when we were finding seats at the movies.

"No," he said, quickly assessing my behind. Because if I had, he would have told me. Just then, a twig-thin girl walked by.

"But I'm not as thin as she is," I wailed.

He shook his head. "That is not attractive," he said instructively. "If a man wants a little boy, he should get a little boy. But if he wants a woman, he should get a woman."

While I was at Yale being schooled by my new best friend in the Romano Theory of Sex and Gender, Bucky, the love of my life, had begun working as a junior account executive at Klein Chapin & Woodruff, a huge advertising agency with offices all over the world. He had passed on the chance to work for his father at the small bank where Mr. Ross had spent his own career, and in return, Mr. Ross never could seem to remember the name of the firm Bucky had chosen instead. Though it was known on the street as "KCW," Mr. Ross referred to it only as "that CW operation." I found it interesting that it was Klein he seemed to consistently forget.

Almost immediately, Bucky started to look like an executive. His thick, white-blond hair thinned on top, extending his forehead in a Benjamin Franklin sort of way. But less hair only highlighted his sky-blue eyes, which, right on cue, sprouted crow's-feet. It seemed he had gone from boy to man in an instant. He still went to the gym every day, though, and kept up the bulging muscles in his arms and chest. I couldn't quite understand the point of it, since he was no longer playing team sports, but it seemed to be a link for him, as it did for so many men, to a time in life when anything was possible. At least that's what I decided it was. But I had no complaints. Anytime I rested my head against that massive chest, I knew the world could get no safer.

Right on cue, Bucky also took on men's behavior. He shook hands heartily and laughed at jokes at just the right moment. He and his friends would go out after work to lift weights together and have a beer, but when wine became the new thing, Bucky was lost. One night he was at a steak house with the guys from his office when his boss said, "Why don't you order the wine, Buck?" Instead of admitting that he didn't know anything about wine, Bucky clutched, as he called it, and ordered a Sauternes, a sweet dessert wine that cost a fortune. When he told me about it I felt terrible for him, naturally. How was he supposed to know? There we were, all of twenty-two years old, and while I was safely tucked away in the sticks, cramming Aeschylus, there he was, out and about with men who were old enough to be his father. Well, they all made terrible fun of him, so he enrolled in a wine course at Windows on the World where he learned to use words like "woody" and "plummy," and soon enough, he was collecting his own Château Margaux. I admired his effort.

When it came time for me to finally get my degree from Yale, we were twenty-four, and though Bucky was about to become an account executive, I found myself still at square one. I definitely wanted to work before I got married, but the three years in New Haven had not taught me what I wanted to do next. I was fifteen thousand dollars in debt, and the only thing I had learned was when to add the fabric softener. Sure, I could have gotten a job for twelve thousand dollars a year in a nonprofit theater filling out grant proposals, especially if I was willing to move somewhere like Hartford or Baltimore. Or I could have joined up with a Broadway producer and tried to convince little old ladies to part with their life savings so that a sitcom star could fulfill his dream of playing Shakespeare. Instead, I made the rounds of employment agencies in New York and took typing tests with all the high school dropouts who did much better than me, in spite of their outrageously long nails.

Eventually, I landed at *Jolie!* I had been an English major at Smith and was reasonably sure I could edit. I would apply the skills I had learned about the administration of actors to the administration of writers and coax them toward their deadlines, building their confidence when they were blocked. Paul was delighted by my decision. "A lady editor," he marveled. "We must buy you a hat."

Bucky was equally delighted, whisking me to dinner at Lutèce, where we drank Champagne and trotted out our high school French in anticipation of my new career. "This is a perfect plan for you until we have kids," he announced, glass in hand.

"Aren't you rushing things?" I asked playfully, but he put the glass down and stopped smiling and seemed to grow pale with responsibility. "I've given this a lot of thought, Sandra," he said solemnly. "We've always talked about our life together, and now that you have such a great job, what I want to do is not to rush things, or you, at all. I've had time in New York to establish myself and my career, and I think you deserve the same, without any pressure from me, because I never want you to look back and resent me. I think we should make a plan: that two years from now, on this exact date, we come back here and sit at this exact table, and at that point we take the next step forward. Together."

I was genuinely moved. Bucky not only loved me, he respected me. He wanted me to have the best opportunities to learn and grow on my own, as he had, even as we remained each other's strongest support. It was the best of both worlds.

Once I left Yale and began the new job, though, I found a glitch in my joy. I hated being separated from Paul. He had moved back to L.A. to work in the mailroom of the William Morris Agency, the first step on the agent/studio executive/producer path to glory. In a strange way, it was even harder for me to be away from him than it ever had been with Bucky. Almost all my time with Bucky was planned, whether it involved dinner, theater, or the movies. When we were together, he would talk about his job and I would talk about school, and after that the magazine, and we both listened intently before going back to doing what we did until we saw each other again—which for me, for three years, had meant spending all day, every day, with Paul. He was the life I lived while waiting for something better. After he left, I missed him all the time.

But Paul and I spoke almost daily as I got more and more enmeshed in the magazine and my routine of seeing Bucky, without fail, three times a week, unless he was in Minneapolis meeting with the brand manager on the account. We were as happy as it was possible to be, apart. Paul approved of my plan with Bucky and almost before I knew it, Bucky was reminding me that we had a date coming up at Lutèce that he had been looking forward to for two years now.

It turned out to be a magical night. We were both nervous, but Bucky ordered Champagne, and after a few minutes of trying to make small talk, he looked deep into my eyes as his filled with tears. He took my hands in his own sweaty ones and said, "Sandra Berlin, this is a moment I've thought about since we were seventeen years old. I love you more than anyone or anything in this life. Will you marry me?"

I managed to say yes as he hugged me, crushingly hard, and the people at the tables around us all applauded and the owner brought more Champagne, on the house. Bucky and I wiped our eyes and toasted each other and decided, since this was already our luckiest date, to have the wedding exactly one year later.

On that particular Thursday afternoon, however, about three weeks after our engagement dinner, I was waiting for Bucky to call with the details of a cocktail party at the Metropolitan Museum of Art, a preview of a Rodin exhibition sponsored by one of KCW's clients. That was the big thing then, having enough money and clout to throw parties at the Met. Gossip columns were filled with stories of wildly extravagant socialites buying fifty thousand roses to decorate the museum's vast spaces, and I could hardly wait to see what it would look like.

I was especially looking forward to seeing Bucky, who had been extremely busy with work and whose friends we hadn't seen since before our engagement; he had left almost immediately for a sailing trip to St. Vincent and the Grenadines. I had declined to go with him: I was afraid of sailing, of not being able to control the boat in bad weather and having it tip over. I was actually afraid of anything I couldn't control, a trait Bucky liked to tease me about. "They named a street after you," he'd say. "One Way." I would laugh, and so would he, and then he'd kiss me.

I was so caught up in my reveries about Bucky that when the phone rang, I jumped. It was Laura Lattimore, finally calling back. Laura wrote about art for *The Village Voice*, and was an occasional *Jolie!* contributor. Even though I found most of her copy impenetrable, everyone else at the magazine would read it, nod, and murmur, "Yes, of course," and then we would print it virtually unchanged. I asked her opinion of a few painters, copied down her dense replies, and, after I hung up, edited them into something that sounded vaguely like English so I could look into Miss Belladonna's perfectly mascaraed eyes the next day and recite them with a straight face.

When the phone rang again and it was Bucky, I practically purred a "hello," I was so eager to see him.

"We can't go tonight," he said abruptly.

"Why not?" My heart felt pinched.

"I have to go to Minneapolis."

I looked at my watch; it was already three o'clock. "Right now?"

"Yeah, there's a big-deal dinner tonight, and the two senior guys on the account decided I should be there."

I sighed. Well, of course. Even though no one at KCW liked to admit it, carting out a direct descendant of Betsy Ross had its distinct dinnertime advantages.

"I'm disappointed," I admitted. "I was looking forward to seeing Ed." Ed was one of our friends, who worked on a different account at KCW.

"I'm sorry, Sandy," Bucky said briskly. "As soon as I'm back, we'll have dinner anyplace you want. You've been so patient these last few weeks, and I really miss you." He lowered his voice so that no one in his office would hear him and slipped into the baby talk we had perfected over the years. "You know I do, Sanny, don't you?" he asked.

"Of course I do," I cooed back. Pimm looked at me over the top of her glasses as if I were deranged. And then I heard one of the guys call out Bucky's name, so he told me he loved me, and I told him I loved him more, as I always did, and we laughed and hung up.

"Oh, well, my plans for tonight fell through," I said to Pimm. "Bucky had to go out of town at the last minute."

"Well, at least you're not married yet," she said. "Then you'd have to go anyway, to be a good wife. This way you can just go home and get into bed."

I nodded, though what she'd said made me think. Maybe I should go anyway, be a good fiancée. It would be fun to see all our friends who I knew would be so happy for us. And Bucky would be impressed to discover what a good sport I was, so readily fulfilling my future wifely duties.

Once that was settled, the afternoon seemed to really drag until I finally realized that it couldn't possibly be 4:20 every time I looked at my watch. My drugstore Timex had died! After all those years.

I headed toward the fashion closet to look for Mimi Dawson, the assistant in charge of accessories—jewelry, scarves, bags, belts—sent by manufacturers for use in fashion shoots, though the merchandise was borrowed so frequently that it spent more time on the employees than on any model.

I liked Mimi: She had no pretensions about fashion and wore leggings and T-shirts every day. She had a southern accent and kept her hair in two little pigtails. She was skinny and friendly and always in motion, giving new meaning to the phrase "bouncing off the walls." Mimi was also exceedingly generous with all of *Jolie!*'s borrowed possessions. When something disappeared, she pretended to look harder for it than anyone else, even though it was she who had lent it out.

I showed her my broken watch, and she flung open the safe and pulled out a drawer.

"Oh, Mimi, I don't need a Rolex, for heaven's sake," I said, laughing. "Don't you have anything simpler?"

She sorted through the pile. "How about a Cartier?" she asked brightly, handing over a tank watch on a black alligator strap.

"Are you kidding?"

"Why not, sugar?" she drawled. "You deserve it, don't you?"

I was dumbfounded. People in the South had a completely different rule book than upwardly mobile New York Jews with iffy stock portfolios. Who *deserved* a Cartier watch?

"The shoot they needed it for is over," Mimi went on, "and I have until Monday to return it. Just bring it back then."

I fastened it to my wrist. Wow. It was beautiful.

"I have lunch with Miss Belladonna tomorrow," I said, "so I'll return it in the morning. I don't want her to get the wrong idea and think she doesn't have to give me a raise."

Mimi smiled. "Okay, hon, you enjoy it now." And she slid the tray of watches back into the safe and sprinted to answer the phone all in one swift movement.

I went to the ladies' room and examined my outfit in the full-length mirror. I had loved the suit I was wearing from the minute I'd seen it at Bonwit Teller: a straight black skirt, a black lace camisole, and a tailored magenta jacket with black velvet buttons and a black velvet collar. It was the perfect sartorial accompaniment to Paul's gold lighter.

Funny, I thought, shifting a cuff back and forth to examine the watch: When I stopped to think about it, I realized that ever since I'd met Paul, I had been shopping to accommodate him. How could I not? His taste was impeccable, after all. The only attention Bucky paid to my clothes was when I was taking them off.

One change Paul had not approved of recently was my hair color, from plain brown to blond streaks. That had been Bucky's suggestion. "You'd look sexy," he insisted.

"I don't look sexy already?" I asked playfully, but then he laughed and so did I, because while he liked to get up and play tennis at six a.m. and I liked to read until three a.m. and sleep till noon, when we did overlap, our sex was sublime.

Paul had sniffed at the prospect of streaks, deeply uninterested as he was in any notion of sex and me in the same sentence. But I thought the blond hair went well with my hazel eyes, and even though I still hated my nose, no matter what angle I examined it from, I was reasonably at peace with my overall appearance — though after growing up with the specter of Twiggy, I was still convinced I was too fat no matter how much I weighed.

I checked my backside in the mirror. Not bad, actually. Bucky could be proud that I was his fiancée. And I couldn't wait to see the two-carat emerald-cut diamond engagement ring he had bought for me. It was being sized, he said. The way he described it, it sounded so lovely, elegant without being flashy. I liked that. It's how I imagined our life together would be. Elegant without being flashy.

I thought about fighting for a cab on Madison but decided against it, and called the magazine's car service instead. Why not? One assistant had even called a car to help her move apartments — on a Saturday. And no one said a word.

Once inside the museum, I was surprised to see how crowded it was. So many people — most of whom I did not recognize. I made my way slowly through the exhibition and seemed to be the only one stopping to look at the remarkable display.

"*The Gates of Hell* occupied Rodin for more than a decade," a sign read. "The work, a monumental portal covered with sculptural relief representing Dante's *Divine Comedy*, was commissioned by the French government in 1880 to be delivered by 1885. However, it was still unfinished at that time and, in fact, was never to be cast in bronze during the sculptor's lifetime."

I sighed out loud. I hated anything unfinished.

At the Temple of Dendur, I finally found Ed, who seemed startled to see me. "What are you doing here?" he asked, hugging me distractedly as he glanced around the room. "Isn't Bucky in Minneapolis?"

"Well, yes, but I thought it might be nice to come in his stead." I looked at him questioningly.

He colored. "I'm sorry, Sandy. It's just I'm supposed to be hosting this thing and I'm a little on edge." He squeezed my arm and left me with a couple I couldn't stand, Biff and Elaine. What were their last names? She was always weighted down with gold jewelry, and the last time we had had dinner, she crossed her legs and waved her foot back and forth just far enough so that I could see the $220 price tag on the sole of her new shoe. I had hoped that that was the reason I nearly fainted after the appetizer, but the reality was that I had been on one of those crash diets, and after a glass of wine, I decided it would be a good idea if I stepped outside the restaurant. We were at one of those snotty Italian places on the Upper East Side, and to the management's unending chagrin, I collapsed in the doorway.

"She got a bun in the oven?" Biff had asked Bucky, who just shook his head and tried to explain that I frequently did this, because I was always on a diet. It was true. It took work to stay a size 4, and I was prepared to keep up my end. Being at *Jolie!* didn't help matters: All day, every day, we were witness to a nonstop procession of six-foot skeletons with million-dollar contracts parading past us to see Jean-Louis.

After a halfhearted greeting, Elaine kept on talking while fingering her thick gold necklace. I pretended to listen and glanced around. A big Egyptian tomb dominated the room, and a few tables were set up as bars in front of the floor-to-ceiling windows. Not a rose in sight. The client must have blown all its dough on Rodin.

I plotted my departure. Was there no one else here I knew? Where were the other people on Bucky's account? They must all have gone to Minneapolis.

I did notice one girl who seemed to be moving against the general traffic toward the bars. She was tall, surfer-girl blond, and beautiful, and dressed mostly in black with a skirt short enough to show some impressive legs and a top low enough to show an even more impressive chest. Maybe someone had paid for her company, I thought as Elaine prattled on about reupholstering her couch. I kept nodding, though certainly not knowingly. Next to art, I knew nothing about decorating most.

"Do you want to escape and get some dinner?" I asked Ed when he returned with a couple of white wine spritzers that he set on a nearby table.

"No, I really have to stay," he said, rolling his eyes. "Clients."

"Too bad. Bucky and I would love to see you soon. Did you know we got engaged?"

"Yes, I did, as a matter of fact. Have I kissed you yet, you sweet thing?"

He put his arms around me and bent me backward. This apparently was too much for Elaine, who turned her attention to another woman who seemed to better appreciate the subtleties of damask.

Then Jeffrey appeared, a nice guy who was always glad to see me. We talked for a while, and across the room I saw JT, another of Bucky's friends, whom I must say I never liked. He was the kind of person who seemed incapable of making eye contact, speaking to my shoulder instead.

After Jeffrey moved on, I put my drink down and was getting ready to leave when I spotted the blonde again. She was too attractive to look so cheap, I noted absently, thinking of the piece for that month's issue I had been assigned to edit, "Posture and the Miniskirt." At least hers was good. She had probably been tall from a young age.

I raised my glance from her hemline and noticed that she was looking directly at me, as if she knew me.

Suddenly she was standing in front of me.

"Are you Sandy?" she asked. Her voice was friendly and somewhat familiar. Oh, of course! She must be one of the assistants who sometimes answered Bucky's phone. I wondered which one she was. Patty? Lucy? My eyes went again to her cleavage. Bunny?

"Yes," I said, smiling broadly. "I'm Sandy."

"You're engaged to Bucky Ross, aren't you." It was less a question than a statement of fact.

My smile grew even broader. It was a smile of pride at my new identity. I remember it being one of the most effortless smiles of my life. "Yes," I said. "I am."

I was aware then that I was standing in the middle of a circle that hadn't been there a moment before. I saw that Ed and JT and Jeffrey had come together, like a little blood clot, ruining the perfect line of the arc. Ed looked stricken, but JT raised his glass — in victory, it seemed — and laughed.

"So am I," she said.

2

The first time I ever saw Buck Ross, he was wearing a skirt and kissing another girl.

We were both in eighth grade—he at Green Hills Junior High, I at the Rolling Ridge School. He was playing Charlie Dalrymple in *Brigadoon* and sang "Come to Me, Bend to Me" in the most beautiful voice. Later in the play, when he got married, he grabbed Christy O'Connell, who had the kind of limp blond hair I would have killed for on a summer's day, and kissed her on the mouth while all the girls from Rolling Ridge went *Ooooooooh*, because none of us had ever kissed anyone before, much less onstage.

I was mesmerized. My friends and I had spent hours trying to figure out just which way our heads should move when the time would come to kiss a boy. To the right? To the left? Did our arms go up around his neck? Or down around his waist? We were certain that there was a right answer and a wrong answer to these questions and passed many afternoons practicing on the posts of my canopy bed. But Buck knew exactly what to do, and—his kilt aside—I was impressed.

Buck Ross, we all soon discovered, played baseball and the

guitar and had actually made out at a party with a girl named Bambi right in front of everyone. He was something, that guy.

The following fall, when Green Hills Junior High and Rolling Ridge sent all their eighth-grade graduates to the same local high school, Buck and I did not have classes together. We were both in the choir, though, and I noticed him every now and then, tall and skinny and pimply where he wasn't pale. I was much more interested in Doug Civecchio, who unfortunately was much more interested in Jane Streit, who was thin as a stick and had the same kind of hair as Christy O'Connell. Doug and Jane used to make out in the hallways and the cafeteria and the parking lot. If I had known then that years later, Jane Streit would be featured in a *New York Times* story about gay pride, I would have felt ever so much better.

High school anywhere can be a horror, but in Green Hills it had a horror all its own. Everything was about money—who had it, who didn't, and what kind was it. There was Jewish money, new and loud, and WASPy money, old and hidden. WASP families belonged to the riding club, their children joined the social-dancing class when they turned twelve, and the girls' wardrobes included short white gloves to wear to weddings. These families belonged to the Green Hills Golf Club, where Jews were not allowed, and their mothers presided at the Green Hills Women's Club, a grand old mansion with vast lawns where they gathered for afternoon lectures on the world's great gardens and a glass, or five, of sherry.

The WASP lifestyle was a complete mystery to me. Most of my friends were Jewish, and while some of them were rich and belonged to the fanciest Jewish country clubs, that particular life never enticed me. At lunches, we would order iced tea and sandwiches and the mother would write on a card with a little red pencil that entitled her to not pay the check. There were pools and tennis courts and golf courses, even martinis.

Me Times Three

But despite the attempted trappings, it never felt much different from being in temple—especially at dinner, when the fathers were there. Everyone nodded and waved at the other tables before commenting sotto voce on how poorly the son was doing at school or how the daughter's nose job wasn't good enough for the money they spent on it. Or how the other daughter clearly had an eating disorder—look at her, leaving the lamb chops on the plate—but with a mother like that, who could blame her?

In my mind, the WASPs had it better. No one said an unkind word, and everyone danced up a storm. They sipped cocktails and wore white tie (which they owned) and rode horses into the sunset.

Never underestimate the power of a good imagination.

With all my efforts to survive socially in school, I didn't think about Buck Ross again until the fall of junior year. He went through one of those metamorphoses possible only during a high school summer, then appeared covered with muscles and clear skin, and turned up—alone—at the drama-club productions on the weekends. He still played the guitar and he obviously liked the theater and now he was also suddenly a football hero, which didn't mean that he was even that good a player (he wasn't), but which *did* mean that every Friday he and the rest of the team could wear their jerseys to school, advertising their elite athletic status. The girls who were cheerleaders wore their outfits, too, and the uncoordinated rest of us sat in class staring at those silver-and-navy getups feeling the glare of adolescent inadequacy in all its blinding glory.

But Bucky was an athlete with an artist's sensibility—or at least that's what I decided he was. He kissed me one night at a party, which according to the rules at Green Hills meant that we were officially going out. I was his date at the football dinner. At George Lowell's New Year's Eve party, Bucky kissed me at midnight in front of everyone. But once the baseball season began—Bucky's true passion—he virtually disappeared. He said he would call, and didn't. He said he'd be at parties, and never showed up.

"How can you do this?" I wailed one day in the high school parking lot. (I was the one with the car at that point, so that I could do Mom's errands after school while she stayed in the lab with the rodents. The Rosses were building Bucky's character by making him work for a car even though they owned two Jaguar sedans.) "I thought we were going out," I said tearfully. "What happened?"

He considered the question carefully.

"You know the song 'The Wanderer'?" he said at last. "Just think of me like that. I'm not the kind of guy who wants to settle down."

So after a week of crying and sighing (when I wasn't eating an Entenmann's cake whole in the front seat of the car, listening to the radio in case they played a song that we had ever slow-danced to), I got over it. I went to camp that summer and fell madly in love with Bobby Levine, who played basketball and whose musical taste tended more to the Grateful Dead than to Dion. He was literally tall, dark, and handsome, and in truth, he was a much better kisser than Bucky.

Bobby Levine was from Brooklyn, but he hung out a lot in Manhattan, going to movies the very day they opened at Cinema 1 on the Upper East Side. He smoked pot and cigarettes and knew all the subway lines, which, coming from Green Hills, I found exotic. But the less great thing about Bobby was that he wanted us to eat together, sleep together, walk together, and breathe together. He wanted me to be with him all the time, a prospect that did not particularly appeal to me. I liked doing what I wanted, when I wanted. Bobby Levine couldn't do something as basic as sitting down to listen to an album unless I was sitting there next to him.

By Christmas of senior year, I had had enough true love. Bobby didn't know anyone I was talking about from my school, and I didn't know anyone he was talking about ever. The Green Hills football dinner had come and gone, and I started to feel as if I was missing out on the most important year of high school. What was I doing, running to the city every two minutes? People had even stopped inviting me to parties, figuring I wouldn't go.

About that time I heard that Bucky Ross, Green Hills High second-base star, had to have surgery on his shoulder. He had lifted too many weights bulking up for football and torn a rotator cuff, and now it seemed that all the colleges that had been scouting him might not offer scholarship money. Not that he needed it, but the Rosses never liked to spend money if they didn't absolutely have to. This much they had in common with my parents.

Bucky had his surgery over Christmas vacation, and I trooped through his parents' house to visit him along with everyone else. The Rosses lived in one of those Green Hills houses where the silver martini shaker and the ice bucket had pride of place on the mahogany bar smack in the middle of the overstuffed living room, and the sounds of a football game were eternally floating in from the den. Some flowered family china cachepots sat empty on the dining room table, and the heavy curtains kept the room dark. At the time I thought the house grand and landed, established in the way I wanted to be.

On one of those visits, after I'd made my way upstairs, past the den bookshelves filled with back issues of *National Geographic*, I found myself actually alone with Bucky and somehow I got close enough to him, propped up in bed, past the sling and the contraption holding it in place, to get another one of his kisses.

"You've been practicing," I said, having noted a marked improvement in his technique.

He laughed, then took my hand and slid it down his stomach into his underwear.

"I don't even want to know where you've been wandering since I saw you last," I said, fancying myself quite the sophisticate, forgetting I had ever even met someone named Bobby Levine. He grinned, while his mother fussed out in the hallway and the dogs thumped around her on the carpet. Suddenly the new movie at Cinema 1 didn't seem to matter. There was something so grounded and independent about these people. They had their own rules. They didn't need to know the newest and the latest in the city. They golfed and played tennis and gardened and swam and never thought the water in the pool was too cold. They ate dessert but never seemed to gain weight, and Bucky called women "ma'am" and held doors open for them. My brother, Jerry, would rather die than do that. In our house, we ate in the kitchen with the television on and bolted as soon as we could, while my father chewed, jaws clicking intently as he listened to the Dow's progress that day.

"I missed you, Sandra," Bucky said softly. He reached for my hand, which was back in my own lap by this time. "Is it true you've been seeing some guy from the city?"

I nodded.

"I know I pretty much disappeared the last time." He smiled tentatively. "But I'm ready now. I think you just scared me a little."

"What do you mean?" I asked.

"Well, with you, there's a whole world out there," he said slowly. "I mean, my parents don't really like going to the theater or to concerts, and they don't read books that much. I like that you do." He blushed. "When I'm with you, I feel like I can be smart, too."

"You know you're smart, Bucky." I shook my head. He was in good classes at school, and he got really good grades.

"Smart enough to know you mean a lot to me," he said, as solemnly as if he were trying to convince a college admissions officer to sign him up. "Could you possibly find it in your heart to forgive me?"

I knew I shouldn't, and I was still sort of hoping that I couldn't, but of course I did.

"I've thought about this so much," Bucky said on my next visit, a few days later. "I know how different we are. But I also know that I don't want to just be like everyone else—play sports, get good grades and the right job, and do everything my parents expect me to do. I want my life to really mean something. I want to learn things, be a better person. You fight for what you get, and I admire that. You study hard, and you do all the drama-club stuff, and you're such a good friend to so many of those jerky girls. You earn what you get. I want to fight, too." He leaned forward, struggling against his cast. "For you."

I stared. How was this happening? All these years of hard work—it was true—and someone had noticed? My parents never had. If a report card had four A's and a B, the only comment was "Why the B?" If any one of the girls I knew who were "popular" ever called or came by with their boyfriend problems or their parents' divorce problems, I dropped everything to listen. And not one of them seemed to remember it past the overblown goodbye hug after hours of spilling their guts on a weekend. By Monday morning, I always felt that I was back to square one. It never occurred to me to talk about problems of my own. I wasn't sure I even had any. I was too busy paying attention to everyone else.

But Bucky had noticed.

He appreciated me.

So I kept visiting. And staying longer. Mrs. Ross would answer the door, hands filled with crochet hook and yarn, apparently in the process of making her son's sling a silver-and-navy doily.

"How nice of you to come by!" she would say with her false cheer, as if I were there to fix the bathroom drain. She never bothered to remove the cigarette jammed into the side of her mouth. Somehow, its ashes miraculously missed her handiwork every time and fell instead on Copper, the Rosses' rambunctious Irish setter, who never listened to one well-bred command she was given. Next to her crocheting, Mrs. Ross's full-time project seemed to be keeping Copper from jumping on guests, a task at which she failed miserably. Beyond that, what she did with her days outside of rose season was anyone's guess.

When school began again and Bucky was no longer bedridden, I started receiving Hallmark cards with beaches and sunsets on the covers. His childish scrawl inside promised his love forever. He waited for me outside my classrooms. Well, in short order, I was smitten. This was the answer to my toiling emptiness, my window onto the secret life of Green Hills: Bucky. He was strong, aristocratic, and sure, and I was the perfect complement, I decided. I was smart, hardworking, and knew a lot about the culture he was interested in, as only the child of immigrants could—having grown up Sundays at museums, and most days at the public library, living in a house where the classical radio stations played continuous Mozart and Beethoven. Together he and I would live in a house with thick Persian rugs, crystal vases, and candlelight. Bucky would provide the bass notes of stability and continuity, while I would contribute the chirpy top notes of color and light.

That's when I first came up with the idea of writing children's books. I figured it would be a perfectly contained activity that didn't require commuting, and because the books would be for kids, how hard could they be? Bucky started buying me blank books, writing SANNY'S STORIES on the title pages.

Our life-planning sessions had taken root—intoxicated as we were by posing as grown-ups—and he asked me to the prom. In exchange, I asked him to my house for dinner. He had met my parents, of course, but this was serious now. This was the prom.

He came one evening in early June, looking impossibly handsome, wearing a white Lacoste shirt and khakis, his blue eyes bright against his tan. My mom had risen to the occasion, coming home for dinner on time and forgoing frozen vegetables for an elaborate salad she made herself.

"What are you planning to do this summer, Buck?" she asked genially.

"Well, I have a job as a busboy near our cottage on Nantucket," he said. "There's this restaurant in town, and the tips there are supposed to be great."

My father said nothing. While any discussion of tips would normally have perked him up almost as much as a mention of Stalin, what soured him was the word "cottage." He knew it was a Christian code word that the Vanderbilts and Whitneys, say, might use to refer to their sixty-room Newport mansions by the sea. While I had been to the Rosses' cottage and had assured Dad that it was nothing more than a small, ordinary house—albeit one with an ocean view—I knew that it was yet one more black mark in the Book of Bucky he had been compiling since the rise and fall of Bobby Levine.

As I was pondering my father's narrow-minded belief that any boyfriend I had could be commendable only if he was fluent in Lenin, I vigorously bit into a cherry tomato, which spurted all over Bucky's white shirt.

I watched the seeds arrange themselves around the grinning alligator at his heart while the textured cotton absorbed the juice as thirstily as any "after" picture in one of those paper-towel commercials. I thought I would fall down dead right there. Thank God Jerry was at boarding school, where he had been sent after earning extracurricular honors as the best botanist in the neighborhood, specializing in marijuana. If he had seen this, I would never have lived it down.

I looked at Bucky, aghast.

"It's okay, Sandy," he said easily. "Nothing that won't come out in the wash."

"I'm so sorry," I sputtered, looking desperately at my mother for help. Trying not to laugh, she brought over a wet dish towel and we both dabbed at Bucky's shirt. She made some reference to all his muscles, another topic that didn't sit well with my father. Not even German Jews were known for their muscles. I hurried the whole thing along as best I could until Bucky and I were finally outside and safely in his car.

"Oh, my God, I'm sorry," I repeated.

"I think your mother likes me," he said, taking my hand. "But I think your father hates me. Is it because I'm not Jewish?"

I nodded. "And because you have no idea what Goebbels was doing at four-twenty p.m. on August tenth, 1941."

He put his arms around me. "Was he kissing the prettiest girl in Green Hills?" he asked tenderly, and I started to bury my face in his neck but pulled back too late and cried, "My lipstick!" And we both surveyed the Cover Girl Passion Fruit on his white collar.

"The only thing left to do is go to Baskin-Robbins and get some cherry-vanilla," he said. "Then it will be complete." We did, and he purposely dropped some right near the tomato stain. I dropped some on my shirt, too. It was like being blood brothers, I thought. We were in it all, together.

The night of the prom, everything went perfectly. I floated down the stairs in an ivory gown and managed not to trip. Standing near the front door, Bucky watched me descend, and his mouth dropped open a little while my mother beamed. My father, reading the CA volume of the encyclopedia in the den, roused himself to see what all the fuss was about. Then our neighbor Mr. Schwarz came over, too, vodka in hand, and offered to take some pictures of us posed outside.

"She's got a nice set of knockers," he confided to Bucky, who blushed and nodded furtively in agreement.

Before the prom, we went for dinner with a group of friends to a fancy restaurant in nearby Greenwich, Connecticut, right on the water. During the second round of sloe gin fizzes, someone made a joke, and while Bucky was laughing he somehow put down his drink on the edge of his bread plate, from which it tipped, soaking the tablecloth and, I noted with horror, the hem of my dress as well. I shrieked.

"I'm sorry, Sandy," he said, stricken, rising from his chair. He had gone completely white. "I'm really, really—"

I never found out what he really, really was because I cut him off with a loud "Goddammit, I can't believe you!" and rushed to the ladies' room with a bottle of club soda and three friends. Scrubbing the stain out, I felt a little ashamed at how harsh I had been, especially since he had been so forgiving about the whole tomato incident. I was always impatient with him, I realized. Maybe it was the way Jerry and I had been brought up. There was no more dreaded question in our house than "How many times do I have to tell you?"—which implied that we children had been in receipt of some defective gene, a clear indication that we had arrived in the home of such smart parents purely by accident.

The lesson I had learned was clear: The worst thing you could do in life was make a mistake. Large or small, public or private, mistakes in our house were all created equal. So, while spilling a sloe gin fizz on a white tablecloth in a fancy restaurant may not have been murder, it was manslaughter at the very least.

The red spot, in fact, mostly came out. The other girls returned to the table, and as I put on more lipstick and started to relax, the door flew open and Bucky walked in.

"What are you doing?" I cried, searching to see if any legs were visible under the toilet-stall doors.

"You are not going to ruin this night because of a spill," he announced with an authority I wasn't used to. "You're always so worried about looking wrong or being wrong, and I'm not going to let this happen. You've got to start giving yourself more credit. You're so smart, but you always treat yourself like you're dumb and worthless. I know I'm not as smart as you, but I can tell you I'm smarter *about* you. You have no confidence about looks and all of that, and I'm telling you that even with the tiniest stain on the hem of your dress you are so much better-looking and just better in every way than any girl out there. Don't you see that?"

"Oh," I managed, leaning back against the counter.

At the prom, we never left the dance floor. As "Stairway to Heaven" came on, Bucky took me in his arms again.

"Do you know what I wished for last winter when I was recovering from my operation?" he asked.

"What?" I asked, pressing my cheek against his shoulder, good as new.

"That I would be here tonight, dancing with you," he said.

I pulled him close to me and looked out through a silvery wash onto the room, where everyone was my friend and looked particularly beautiful and I was certain that after we all went away to college we would still know one another forever.

When we left for the midnight breakfast, sitting in his car, Bucky gave me a bracelet—a graduation gift, he said—of gold links with tiger's-eye beads. I would die for him, I thought.

The breakfast, sponsored by the parents of the senior class, was held at the Green Hills municipal pool in a tent whose walls had been decorated with baby pictures of all the graduates. My mom was there and so was Bucky's; everyone ate scrambled eggs and jumped into the pool, some in bathing suits, some in their dresses and tuxes. Bucky and I left just before the second round of eggs came out. His neighbors were gone for the weekend and had given Bucky their keys so that he could walk their dog. Our secret plan all along had been to go there while his mother was still at the breakfast. (His father was at the cottage with Bucky's older brothers, back from college.)

We ran giggling though the dark upstairs hallway to an empty guest bedroom, where we had sex for the first time. After we'd got into the single bed and he was inside me, he pulled his head back, and in the half-light from the window I could see a child-like surprise on his face.

"It's warm!" he said, and I knew then that, for all his talk, this was the first time he had ever done this. (Not that I could say the same, thank you Bobby Levine.) The hour seemed to pass in one ecstatic minute until the alarm clock he'd brought went off, and after hurriedly putting our clothes back on, we returned to the pool, which was quiet by then, both our mothers having gone. Perfect timing! We lay on the grass, which smelled clean and good, quite pleased with ourselves, with our dangerous escapade undertaken while both our mommies were a few blocks away pouring juice and buttering toast. We fancied ourselves wild sexual adventurers. And we looked up at the stars, drunk with the certainty that every night of our lives would feel like this, protected and victorious, that we were bound together by a secret that made us more special than anyone we knew.

It was this cocoon we shared throughout our college years. We were free and independent; we were homebound and family-tied. Sometimes he was my family, sometimes my liberty; and I was his; we slid between the two points like mercury, all nestled within a world bounded by Green Hills, the campuses of Smith and Amherst, the coziness of the cottage and periodic jaunts to the theater and the Philharmonic in Manhattan. Wherever we went was home, with living rooms, dens, and bedrooms at our disposal, friends and friendly acquaintances, windows that overlooked only leafy trees and thick lawns. And to top it all off, sex with Bucky had quickly developed into one of the world's wonders, sometimes as often as four or five times a day, a pattern I was confident would continue well into our old age.

Granted, our lives weren't always idyllic. Bucky's father drank, and he could get nasty when he did. He once punched Bucky in the face for coming home too late. And when Mr. Ross's favorite Irish setter, Baxter, died, he locked himself in his bedroom and cried for two days. I think Bucky was more upset about that than about getting punched. At times like those, Bucky would leave his house to seek shelter at mine, where the conflicts were more subterranean, cloaked as they were in scientific or historical debate.

For the most part, though, we were pampered by the suburban peace that was all our parents' birthright, and so, by the laws of inheritance, it was our own. It didn't matter if the parents were descendants of American royalty or the spawn of horse thieves; they had all signed up for the promise of the electric can opener back in the 1950s, and through the fruits of their labors their children could ski in Vermont, sun in Puerto Rico, and see the doctor every fall for checkups that were always normal. Yes, there were rules to be followed and chores to be done, but as long as we were good children and did the right thing, we would all be safe.

When Bucky started work at Klein Chapin & Woodruff, he moved back to his parents' house in Green Hills until he received his first bonus, with which he bought an apartment nearby. The city was too dirty, too noisy and expensive, he said. It was a much better value to buy in Green Hills, he insisted, because you could get so much more space. And his place *was* huge—at least by New York City standards. He would take the train home from the office every day, and run on the track at Green Hills High with other guys from our class who had also found themselves so rudely thrust into the working world. They, too, had been lulled by their upbringings and shunned the city, finding a way to still go to school every day, the way they used to. They would slap one another's hands in greeting, swaddled by memories of athletic triumphs past. They ran with their heads thrown back, as if relieved to find the trees all in the same place they had left them just a few months earlier, before the mail started coming with bills and tax returns addressed to them instead of to their parents.

Mrs. Ross immediately set herself to work furnishing her son's apartment, which meant that matched sets of brown plaid couches began appearing, covered in all manner of crocheted doilies and knitted afghans. Once we were married, I knew, I would burn them all.

But after a year of living in Green Hills, Bucky started having second thoughts. I wasn't there, for one thing; at best I turned up for the occasional weekend. Plus, he often had to go out with his co-workers, and the idea of getting on a late train every night when they all stayed in the city was becoming more and more impractical. He brought some of them to his apartment once, and they were stunned by his refrigerator, bare but for a quart of milk. They dubbed the place the Bobby Sands Hilton, in honor of the Irish hunger striker.

So before I could even graduate and snuggle into Suburban Living, Part One, Bucky sold the apartment—at a tidy profit, as he had predicted—and moved to the Murray Hill section of Manhattan, to a brownstone where he could walk to his mid-town office. I liked the place, a duplex, and started making lists of things I would need to buy as a newlywed—a lasagna pan, for instance. I had never actually made lasagna, but I was sure I would soon.

#17   *The Tale of the Gravy Train*
by Sandra Berlin

Once upon a time there lived a Prince who was the apple of his mother's eye. Her husband, the King, had been thrown from his horse at the segregated riding club and killed, so the Queen raised the Prince herself. Because he was a sickly child, she took extra-special care of him, and made sure that he never left the castle.

But as the Prince grew to be a young man and the Queen's advisers wondered when he would finally ascend to the throne and become King, the Queen knew that she would have to improve her son's health. For starters, the Prince had a terrible appetite, eating almost nothing but cherry-vanilla ice cream. So the Queen sponsored a contest for all the maidens in the land: Every Sunday night she would open the doors to the castle, and whoever made the dish that enticed the Prince to eat and grow strong would become his new Princess.

A long line formed outside the palace door, of maidens wielding baked hams, scalloped potatoes, and steamship rounds of beef. The Prince sat in his chair, his lap covered by the brown afghan his mother had made him, and although he was exceedingly polite, he ate nothing at all.

Then one Sunday a maiden appeared with an aromatic lasagna, bubbling in its pan, and as she set it upon the table, the Queen rang furiously for her servant. "I said olives, not onions," she huffed, holding up her martini glass.

"But, Your Majesty, we are out of olives," the servant said.

"Nonsense," the Queen yelled. "Why must I do everything myself?"

As she stomped to the pantry to find the olives, the maiden smiled at the Prince and said, "You know, it's really hot in here. Why don't you lose the afghan?"

And before he could say a word, she had slipped it from his lap. Almost instantaneously, the Prince grew larger, great, and strong. He reached across the table and took a huge helping of lasagna.

"Why, this is the most delicious dish I have ever eaten!" he proclaimed.

"No kidding," the maiden said. "You should taste my kugel."

And at just that moment the Queen returned, and when

she heard what the maiden said and spied the cast-off afghan, she snatched it up and began to moan. "I'm melting, I'm melting," she wailed. Soon she lay upon the floor, a puddle of brown gravy, and the royal Irish setters gathered round and lapped her up.

The Prince promptly married the maiden and said, "Every Sunday from now on, we must have your lasagna for dinner, my dear."

"My darling, I love you," she said. "But in the castle where I grew up, we had Chinese on Sunday nights. And if you think lasagna is great, wait till you try shrimp with lobster sauce."

He loved it. And they lived happily ever after.

The End

3

While Bucky made the move to the city, another year passed at the drama school. I was having such a good time that my always vague plan to move to Murray Hill and commute somehow evaporated.

My good time, of course, was being had with Paul, who continued to instruct me in the art of seeing life as a perpetual first date—which he also seemed to have late every night, after safely depositing me back in my apartment. How many gay men can there be in New Haven?, I would ask, and he would just laugh. Hundreds, apparently.

But until the clock struck midnight, we were always together. Paul spent hours at my apartment, cooking dishes like fettuccine Alfredo and teaching me to throw a piece of pasta against the wall to see if it was ready—it was if it stuck. We drank wine and invited other people, who brought salad and dessert, and the party went from night to night. Except when it went to the city to take advantage of what seemed to be limitless opera and theater tickets Paul got through Dennis, an older guy he dated. Sometimes, when Dennis was out of town on business, I would accompany Paul.

Paul also managed to do what no man before or since has dared attempt: surprise me. For my birthday during our final year at Yale, Paul and a few friends took me to dinner at a place I loved called Leon's: an old-fashioned Italian restaurant where the bottom of my stomach invariably disappeared and I attempted to eat everything the kitchen made in one sitting. That night, Paul seemed incredibly jumpy. Laughing too often and chattering about things that made no sense, he seemed to be drunk.

He insisted we go back to his apartment for a nightcap, something we never did—he much preferred my place, since I seemed to go to the supermarket daily. And when I walked in the door, I truly thought I would die: Bucky was there, and all of my friends from school, even some friends from Green Hills. I thanked Paul profusely for the planning that had gone into it all, but he seemed more relieved than pleased—he even waited until it was over to go boy-hunting. I'm sure, though, looking back on it, that I didn't thank him enough. Then again, he wouldn't let me. Anytime I reached toward him with a warm emotion, he would jam right up.

"Romano, what is your problem?" I would say. "You cry at the opera, you cry at the theater, and if all I want to do is say thank you or something else equally deep, you go crazy." He would grimace, and I would invariably add, "This is about Marie."

Marie Romano was Paul's mother, and from what I could gather, she was not a woman given to spontaneous outbursts of emotion. She was, according to Paul, devout and regimented and had raised her only son to be a good Catholic boy, entrusting him and his education to the nuns, who worked overtime to keep him in line. She was counting the days until her prize child would marry his childhood sweetheart, Sally Pozzo. Sally's father was also incredibly rich, Paul explained, from patenting some gum base used in the mass production of ice cream. The Pozzos of Los Angeles were such a prominent Catholic family that the walls of their home were covered with photographs of them posing with the Pope. Paul had a copy of one that showed

Sally, attractive enough, with her black hair pulled into a severe bun, wearing a plain white suit. She looked like an executive nurse.

"Romano," I said during one of these tête-à-têtes about Marie, who, from her own pictures, looked as if she must have weighed at least three hundred pounds, "does your mother truly have no idea that you're out every night boffing boys until the sun comes up?"

Paul covered his face. "Don't even *mention* sex in the same sentence as Marie," he said. "She's a holy woman, my mother. She wears those white sandals with the toes cut out to church every Sunday when she prays for me. A lovely person. The best."

I reminded him of this exchange one morning—or, I should say, one afternoon—when he didn't appear for class. Though this happened occasionally (how could it not when he'd start bar-hopping at midnight and get home at six a.m.?), it was not the norm.

Around one o'clock, I'd gone to his apartment and rung the bell. No answer. I got scared then and started pounding on the door. Finally, I heard something inside, an awful noise between a groan and a roar.

"Open the door," I yelled in a panic. "Right this minute!"

It took more screaming and pounding before Paul finally did open the door, at which point he turned abruptly and fell face-down onto his bed.

"Romano, what is the matter with you?" I yelled, following him, trying to get him to sit back up. He clutched at his pillows and squealed into the mattress, imploring me to leave.

"Okay," I said, suddenly, in the calmest tone. "I'm just going to sit here and say nothing, and when you're ready, you can tell me what happened."

He was silent. And I sat, for almost ten minutes, while he seemed to be praying, with all his soul and all his might, that I would disappear. When he eventually realized that God wasn't listening, he turned the slightest bit toward me.

"What is wrong?" I was almost whispering.

"Bad night," he muttered.

"Do you need a doctor?" I asked.

He groaned. "No," he managed, before putting his face down again.

"Do you want me to leave?" I asked.

About ten seconds passed. "No," he said.

I was encouraged. "Okay," I said. "I'm going to stay here, and you can tell me what you want to do next."

He thought about that awhile, then turned over. There was a swelling bruise next to his mouth that was turning reddish purple.

"Will you let me put ice on it?" I asked, and though he shook his head no, I got up and filled a plastic bag full. I handed it to him, and he moaned when it touched his face. I went back into the kitchen and opened the refrigerator. Two bottles of vodka.

"Okay, here's the deal," I said, returning to the bedroom. "It's two o'clock, and I'm leaving now. At three I'll be back, and we're going to get some coffee and food and make sure everything on you works."

He glared.

"That means when I come back there's no banging on the door, or I go straight to your super. Okay?"

His eyes shone with hate, and with love.

"Okay," he said.

An hour later he was waiting for me on the street, cleaned up and dressed. We went to a crummy luncheonette, where he had coffee and toast, which I buttered for him. But after eating two pieces, he stopped.

"You don't have to tell me," I said, lifting my glass of ice water to his mouth.

He shrugged. "Too many drugs," he said. "And the guy took my money."

"Do you need to cancel your credit cards?" I asked, instantly efficient.

He half smiled. "He only took cash," he said. "My money clip."

We sat for a while without speaking. He started to look less gray, and even ate a third piece of toast. When he pulled out a cigarette and his gold lighter, I felt better.

"Well, at least he left the lighter," I said.

He nodded, seriously. "I was glad about that," he said. "It was my grandfather's. From Italy." The lighter was a deep shade of gold that looked foreign and aristocratic. I liked the sound it made when he closed it, a quick, resonating clunk.

I pulled out a cigarette too, and he lit it.

"Romano, let me ask you something," I said. "Does Sally know anything about this part of your life?"

He looked as if he might cry. "Well, no," he said. He waited a moment and added lamely, "You know, we're just friends, really."

I looked at him hard. "And you're telling me that your mother has no idea you're gay?"

He flinched. "No," he said. "And she never will. I'm going to marry Sally."

"Even though you're just friends?" I asked as the waitress arrived with the coffeepot to give us refills. He didn't answer, and I didn't push it.

He looked up from his coffee, wincing from the weight of the cup on his lip.

"Come over to my place," I urged. "You'll take a nap, and we'll watch *Brideshead Revisited* and order in pizza, and if you can't chew, I'll make you soup. And you can keep ice on your face and no one will see you but me."

He looked unsure, and I started to laugh. "Do you think you're going out tonight and showing that puss in a bar?"

"Okay," he said. As we got up to leave, he turned to me. "Sally and I really are getting married."

"Great," I answered lightly. "I just think you might let her know there's a possibility you're going to come home like this, sometimes."

Like most people leading a double life, Paul counted on the notion that one day he would simply wake up and choose, just like that, and everyone would embrace his decision. I wondered about Sally. I could only hope she was having wild sex with someone, anyone, in between papal visits. Life was too short for this type of deception.

Meanwhile, my own double life was progressing unchanged. Every time I was in the city, I felt I was missing something in New Haven. And more often than not, Bucky had to have dinner with the client and I was left sitting in the brownstone by myself, reading. When he got home he was usually exhausted and fell into bed, then got up for work at six a.m. Finally, I opted for meeting him in the city, or in Green Hills on the weekends, instead.

Toward the end of my last year at Yale, Bucky decided to "trade up," as he called it, on apartments. He had been sweating out the final weeks of the year, waiting to be summoned and told what his bonus was. The eighties were in full flower, one of the senior executives had left, and I remember numbers like $100,000 being bandied about. For a kid. But he was working day and night, Bucky kept saying. He deserved every cent. When his check arrived, he wasted no time finding a beautiful place around the corner from where he was, in a nineteenth-century brownstone. It had tin ceilings, tile work, and oak floors. It was gorgeous, perfect, as if I had chosen it myself. And the best part was that the brown plaid couches disappeared without my interference. Bucky had a decorator now, an older British woman with whom he would drink tea at the Regency. Each appointment would end with his signing more checks. Though I wasn't thrilled about how much money he was spending, it turned out that his decorator actually had good taste. Mrs. Ross was genuinely furious when she was informed that there was no place for her needlework except, as the decorator sniffed, "bundled off to the Goodwill."

When I got my degree, I moved back in with my parents. The idea of living with Bucky before we were married had always made me uncomfortable—like cheating, somehow. I wanted to do things right, in order. I knew that we would be spending the rest of our lives together, and I trusted him completely. When he told me stories about how his married friends went to golf tournaments just to pick up women, we scoffed in unison. How bored they were, how pathetically unfulfilled.

Later that year I planned to move in with my friend Sharon, down in the Village. Sharon was another student from the drama school who couldn't find a paying job in the theater; she was now studying to become a therapist. She was an only child, and her widowed mother still bought all Sharon's clothes and cooked full meals that she delivered weekly to her daughter's refrigerator. That unyielding attention had sent Sharon into individual and group therapy long before she surrendered to it as a profession. She was a small girl, with sallow skin and masses of dark orange ringlets, who seemed to cry hourly—the kind of person you see on the bus, red-rimmed eyes fixed on the floor, an advertisement for the misery of city living. On an up day, she wore a beret.

Our agreement was that she would have the bedroom and I would pay less to sleep in the living room. Though Sharon never seemed to find the right guy, lately she had been seeing a gynecologist named Dr. Hyman.

"Don't you think he should change his name, or at the very least his job?" I had asked after their first date. We were collapsed in laughter. "Really!" she gasped, but I also knew she had no bargaining chips, because it was Sharon's specialty to bring guys back to the apartment, suggest they take off their clothes, get into bed, and "just sleep." Though for a gynecologist, that might constitute its own eroticism.

None of that concerned me, of course. Living downtown, I would be only a few subway stops from midtown, where I would certainly spend most of my time.

By this point, Bucky was pretty well entrenched at Klein Chapin & Woodruff. All the right people liked his work, he said. He had dinner during the week with all those right people, and played tennis every weekend with them. We also went to some right-people parties, the idea of which excited me no end. This is what I had been waiting for my entire life! To be a right person. Even by association.

The party I remember most clearly was at a big-deal country club near Green Hills. I borrowed a grown-up silk dress from my mother and arrived in high spirits. Most country clubs I'd seen, including the Jewish ones, tended to look nice but never nice enough, as if their members hadn't wanted to cough up funds to replace the worn carpet in the hallways or repaint the flaking heating vents in the ladies' rooms. This one was no different. But there was a genuine buzz near the bar, and the lighting set off the wood paneling in the library, where the drinks were served, and I felt the same release as at the end of a good bedtime story. Everything was as it should be. I was in the right place with the right guy. I was safe.

The men soon broke off into one group, the women into another. I was welcomed by Nancy Dickinson, the wife of Bucky's good friend Arthur. The Dickinsons were the epitome of right people, as far as I could tell, with a huge apartment on Fifth Avenue and an estate in Oyster Bay, where they went on the weekends, complete with stables and a well. Nancy was big at the Junior League, and we chatted about that for the longest time, or at least she did, telling me all the good deeds they were doing for poor children in Harlem. I nodded knowingly and what I hoped was enthusiastically.

At dinner I found myself next to Arthur. We had a merry time rating New York restaurants: Arthur was the rare WASP who not only liked to eat but genuinely knew a lot about food. Nancy pre-ferred peanut-butter crackers, as she would be the first to tell you, but Arthur ate out every day for lunch and for as many dinners as he could manage. While the country-club food left much to be desired, we talked so much about good food that I barely noticed it until the plates were cleared away.

It was time to dance then, and Bucky spun me around the pol-ished floor until Arthur cut in. Then it was Bucky again, and then the men went back to talking together and drinking brandy and Nancy introduced me to some of her friends, who mostly talked about tennis, so I stayed quiet. But I looked at the floodlights outside the window, illuminating the lush sweep of lawn, and watched as the valets drove the cars up to the front door, helping the women tuck their mink coats inside, and I saw the long warm bath of my future life before me. I smiled at Bucky and he smiled back, pleased to see me so happy.

It was actually one of those men sipping brandy that night who recommended to Bucky that we visit Seven Maples, a resort in Vermont. So a few weeks after I started at *Jolie!*, we packed up the car and headed north for the Fourth of July weekend.

As promised, it was lovely. We wandered through crafts fairs, watched Wimbledon on television, and went to a steak house in a real log cabin just over the border in New Hampshire. I remem-ber that the menu had a description of how the steaks were cooked, and medium rare was described as having a "hot pink center."

"That's just like you," Bucky said, and I blushed and laughed and thought how good my life was, how fortunate I was to have this through line, this person I had known since high school who knew me so well, who was always on my side, who was so success-ful in the world that he could afford these extravagant weekends. I started making lists in my head of all the places I wanted to go, all the islands, the inns, the exclusive, beautiful hideaways the world had to offer. True, I had no interest in sailing, Bucky's latest hobby, but I could go along and lie on the beach while he was off-shore. There wasn't a situation in the world that could trouble me; I could adapt to anything. Being an editor meant reading manuscripts, and I knew I could do that anywhere. And my blank books, filling slowly with practice tales, were always with me. The stories I had written so far didn't seem quite right for children, but I knew that would change once I had some of my own. Everything was working out fine.

On our last day in Vermont, Bucky went into town without me and came back with a copy of *Ancient Evenings*, by Norman Mailer.

He showed it to me by the pool, where I was sunning, waiting for him. "Doesn't this look great?" he asked.

"It does, but you'd like John Irving better. I told you that. *The World According to Garp*."

"Well, this looked harder," he said valiantly.

"Okay, you'll tell me how it is," I said. "What else did you get?"

He smiled and handed me a small stuffed bear and a big stuffed porpoise. "They're going to be your company on all the nights I have to do business and you have to do business and you're by yourself," he said. "They'll keep my place warm until I come back." I cooed over them, and him, and we cuddled for a while before jumping into the pool together.

We swam laps side by side until finally I clung to one end, breathless. A man in lime-green pants sitting poolside smiled down at me and I smiled back, feeling the heft of the riches my future life had in store. A brand-new porpoise *and* valet parking. Their world wasn't so mysterious, after all. It would soon turn into the world according to me.

4

There are certain moments in life when you realize that nothing will ever be the same. They can thrill you, those moments—like the morning after Bucky proposed, when I woke up and remembered that something wonderful had happened.

The moment that came that night at the Met, though, was of a different sort. It wasn't when I expected it. Not when Carla Jones first stood in front of me, when Bucky's friends gaped, when I realized that somehow I had been left out of my own life.

It came outside the museum, a little while later. After Carla had presented herself and we sat down in the midst of the party and the noise resumed and the girlfriends and the wives who knew better prevailed upon their lesser halves to go and get them another drink pronto, we got up and left. That was Carla's idea. She walked and I followed, eyes down, the smooth marble floor beckoning the way tile does in the bathroom after you've been sick and there it is, so close and cool, a place to rest. But my feet kept pace with hers, and aside from the rushing in my ears the only sound I could hear was that of our heels, clacking.

On the steps of the museum she turned and faced me. "Do you want to come back to my apartment?" she asked. "There are a few things I think you should see."

Me Times Three

That was the moment. I didn't look at Carla then but at the steps, stretching out, it seemed, for acres. Ghostly gray cement. And I knew that this was it, knew in some hard part of my brain that if I accepted her invitation I was taking nine years of patty-cake bliss and throwing them away. I knew it whole at that moment, that small, hard part of me standing there, nodding and saying in the clearest tones, "Yes, I will go with you."

Carla Jones lived in a high-rise in the West Fifties with a roommate, she said, who was not home that night. I couldn't see much of the apartment as she led me straight to her bedroom, but the living room looked, well, efficient, with its track lighting, glass coffee tables, and cubed couches. There was probably an expensive stereo behind the cabinet doors of the mammoth wall unit. Stew coop, I thought. Isn't that what they used to call those apartments that stewardesses shared back in the sixties and seventies? A perfect place for a drink and a screw on the way out to dinner?

She switched on the lights in her bedroom, and the first thing I saw were the stuffed animals littering the pillows on the single bed. I felt a stab in my stomach. There was a bear, different from mine but a bear all the same. No porpoise. A monkey, instead. And though there were no flowers, I saw that she had saved, in the frame of her mirror, a note card from a bouquet. This was a recent habit of Bucky's—ordering long-stemmed roses over the phone, charging them to his American Express card, and having them delivered with a note that declared all his love in the florist's handwriting.

Somehow I'd thought a girl like this would have had a king-size waterbed and a few whips and chains tossed nonchalantly over the closet door. But there were only lamps as decoration, with frilly, bowed gingham shades. I don't remember a desk or a bookcase, but the carpeting was thick and creamy, wall-to-wall. They must have fucked a lot on the floor. That was Bucky's idea of avant-garde.

We proceeded inside with the intimacy of friends, throwing our coats on the pink velvet chair, sliding off our shoes, sitting cross-legged on the bed. I noticed her checking out my legs, which were shorter than hers, and I could see her tally one for her side.

She leaned over and pulled a file from a drawer in her nightstand. She was incredibly prepared for this, it seemed. She had collected evidence. She was laying out her case. Now she was about to present it.

But first, as they say in the kind of books I save to read on the beach, she let the other shoe drop.

"Do you know Beth Brewer?" she asked, settling against the headboard.

"Yes," I said. She was also an account executive at KCW, as I recalled—in any event, Bucky called her his friend and I had met her once or twice. She was short—her legs were shorter than mine, as a matter of fact—and plain in a way that was only accentuated by her bow-tie blouses and shag haircut. I thought it was nice that Bucky had a woman friend in that piggy world where men reigned supreme.

Carla Jones looked at me. Was that the slightest glimmer of contempt?

I stared back, feeling foolish without knowing why. Everyone seemed to know the password but me.

"He's engaged to her, too," she said flatly.

I waited, as if there might be more. As if that was only the preamble. Carla looked a little let down by my lack of response. I turned my head away, back down at my friend the floor. I was really ready to lie down now. The carpeting could be comfortable, I thought, sort of like a bed. But I sensed that if I sank there, I would choke. I also envisioned, half hidden in the fibers, Bucky's yellowed toenails. He liked to peel them.

Trying to raise my head back up, I flashed onto how I'd run into Bucky and Beth just a few months earlier, in midtown, and how jumpy he'd been. She was scowling, I recalled, bargaining, it appeared, for something she wanted that she wasn't getting. I said hello, and it was all very awkward, and when I asked him about it later he said that they were just going to dinner, she was unhappy at work and wanted to talk, that was it. I truly hadn't thought about it again, and why should I have? Beth Brewer was a dumpy little thing who sewed. I knew that last part from Bucky. If someone sewed, Bucky knew about it. And she came from someplace like Maine. All of which was fine. But competition? Please.

Carla Jones was competition. She was every woman's nightmare come true. She must have been five foot ten, with a showgirl's body and a model's face. Her blond hair was lush enough for a Clairol commercial, the kind where she'd hold it up and release it, letting it fan into slow-motion waves that would fill the screen. You couldn't find a pore on her face without a magnifying glass.

It turned out that she worked at a competitor of KCW's, where she was some sort of assistant. She wasn't quite clear, but said she did business with Ed, who had introduced her to Bucky six months earlier. I heard some of what she was saying as she spoke, but I was thinking again about Beth Brewer, recalling a strange incident when an uncle of Bucky's had died the previous year. There was a reception at the Rosses' house after the service, and one of his relatives had come up to greet me.

"Are you Beth?" he had asked. He was an older man and he smelled of whiskey, so I figured he was just mixed up. But when I said no, quite politely, that I was Sandra, another relative I'd never met before, a woman, appeared and bustled him away, embarrassed.

I shifted around on the end of Carla's bed. So, it wasn't the drunken man who had mortified that woman after all. It was the mention, in front of me, of Bucky's other girlfriend. The one whom all the descendants of Betsy Ross surely knew about and, given her prowess with a needle, were doubtless rooting for.

I looked at Carla. "How long have Beth and Bucky been together?" I asked.

"Almost two years," she answered coolly, her gaze still level. No matter how much I clutched, she seemed just fine. And why not? What did she have to lose, really? She had invested all of six months in this guy. She could just wake up tomorrow and fan her Clairol hair at the next guy who came along.

Carla continued to study me, her expression unchanged, intent yet somehow unobtrusive. She had waited a long time to examine me at such close range; she didn't want to do anything that might scare me off just as she was getting started.

I tried to concentrate on what she had told me. If Bucky and Beth had been seeing each other for almost two years, then they'd started when I was still at Yale. Then they were already a couple when he and I were at Seven Maples together. Impossible.

"You and Bucky first met six months ago?" I asked slowly.

Carla nodded. "We got engaged three weeks ago, right before he left on the Grenadines trip. But that's when I figured out about Beth."

I felt dizzy. "What do you mean?"

"She went with him," Carla announced.

"Beth went to the Grenadines?" I shook my head. That couldn't be right. But wait! Maybe *nothing* Carla was saying was right. I looked at the stuffed monkey, lying on its side.

"Bucky went with JT and the people in his sailing class," I said calmly.

Her gaze stayed even. "Beth *is* in his sailing class."

My gaze returned to the monkey.

"She's in the class," Carla went on, "even though Bucky told me she wasn't. He told me she was afraid of sailing, of the boat tipping over in bad weather. I finally found out the truth from JT's girlfriend. Anyway, the first stop was St. Vincent. They had to stay overnight before getting the boat. So I called every hotel on the island asking if Buck Ross was there, and when one operator said yes, she rang the room and a woman picked up. That's when I knew he had been lying. Because I thought it was weird that right after we became engaged, he would just take off on a two-week sailing trip without me, even though I had told him I wanted to go and try it. I also thought it was weird that he made such a point of telling me to keep our engagement a secret until he came back."

She smoothed her hair—self-righteously, I thought. Her nails were manicured, with light pink polish, each one a perfect half-moon. Her fingers were long. A two-carat emerald-cut diamond ring would only complete the picture.

"At first I thought that *you* had gone with him," she said. "That's why I called you."

"You called me?" I echoed.

"Two weeks ago. On a Saturday morning. I wanted to see if you'd answer the phone."

That's where I knew her voice from. The phone had rung about eight-thirty in the morning, and a woman had asked for me by name; she seemed to be an operator. When I said, "Yes, this is she," the line went dead. I gave it about two seconds of thought before turning over and sleeping till noon.

Carla opened her file. Time for show-and-tell. "Look at this letter," she said, handing me a sheaf of yellow legal sheets filled with Bucky's childish scrawl. I handed it back.

"What does it say?" I asked weakly.

She read excerpts. It was practically identical to a letter he had sent me after our engagement dinner: how we would go to Vermont and stay at Seven Maples, our special place, to celebrate, and how he was having that diamond ring sized, and how much he had always loved me. Only in this letter, me was she.

"Look," I said, trying desperately to focus, "I've known this guy since we were sixteen. He was my prom date. We've named all of our children, all of our dogs. He took me to the football dinner. I typed his term papers. Whenever I had a fight with my parents, he drove to my house and picked me up and we went out for ice cream." I thought of the cherry-vanilla and my eyes filled. "He was my friend."

The words hung there. I flushed. What a stupid thing to say. If nothing else, a friend is loyal, caring, true. When was the last time Bucky had acted like my friend? I thought about the day after our engagement dinner, when he appeared in the lobby of *Jolie!* with a monogrammed black leather Filofax, a present in honor of the promotion he just knew I would get while he was in the Caribbean.

See? I wasn't nuts after all. Okay. When else? When *time* was freely spent, and no thing, no object, was given?

Shit. I couldn't remember. Vermont, maybe. Two or three other long weekends since then. Work for him, it seemed, had become all-encompassing. During the week, we usually saw each other only once or twice, for an early dinner. He needed to get to sleep, to be at the office by seven. I didn't mind. Sure, I would have liked to see him more on weekends, but he played a lot of tennis, which I didn't, and he liked to watch football games and drink beer with his friends, and this sailing thing seemed to have taken off.

At the same time, I was fielding a new job, reading tons of magazines every weekend in a crash course in what it meant to be an editor who had ideas, who kept up, and who could still read enough books to catch whatever literary reference Susie Schein threw into the weekly meeting. I was busy, too.

Truth be told, the entire arrangement seemed like an extension of our college relationship. For me boys had always been like dessert, not an everyday occurrence but a sometime thing, a reward. I worked hard. I saw my friends. And Bucky. Everything was fine. Our future, with our wedding less than a year away now, was secure.

Carla had the phone in her hand.

"What are you doing?" I asked.

"Calling Minneapolis," she said. "I want him to know that we've met. I'd like to know what he plans to do about it."

I stared. What did she have in mind? That Bucky become a Mormon?

"Do you know where he's staying?" I asked. It had never occurred to me to ask. He'd be back in the morning.

She shook her head. "No, but I'll find him."

She got a sympathetic operator who just loved hearing about what an emergency it was while Carla ran through all the hotels where KCW might have a corporate rate. Each chain seemed to have ten local branches, so she started making lists on a pad.

"What about Beth?" I blurted when Carla finally hung up. "Does she know all this, too?"

For the first time, Carla looked uncomfortable.

"Well," she hedged, "I don't know what she knows about me. But I'm sure Bucky told *her* the same thing about you that he told *me* about you."

"And what's that?"

"That you guys broke up almost two years ago, but you still couldn't let go. He said that no matter how much he explained he was in love with someone else, you wouldn't stop calling. That's why he said he agreed to see you every once in a while. To help you along. When you would call and I would be there, he would cover the phone with his hand and shake his head like you were crazy."

Wasn't it time for the punch line, right about now?, I wondered. For Bucky to come out from the darkened living room with Ed McMahon and a camera crew and a king-size check for ten million dollars and tell me that this, all of this, was an enormous joke—no, an enormous test, of my will, of my sanity and love, and that I had passed with flying colors? And now I could take my prizes and go home and live happily ever after?

I tried to laugh. Carla continued to look at me, with a hint of pity now, and I knew it was true. All of it. I had called Bucky a month or so ago, on a Sunday night, screeching, because I had gone into my kitchen to turn on the oven, which I hadn't done in a while, and a mouse jumped out from behind it. "Can you come over here?" I wailed. "There's a mouse!" He seemed distracted. "Oh, come on," he said. But I was genuinely upset.

"I'm invoking The Clause," I declared, surprising myself; I hadn't thought of it in so long. The Clause, as we'd dubbed it, had started in our freshman year of college, during exams, when we were both studying but had had a fight. I was heartbroken. Bucky drove from Amherst to Smith, and we promised each other that no matter what ever happened in our lives, even if we ended up with other people, all either of us had to do was invoke The Clause and the other would immediately come.

The night of the mouse, Bucky had laughed. "You can't invoke The Clause for a mouse," he said.

"Yes, I can," I cried. "I'm scared."

His tone had remained amused and, yes, now that I thought of it, more than a little patronizing.

"You should call your super," he said. "Besides, I have a co-op board meeting tonight that I can't miss. You'll be fine, Sanny. It's only a mouse."

And now, staring into Carla Jones's light green eyes, I could just imagine her as he hung up the receiver, wrapping her arms around his neck, saying, "Oh, Bucky, your old girlfriend loved you so much that even all this time later she still has to call you about a little old mouse. Poor thing." And she would kiss him and he would laugh, gently this time, and off they would go to have rollicking sex while I stomped around my apartment in the rain boots I refused to take off.

I looked at the clock on Carla's bedside table. It was almost two in the morning. She was back on the phone, working her way through every hotel in the greater Minneapolis–St. Paul area. Nothing.

"About Beth," I persisted. "Did you meet her? Did you confront *her* with all of this?"

Carla shook her head, and I realized that she hadn't bothered with Beth for the same reason I hadn't. Beth was a dull little thing who scowled and sewed. Now that I thought about it, she was eerily similar to Mrs. Ross, with her cardigan sweaters and sturdy shoes.

Okay, I had been raised in a household where psychology was served up with the frozen vegetables. If Beth was Bucky's mother, and Carla was the *Playboy* centerfold every twelve-year-old boy wishes was his—

"What did Bucky say about me?" I demanded artlessly. "Tell me. I want to know."

Carla hung up the phone and crossed another hotel off her list. She twirled the pen in her hand, tracing over the doodles she'd made in the margin: daisies. When she spoke, her tone was flat.

"He said that you always believed in him when he was growing up. That when you looked at him, you saw what he could be. That you always said he had great potential, that he could do anything he ever wanted in his life. That you actually believed that. And because you were always so smart, so much smarter than Bucky, he didn't want to let you down."

I waited for more, but she was silent. "What else did he say?" I pressed. I knew from the look on her face that I should keep my mouth shut, that she had told me the nice part already—but I couldn't stop. "How did he describe me?"

She didn't even flinch. "He said you were pretty, not beautiful. He said that you worked at it. He said that you looked like a finished Jewish girl."

"Finished?"

"Yes, like your makeup was always right and your hair was always done and your outfits always matched."

She had the air, it seemed to me, of a court reporter, dispassionately reading back her notes. There was not even any of the gloating that was her prerogative as the resident babe. But there was something else going on, something I couldn't quite place. She just kept watching me, almost baiting me to figure something out. But I couldn't; I couldn't think at all. At that moment, I wasn't even sure what Bucky looked like. And there I was, hunched at the foot of a stranger's bed, while she sat, tall, self-assured, in control. Why? Why wasn't she upset? Obviously, she had had more time to digest the situation, but she seemed so clinical. I mean, this was a girl with bows on her lampshades. You would think she'd be destroyed.

I looked at her again. She was tapping the push buttons on the phone with her pencil. Maybe she was in shock. It had been her engagement, too, after all.

"Tell me about you," I said when she hung up.

"What do you want to know?" she asked, with a hint of surprise.

"Well, for one thing, how come you're not more upset about this?"

Tears sprang to her eyes. "Of course I'm upset!" she exclaimed. "I thought this was it. That I was going to spend the rest of my life with this man. I was already looking for the dress, and we were about to buy a dog from a breeder in Connecticut. We visited there a few times and fell madly in love with a yellow Lab that was about to have puppies."

I felt myself go cold.

"You were going to name her Snowball, weren't you?" I asked, and for the first time all night, I watched *her* jaw drop, *her* shoulders slump, *her* mouth twist into what I must say was a most unattractive arc.

"He told you that?" she half whispered. Her cheeks flushed.

"No," I said, feeling instantly less stooped. If I just kept thinking of him as a human copy machine, everything would make sense. This was me times three.

"It was the same name we were going to give *our* dog," I said. "But that one was going to be a Samoyed, which would at least make sense."

She looked confused. "What do you mean?"

"A Samoyed is white. So it would make sense to name one Snowball."

She stared.

"Didn't it seem like an odd name to you for a yellow Lab?" I prompted.

She shrugged. "I guess. I just thought it was cute."

Dear God.

"Forget about Bucky," I said. "Tell me more about you. Before you met him." She looked suspicious. "I mean, here we are in the middle of the night," I went on. "It's an unbelievable thing. How did this happen to you?"

I really wanted to know. All night, I had assumed she had all the answers. But the dog thing had wounded her. She had trusted him. Why did he betray her? How? Why had she let him? Why had I? It's always easier to figure it out on someone else.

Finally she relented. The chance to talk about herself was too good to pass up. The one thing I've noticed about the very few superhumanly beautiful women I've met is that they have the same level of entitlement and self-absorption that men do. Nothing on earth is ever quite as beguiling as themselves.

She was born and raised in Oklahoma, she said. Her father owned a hardware store, and her mother was deeply religious—only her religion was always changing. She had tried everything, including being a Jehovah's Witness. Then one day she up and joined the Hare Krishnas. Carla's father took up with a neighbor woman then, so Carla dropped out of community college and moved with a friend to Hilton Head, where she got a job bartending.

I tried not to gulp. The descendant of Betsy Ross was going to marry a bartender from Oklahoma whose mother chanted at airports?

Carla kept on. She liked her story. It starred her as Everywoman, who, to hear her tell it, might as well have looked like Godzilla for any good her looks had ever done her. In Hilton Head she had had a boyfriend twenty years her senior, a former professional baseball player. He was wealthy and he wanted to marry her, but she—toss the hat high, now—had wanted to make it on her own. She moved to New York. She zeroed in on advertising and landed herself an assistant's job at one of the top firms.

Then along came Bucky, American royalty with his big blue eyes and impeccable manners. They were instant soul mates, she said. Not only did they both love the business, but (incredibly enough, in spite of those tits) she even played tennis and liked nothing better than to get up at six on a Saturday morning and start bouncing. And when they were done, they went straight to the gym, where they both worked out as hard as they could. Sometimes they would have a rollicking night out, like when the Judds played Radio City. And even though the old baseball player flew to New York to implore her to come back to him, she stayed loyal to her new true love and was even considering leaving the firm to get down to the serious business of making little Betsy Rosses.

But then the Grenadines trip happened and she had found a new hobby. She showed me her folder filled with notes documenting how Bucky lied to her about the time he spent with me (she had discovered from Ed that I was not in the past tense—Ed's motive for sharing that information wasn't mentioned, but, looking at Carla up close, I could guess), and then she showed me her notes about the times Bucky had spent with Beth. They were arranged in chronological order.

So, yes, she was crushed that all this had happened. Maybe New York wasn't really for her after all, she had been thinking lately. Vast sigh. A close friend of hers worked in Miami. She would just have to wait and see what happened next. Obviously, she stressed, she would never marry Bucky now. She could never trust him again, and the one thing she had learned from her parents' unhappy marriage was that trusting someone after they betrayed you never really worked.

I nodded, as if I knew what she meant.

She drew her knees up to her chest, flaunting a mile of calf, and yawned. We sat for a while in silence.

"He talked about you a lot," she finally offered, perhaps feeling guilty. "He said you were the smartest person he had ever known, that you had influenced him more than anyone. He took harder courses in school to prove to you he could. He went to the theater and listened to classical music because you did those things and you didn't make fun of him for liking them. You made him read books, just for fun. He said that *Ancient Evenings* changed his life."

Finally, I laughed. She looked at me oddly, but I didn't bother to explain. What a literary giant he fancied himself now, all on the basis of one book. I could just hear the meaningful conversation about it they could share—though Carla seemed like the kind of girl who'd rather wait for the movie.

Oh! But that was it! That was the real reason I was here. I felt some relief at the realization. My brain must still be alive.

This girl obviously didn't care what I looked like, because physically she was ideal. There would never be any contest on that front with me. But Carla Jones, college dropout, *community-college* dropout, had outsmarted Sandra Berlin, Yale graduate. That was her victory. Forget Beth; Beth was a bore. But Sandra? Sandra was the smartest person Bucky had ever known. And after all these weeks of sleuthing, Carla had waited for the perfect moment to play her hand, to do it in the most exquisite way. Why bother to appear at my apartment or at the magazine for a confrontation? Who would know except me? No, this was a girl who had mastered the fine art of turning heads. The only thing she hadn't counted on was Bucky's last-minute defection to Minneapolis. Think how much juicier her party scene would have been with two supporting players.

It was almost four-thirty. I stared down at the Cartier watch on my wrist and, for a moment, had the heady sensation that I was someone else—there was the proof that this was not happening to me. But I could hear Mimi Dawson saying, "You deserve it, don't you?" and then suddenly I couldn't hold my head up one more minute.

"I think I'd better go home," I said, pulling myself up from the bed. "Listen. I appreciate your telling me. I, um, I guess you've saved me a lot of trouble."

She smiled. "We'll talk tomorrow," she said, warmly, conspiratorially, walking me to the door. "After he's back. Get home safe, now."

I stumbled from the elevator through the lobby and onto the empty street. The beginnings of dawn showed in the sky. I walked several blocks without seeing a cab. The street stayed empty. You could hear the grinding when the traffic lights changed. How foolish they seemed, hanging there heavily, signaling no one.

It was past five by the time I got home. Without even taking off my coat, I dialed Paul. It would only be two a.m. in L.A. Maybe he had gone out and would just be coming in.

No answer. No machine.

I didn't really lie down on the couch so much as fall onto it. Numb. Numb wasn't necessarily bad, I thought, the tweed of the cushion against my face. I had never realized before that numb came from the head as a direct command, not from the body part you imagined to be numb. I could feel the numb message thrumming on the switchboard, sending itself out, over and over, though my hands, wedged underneath my chin, stayed icy.

Me Times Three

I tried Paul again.

"Hello?" His voice was sharp, pissed.

"It's me," I said.

"At two-thirty in the fucking morning?" he asked. "Who died?"

"I did."

5

It must have been near six when I hung up with Paul, and remembered that my long-awaited lunch with Miss Belladonna was at one. First I cried, convinced I should cancel. That lasted about ten minutes, until I realized I wasn't getting married anymore and needed a job.

The restaurant was crowded and Miss Belladonna was late. Not that it mattered, but her assistant, Kate, kept calling the maître d' with updates every three minutes. I knew that Miss Belladonna was making Kate call only to torture her, keep her jumping, just for fun. Kate was a solemn, bottom-heavy girl who fought her weight constantly. During her thinner phases, she told us, Miss Belladonna was exceptionally nice to her. Whenever she gained weight, however, Miss Belladonna either completely ignored her or worked overtime to make her crazy—like the time a hot new restaurant opened in TriBeCa and Miss Belladonna *had* to be there that very day and she *had* to have a fabulous table since she was bringing Calvin Klein. Kate called for hours and got only a busy signal. By noon, Miss Belladonna ordered her to type up a request and take it to the restaurant in person, with a warning not to return until the correct table was secured at the correct time.

Kate's weight must be up, I figured each time the host came by. Miss Belladonna finally appeared, spouting airy apologies as she looked at all the other tables to see who was there. I was surprised that she even remembered my name.

There was indeed Perrier. And salad. I couldn't remember a word Laura Lattimore had told me and I didn't need to. Miss Belladonna, it turned out, didn't know a thing about art either—or theater, or movies, for that matter, unless someone French was in them, and then she only knew who they were sleeping with when they weren't onscreen.

While she was talking, I caught sight of my reflection in a mirror on the opposite wall. Hair combed, sitting up straight. Sometimes nodding, sometimes speaking. By the time coffee was served, she asked if I wanted the job, and I said yes, working up some real enthusiasm, gushing about how much I loved the magazine. She nodded, satisfied, while renewing her lipstick, studying herself in her compact mirror. Good. Done. Onto the next.

They could only give me an extra two thousand dollars, she added, almost as an afterthought, as we rose to go. She hoped I understood. I said I did. As much as I understood anything in my life.

Though I wanted nothing more than to catch the next train to Green Hills, I still had to go back to the office to return the Cartier watch, safe inside my purse. Also, it would be nice to share my promotion with Pimm and Coco. Pascal wouldn't care because Pascal cared only about Pascal—and the free international calls he could make from his desk. Every morning when I came in he was already speaking to "Papa," who lived in London and to whom he spoke in French—even though they were both American. I guess it was his bid for privacy, sitting in an office with three nosy women.

When he wasn't chatting with Papa, or anyone else to whom he could say "Oui" and pronounce it "way" in a manner to assure any eavesdropper that he knew French and she didn't, he would stand in the middle of the room and tell tales, gesticulating grandly as he described whatever cocktail party he had been to the night before. Coco and Pimm loved his stories and begged for more. I would watch him perform, like a poodle begging for treats, as I answered my phone and tuned him out.

But one day I came in early and he was not chatting with Papa and no one else was in yet. He was sitting at his desk, drinking coffee, with the gray face of someone who hadn't slept. He looked awful.

"Pascal, are you okay?" I asked.

He glanced up, surprised. He knew I didn't like him, just as I knew he didn't like me, with my abrupt New York manner and intense lack of interest in all things Eurotrash. But he was in bad-enough shape to want to talk, even to me.

It was a girl, he said. A girl whom he had loved for more than a year now, who cared for him not at all. He had never told her about his feelings, just loved her from afar, but it was hopeless, he sighed. Entirely hopeless. I listened with as much sympathy as I could muster, and then in my own irritatingly pragmatic way asked if he could just stop feeling bad about it and come right out and tell her his feelings. Really go for it.

He looked at me, thoroughly miserable. "I would," he said slowly. "Except that she's having a rip-roaring affair with her brother."

I almost laughed, but quickly realized he wasn't kidding. Thankfully, at that moment Pimm arrived and took over, endlessly sympathetic. After that, for a few days at least, Pascal and I smiled and said good morning, but I stopped asking questions and offering advice. Green Hills had certainly never prepared me for a dilemma like that one.

After the lunch with Miss Belladonna, I arrived at the office midafternoon, full of my news triumphant and tragic, but no one was around to hear either. I sorted quickly through the mail and headed to the fashion closet to look for Mimi. Instead I found a convention.

Except for Susie Schein and Miss Belladonna, everyone on the staff seemed to be there. A few of the girls looked as if they'd been crying.

"What happened?" I whispered to Pimm, who was standing near the door.

"It's Mimi," she said solemnly. "She was fired, and there's going to be an investigation." I reached nervously for the watch. Could this be my fault?

It was even worse than that. It seemed that Mimi had had an elaborate barter system going with a boyfriend with whom she traded *Jolie!* luxury items like Rolex watches for cocaine. At least ten thousand dollars' worth of borrowed merchandise was gone.

"The magazine has insurance for things like that, doesn't it?" I asked.

Pimm looked horrified. "I'm sure it does, but that's not the point, Sandy. Mimi was stealing from the company. And making herself sick in the process. Didn't you realize how skinny she was, how hyper?"

Well, sure I did. But I thought being skinny was every girl's dream come true, and I thought she was hyper just because some people are, and I believed that anyone from the South had to be as different from me as possible. I was happy to sit on my behind and read for hours on end, so I figured that Mimi was just a latter-day Scarlett O'Hara who was running the accessories closet instead of the plantation.

And while we were talking about judging appearances so expertly, why was no one rushing toward me with concern, saying, "Oh, Sandra, what's wrong? You look like you haven't slept all night, your life must be absolutely ruined!" Well, as *Jolie!*

could tell you, never underestimate the power of a good under-eye concealer.

"Are they going to press charges?" I asked.

Pimm shrugged. "No one knows. But Susie says they are."

I'll bet she did. I sidled through the crowd over to the safe, where Buffy Parks stood guard. She was one of the fashion editors I loathed, the kind of woman who talked with a clenched jaw, like a character from one of those fifties teenage movies—the priss who ran the sorority. She had a list, handwritten in that Miss Porter's School rounded penmanship—feminine yet insistently childlike.

"Buffy, Mimi lent me this watch last night because mine broke," I said, handing it to her.

"Well, what took you so long?" she chided. "We told everyone this morning to bring back whatever they had."

I stared at her coldly. "Sorry," I said. "I was having lunch with Miss Belladonna."

"Oh." She barely even spoke, practically breathed the word, so awed was she by my brush with greatness. "That's all right, then," she added meekly.

I turned around and left the room. What the hell was going on? I really liked Mimi Dawson. I truly had no idea that she was taking drugs. I felt a stab in my stomach, thinking about this, and about the night before. For a smart girl, I seemed to miss an awful lot.

I gathered my things together and left.

My mom picked me up at the Green Hills train station. When she pulled her car to the curb she took one look at my swollen face, makeup be damned, and I saw her own face turn pale. I can't say I was ever that close to my mother. We were so very different—I eternally trying to figure out every last detail of how the world worked and why, and she resolutely escaping the world for the confines of her lab and her classroom. Although we had very few interests in common, she was always great in an emergency. And this qualified.

I immediately started crying and told my story all the way home—punctuated by her indignant yelps—and on into the garage, through the door, into the den, and onto the couch, where I sobbed with the fiercest sobs I could muster and all my tears fell on her cashmere sweater. I finally stopped long enough to finish the story, every last detail, as if someone might be listening who could stop and reassure me that I was indeed wrong. She clucked me on, all the way until I got to "finished Jewish girl." Then her eyes darkened, and her mouth tightened, and she shook her head with a terrible finality that seemed to make the phrase sound that much worse.

She fixed my father a plate for dinner, but we stayed in the den, smoking and talking. She drank vodka, I drank Scotch. We chewed over every detail for hours before she switched to assuring me that my life would go on. I assured her it would not. The conversation lasted throughout the weekend, during which time my father stayed mostly in his bedroom, emerging only to go to the library. He seemed to know what was happening, but he kept his vow of silence, for which I was grateful. There was noise enough in my head, with the continual replay of the call Bucky had made the morning after the Met. At 7:38 a.m., to be exact.

"Sanny?"

I had picked up the phone and said nothing, blowing my nose.

"Sanny, is it you?"

"Yeah." It came out like a honk. "Where were you?" I couldn't believe I asked, but I was so damned anal, I had to know. Forget the betrayal. All I could think of was how long I had sat on Carla's bed, looking at the pad with the daisies in the margin. "What hotel?"

"We weren't at a hotel," he said. "It was a country club somewhere outside of Minneapolis."

Oh, how perfect. More right people.

"Sanny, I'm sorry," he said. "You have to let me explain."

"Never," I said. "Never." And hung up the phone.

When it rang again, I let the machine pick up. Another heart-felt plea. He was calling from the airport, he said. He knew what had happened at the Met because Ed—that fucking double agent—had called his machine to tip him off. Along with all the gory details Ed had offered the advice that maybe Bucky should think about staying in the Twin Cities, that real estate there was looking good, ha ha. When Bucky repeated that to me, he tried to laugh, but all that came out was a harsh rush of air. I still didn't pick up. We both waited, each listening to the other's silence. Finally he said "I love you" and hung up.

I stayed true to my word and refused to speak to him. He delivered to my apartment a mostly incoherent ten-page letter in a shopping bag that also contained his Amherst baseball jersey. What was I supposed to do with that? I almost cut it up into little pieces and sent it back, but I put it on instead and wore it every night for the next few weeks, which I mostly spent eating Ben & Jerry's Coffee Heath Bar Crunch ice cream and not sleeping. He kept calling, and I kept hanging up.

I refused to read the letter. Sharon read it to me instead, even volunteering to call her mother back rather than talking to her the moment she called. Now Sharon had another full-time lunatic to take care of. Between the two of us, a family-size box of Kleenex didn't last a week.

Sometime after the letter and the jersey arrived, Sharon came home late one afternoon with a present. We had recently gone out for brunch, where she espoused her pet theory that all the women we knew should band together and file a class-action suit against MGM for producing a lifetime of movies about men in tuxedos loving women in evening gowns that only fostered unrealistic expectations for those of us in our pajamas. Then we shopped. I saw a pink flannel shirt that looked pretty and warm—

safe, somehow. But it was forty dollars, which was a ridiculous price for a flannel shirt, and I left the store without it. Sharon had gone back and bought it for me, and had it wrapped as if it were my birthday. I cried. "Everyone should have a pink shirt," she said. I hugged her, then put the shirt on over the jersey and wouldn't take either one of them off except to go to work.

This lasted a few weeks, until Paul called one day and, instead of giving me a chance to talk, announced that the moping was getting old, the whining even older. He demanded that I meet him in Palm Springs for a complete overhaul.

We agreed on Memorial Day weekend, and then it became something I was actually looking forward to. So what that the town was filled with ninety-year-olds waiting to die? I knew just how they felt.

At the Los Angeles airport, I checked my answering machine before catching the connecting flight. There was the requisite daily message from Bucky: "I know you hate me, I know you'll never forgive me, but you've got to see me, you've got to let me explain." I erased it.

In Palm Springs, the desert air hit the doorway of the plane with a weight of its own. I headed for the baggage claim, determined to enjoy my R and R. Paul had explained that we didn't have enough money to go to Two Bunch Palms—the best spa in the area, which only William Morris clients could afford, not William Morris mailboys—but he knew another place that used to be a tennis club. It also had a pool and a view of Bob Hope's house on a hill nearby. The house had a roof that slid open, Paul said, so that you could see the stars.

Well, I wasn't crazy about the tennis part, but the price was right for my majestic raise, and the only thing that really mattered was seeing Paul, talking to him, centering myself somehow.

I checked in and found a message waiting for me. "Running late. Paul."

That figured. I headed to the room—a suite, actually, and, given the rate, kind of nice. I ordered an omelet from room service and called my machine. No more messages from Bucky. Well, it was a holiday weekend, after all. He was probably up at the cottage with his sainted mother, nursing his own wounds.

True to her word, Carla had dumped him. A week after we met, she called me at work and invited me out for a drink so she could tell me all about it. I don't know why I accepted—I didn't want to see her, or Bucky, or Beth. But even people in earthquakes have to confront the wreckage before they start cleaning it up. This earthquake was mine.

We met at Café 43, a place near the magazine that had a wine bar and one of those Cruvinets that were the new big thing. We had Chardonnay, two different kinds. She was just as beautiful as she had been the week before, and she was filled with plans for things the two of us could do together. We could be best friends and find other guys and make Bucky's life a living hell. She went on and on. I listened, or I thought I listened, but just as in her apartment, I couldn't seem to register what she was saying.

I went to the ladies' room and glimpsed myself in the fluorescent-lit mirror. My face looked bloated; my hips looked wide; my arms looked short. I wanted to go home.

I promised to call her.

I didn't.

That evening I got Beth Brewer's number from Information and phoned her house. The machine was on. She had a nice-enough voice, now that I listened to it, sort of settled, with a New England accent. I didn't leave a message; what was there to say? "I don't want him, Carla doesn't want him, you can have him"? The one thing I had heard Carla tell me between sips of Chardonnay was that Beth had been furious when, through the office grapevine, she discovered Bucky's triple crown, but she still hadn't officially dumped him. She had gone to see her parents and she was hurt but she hadn't made any decisions. At least that was according to the guys in her office.

Well, I had gone to see my parents, too. I was hurt. And since I hadn't spoken to Bucky, I hadn't made any decisions, either. So—the thought hit me then, in my Palm Springs hotel room—what was stopping *me* from just changing my mind? Yes. After all these weeks of suffering and uncertainty and regret, what if I just decided to forgive him and let everything go back to how it was before—before Beth did it first?

I left the omelet on the room-service cart, went out onto the terrace, and lit a cigarette. From where I stood, I couldn't tell if Bob Hope's roof was open or closed. His house was one of those modern things that look like a dumpling with edges. The lights were on inside, and the place seemed warm and homey. I tried to picture Bob Hope in there. I knew he had been married forever to a woman named Dolores and that they had lots of kids, and after he entertained the troops and made everyone laugh he would unwind at this haven on the hill. They were perfect Americans living there, I supposed, in a house you could open and close like a box of Cracker Jack, with the family the prize inside.

I finally turned away and, for the first time, opened Bucky's letter myself. Even though I'd carried it with me every day, I hadn't looked at it since Sharon's reading. But after all, I thought, if I was going to forgive him, I should be better acquainted with his apology. I unfolded it, feeling the indentations of the pen on the paper.

"Written on plane from Minneapolis" was scrawled across the top right-hand corner, instead of the date. "Dear Sanny: Whatever you chose to do with this letter is none of my business—burn it, not read it, mail it back, or even share it with your newfound best friend, Carla Jones."

I read the sentence again and noticed that Bucky had written "chose" instead of "choose" and I hadn't even seen the error. I had corrected it automatically. As I kept reading, it happened again and again.

"This woman merely tried to destroy every memory and dream we've ever had for each other to make herself feel better, because she knew how much you really meant to me."

Yes, but you could hardly blame her. It's every bartender for herself.

"You will be wrong for the rest of your life if you believe that I have not and do not love you with the greatest intensity of feeling that any human being can share with another. It is this almost torturous love that I have held for you since I've been 17 years old that caused so many emotional confusions inside me —"

The terrace door opened. "Romano!" I dropped the letter onto the glass-topped table and flew into Paul's arms. He laughed as he hugged me, his crisp white shirt seemingly the same one he had been wearing when I last saw him. His cologne was the same, his tight jeans were the same, he was even wearing his cowboy boots with the pointy toes. I felt as if a genie had granted me a wish, to have him suddenly in front of me like this. And gorgeous! He looked as if he'd walked off a magazine cover.

He lit a cigarette. "Did you eat?" I asked.

He shook his head. "Not hungry." He gestured toward the hill. "So, what do you think of Bob Hope's house?"

"I don't know, really. Is the roof open or closed?"

He squinted. "I'm not sure. But it's a nice night. I bet it's open." He saw the pile of yellow legal sheets on the table.

"What's that?"

"Oh, just Exhibit A of *The People versus Bucky Ross*."

"Well, I would say we need a drink first, wouldn't you?" he asked, going back inside to retrieve a large brown bag containing two bottles of vodka and a carton of grapefruit juice. We drank for a while, and both of us talked almost at once, each sentence bumping into the next in our haste to say every last thing that we had forgotten to mention by phone: the scummy actor from the Rep who had complained about the laundry now trying to get William Morris to represent him, and Paul filching the letter from the pile to answer it himself; Susie Schein seeing Paul's picture on my desk and wondering what TV show he starred in.

Paul never mentioned Sally, and neither did I. And we seemed to have an unspoken agreement to leave Bucky for later. That night was just for us, to sit and gab, for me to hear more about his new job offer: to be an assistant agent, not at William Morris but at a smaller place, Advancing Artists.

"A big queen runs it who *loves* me," Paul said. "They need to build up their television department, and I can do film there, too." We toasted him. We toasted my promotion.

Eventually, he went back inside and emerged with my omelet, eating the bacon and leaving the green peppers while I steadily worked my way through the bread basket. Just to hear him laugh was restorative. I didn't even care that we were looking onto tennis courts. I felt that I could breathe again, that I knew where I was even though I had never been there before.

Hours later, when I finally couldn't keep my eyes open one more minute, he kissed me good night and said he wasn't tired yet, that he wanted to go out and see what was happening. I knew that meant boys, so I wished him good luck, slid into the air-conditioned sheets, and, for the first time in weeks, slept all the way through until morning.

In the sunlight, I had to admit, the place didn't look as good as it had the night before. Twigs and scraps of paper floated in the corners of the pool, and I was the only person sitting out there, even though it was already noon. I had left Paul in bed. I hadn't heard him come in, but when I left an hour earlier he was showing no signs of life.

Feeling the sun bake me, I thought again of the option I'd come up with yesterday: What if I went back to Bucky? What if I just chalked the whole thing up to his being young and confused? He'd gone out and sown his oats and now he was deeply sorry, completely changed, and ready to get down to business. We could get back on track with the dogs and the kids, the summer house and our lives.

Just the thought of it swamped me with relief. All I needed to do was say yes and I would have my life back. Why had I been fighting it all these weeks? All I had to do was say yes.

A shadow fell over my chair. Paul was standing there, wearing sunglasses and shorts.

"We're out of here," he said, peering distastefully at the debris floating in the pool.

"What do you mean?" I asked, squinting up at him. "You want to check out?"

"No, but we're definitely not staying here during the day. There's a really good hotel nearby—some kind of Marriott, I think. Let's go there."

"Any takers last night?" I asked in the parking lot.

He shrugged. "Do you really have to know?"

I shrugged back. "No, I guess I don't. Touchy-touchy first thing in the morning. Or afternoon."

We climbed into his car, a red Karmann Ghia convertible he said he had named Walt.

"As in Disney?" I asked.

"As in Whitman," he said, smiling.

"Ah," I sighed. "Very fancy."

The Marriott was gorgeous, all terra-cotta, built close to the ground, surrounded by lawns and bushes, an oasis of green. We walked around to the pool. The gate was locked and had a sign on it that warned, FOR HOTEL GUESTS ONLY.

"Oh well," I said, turning to go just as a hotel guest walked past us and opened the gate. Paul slipped in behind her and I nervously followed. The guest never looked twice. Paul just had that way about him, inhabiting a place as if he naturally belonged there.

Noticing my hesitation, he turned toward me. "What's the matter?"

"Well, I mean, I didn't think we could just come in here, if we're not staying here is all . . ."

He lifted his sunglasses, and his expression was gentle. "You've really had a hard time, haven't you?" he asked.

"What do you mean?" Suddenly I felt wobbly.

"Normally, you would have walked right in and given attitude to anyone who tried to stop you."

I felt flustered, as if I had done something wrong. He put his arm around my shoulder and squeezed.

"It's okay, doll," he said tenderly. "It's okay, and you're okay. And if you're not yet, you're going to be."

My eyes filled. "Promise?" I asked, trying to laugh.

"Promise," he answered firmly.

We staked out chaises, and Paul sashayed his tight butt past the pool attendant, who promptly rushed right over with plenty of towels.

"How about some lunch?" Paul asked, signaling a waiter, and soon I was eating a huge burger with lettuce, mustard, ketchup, and mayonnaise. I didn't think about Carla Jones and her perfect body for one second. Paul loved me—I had forgotten how much. And Bucky loved me. No matter how many things happen in life, the people who love you don't just stop. It takes a lot to love someone. And not only did Bucky love me—had always loved me, in fact—but he was begging my forgiveness on a regular basis, so it absolutely didn't matter that I had gained at least five pounds— okay, eight—on the Ben & Jerry's diet over the last few weeks. All right, ten. It would come off.

Paul sipped a margarita, gave the waiter a phony room number and a wad of cash, and fell asleep. I opened a magazine, but before I could focus, I noticed that a few chaises away, a girl was reading *Jolie!* I had never actually seen anyone do that before. I felt sort of proud, actually. That was *my* magazine.

I watched her flip a few pages until she got to the Burt Reynolds interview. After a glance at the headline and caption, she moved on. I was incredibly annoyed. That piece had cost me almost two weeks of work, and it was one of the reasons I couldn't even consider hanging around the lobby of my office building, in case Bucky tried to waylay me there. The writer, Nina Martini, had gotten paid an unprecedented five thousand dollars for it, and all she did was send me four hours of tapes to have transcribed.

Take a breath, Sandra, I thought, imagining my face thrust forward, East Coast white with a grim, set jaw. What was the big deal? This was *only* a job, after all, not my life. But without Bucky, I had to admit, it had rapidly become my life. If it wasn't Burt Reynolds, it was some other actor or actress—anyone but me. Because when I stopped to think about me, lately, the terrible truth was that I could not shut up. And I wasn't only talking to people I knew. Strangers were fine. At the bank, say, waiting on line for a cash machine. Outside, some man would bang on the door for someone to open it instead of taking out his card, and the woman would say, "How entitled do you think they can be?" and I would burst out with "How about being engaged to three women at the same time?" And she would step away sideways, smiling vaguely, the way people do when a homeless woman stands on the corner singing Piaf, for money.

Business lunches were also good opportunities. I had had one recently with an older woman, a motherly sort who owned a modeling agency. She didn't want her girls only in photos, she told me, but thought they should be written up in features. But before she could get out another word, I started in with the night at the Met and went from there. I was describing my prom dress when she began waving down the waiter, frantic for the bill.

The only person I couldn't bear to keep talking to about Bucky was Sharon. She was so understanding, so *with* me, feeling my feelings, while I felt so utterly alone that I couldn't stand it. And I couldn't talk to Mom after that marathon weekend. She had turned against Bucky with nuclear force.

I looked over at Paul, who was still asleep. He would give me the best advice. In the meantime, though, maybe I should finish the letter. Refresh my memory.

I wiped my hands carefully on a towel before pulling the yellow sheets from the envelope and picking up where I'd left off: "Damn it, Sanny, my life is not worth a shithole without you and I was so scared to be 100 percent with you because you were the only person in this world that I did not want to fail in front of."

See? What was I worrying about?

"I can live without you, but not if you for one second believe that I fell out of love with you and that I am a sick, lying scumbag."

How nicely put. But wait a minute. *He could live without me?*

"Sanny, if this is to be my last letter and last communication with you, thank you and I will love and have the most intense emotional commitment to you for the rest of my life, notwithstanding whomever you or I chose to be with."

How could I have forgotten that part? After all, Sharon *had* read it to me. This was not good. Could it be that he wasn't home this weekend because he had found someone else to "chose"? But how could he have found someone so quickly? Who was she? Carla had dumped him. I had dumped him. Beth Brewer had—

I felt cold suddenly, as if someone in the pool had splashed me. Of course Beth hadn't dumped him: Bucky Ross was the catch of her life. Her entire hometown was probably waiting for her to creep off the next plane and admit that the big bad city was a big bad idea and dash down the nearest aisle with a fine, upstanding sales manager for L. L. Bean as fast as her little legs could carry her.

Finally, Paul opened his eyes.

"Listen," I said, frantic. "I think Bucky is with Beth."

"What?" he asked groggily.

"Beth. You know—Door Number Three. I think Beth forgave him. And because I didn't, she's going to get to marry him and make little Betsy Rosses and I'm going to have to start going out with doctors and rabbis. I fucked up. I should have forgiven him sooner."

He yawned. "Sandra, I always thought you were too smart for a girl. But now I know you're not."

"What do you mean?" I asked, flustered.

"Bucky didn't just cheat on you the way a husband would cheat," he said. "He's at the beginning of his life, not bored in the middle or desperate at the end. There's no explanation for what he did—that I can see, anyway—other than something so deeply screwed up I would think you'd do anything to avoid it."

"But maybe it's different because we've been together for nine years," I argued. "Maybe it *is* like we're an old married couple. Maybe we're the exception to the rule, and maybe that's why I should forgive him."

Paul lit a cigarette with an air of exaggerated patience. "I think it's noble of you to want to forgive him, Sandra. People need to forgive each other more."

"Just like Dennis forgave you," I said, more sharply than I intended.

Paul frowned. "Sandy, do you remember when Dennis and I broke up?"

I certainly did. Dennis was the older man, the one with the opera tickets, and he and Paul had been the loves of each other's lives, but Paul was such a maniac, drugging and drinking and screwing all the time, that Dennis couldn't take it anymore. He left.

"And remember I was devastated," Paul went on, "and you told me to keep my chin and my cheeks up because sooner or later someone else with a million bucks would be glad to give me a roll? Well, you were right, they have. But I lost the one guy I cared about, and I was the one who fucked it up. Now he's moved back to Australia and it's completely my fault. I told you when it happened that I was going to fly to Australia, that I was finally going to see a shrink, make it work. But you never heard me, because you had the official best relationship on the face of the earth." He sighed. "The point, Sandra, is that I actually could have done something to change and I could have saved that relationship. I just don't think you're in the same position."

My face burned. "Paul, I'm sorry. I'm sorry about Dennis. I had no idea how horrible I was. It's just that— Well. I had no idea, I guess. About anything, including the official best relationship on the face of the earth."

"It's okay," he said, jabbing at his hair. "You're an evil bitch, but you're *my* evil bitch."

When I didn't laugh, his tone softened. "Don't feel bad, Sandy. No matter what you said, I would have done what I did. I fucked it up all by myself."

I felt ashamed. I thought back to an afternoon when my mom had come up to visit me at Yale and we had lunch at the restaurant next to the theater. She looked outside and saw Paul and Dennis walking down the street.

"They look so connected, so together," she marveled. "It's as if the rest of the world doesn't exist; only they do."

"Yeah," I answered, barely looking. I knew what Paul was up to in his spare time, so none of the rest of it impressed me. His relationship with Dennis was nothing like mine with Bucky. We were the ones who were really together. Maybe it was easier for my mom to appreciate Dennis and Paul because neither one of them was Jewish.

Well, that was a brilliant assessment, I could see now. I had only thought of them in terms of me—my rules, my goals. I had never thought of myself as a selfish person before. It would seem that I was wrong.

"Paul," I started, but he cut me off.

"It's over, Sandy, forget it. But the bottom line about Bucky is: People don't change. Five years from now, or ten years from now, when you've got two kids and he does it again, what are you going to do about it?"

"Kill him?" I offered.

He smiled. "Did he ever actually say *why* he did what he did?"

I shook my head. "Not really, aside from some double-talk he wrote in a letter. And I think it's because there *is* no explanation — unless temporary insanity can last for two years."

Paul lit a cigarette. "Look, Sandy, you're all of twenty-six. Why don't you go out with some other people? See who else is out there."

I looked at him uncomprehendingly. *No one else* was out there. There was only Bucky. For my whole life, or at least since high school, there had been only Bucky.

I wondered if someone like Dolores Hope would give Bucky another chance. People who want to see stars badly enough to have a removable roof couldn't possibly classify the world so rigidly. They knew that there was youth, romance, passion, confusion, anger, sadness, and sorrow out there, sometimes all at once. To forgive was divine.

I suddenly noticed that we were among the last people poolside; the *Jolie!* reader had left along with the sun, which had dropped down behind the palm trees surrrounding us. I felt chilly.

"Romano, I need a drink," I said. "Let's go."

He looked at me quizzically.

"No, I'm not mad at you," I said. "I appreciate everything you're saying. I, well, I guess I just don't want to hear it."

"Fair enough," he said easily, and we went back to our own hotel, showered and changed, then drove around town until we found one of those Mexican places with something for every-one—wishing wells, miniature bridges, strawberry daiquiris whirring in the blender. We ordered beers, and Paul stretched out in his chair, throwing back his head and yawning.

"What's with your teeth?" I asked.

He closed his mouth, immediately self-conscious. "What do you mean?" he managed to say, practically without moving his lips.

"I mean that they look dingy, or something. Not like they usually look."

He shrugged, resigned. "I don't know. Maybe it's the crystal meth."

"Jeez, whatever happened to just plain booze?"

"It doesn't keep you up and screwing for twelve hours, for starters." He had his arms crossed in front of him, his mouth set.

"Romano, no one screws for twelve hours. They stop to talk or eat or sleep and do it again later."

He laughed without smiling. "These are not people you want to talk to," he said curtly.

My eye went to his Marlboro pack. There was no gold lighter on it, just the kind of matches that offer a good deal on a muffler.

"Where's your lighter?" I asked, suddenly feeling afraid.

Another shrug. "Some trick took it," he said, draining his beer. "No big deal, Sandy. I can always get another one."

"But it was your grandfather's!"

He lit a cigarette. "Another reason I haven't been home lately." He looked me square in the eye. "Because everyone asks me too many questions."

"Does that include Sally?"

He turned away, exhaling his cigarette smoke toward the ceiling beams. I turned away, too, and watched a little girl throw a penny into the wishing well. Her father smiled, scooping her up and kissing her on their way out. She wrapped her arms around his neck. Now that I noticed it, every table seemed to be filled with kids, eating chips and dripping sauce on their T-shirts while their mothers drank margaritas and batted eyelashes at husbands who looked suitably surprised by the attention.

But at our table, a cold wall had come up between Paul and me, which I didn't remember ever happening before. I switched to Scotch.

When our entrées came, I stopped trying to make conversation. My plate was filled with chicken enchiladas covered with guacamole, black beans, sour cream, and a thick layer of melted cheese. I ate almost half of it without putting down my fork.

Paul picked at his dinner and watched me with distaste. "Do you think someone's going to take it away from you?" he finally asked.

"They've taken away everything else," I said sharply. "Why should this be different?"

He shifted in his seat.

"And while we're criticizing," I went on, "why are you eating nothing? At every single meal?"

"I'm not hungry." He motioned toward the waiter. "Check."

"Is this a new diet for me?" I asked. "Pay the bill before I'm done eating?"

"I don't know, Sandy, this place is giving me the creeps." He half smiled. "All these happy families."

I half smiled back. "I know what you mean."

When the waiter returned, Paul reached for his wallet.

"Let me get this," I said.

"No, it's mine," he answered, holding up an American Express card.

"Sorry, señor," said the waiter, "we no take credit cards. Cash or check only."

"You take checks? And not credit cards?" Paul looked incredulous. "Well, okay, since I left my cash at the hotel." He wrote out a check and handed it to the waiter, who smiled and said, "We see identification. Driver's license or passport."

Paul blanched. "I don't have it with me," he said. "I didn't realize I was going to a foreign country."

The waiter kept smiling. "That's okay, sir, driver's license." I could see him eyeing the valet parking ticket on the table. Paul seemed frozen.

"Oh, I drove here," I said, a shade too loudly. "But I don't have my checkbook with me."

The waiter's smile disappeared. I pulled out my wallet. "I'm going to pay cash," I told him with an edge in my voice that all but demanded he put the goddamned smile back on his face. Which he did.

"What's the matter?" I asked Paul after the waiter had left the table.

He looked somber. "Sandy, I was going to get around to telling you this, but, well, I don't know, I guess I didn't."

I waited.

"We're going to have to take a taxi back to the hotel."

I looked blank. "Why?"

"'Cause you can't drive a stick, right?"

"Right."

He took a breath. "I'm actually not supposed to be driving."

I stared. He stared back.

"I've been arrested twice for drunk driving," he said, speaking quietly and directly. "The first time it happened, Sally bailed me out, but the second time, she refused. I had to spend the night in jail." He sighed. "And if a cop picks me up driving when I've been drinking, I'm going back to jail and staying there."

I could tell how this had been weighing on him, how worried he had been that I would think less of him. But somehow, I felt better. The barrier that had risen so quickly between us was down. This was my fault, I thought. All I'd done all day was talk about Bucky. I hadn't asked Paul anything about himself at all.

So I would now. But first we got up and went into the bar, filled with forlorn singles just like us.

Okay, I asked. How? Why? What was going on?

Slowly, he told me. About how the partying was such an unavoidable part of life in L.A., whether it was showbiz life or gay life. About how glad he was that it really hadn't affected his work, because so many other people in the business partied, too. I asked him three times if he thought he needed help—shrink help, AA help. He assured me he did not. He talked about how Sally was so patient—most of the time, at least—but no, he admitted, he hadn't really told her what he was up to—about the guys, that is. But she was a grown-up, he insisted, she knew it and loved him anyway, loved him for who he really was. Marie, of course, didn't know a thing about any of it. She was still a saint, and her shoes were still toeless.

I ordered another round of drinks. "If you can't drive anyway, you might as well have a good time," I said, and we both just laughed.

Then he assured me that the partying really was under control. He had also enrolled in traffic school, as required by California law. Only he was going to gay traffic school, he said. Yes, there really was such a thing. And somehow we got onto the topic of stick shifts, and we laughed until the tears were rolling down our cheeks. The other customers looked at us, then away, shaking their heads at our making a scene. I couldn't have cared less. We were together and talking and we were back on the same side and somehow all of these glitches—Bucky and partying and Sally—would work themselves out and we would be fine. Finally, we staggered out of the bar to call a cab.

"You have to think about moving on now, Sandy," Paul slurred earnestly, as he pulled open the huge carved door. He threw an arm around my shoulders. "Get married. Help your kids with their homework. Have a normal life. Then you can come back to this restaurant."

I nodded, which sent me falling into the door frame.

"Give someone else a chance," he went on. "Don't only see Bucky wherever you look. No one else will be that fucked up. They don't have to be perfect, remember. People do stupid things they don't mean sometimes," he said, holding me up. "It doesn't mean they're bad people. You should be softer about that."

"Okay, Romano, I will," I said. "But I have to tell you that I'm still worried about you and I don't know how to help." I grabbed his shirtsleeve for balance. "I liked it better when we lived close by and I could see you every day."

He nodded and we were entwined, leaning against the building, and he smelled from cigarettes and the stuff he put in his hair. I was overcome with feelings of love and frustration in equal parts, wanting to turn back the clock on my entire life, so I could be with Bucky again, and I could be with Paul all the time and be there to break down the door if something went wrong. Too much time had passed. I wanted to see the gold lighter again. I wanted to feel Bucky's chest against my cheek. I breathed in the night air and thought my heart would break.

"I love you," Paul said earnestly, then the taxi came and we went back to the hotel, where he stayed in our living room watching TV and I fell into bed.

When the room stopped spinning, or almost stopped spinning, and I was under the covers while holding on to the night table for balance, I called out to him. "Romano! Tell me the name of that day spa. The cheap one we can afford. Because we're going there, first thing in the morning. I need to lose five pounds fast, or no one is ever going to look at me again."

He didn't answer, but I could practically hear him smiling. Next to boys and shopping, Paul liked diets best.

"So, first we're going to fix me," I went on, "which means I have to starve to death. But if I lose my weight and promise to do exactly what you told me to with Bucky, that means you're going to cut out the partying and be a good boy too, right?"

Suddenly he was standing in the doorway. He nodded.

"And next time I'm here, you'll have your license back, okay?"

He nodded again.

"Good." And then I felt my throat start to close and I threw off the covers and dashed to the bathroom. Paul stood there and laughed. "That's a good start, Sandra," he said. "That's a few pounds right there."

6

By the end of July, I still didn't have my own office. Not that I minded—mostly I appreciated having the company—but at certain times when I was rushing to leave and my slip was stuck, I would have loved not to fish for it under Pascal's watchful eye.

"Big date?" he asked, amused, one night when I was busy fishing.

"Blind date," I answered, finally shaking it free. "I don't suppose it's the same thing."

He cringed sympathetically, but Coco perked right up.

"Oooh, that's great, where did you find him?" she asked. I hesitated. She had just returned from a long weekend with a French novelist she'd met at a Hamptons cocktail party. He had a beard and an earring, and they'd shacked up in someone's empty house while he read aloud to her in the bath and wrote poems to her while she slept. She'd showed them to us, and even though they weren't very good, it was poetry all the same.

For a desperate second I thought about inventing a novelist of my own, but I didn't have the nerve. "I found him through my parents," I confessed miserably; she and Pascal groaned. "His father and my father go to temple together." More groaning. Only Pimm was optimistic.

"I think you have to give everyone a chance," she said staunchly. "Maybe he'll turn out to be wonderful."

"I don't think so," I said. "When he called me, I asked him what kind of doctor he was, and he said a radiologist, and then he asked if I knew what a radiologist does. And when I said no, he said, 'Well, it's not about radios!'"

Even Pimm groaned.

"Listen, you guys," I said, "give me a break. As my loving mother has pointed out a million times, I have not been out on a proper date with anyone besides Bucky Ross since I was seventeen. Which is nine years, for those who are counting." I sighed. "She told me I have to polish my dating skills."

"She's right," Coco said emphatically. "And your dumping skills. If you think he's thoroughly wretched by the end of the first drink, tell him you're on deadline and have to run."

"This issue doesn't close till next week!" I said.

"So? He doesn't know that. Just say you're terribly sorry and get up and go. Then you can come to the Limelight. My friends are giving this really fun party that starts at nine."

"'Fun party' is an oxymoron," I said, checking my reflection in the window and fixing my hair. "What's it for, anyway?"

"It's a party, Sandy. It's to have a good time."

I blushed. "You know what I mean."

"It's a few friends who pooled their birthdays," she said. "They're a terrific group, actually. One just opened a restaurant in the Village, one is an architect, and one is an art dealer in SoHo. So if you're already dressed and made up, don't waste it by going home. Come meet us. You might even have fun. Pimm is coming, aren't you?"

Pimm smiled nervously. "I guess so, Coco, if I can bring my sister. I promised her we'd have dinner tonight." I had only recently discovered that Pimm's real name was Theresa; she had been conceived in London during her parents' honeymoon after they'd had Pimm's cups. Her sister Linda was called Breezy—

because when she was born, it was a breezy day on the Vineyard. That's WASP for you.

Anyway, I was glad Pimm had company. Her boyfriend was in graduate school in California, and she seemed to be alone a lot.

"Of course you should bring her," Coco said easily. "Everyone's bringing someone." Then she turned toward Pascal. "*Et toi, mon cher?*"

He sighed. "Another dinner party where I face my fate again," he said dramatically, referring to his incest-impaired paramour.

Looking at his sad-sack face, it occurred to me that some people just love being miserable, no matter how much they deny it. It's a hobby, like chess.

"Well, maybe I'll see you later," I said halfheartedly. "Unless I fall madly in love, in which case I'll see you tomorrow." I left the office, calls of "Good luck" bouncing behind me.

Howard Barad was my first blind date. And if anyone told me I would ever be fixed up by my parents, I would have slit my throat. But Mom was insistent, and not entirely unreasonable. "You have to get used to meeting new people," she said. "You don't have to marry them. Just eat with them. Talk to them. Give someone else a chance. It's one night."

He was driving in from Long Island, and his car pulled up, right on time. I got in and found a not-terribly-attractive guy about my age, with brown hair, brown eyes, glasses, and a polyester-blend tie from a Christmas clearance sale. He shook my hand with curved, damp fingers, and I smiled enthusiastically when he mentioned the Edwardian Room at the Plaza Hotel. No, I had never been there. And the reason why, I couldn't help thinking, might be that no one under the age of one hundred *ever* went there unless they were in from Kansas and didn't want room service.

"Sounds great," I said.

"Fasten your seat belt," he instructed.

"It's going to be a bumpy night," I responded automatically, then smiled again. He looked blank. My heart dropped, but I caught myself. Maybe only pretentious drama-school graduates went around quoting from *All About Eve*. Just because he didn't get it didn't mean he was a bad person. Maybe he could quote from *Dr. Kildare* and I wouldn't get it either. Meanwhile, he was still sitting there waiting for me to fasten my seat belt. So I did.

Once we were ensconced at a table near the window (the only other diner was a John Gielgud type across the room who I would have sworn was wearing his slippers), I knocked back a white wine in record time. My date presented a floor show à la Pascal, only his stories were about the hospital and its chronically ungrateful patients. I kept on smiling, had a second drink, and never mentioned a deadline, for which I gave myself ten bonus points. I excused myself prettily to go to the ladies' room, but as I passed the revolving door in the lobby I had to physically restrain myself from leaning into one of its spinning panes and fleeing onto the street. Why was I doing this? Was there a rule somewhere saying that everyone had to get married? Or be in love? Some people actually managed to live happily ever after all by themselves—didn't they? Someone, somewhere, must. I could always start a trend. We could run it as a cover line: "A Spinster's Life: The Ultimate Relaxation."

I returned to the table in time to see Howard Barad, M.D., aim his fork at my just-served veal scallops, spear one, and fold it whole into his mouth. "Mmmm, good," he pronounced. "You'll like that."

I looked at the long drips of sauce on the tablecloth and then, as surreptitiously as possible, at my watch. It wasn't even eight o'clock.

A full mouth proved no deterrent to Dr. Barad's conversation, which encompassed radios (he actually collected them) and snorkeling, one of his favorite pastimes. I groaned inwardly. Another water sport that had never appealed to me. At least it wasn't sailing.

I looked out the window as Howard droned on. The horse-drawn carriages were lined up in the street waiting to take tourists and romance seekers for a twilight spin through the park. I had never done that with Bucky, I realized, though we had always planned to.

When I'd returned from Palm Springs, I must have picked up the phone to call him a hundred times, but always managed to stop myself. I got into the habit of calling his desk at work, just to see who answered. He never did, and I always hung up.

I also called his home machine during the day and found that he had changed his message. Suddenly he was sporting some sort of country-western twang, saying, "If you would be so kind as to leave a message," he'd call you back. I didn't get it. Here was a guy trying to look like Arnold Schwarzenegger who talked like Kenny Rogers and, with his new wardrobe of custom-made suits, dressed like James Bond. Who the hell was he, anyway?

He left me a few more messages—at times of the day when I would never be home—but I didn't return them. Finally, they stopped.

Which is how I ended up in the Edwardian Room with Howard Barad, who, unfortunately, was still talking. Over coffee, the conversation turned to food, which was at least a step up from radios.

"What would you say is your favorite meal?" he asked.

"Pizza," I said immediately. "Double cheese, pepperoni, and mushroom."

He clapped his hand on the table. "Well, if I had known that, I could have saved a lot of money," he exclaimed, vexed.

"Sorry," I said, narrowing my gaze, but he was already searching for his car keys, insisting on driving me home.

"Actually, I'm going back to the office," I said quickly.

He looked at his watch, aghast. "But it's almost nine-thirty," he said. "The office is closed now, isn't it?"

I sighed and shook my head mournfully. "Not for those of us on deadline," I said. There went my bonus points. "Actually, in Los Angeles, it's only six-thirty, and I still have to call someone and interview them, because the piece has to ship tomorrow. But I had a lovely time. Thank you." I got up and started to walk.

"Well, at least let me drop you there," he said anxiously. He must have promised his father he'd see me home. "That would be great," I said, and this time I put on my seat belt without being asked.

I managed to elude the wet lips in the driver's seat and ducked inside the *Jolie!* lobby. The nighttime doorman looked up. "Forget something?" he asked amiably, so I said yes. My dignity.

I waited until I was sure the car was gone, then decided it was probably against my better judgment to walk into the Limelight, alone, for a party inhabited by the kind of people Coco Church hung out with. But I was also desperate to prove to myself that there was more to life than Howard Barad. I forced myself back outside.

When I arrived at the club, there were a handful of people at the door who didn't want to be told that a private party was in progress, and they were none too happy when I handed over the slip of pink paper Coco had given me to gain entry.

Inside, it was very dark and very loud and, in truth, very empty. It didn't take me long to find Coco.

"Hey, you made it, how great!" she enthused. "Was the date just pitiful?"

"That's the word for it. I'll give you the gory details tomorrow. Where is everyone?"

"Oh, it's early yet," she said, not even looking at her watch. "They'll start coming soon. But in the meantime, you know, we have some fabulous coke."

I shook my head. "No thanks," I said. I may be the only person in New York to have lived through the eighties without ever trying cocaine. The idea of inhaling something directly into my brain simply unnerved me. If it had come in suppositories, I might have considered it.

"Okay, then come meet some people," she urged, dragging me toward a small gathering. "This is Sandy, everyone," she announced. A few of them smiled and said hi, though most of them ignored me.

"Is Pimm here?" I asked, but Coco was already off with some musician type, arm draped around his neck, laughing and dancing. Her halter top was almost untied.

This had been a mistake. I started sidling toward the door.

I had almost made it outside when someone called my name.

It was Peter Darby, who I knew from drama school. He was gay and used to accompany Paul to some of New Haven's finer bacchanals, when he wasn't practicing transcendental meditation. He had always seemed the picture of calm to me, but now that he had taken a job with a Broadway producer, he said, he found spiritual nirvana more elusive than ever. He was a friend of the architect, it turned out, who hadn't arrived yet for his own birthday party. We talked for a while, until a large group poured in, pushing past us, drunk and rowdy. One guy practically mowed me over, stomping on the heel of my shoe, pitching me forward. Peter caught me by the wrists.

"Jesus!" I bellowed indignantly, though the guy never even turned around. "I think it's definitely time to go home," I told Peter, working the mashed shoe back on. Another man came through the door and approached us with a tentative smile.

"Um, hi, is this the party for Claire?" he asked pleasantly.

"If it is, she has some rotten friends," I said curtly, turning my back on him. "Give me a call sometime," I said to Peter. "Gotta go."

After almost breaking someone else's foot in a struggle to get a taxi, I sat back and made a post-Bucky resolution. No more parties. I was too old to feel this meaningless and humiliated.

At thirteen you have no choice, but as a grown-up you do, and goddammit, I was going to be a grown-up if it killed me, as it certainly promised to. Blind dates, I decided, were a definite maybe from now on, depending on the referral. My parents, however, were permanently disqualified.

In the following weeks I discovered that, my parents aside, it seemed that everyone I knew had someone I *had* to meet, the perfect person just for me. It was like a community project in New York to fix people up, play fairy godmother and get all the credit. It had nothing to do with love, and it had nothing to do with the hapless souls involved. It was all about the fixer-uppers savoring the ultimate control freak's triumph: deciding what was best for everyone else.

The procession of dates seemed endless. First, there was the real estate entrepreneur—highly recommended—who sent me a bouquet of balloons at the office with a note telling me how much he looked forward to our dinner. As the balloons bobbed along the ceiling, we all spent the better part of an afternoon planning my wedding—and then the guy stood me up.

Next was a book editor who took me to Memphis, a loud, happening restaurant on the Upper West Side where everything was served with the Cajun spices that were so trendy then. But before the blackened redfish arrived, he left the table to do coke—without telling me and without offering—and returned twenty minutes later with a bloody nose. So much for the redfish.

Then there was the lawyer from Sullivan & Cromwell whose name I actually forgot by dessert. I did my best to cover it up, but when he walked me home and called me "Sandy" twice and all I could come up with was what a *great* time I had had and thank you so much, I think he figured it out. I was so mortified that, once inside, I ate an entire bag of Mint Milanos.

Another night I had to go to a silly event for *Jolie!*, a screening of some public-television thing at the Guggenheim Museum, where a semi-famous actor, very tall with a long face, sat next to me and eventually asked me to dinner. That was fine until he insisted on driving me home. While stopped at a red light he reached over, took my hand, and started kissing my palm, picturing himself the soul of romance. He looked so much like a nag going for a sugar cube, it took all my willpower not to laugh.

In retrospect, of course, I should have dated no one until I had regained some sense of equilibrium. No matter where I went or whom I was with, I always had the sensation of being outside myself somehow, watching, and none too acutely at that. I wasn't happy alone, and I wasn't happy with anyone else. Though my instinct was to stay away from men in general, everyone *insisted* that that was the wrong choice. And having made the wrongest of all wrong choices imaginable, well, I didn't consider myself much of an authority. So I kept dating, believing that the ritual would heal me eventually, like antibiotics.

Next up on the hit parade was Bart Canaday, an Australian business executive recommended by my drama-school friend Dara Richards, another theater refugee who was now an aspiring movie producer. Bart was a year or two younger than me but very smart, Dara insisted. And because he gave money to struggling nonprofit theaters in leaky basements in the Village, she declared, he had the soul of an artist.

I met him at a charity polo match, of all places. It was in Connecticut, and a group of us drove out there, dressed in our drama-school idea of polo-match finery: large hats that looked stagey—there were tents to keep out of the sun—silk dresses we sweated through, and high heels that sank into the grass and were stained forever. We looked ridiculous. The real habitués, who were dressed in cotton, khaki, and Keds, stared us down, so except for occasional forays to the buffet table, we kept to ourselves. Bart met us there. He seemed older in the way that most non-American boys did, better educated somehow, wiser in the ways of the world. He was pleasant company, he did like the theater, he even knew about *Jolie!* And if he realized that our hats were stupid, he never let on.

He and I met a few nights later, for dinner. It was perfectly fine, but that was also the problem. Our date, like so many of these dates, felt no different than a business lunch. Everyone always says you *know* when it's right with someone, which may be, but when it's not exactly *wrong*, there's the trap. You start thinking, Shouldn't something be happening here? And when it's not, you think, Maybe *I'm* not giving it a chance. (When in doubt, always blame yourself.)

So then you agree to two or three more of these completely eventless evenings where both of you gamely stick it out though he would rather go home and take off his tie and you would rather go home and take off your pantyhose. But you order coffee while he talks about how Outward Bound changed his life, and you wonder what kind of life can be changed by a camping trip.

After dinner, Bart and I walked along Columbus Avenue. It was a beautiful night.

"Look," I said. "There's the Big Dipper and the Little Dipper. It's so rare to actually see them in the city."

He followed my gaze, seemingly confused. "Where?" he asked. I laughed, thinking he was making a joke, but he shook his head. "In Australia, we have a different set of constellations," he said.

"What?" I couldn't tell if he was putting me on.

"Yes," he continued. "Our stars aren't like these. The whole setup is different."

I felt unexpectedly crushed. Lackluster dinner conversation was one thing, but how could I fall in love with someone who didn't even know the same stars I did? He called, but I didn't call back. There are just some givens in life. A pulse and the Milky Way. Next.

By August, my patience with the entire dating process was

running out. I was bored to death and hadn't had sex in months, a strange and unappealing situation. Dara Richards then introduced me to Roy Toner. Roy was a development executive at TriStar Pictures, which meant that he spent his time doing pretty much what Dara did, turning up at meetings with just about anyone with even the slightest crackpot idea for a screenplay. Though he at least had a few pictures actually threatening to go into production, and had co-produced one already, albeit a flop.

Roy was very smooth, tall and slim and nattily dressed, with a handsome face and the unctuous manner of a Hollywood executive—no depth and no apology—which, at that moment, beguiled me. Beside the fact that he seemed to disappear periodically, I decided that the time had come to sleep with someone who wasn't Bucky.

I made the monumental effort to clean my apartment—I actually folded the futon up off the floor for the first time in months—and invited him over. Beforehand, we got suitably smashed at dinner at Orso, a showbiz hangout, where Roy shook hands with just about everyone at every table while I smiled from a distance. Back at my apartment, things moved right along— though, of course, I had to pull the futon right back down again. As I did, I willed myself not to think, just to do it. I hate to say that I wanted to get it over with, but I did.

Meanwhile, Roy Toner had no sense of what I was thinking or feeling, because he seemed suddenly possessed by the ghost of Errol Flynn. He was quite the swashbuckler, all pose and swagger and a well-choreographed technique, which, in his defense, included a clitoral homing device he could have marketed to a fare-thee-well.

But, alas, sex with Roy Toner was about Roy Toner, expert seducer, with none of the sloppy authenticity or charm of an inadvertent tooth or an errant elbow. What an operator he was. And what a bore.

When he had finished his performance, we settled onto the pillows and under the covers. I turned to him, alarm clock in hand. "What time do you want to get up?" I asked. He flinched, as if I'd slapped him.

"Oh, I'm so sorry," he said formally, as if addressing the Queen Mother, "I have such an early breakfast meeting tomorrow, I won't be able to stay."

I thought I might die of humiliation. I had no idea that I could be a one-night stand for someone who didn't even stay the night.

We spoke on the phone a few more times but never managed to actually connect, and then Dara called me. "I thought I should apologize, but I had no idea," she said timidly.

"What do you mean?" I asked.

"Well, about Roy," she said.

"What? What about Roy?"

"I found out from someone he works with that he's been seeing the same woman for years. And she's about ten years older than he is."

I laughed. "Well, at least now I understand the performance aspect of the evening," I said. "The part of the young, full-service stud will be played by Roy Toner. At least the old broad did the rest of us a service and gave him a geography lesson."

She laughed with relief. "You're not mad?" she said.

"No," I said truthfully. "I have to say, I really don't care."

And I didn't.

Enough so that over the next several weeks I had three drinks dates, two lunch dates, and four dinners. I kissed two, slept with two, and the rest didn't even get a handshake.

About six weeks after the party at the Limelight ("Fabulous," Coco had pronounced it, "you definitely should have stayed"), I got a call from Peter Darby.

"I have a friend you might be interested in," he told me.

"God, do I have to?" I wailed. "My life has been a living hell."

"No, this one's different," he insisted, launching into a hard sell of Michael Victor, a financial whiz who was also on the board of the New York City Ballet. When I finally said okay, mostly to make Peter stop, he sounded relieved.

"You shouldn't be so angry, Sandy," he said.

"Are you going to give me a TM lecture now? Because I am truly not in the mood."

"Look," he went on, unperturbed, "I know every breakup is hard, but this is a big city and there are opportunities everywhere. Like that night at the Limelight. I couldn't believe that."

"What are you talking about?"

"Remember that guy who asked us if it was the party for Claire, the one you totally blew off?"

"Yeah? So?"

"That was Mark Lewis."

"The art writer?"

"The very one. Who, I might add, has been separated for more than a year now and dating like crazy."

"I'm not interested in anyone who dates like crazy," I huffed. "Including me."

"Well, you certainly made an impression," he said.

"What do you mean?"

"He wanted to know who that really cute woman was and why she was so incredibly pissed off."

"Did you tell him that someone had just mauled my shoe, not to mention my foot, and I couldn't wait to go home?"

"No," he said. "I told him that you had just broken off an engagement and were a bitch in general. Nothing personal."

"Thanks for the support. Don't you think then that you should wait before letting me meet your friend? Let me cool off a little?"

"Nah. He's lonely. And if the date doesn't work out, you guys can always be friends." Every matchmaker's favorite line.

"I have enough friends," I growled.

Peter laughed. "I know, I know, but if you keep behaving this way, you're going to run out."

He told me that Michael Victor would call. I hung up and lit a cigarette. Okay, I was angry. Why shouldn't I be? I'd been totally betrayed by the love of my life. And the only remedy seemed to be enduring this endless procession of bad meals and deadly men.

I thought about Mark Lewis. He probably wasn't deadly, I'd give him that. He was *the* art columnist for *Art and Our Times, the* prestigious art magazine, and a hot writer everyone wanted. He always seemed to be on PBS expounding on Pollock or Klee — which is why I hadn't recognized him, since that was usually when I changed the channel. I let go a plume of smoke. Fuck it, I decided. I knew nothing about art and would have nothing in common with him, anyway. Let him date until his dick dropped off. What did I care?

Michael Victor called the next day and was extremely nice. He was also allergic to cigarette smoke (I was puffing away when we met), allergic to perfume (I was wearing Chanel No. 5), and after I'd ordered the rack of lamb at the Quilted Giraffe, he broke it to me that he wouldn't be eating dinner. He was on Optifast. So while I made my way manfully through six chops, he sipped from a frosted glass through a straw.

After he didn't kiss me good night (allergic to makeup?), I went home and stayed in bed for the rest of the weekend with hot towels and a heating pad around my neck. I couldn't move it at all. Sharon, who had turned into the typically absent New York roommate who left me notes like I was the cleaning lady with instructions on her real whereabouts versus the version I was to tell her mother, was actually in residence and served me roast chicken and kasha varnishkas. She lent me her sympathetic ear, and together we decried the quality of men worldwide. Her Dr. Hyman was history, and she was now onto a scenic designer she knew from the drama school who had never spoken once in the three times I had met him.

"Is he a deaf-mute?" I asked, only half joking.

"He has issues with his mother," she said tersely. End of discussion.

I could sympathize, actually. I was having issues with my own mother. She couldn't understand why I hadn't fallen in love with someone else yet, since that night at the Met had happened an eternal four months ago. Every minute I spent unattached was a direct insult to my ovaries.

One night on the phone when I found her to be exceptionally prickly, I finally mentioned Fred Salzman and heard her start to smoke. Fred Salzman had been Mom's fiancé before she met Dad. He had been her boyfriend starting in eighth grade. His mother had wanted him to go to Yale Law School and become a big shot and leave my middle-class, Bronx-born mother in the dust. The fact that Fred Salzman was also middle-class and Bronx-born had escaped his mother entirely. The daughter-in-law she envisioned had grown up on Park Avenue, the kind of girl who spent her days shopping for gloves and perfecting her beef Stroganoff. That kind of girl did not train rats to roll over three times before pressing the lever in their cage and leave broccoli defrosting in a pot for dinner.

I once saw a picture of my mother taken right after she and Fred broke up. In it, Mom had a cigarette in her hand, and her eyes looked wounded and powerful all at once and she was incredibly beautiful. She probably ripped it up; I never saw it again, and whenever I asked for it she made a big fuss about how she couldn't find it. So she knew better than she liked to let on about loving someone from childhood, dreaming about everything you might do in your life together, and watching it come apart once you grew up. And she was furious with me for reminding her.

After I invoked Fred Salzman, I noticed that she eased up on me and criticized my brother, Jerry, instead. He was now a doctoral student in microbiology at Harvard and seemed to have inherited Mom's tendency to hang out with the rodents rather than dating marriageable women eager to have children. The older we Berlin children got, it seemed, the drier the promise of Green Hills became.

As I lay in bed one Saturday in early September—or, rather, as I lay on the futon on the living room floor—I thought, yet again, about Bucky. It had been his birthday the day before. It had also been his mother's birthday, the very same day. Every year she would say how he had always been her best present, blah blah.

The previous year, we'd spent Bucky's birthday at the cottage. Neither of his brothers were there, so it was just his parents and the two of us.

I'd gotten up that morning and gone down the hall to the bathroom. By the time I got back to my room, Mrs. Ross had been there and made my bed—tight, like a coffin. I brought Bucky in to see it.

"Is she trying to erase all signs of me?" I asked, and he laughed helplessly at the hospital corners and the knifed pleat under the pillow that she had managed in three minutes flat. She had already gone back outside to her folding chair, where she sat with a mound of yarn, knitting sweaters for Christmas. There was a new dog now to replace Baxter, a black Lab named Maggie—or, as Mrs. Ross liked to call her, Margaret Ann Ross. Mr. Ross didn't seem to even notice her.

Or me. He nodded good morning, passed the sugar, and mentioned the Yankees once or twice to Bucky. Mrs. Ross, in contrast, spoke constantly, to no one in particular, as was her way, but she also directed her questions only to Bucky. They were good, these people. Lying on my futon a year later, I realized that they had decided on Beth Brewer as their candidate for the job of daughter-in-law, and they aimed that WASP technically-polite-freeze-thing right between my eyes. While you couldn't fault a word they said, they managed to make me feel invisible.

Until dinner. In celebration of her and Bucky's shared birthdays, Mrs. Ross had made a roast beef, instant mashed potatoes from a box, and canned peas and carrots—this in late summer, when the farms were bursting with fresh produce. I had to really choke that meal down. There was no wine, though Mr. Ross nursed his drink at the table and smoked, leaving most of the abysmal food sitting right on his plate. Mrs. Ross urged him to finish, more than a few times, until he fixed her with an icy stare and said in a deadly quiet voice, "I have."

I felt so bad for her that I started to talk, just for distraction, about a biography of Eleanor Roosevelt I was reading, and what an inspiration she was, a real role model for the women's movement. I went on and on and eventually realized that no one had said anything in the longest time and that the potatoes had hardened on the plates.

Bucky wouldn't meet my eye, Mr. Ross lit another cigarette, and Mrs. Ross said, "Well, yes, dear, isn't that interesting," as she stood and started to clear the table.

I suddenly felt as I had that morning, when I'd seen the tightly made bed. Had I done something wrong? I stood and helped Mrs. Ross clear, and looked at Bucky again, but he stared down at the table. Finally, it was time for the cakes, two of them, and Mrs. Ross also set out a box of chocolates that a neighbor had dropped off. I had the distinct sense that I was now in the doghouse, but I couldn't figure out what I had done other than try to make conversation to divert a scene, and no one wanted to help me, including Bucky. Slowly but surely, I was starting to get pissed.

While Mrs. Ross was busily cutting pieces from both cakes, I slid the candy box over to my place. Out of the corner of her eye, she followed my every move, as if the box were filled with gold.

"Did you ever play 'guess inside'?" I asked innocently, my hand poised over the chocolates.

"No, dear," she said nervously, trying to finish with the cake so she could rescue the candy. "What's that?"

"Oh, when we were little, we used to try to guess what was inside the candy, and if we took a bite and found we guessed wrong, we didn't have to finish it."

Even in the twilight, I could see her face flush red. Finally, after all these years, I had found something that Mrs. Ross cared about as much as her yarn and her dogs and her cigarettes.

She sat down quickly and grabbed for the box. I almost fought her for it but Bucky kicked me under the table.

Her hand hovered.

"Guess," I said, more loudly than I'd intended.

"Oh, well, that's silly," she said, "but I love my chocolate cherries, and I just know that this is one of them." She put the piece whole into her mouth. Her face changed, and I waited for her to spit the candy out, but she lowered her eyes and swallowed instead.

"Coconut," she said grimly. "I *loathe* coconut."

"What a shame," I said solicitously. "If you had played, you wouldn't have had to finish it."

"Time for presents," Bucky boomed, bringing the gifts to the table. He opened his first—two polo shirts, whoop-de-doo—and then Mrs. Ross opened hers, exclaiming over a gold chain with a gold heart that had a tiny diamond chip in the middle. I raised my eyebrows at Bucky while his mother cleared the dessert plates, this time without my help.

"Does that mean you're going steady?" I asked once Mr. Ross had gone out onto the patio.

"Christ, you're a bitch," Bucky said glumly.

"Can I have some dinner now, please?" I asked, and after a chirped goodbye from the kitchen, we went straight to a place near the water where I polished off two lobster rolls in minutes.

"Okay, explain that scene to me," I said finally. "What did I do wrong?"

Bucky shifted in his seat. "Nothing, really. It's just that with my parents, when someone talks about a book they've read that no one else has, they consider it showing off."

"Excuse me?"

Bucky blushed. "I know it's not what you're used to, but that's the way they are. They think that if you're going to talk about something, everyone should be able to be part of the conversation."

"That's the stupidest thing I've ever heard," I said. "What's more, I don't believe it's true. In all the years I've known you, why would this be the first time I've heard about this philosophy?"

"I guess it just never seemed that pronounced before," he continued. "And, well, there you were going on and on about Eleanor Roosevelt and women's rights. I mean, I guess the point really is, Sandy, they don't believe in things like women's rights."

"Oh, sure they do. Your mother feels she has the right to serve instant potatoes instead of real ones she has to cook herself. She's a radical feminist."

"And why did you have to do that to her, with the candy? You made her take one she didn't want. It is her birthday, after all."

"A catastrophe," I said. "Certainly, the last thing anyone in your house wants to do is look at the inside of anything."

An awful fight ensued.

I lay on the futon in my apartment trying to remember all of it, but couldn't. What dominated my thoughts was: He was seeing Beth Brewer then. I did recall saying, "I don't know when this started to be so hard," and genuinely feeling that way, because ever since Seven Maples, something always seemed to mar our time together. And I remembered him saying, "You want everything, but only how you want it and when you want it. You want me to appear when *you* want me to. When you're done with *your* work, when *your* magazine issue is closed, when *your* test is taken, when *your* mommy yells at you. That's when you want me to appear, magically, and make everything better. But then afterward, you want me to get lost and give you your freedom until the next time."

I heard his voice in my head and felt a flush of shame. After all these months bemoaning his betrayal, I had somehow forgotten there had been anything else. The religion issue, the parent issue, and, most important, the fairy-tale issue: my holding tight to the simpleton's notion of him as the conquering hero, as steadfastly as he regarded me the mighty queen whose favor he needed to win. We weren't young adults, I realized, so much as very old children. I felt my victimhood shed, like a snake's skin.

He had kept on yelling. "Are you there for me when I'm sitting at that desk and I'm supposed to make a decision worth millions of dollars and have it be right the first time? If I call you, you tell me to work harder. You tell me that if I only applied myself, I could do anything I wanted. Well, what if I *can't?* Don't I still deserve to be taken out by you sometime and comforted? To get my own ice cream and have you say, 'Yes, Bucky, *you* are right and *they* are wrong,' instead of telling me how much work you have to do so you can't see me right now and why don't I use the time to devise a long-term strategy instead?"

Tears shone in his eyes. "Fuck a long-term strategy," he said. "I don't know if I even want to be doing this job next year. And you're moving straight ahead to run that magazine, and if we ever do get married, I'll be lucky to get you on the phone." A fat tear rolled down his cheek. "I want a partner in life," he said. "Do you really think you can be a partner for me?"

I closed my eyes and winced at the memory, a fat tear of my own sliding past my temple, into my hair.

Apparently not.

Me Times Three

#31 *The Mystery of the Golden Box*
by Sandra Berlin

Once upon a time, there lived a baker and his wife in a small village at the foot of a great mountain. One summer's day, the wife set out to pick some blackberries, and as she knelt among the bushes filling her bucket, she saw something shining in the dirt. She dug and dug until she unearthed a beautifully scrolled golden box that was so heavy she had trouble lifting it.

But lift it she did and, along with the berries, hauled the box home.

"Look, my husband," she said. "Have you ever seen such a beautiful thing? I'll bet it's worth a fortune."

The baker nodded. "It looks like solid gold," he said. "But what is inside that makes it so heavy?"

He tried to pry the box open, but alas, the clasp had broken off and the box was sealed shut.

The next day, a village woman came into the bakery to buy a blackberry pie and spied a golden gleam from the back of the shop. "What is that?" she asked with interest, walking toward the box. The baker grew alarmed, thinking that someone would discover his gold and try to rob him.

"Only a trinket my wife found while picking berries at the foot of the mountain," he said.

But when the village woman went home and tasted the pie, she exclaimed, "Why, this is the most delicious pie I have ever eaten! There are no berries at the foot of the mountain that taste this good. Whatever is inside that golden box has made this the best pie in the kingdom. I just know it."

So off she went, back to the bakery. Along the way she told the other villagers about the pie, and a large group of them arrived at the bakery together. "Tell us your secret ingredient," the villagers demanded. "What is inside the golden box?"

Well, business had never been so brisk for the baker, so first he sold everyone a pie, and then he smiled. "I will never tell," said he.

The next day, the baker baked his bread, the same bread he had always baked, and when the villagers tasted it, they all exclaimed, "This is the best bread we have ever tasted. What is the secret ingredient?"

Again, the baker smiled and said, "I will never tell."

A few more days passed, and one villager got an idea. "Why should we stand by and let the baker keep the golden box and its magic for his own?" he demanded. "We must take the box and split what is inside it equally amongst us."

By the time the group arrived at the bakery en masse, they were mighty mad. They woke the baker and his wife from a sound sleep, shouting, "You must give us the golden box! It is not for you alone."

"We know that," the baker answered. "Which is why we bake the magic into the pies and breads that you buy from us."

"Not everyone buys from you, and the magic is for everyone," the crowd cried. Then they ran past the baker and dove for the golden box and carried it outside, where they commanded him to open it.

"But I can't," the baker was forced to admit. "Look and see for yourselves. The clasp has broken and the box is sealed shut."

Well, that made the crowd even angrier. They jumped on the box, and they battered it with sticks, and when nothing else worked, they finally thrust it into the baker's oven to melt it. And when one corner gave way, they held it aloft and everyone peered inside and a great gasp went up from the crowd.

"You tricked us!" they shouted at the baker. "It is empty!"

And they killed the baker and his wife, and melted the box all the way down so they could divide it equally amongst themselves. Then they headed back to the foot of the mountain to see if they could find any more.

But, alas, they could not. And so, over time, the villagers started to tell the story of the Golden Box and how the baker and his wife had once made the best pies and bread in the kingdom because of the secret ingredient inside.

The End

7

Susie Schein was angry. I could tell because red splotches were bursting out on her neck, but in some weird internal contract with her chalky face, they never ventured above her jaw.

We were in yet another interminable story meeting where no one's ideas were good enough. A cold December rain hit the windows; on our high floor, it seemed as if we were encased in a cloud. The conference room was filled with gloomy faces, each one of which wanted to be back in bed, but Susie was having none of it. Evan, our publisher, was alarmed by the fact that following *Jolie!*'s spectacular debut, sales had leveled, so he kicked Miss Belladonna, who kicked Susie, who was now kicking us. Even Jean-Louis found himself defending his covers to Evan in closed-door meetings that invariably ended with Jean-Louis slamming out of the office yelling French obscenities and taking every model he could find clubhopping in limos stocked with Cristal.

The magazine was getting stale, Evan decreed. Jean-Louis used too many of the same girls, he complained, and the other magazines all had models jumping off the page now, so we had to do something different. That meant using less of Jolie, the model who had named herself after the magazine and who was married to its top photographer. Jolie had seemed like a perfectly nice girl to me until the day I was in the art department fighting with Jean-Louis about a layout of Colleen Dewhurst, who had just played the morphine-addicted Mary Tyrone in *Long Day's Journey into Night* on Broadway and had given us a smart, insightful interview. But Jean-Louis took one look at her photo and snorted. "Too old," he said disgustedly, and reduced it to one third of its size.

"But that's Eugene O'Neill's mother, his *mère, très dramatique*," I wheedled, while I mimed shooting up with a syringe. "*Elle est très important*," I insisted, but Jolie appeared then and Jean-Louis gladly forgot the shrunken picture to embrace her. Jolie had barely kissed both his cheeks in return when she spotted The Wall, filled with shots of her in an array of tiny bikinis. Her eyes widened, and she walked closer, intoxicated, to get a better look.

"*C'est moi! C'est moi! C'est moi!*" she cried delightedly, pointing a finger at each new image.

"*Ah, oui,*" Jean-Louis cooed.

I left, forgotten. I'd have to cut the story now to match the postage-stamp-size picture. And then I'd have to listen to complaints about how our features weren't selling the magazine. Could it be possible that even women, those masochistic creatures, could get sick of looking at paragons like Jolie? Did it occur to anyone here that someone, somewhere, might want to read a story about an actual grown-up who had worked for decades and had something to *say*? When Jolie was Colleen Dewhurst's age, what would she be doing? Paging through her scrapbooks, still chanting "*C'est moi?*"

In the gloomy conference room, I sighed out loud, louder than I'd meant to, drawing Susie Schein's annoyed attention.

"Nothing, sorry," I muttered. But the damage was done. Consulting her notes, she squinted at me and demanded, "Why are you using the same writers over and over?"

"Because any time I suggest new ones, you reject them," I snapped, though I caught myself before I could add, "And because they're the ones so desperate for money that they'll let you, through me, destroy their work."

"Well, I think it's time for a change," she said crisply. "What we have to do is stop thinking the way we've been thinking. How about using some men, for a change?"

Everyone murmured eager assent, even though we already used men. But maybe this was a way to get her off our backs.

She turned to me again. "What about Mark Lewis?"

"Mark Lewis?" My heart sank. I could practically hear him saying to Peter Darby: *Why was she so incredibly pissed off?* "Uh, sure, what about him?"

"Miss Belladonna met him at a dinner party last week," Susie said, pulling out a sheet of paper. "She sent me a note on it: 'Charming company, funny stories.' Why isn't he writing for us?"

"Well, no offense, Susie," I said slowly, "but why would he?"

"Because this is a national publication with a readership of one million people," she said impatiently. "*Art and Our Times* has a fifth of that."

"Okay," I said, conciliatorily. It was probably best not to introduce the notion that Mark Lewis might not cotton to writing for a magazine most frequently read under the hair dryer. "Do you want an essay on something in particular?"

"Not about art," she said. "Try something different. Call him up and ask what he's passionate about, what his hobbies are. Maybe he races sports cars or has a summer home in the Vineyard that gives him a spiritual lift. Maybe there's some city he's madly in love with. Didn't he grow up in Chicago? Maybe he could write about that."

To argue would be pointless. I would now have to pick up the phone and admit to Mark Lewis that I was the bitch who had snubbed him at the Limelight. Not to mention having to call the other big names Susie was reeling off now—everyone from a food writer at *The New York Times* to a movie executive who wrote book reviews in his spare time—none of whom would be caught dead writing for us. I nodded dutifully and said nothing. My life sucked.

Back in my office—yes, my very own office, as of three days earlier and bare of everything except my computer and the requisite white orchid sent to anyone who got a promotion—I closed the door and lit a cigarette. Then I threw self-respect to the wind, picked up the phone, and left cheery messages far and wide, saving *Art and Our Times* for last. The receptionist there referred me to Mark Lewis's agent, Victoria Segal, which was an immense relief. Maybe this way he would just say no in principle and never realize it was me who had asked.

I checked my watch: 11:41. Paul's plane was due at five-thirty, and I didn't care what Susie Schein said, I was walking out of this office at six sharp.

Paul had called a few nights earlier to tell me that he had joined Alcoholics Anonymous. His boss had taken him out to dinner and told him what a bright future he had, or could have, with the company. But it had come to his boss's attention that the partying was, after all, out of control. Meaning what?, I had asked Paul suspiciously, but all he'd say was that he'd tell me when he saw me.

He was arriving that night for a week's stay. Maybe he'd do some Christmas shopping, he'd said, though I didn't see how. His every minute was already booked. As a rule, Hollywood agents have breakfast, lunch, tea, cocktails, and dinner each day with anyone they can get their hands on. Paul also had theater or opera tickets every night, and somehow had to squeeze in AA meetings, to which I agreed to accompany him.

I certainly had nothing better to do—except work, to which I was now devoting a minimum of twelve hours a day, six or seven days a week. In addition to editing, I had started writing, too—

little pieces, mostly, but I enjoyed it. They were certainly easier than the fairy tales I'd been writing at home (I had kept the books but ripped out the title pages). Without Bucky and the prospect of children, the stories had lost their urgency, somehow. I tried keeping a journal instead—everyone said it was great writing practice—but I had no appetite for reality, either. I would start out with Susie and Miss Belladonna and end up with the Wicked Witch of the West and Glinda the Good. My writing was as mixed up as the rest of my life.

I hadn't heard from Bucky since the end of the summer. After the unreturned phone calls, he sent a few more letters written in his baby script on yellow legal paper. "Sitting here thinking of you," they inevitably began. He dotted his *i*'s with circles. I thought only girls did that. In seventh grade.

Yes, I was bitter, and it was a dark, ugly emotion with a taste all its own, one that even Ben & Jerry's Coffee Heath Bar Crunch could not obliterate. I tasted it all the time. I tasted it whenever I wanted to take one more bite, smoke one more cigarette, drink one more drink. I tasted it whenever I was overindulging in something I only thought I wanted and then thought about why I was wanting it. I tasted it in the back of my mouth, right near my brain, bitter.

I worked and walked and paid my bills, took my shoes in to be resoled, read the paper. I did everything I was supposed to do, only with an extra weight pressing right against the spot between my ribs where you get the wind knocked out of you.

After my brief flurry of social activity, I did not go on any more dates. I had freed myself of that obligation as my own extra-special birthday present. I didn't care what anyone else said or what they advised. I was sick of every man on the face of the earth, and if I could kick each one of them in the balls and watch them keel over in pain, I would levitate with sheer delight. Did I mention that I was bitter?

When Paul told me he joined AA, I actually felt jealous. Why wasn't there someplace I could go that would fix me? Some group of jilted women where I could stand up and say, "Hi, I'm Sandra and I'm a gullible, pathetic sap. I believed every word my prom date ever told me and I've just turned twenty-seven and I'm totally alone." Everyone would smile kindly and say, "Hi, Sandra," then we would drink coffee together, and each time I had the urge to walk over to Klein Chapin & Woodruff with a loaded shotgun, I could call my sponsor, Miss Havisham, who would adjust her tiara and talk me down.

The phone rang as I was grinding out my cigarette. My brother, I suddenly thought, always teased me about smoking cigarettes like a Friendly's waitress, right down to the end.

It was Victoria Segal, Mark Lewis's agent, and she sounded vaguely amused. I took a breath and launched into my pitch.

"I'll ask him," she said, surprising me. "He could probably use the cash. Divorce always means needing cash. I'll call you back."

Swell.

The afternoon dragged on. I had arranged to meet Paul at Joe Allen for a burger before the theater. I got there early, had a glass of wine, and relaxed. I always felt better when I went to the theater district. I usually ran into people from school, and I liked the us-versus-them feeling of watching the civilians gulping down their dinner and running to the theater at seven-thirty for a curtain that wouldn't rise until five minutes after eight. Tonight, though, I knew very few people and nursed my wine alone, waiting for Paul to appear, which he did, finally, at almost seven o'clock. He had a new, short haircut I didn't like at all: It made his face look square and drawn, at odds with his ebullient smile.

"Feel this," he said as we hugged, moving my hand to his stomach, which was sticking out over his jeans. "I'm eating ice cream all the time, 'cause when you quit drinking you need to replace the sugar you'd been getting from the alcohol." He looked at me expectantly. "Is it bad?" he asked sweetly.

"No, of course not. It's fine. I wouldn't even have noticed if you hadn't told me. Don't panic, Romano, you're still pretty." That part was certainly true. Every chorus boy in the place was panting. "But what's with the hair? Are you joining the military?"

His hand flew up to fluff it, as he always did, but he didn't have much to work with. "I don't know why I cut it, I just did. A new start, I guess."

"Cutting your hair is a new start? What happens when it grows out?"

He ignored me, sitting down and ordering coffee and a burger and launching into a sermon on AA and his new favorite word, "co-dependency," which seemed to mean that when Sally bailed him out of jail for drunk driving, she was encouraging him to drink.

"Wait a minute," I said suspiciously. "You drink and it's *her* fault? That's a neat equation."

He smiled the smile of an apostle. "It's a good thing I'm here for so long so I can explain it to you."

Not that he ever did. The days flew by, packed with activity. Fun activity, in spite of my job—and his. We laughed at the theater, cried at the opera, window-shopped Madison Avenue. We descended on the men's department of Saks Fifth Avenue, where I sat in an overstuffed chair, like one of those husbands in the dress department, while Paul modeled the most fabulous suits, jackets with broad shoulders and pants with crisp pleats, and I fingered the sumptuous material and nodded approvingly. He flipped through piles of cashmere sweaters and chose a handful. When Peter Darby joined us for drinks one day at the Plaza, Paul made us howl with tales of a priest he had had sex with, and the very large cross the priest kept above his bed that Paul could never take his eyes off.

One night, finally, at an early dinner before an AA meeting, I made Paul tell me what had prompted his big cleanup.

He sighed. "It was because of that jerk Richard Whitford," he said.

"The actor?" I asked, surprised.

"Yeah. He's a new client, and I was at a party with him where there was this huge bowl of coke on the dining room table. Everyone was doing lines, and he made a pass at me, and I wasn't interested, so he narc'ed me out to my boss."

"But are you really supposed to do *anything* to make a client happy, including fuck him?" I asked.

"Sure," Paul said glumly. "And if you don't, you shouldn't then be stupid enough to fuck a more famous client instead."

"And who's that, dare I ask?"

"Do I really have to tell you?"

"Yes."

"John Bean Marshall."

"That old thing? What did he direct last, the *Ziegfeld Follies*?"

"You are a witch. He has six projects in development."

"He's old enough to be your grandfather."

Paul cackled. "And you should have seen him when he was getting ready to come, with all the rolls on his stomach just shaking. Shake, rattle, and roll!"

"*Eeeeyooooh!*" We both hooted with laughter.

I put down my fork. "Paul, really, though," I said, "is this the kind of thing you want to be doing? I mean, is this business the right place for you?"

He smiled benignly, as if I were a child. "Sandra, you're dear to worry about me," he said. "But if I'm going to sleep with these men anyway, why not get a picture out of it?"

"That's lovely."

"Well, it's true. It's not such a big deal, you know. A lot of it's amusing. Most of the time, anyway. And also, well, truth be told, I guess I felt sorry for Marshall. He's lived with this woman for years, and I think he's only able to get out for some fun once in a while. So, you know."

"And figuring you're about to enter into the same kind of arrangement, you thought you'd give him a tumble? So when your karma comes around, someone else will return the favor? I mean, Paul, do you ever sit down and think of *how* you're going to balance all these flings when—and if—you do marry Sally?"

He looked hurt. "Yes, I've thought about it, Sandy. I've thought about it constantly, and I've decided that I don't want to be alone. I look at Louis, the president of my company, who's like sixty, now. He's been this big queen forever, he still hates his mother, he flirts with waiters who laugh at him in the kitchen, and he lives in this huge house all alone. I don't want to end up like that."

"I don't blame you," I said. "But does it have to be Sally? It is possible, you know, for you to meet a *guy* you could be happy with."

"No, it's not," he said decidedly.

"Why?"

"Because it's not. Could you see me living with a guy? Marie would have a heart attack. She wants grandchildren, poor thing."

"And what about your father?"

"What about him?" he asked sharply.

"Well, usually, one parent is more flexible. Your father's been out in the world, done business, made a success of himself. Do you really think he doesn't know you're gay?"

"Yes, Sandra, I really think he doesn't." He snorted. "As if business has anything to do with it."

"You know what I mean. He wasn't born yesterday."

"Enough," he said, going for a cigarette. "I can assure you beyond a reasonable doubt that this is a devoutly Catholic man to whom God gave only one child, so he expects molto grandchildren. End of story."

"Okay, then. Don't you think you at least owe Sally the courtesy of the information? The truth? She may decide it's no problem, but at least you won't be like Bucky, lying to her."

"Sally is why I joined AA," he said.

"I thought Richard Whitford is why you joined AA."

"Jesus, who are you, Perry Mason? They're *both* why I joined." He sighed. "Sally told me that this was all too hard for her, and she wouldn't be able to see me anymore if I didn't stop. She's put up with so much. I owe it to her."

"You do," I said. "You also owe her the rest of the truth."

"One thing at a time, Sandy. Okay?" His expression was pleading.

"Okay."

We went to the meeting, in a church basement with folding chairs and Styrofoam coffee cups. Everyone seemed friendly and genuinely supportive. We left as soon as the speaker finished and ran to the theater. We seemed to run everywhere, as Paul was his usual combination of manic and euphoric, fueled by avoidance, Christmas cheer, and king-size hot-fudge sundaes, which we ate every night at David's Potbelly Stove on Christopher Street.

He had very generously agreed to cancel a dinner to come with me to Green Hills for my parents' annual Chanukah party, an event I couldn't bear to face alone. Not that Bucky had ever attended—probably because he had never been invited, and I never pushed it. I knew he would rather die than be whispered about by the assembled congregation of Ahavas Israel—and frankly, I didn't blame him.

Paul and I arrived early and helped my mom set up. She loved Paul, and the feeling was mutual—he made her laugh with his outrageous-boy stories, and she mommied him, which he loved. My father was civil enough, though he considered my fraternizing with faygelehs instead of husband-hunting a clearly inferior decision.

The house looked great, buffed and polished, and the good china was making its annual appearance. The dining room table was loaded with lox and whitefish and bagels, and Mom had spent the past few weeks making and freezing hundreds of potato pancakes, which she now reheated—her favorite activity. I armed myself with a double Scotch and hid in the den once the doorbell started ringing.

"Everyone's going to think I'm an old maid who was thrown over by the big goy from the baseball team," I whimpered. "And they're going to think I'm fat and that my skin is bad and that no one will ever go out with me again. And they'll tell their kids what a mess I am and how they all knew from the start that this relationship would crash and burn because anyone who is descended from Betsy Ross would never marry someone whose mother freezes potato pancakes in Scott towels *and* waxed paper *and* aluminum foil. I never should have come."

Paul laughed. "You're nuts," he said comfortably.

"Easy for you to say," I answered. "Think if our roles were reversed and I was the one coming to your family's Christmas party."

He stopped laughing.

"My point exactly," I said. "Just hang around with me, okay?"

"Of course," he said. But I could tell that he was already scoping the student Mom had hired to tend bar, some tall, awkward guy with chewed-up fingernails.

"Look, it's Sandy!" Mr. Schwarz boomed from across the room. He of "knockers" fame, from the day of my prom pictures.

"Hi, Mr. Schwarz, how are you?" I introduced Paul to him and his wife, who took me in from head to toe with one shrewd glance. I gave her one of my own. She bought most of her clothes at Loehmann's—they were all stylish but often came in peculiar colors, which is why they were sold there instead of Saks. So she was always well dressed, except that something would invariably be aqua.

"Sandy, you look well," she said, shaking my hand. My eyes narrowed. What did that mean, exactly?

"I'm fine, thanks," I said.

"Enjoying the magazine?"

"Yes, very much."

"And how's everything else?" Aha. Down to business.

"Great."

"Good. You're having fun?"

I could have killed her. Why didn't she come right out and say, "So, are you dating? Have you gotten over that inappropriate boy? Who are you marrying instead? Where will you be registering?"

"Yes, I'm having lots of fun. Just going to get another drink," I said, turning and hightailing it to the bar, where Paul was loitering.

"Thanks for being there," I said to him. And then, to the bartender: "Another double and make it strong."

"Time to eat," Paul announced, putting my glass down and steering me toward the dining room, where the Salton hot tray was loaded with potato pancakes. "Ah," he said, piling his plate. "Heaven."

I followed suit. We sat and ate and I started to feel better. More people came and went, and I introduced Paul and answered the same meaningless questions over and over. Mrs. Stein wanted to know why the clothes in *Jolie!* were so expensive. Mrs. Dubinsky wanted to know if I got any designer discounts. Before I could get away, Paul had disappeared again.

"Hi, Sandy, how are you?" It was Dr. Lipton, a shrink who worked at the same college as my mom and who had the distinction of living a block away from Bucky. Unlike the other women here—teased, sprayed and lacquered—she wore her hair in a braid, and her glasses hung on a chain around her neck. I had liked her ever since a conversation we had once when I was in college: We were talking about avoiding feelings of depression. "What makes you happy?" she had asked. I considered a moment. "Sex," I answered. She nodded, unfazed. "So have more sex," she said. "You'll feel better."

"Hi, it's nice to see you," I said, rising.

"Oh, you look wonderful, dear," she said. "I haven't seen you in ages."

"Thank you."

"What have you been up to?"

"Not much, just working, really."

"Your mom told me that you and Bucky broke up." I snapped into consciousness. Someone had actually said the B-word.

"Yes, a while ago. Before the summer."

"I figured as much," Dr. Lipton said, "when I met his new girl-friend."

"Oh?" I tried keeping my voice casual. "When was that?"

She cleaned her glasses with a cocktail napkin. "Around Labor Day weekend, I guess."

That would be Beth Brewer.

"Yes, I think I know the one," I said. "Shag haircut, bow-tie blouse?"

Dr. Lipton shook her head no.

"Well, I mean, I guess she wasn't wearing a bow-tie blouse on Labor Day weekend, but—"

"Actually, she was a tall girl with long red hair."

"Beth? Tall?"

"No, her name wasn't Beth. I believe it was Wendy."

"That's a new one on me," I said, my voice loud and bright. "He sure does go through 'em, doesn't he?"

Dr. Lipton looked at me. "His mother says he's marrying her next summer," she said quietly.

I felt as if I'd been punched. I thought I might even fall over, until I saw Mrs. Schwarz out of the corner of my eye. That straightened my spine.

"Again?" I snapped.

"Again," she said. "This one is an interior decorator."

"Really?" I said, trying to laugh. "I don't think his interior can stand any more decorating."

"She works at Hargrove Hadley on Wall Street," Dr. Lipton

went on, "in charge of executive offices and things. That's according to Leila Ross, anyway."

"Um . . ." I stopped.

"What?" she asked.

I opened my mouth, but nothing came out.

"The wedding? It's going to be at the Green Hills Golf Club," she said, taking me by the elbows. "You can do so much better, Sandy." Dr. Lipton's voice was warm, her tone firm, and her brown eyes focused on mine. "Trust me. I have daughters, too. You think the world has come to an end, but it hasn't."

I sank into a nearby chair. "I'll take your word for it," I said.

By Paul's last day in New York, I had gained back the seven pounds it had taken me all summer to lose. The news flash on Bucky's latest engagement hadn't helped. Even though I didn't have time to lie in bed and devour the harvest of America's heartland, I made up for it at work and with Paul, instead. I would write a book of love poems dedicated to Hellmann's mayonnaise, I decided. It was the perfect life partner—so very versatile, yet always reassuring. I only agreed to be separated from it by the prospect of a trip to John's Pizza on Bleecker Street. I sat with Paul on the eve of his departure, close to tears.

"You don't have to leave yet," I said. "There are more than two weeks until Christmas, and anyway, L.A. is no place for Christmas. I'll miss you. This is my first Christmas without Bucky."

He squeezed my hand. "I'll miss you too, Sandra, but you know I have to go home to Marie. And it's time to forget about Bucky. You've got to realize that *nothing* you did warranted the way he treated you. You're immature and selfish? You and everyone else. That doesn't mean Bucky gets engaged to three people and you're supposed to say 'I deserve it.' "

I smiled gratefully. "Thank you," I said.

"Sure," he said. "But it's time to move on now, Sandy. It's going to be a new year soon."

I sighed. "I just can't bear the thought of the next few weeks," I said. "Everyone in the office will be going someplace with their husbands or boyfriends, to ski or to the beach. Or they'll stay home and have all their friends visit, and serve them cocktails and buffet dinners with chafing dishes filled with Swedish meatballs and turkey Tetrazzini."

He laughed out loud. "What fifties fantasy is this?" he asked.

"It's not," I insisted. "Bucky and I went to a party just like that a few years ago. This couple we graduated from high school with got married and had all their friends come to her parents' house in Green Hills, and everyone got dressed up and had gin and tonics and there was Christmas music on the stereo and a big tree with all the trimmings and a fire in the fireplace. And the china was stacked up on the buffet with the good silver, and everyone ate that food, and the hostess was pregnant and wearing these velvet evening pants with an elastic waist and a silk tunic, and I thought how great it would be when I was the one giving that party and I was the one serving that food and I was the one wearing that tunic."

"Sandy." Paul regarded me seriously. "Is that the life you really want?"

My eyes filled. "I don't know," I said honestly, looking down at the wooden table, which jiggled in stripes. When I was growing up, Christmas was so desolate. "For us, it's a day like any other," my father would say in his utilitarian way. And if something like *Mary Poppins* was playing at the movies, we would go and see it, but more often than not we would stay home. Dad would listen to the radio, and there was no one to call because other Jews either celebrated Christmas or went away, daring to have fun. I would read, but somehow not even a great book could distract me from the fact that in other homes, people weren't reading alone, they were talking, laughing, rejoicing together. I wanted that, too.

"What have you planned for the holidays?" Paul asked.

I shrugged. "Work, I guess. A friend is having a party on New Year's Eve. I don't know." This time the tears spilled over and I tried to laugh. "Do you think I'm feeling sorry enough for myself? Maybe I'll go back to the AA meeting and listen to everyone else's problems."

"I don't think so," he said. "I think one of the things you have to do in the next few days is make plans. I want you to schedule at least one activity every day for the next two weeks. And no days in bed feeling sorry for yourself."

"Does reading a book count?"

"No. You know what I'm saying. I want to see a schedule."

"I could always fly out and spend the week with you and Marie," I said. I could see him starting to vibrate. "I could watch you kiss the Baby Jesus good night. I'm an expert at that."

He put on his coat and didn't answer.

"Are you ignoring me?" I asked.

"Yes," he said. But as we left the restaurant, he hooked his arm through mine and we started down the street, stopping to look in a store window filled with leather bags and briefcases. I caught his reflection in the glass. He was looking at me.

I turned to him. "What?"

He took my arm and kept walking. "Well, you know, Sandra," he said, "I was just thinking that it probably wouldn't kill me to stay a few more days." I stopped, and he tried to suppress a grin. "There's this actor I've been meeting with who may not sign as fast as I thought he would, and you know there are at least four plays I didn't see with people in them we might really want."

I started to cry. He looked away, jabbing at his hair.

"I never cry," I yelled. He raised an eyebrow. "Or at least I never did until this year."

He threw his arm around my shoulders and turned us in the direction of the Potbelly. "Time for dessert," he said, rummaging in his coat pocket for a cigarette.

As we passed under a streetlamp, I wiped at my mascara. "Am I a mess?" I asked.

He nodded reassuringly. "The worst."

"Good," I said. "Then it won't matter if I eat a sundae."

"Yes, it will," he said sternly. "Project New Year is coming up, and that means we're forgetting Buck Ross and finding you a fabulous new man, so you are not allowed to look like a cow. You ate too many potato pancakes the other night, and tonight you had pizza, and this idea about the mayonnaise book is completely insane. You can watch me eat a sundae, but you are having water."

"Well, what about your own potbelly, while we're on the subject?"

He drew himself up. "The guy I was with last night didn't seem to mind," he said.

I sighed. "You meet more men than any woman I know."

He smiled. "That's the point, dearest."

The following morning I was up at six-thirty for my first freelance writing assignment. One of the British editors who had been at *Jolie!* early on had since returned to England and was working for a newspaper as a features editor. She had called, asking if I would write a piece about Ira Baumgarten, a lawyer who worked for the Justice Department and a bona fide Nazi hunter. He was also— the editor mentioned helpfully—single and in his thirties. He had been involved in uncovering the Kurt Waldheim scandal, and she thought he would make a good piece for her readers. It seemed like an awfully grown-up subject for someone who spent her spare time writing about spells and princesses, but it was time for something different. I agreed to meet him for breakfast.

I arrived at his office at seven-twenty; to my surprise, other people were already hard at work. His secretary poured me coffee and seated me in a conference room with a large platter of danishes and croissants. I set up my tape recorder, opened my notebook, and perused my questions. I was in good shape. I sipped my coffee. Maybe he'd be fabulous, I thought, looking out the window. Sandra Baumgarten. I wouldn't even have to change my initials.

The door opened. Never mind. He was the ultimate geek, so much so that he reminded me of Henry Cain in third grade, who used to steal my bus fare every time I went into the coatroom. Here he was again, I thought, all grown up and looking for Nazis.

We shook hands and sat down. He offered me a croissant, which I refused, and then I sat there a moment before it occurred to me to look at my notes. Good news, Sandra, I thought. You're not on a date. It's time to work.

The hour flew. I was well prepared, and Henry Cain—I mean, Ira Baumgarten—knew it. He was very smart and very eloquent and very anal, showing me all sorts of documentation to prove the most basic things that I never would have questioned, official papers from Austria proving where Waldheim had been and when. As he spoke, staring out from behind his thick glasses, what I liked about him best was that he was a bigger dweeb than me. There I was, working at this slick fashion magazine in the middle of the eighties, surrounded by toned twigs who club-hopped and had strong opinions about *Dynasty* and who looked at me as if I were Emily Dickinson's idiot cousin, stumbled in from the wrong century. Compared to this guy, I was some happening chick—if anyone even used that expression outside a sketch on *Saturday Night Live*.

He moved on from Waldheim to escaped Nazis who were now living in America, and showed me parts of their files.

"How do you find these things out?" I asked.

"All kinds of ways," he said. "We have them followed, tap their phones, go through their garbage."

"You do?"

"Yes, we've actually found some relevant evidence that way. Old papers they've thrown out, letters, pictures."

His secretary came to the door. It was eight-thirty sharp.

"Thank you," I said, standing. "I appreciate your time."

"You're welcome," he said. "When will this run?"

"I'm not sure, but as soon as I know, I'll call you," I said.

"Great," he answered, walking me to the door. "Maybe we could have a drink sometime."

I smiled. "Sure," I said. "We'll talk."

I could always slot him in over the holidays so I could have something to put on my list for Paul, I thought. We could see *Mary Poppins*.

When I got to the office at five minutes to nine, I figured I would be the first one in. But no, there was Susie Schein, already on morning patrol. She raised her eyebrows at the sight of me.

"What's happening with Mark Lewis?" she asked in lieu of "Good morning." "Miss Belladonna asked me about him again last night. I think she wants to call that dinner-party hostess and tell her she's using him in the magazine."

"His agent said he was out of town giving speeches. She wants me to call after New Year's, when everyone is back."

Susie twisted her mouth in annoyance; holidays were a personal affront to her. She didn't have to ask about the other marquee names; they had all said no, as I knew they would. Frankly, I was surprised we had lasted this long with Mark Lewis. He must have really been broke.

I went to the coffee room, where the chief copy editor was using a plastic stirrer to scrape the excess butter from her roll. We talked awhile about our holiday plans. Things weren't too bad, she said. She was dating an executive from Wall Street who seemed like a real human being.

"That's so great," I replied automatically. "Where does he work?"

"Hargrove Hadley," she said.

"You know, I was just talking about that place with someone," I said, managing to keep my voice steady. "She knows the woman who designs it, or something. Isn't that the strangest thing you ever heard, being a bank designer?"

She nodded. "Actually, it's funny you should say that, because it's the only bank I've ever been in that looks like a bed-and-breakfast. The offices all have lots of baskets and dried flowers, and the pencil holders are wrapped in fabric to match the curtains."

"That's hilarious," I said. "I guess they're just trying to make it homey. The bank with a hearth. Uh, heart."

That afternoon, Paul called. "My tea canceled," he said, aggrieved. "Can you believe it?"

"Honestly, Romano, how do you sit through all these meals every day? You should be glad to skip one."

He sighed. "I guess I'll do some Christmas shopping instead."

"Well, what if I met you?"

"Sandy, it's only two-thirty. You can't leave now."

"I think I can, actually. Meet me on the corner in fifteen minutes."

I grabbed my coat and stood in the doorway of Susie's office. She looked up impatiently from her computer.

"Susie, I have to go and meet with Victoria Segal," I said quickly. "She has some questions to ask before she lets me sit down with Mark Lewis."

Susie looked at her watch. "You can't talk about it on the phone?"

I shrugged helplessly. "That's what I suggested, but then she said if I didn't think it was important enough to meet face-to-face, she wasn't sure it was something he should do. So what could I say but yes?"

After she grudgingly nodded her approval, I practically ran to the elevators and out to the corner where Paul was waiting. I hailed a cab.

"What are you doing?" he asked.

"We're taking a field trip," I said, leaning toward the driver. "Thirty-fifth between Park and Lex, please," I said.

Paul looked confused.

"I met a man this morning who hunts war criminals," I said. "And he told me that one of the ways to discover the truth about people who lie is to go through their garbage."

"So?" he asked warily.

"So we're going to look through Bucky's garbage and see exactly who he's marrying."

"What? How?"

"Last night was Bucky's company's Christmas party," I explained. "That's always the night he likes to begin exchanging gifts—make Christmas start early, he says. And I'll bet you anything that the wrapping of whatever she gave him is still in the garbage outside his house."

Paul gripped my arm. "Sandy, for God's sake, what are you doing? Why do you care who this woman is or why he's marrying her? I thought we agreed that it was time to move on."

"We did, and I will. But I cannot for one minute believe that after nine years with me he can turn around and marry someone else and I don't even know who it is. I have known every single thing he's done during our entire lives."

"*What?*" Paul yelled.

"Well, except for the last part."

"Hello," he called, "are you in there?"

"Listen, for the last eight months, nothing in my life has been right. I want to see what's going on. I know you think I'm crazy, and I probably am. But at least I'll be getting information."

"Sandy, between the two of us I think we can find out some other way, if you need to know that badly. But don't do this. It's demeaning."

"It is not. The guy who works for the Justice Department of the United States says it's a legitimate way of getting evidence."

"Against Nazis. Not ex-boyfriends." He covered his eyes with his hand.

"Look, that's his house," I said, pointing through the window at the brownstone. I paid the driver and scrambled to the sidewalk, Paul sliding out after me.

"Now what?" he asked, distressed.

We stood across the street from the house, gazing up. The shades to Bucky's apartment were drawn. The garbage cans were lined up behind a railing a few steps down from the street. We crossed. "Just stand there and make sure no one's coming," I said, heading toward the first can.

"It's broad daylight, Sandra," he wailed, poking at his shorn hair.

I turned my back on him and lifted the cover. Empty boxes of animal crackers. Disposable diapers. Damn. This garbage belonged to the Cohens, the people downstairs with kids.

I opened the next can, which was filled with tightly tied white plastic bags. I took off my black cashmere gloves. Somehow, in my master vision of espionage, I hadn't planned on actually having to *touch* the garbage.

I turned to look at Paul. His face was a mask of disbelief. "You aren't really doing this," he muttered.

I untied a bag and saw an envelope addressed to Bucky. Bingo. Beneath it was an empty Ragú tomato sauce jar and a dented Ronzoni spaghetti box. Since Bucky didn't cook, it must have been the designer. What a gourmet. Foil, balled up, that felt oily. Garlic bread, no doubt. Ah, here was something: a receipt from the bookstore down the street. It was stained with grease, but I held it up to the light: *Ancient Evenings*. Unbelievable!

"Are you done yet?" Paul whispered loudly from the pavement, where he was trying not to pace, trying not to stand still, trying to disappear into thin air.

"No," I whispered back, struggling with the next bag, through which I could see the curly red and green ribbons and shiny wrapping paper I'd been hoping for. Inside were a few little envelopes, empty. Three chestnuts. A candy cane still in its plastic, broken. She must have done a stocking. But where was the real present? There were no boxes, nothing. The next bag was filled with canceled checks, but they were from the man who lived on the third floor.

I lifted the Cohens' bag to get at what was underneath and it broke, spilling leaky boxes of apple juice onto my coat.

"Sandra!" Paul practically yelled. "Please stop this!"

"Shut up!" I yelled back, grabbing the wrapping paper. Bucky would never have folded it so neatly. The girl must have. I undid it, and a yellow slip fluttered out. I picked it up off the ground and read: "Deerfield Antiques Fair. One butter churn, c. 1690. Certificate of Authenticity not available."

An ersatz butter churn. What the hell was he supposed to do with that? I threw the remains of the Cohen garbage back into the can and stuffed the wrapping paper on top of it.

"Watch out, watch out!" Paul called in a panic. I looked toward the corner and saw a mother leading her daughter away from a school bus. Jamming the cover back on, I rushed to join him on the sidewalk. "Just walk," I ordered.

"That was a major mistake," he said, looking at the juice dripping down the front of my coat.

"It was not," I said excitedly. "Because now I know that the designer gave him an inauthentic butter churn for Christmas. And not only that, she *wrapped* it. And he gave her the only book he's ever read. A phony intellectual and a phony butter churn, a match made in heaven. But he must have given her jewelry, too. Then again, he probably gave her the two-carat emerald-cut diamond ring."

Paul's face softened. "Yes, Sandy, he probably did," he said, "since he is marrying her. And he is not marrying you."

I drew my breath in. He was right, after all. Whether I wanted him to be or not.

We walked a few blocks; I could feel my heart gradually stop thumping. I could see from the gray cast of the sky that it was going to snow. We passed neat rows of brownstones, some with picture windows framing Christmas trees, others with curtains drawn in swoops. And just as if I were in a museum and had come to the end of an exhibition, I snapped back, suddenly, to the present. This was a place I did not belong.

I linked my arm through Paul's. He had remained mercifully silent.

"Hey, handsome. Come here often?"

He smiled. "Every chance I get." A cab turned the corner, and he held up his arm. "Though I think we've had enough Murray Hill for one day, don't you?" he asked.

"Yes," I answered. "Maybe even a lifetime."

8

I almost honored the schedule I had presented to Paul. I bought tickets to an organ recital, said yes to holiday parties I never would have considered otherwise, even made dates for brunch, an activity I detested. In post-Depression America, I refused to stand on line to be fed, especially with people who had plenty of money and Cuisinarts they were just too lazy to use.

Another thing I hated about brunch was its unmistakable smell of post-Saturday-night defeat; women and men in separate packs, wielding the *Times*, the women bolstering one another by making plans—a new diet, a new lipstick, any piddling thing would do—the guys trapped in a fraternity-house time warp, talking sports and noisily hoisting watered-down Bloody Marys.

The only thing worse was the smell of envy when a happy couple appeared, the woman wearing the man's sweater, he preening while she tore a croissant to bits and fed it to him. Those people should have the decency to lick each other's fingers in the privacy of their own homes. Who wants to see that when all your own Sunday offers is an hour on the StairMaster and a well-meaning mother on the line wondering if by any chance you just happened to meet Prince Charming last night?

Me Times Three

I filled one of the free evenings on my schedule by inviting Pimm and Coco to join me in my new office for dinner, drinks, and decoration. We each brought a bottle of holiday cheer—vodka, bourbon, and gin—and Coco presented me with chipped highball glasses from a home-design shoot that she said I could keep. We ordered in filet mignon from Between the Bread, where *Jolie!* had an account, and then we went through all the giveaway piles of newly published books and assembled a mini-library for my empty shelves. Pimm brought in a plant from our old office, and suddenly the room looked cozier.

"Here's my housewarming gift," Coco said, handing me an ashtray with a removable top, ingeniously designed so that I could dump the ashes into it and cut down on the telltale smell. "It's Susie Schein–proof," she said.

We sat around my desk, eating and drinking. Pimm said that her boyfriend was finally coming home from California, so they would spend the holidays together, and Coco said that she had a brand-new beau, a rock star famous enough that even I had heard of him, who wanted to take her to Anguilla for Christmas, but she wasn't sure she should go.

"Why not?" I asked.

"Well, if you fall out of love with a rock star on an island over the holidays, I'm not sure you can get back to New York even if you want to," she said sensibly. "And playing hard to get never hurt anyone."

"I wish I was as smart as you are about all this stuff," I said.

"You're doing fine," she said staunchly. "You just need to loosen up a little."

"So I've heard," I said.

But before we could say any more, Jean-Louis was at my door. "Ah, Coco!" he cried, coming in and kissing her on both cheeks. "Jean-Louis," she crooned, pulling him over to the filet mignon and the booze, but he laughed and shook his head and chattered to her in rapid-fire French.

"There's a fun party downtown that Jolie is giving, and Jean-Louis is going and thinks we should go with him," Coco translated. I understood enough French to know that Jean-Louis had said no such thing. He had asked Coco to go, period, which was fine with me and with Pimm, who was signaling me wildly. Neither of us wanted to end up in a loft filled with models and the men who chased them. Those guys were a creepy breed I'd seen at fashion shows, usually handsome themselves and well dressed. But they had a particularly demeaning way of looking at an exquisitely beautiful woman—as if she were a car and the only way to judge her beauty definitively was to see how good she would look with him driving.

"You go on without us, Coco," I said, as Pimm nodded and Jean-Louis looked relieved. In his book, we were the office librarians.

"You don't mind?" Coco asked, already swinging her bag up from the floor, her adrenaline pumping at the mention of a party the way mine did at the mention of a pizza.

Pimm and I cleaned up the remains of the dinner and left, walking up Fifth Avenue to Rockefeller Center, where we stopped to see the Christmas tree and the ice skaters. "Isn't it beautiful?" Pimm asked, beaming.

"It really is," I agreed. I felt that old childhood thrill at the notion of Christmas. No matter that it wasn't mine to celebrate. Everything else was.

My elation lasted until I got home. Our super had made a dismal show of decorating the lobby, hanging red velvet bows near the part-time doorman's station and parking a few poinsettias on the floor. The doorman, however, was nowhere to be found, and there were already dead leaves surrounding the foil-wrapped pots. I got my mail and went upstairs, yet again, to an empty apartment.

Sharon had been out a lot lately, and when I'd finally seen her one recent morning, it had occurred to me to ask if she was avoiding me as well as her mother. She seemed uncomfortable. "Sort of," she said, hastily explaining that her mother's lawyer had determined that the time was right to invest in real estate. Sharon's mother was buying a co-op for Sharon to live in.

"Will she have the key?" I asked.

Sharon looked panicked. "Over my dead body," she said, adding that she felt ready to live on her own. As if with that mother she ever would.

There was another year left on our lease, so I would have to find a new roommate. That would mean living with a stranger, placing an ad in *The Village Voice*, starting over with someone else's bathroom habits. But I couldn't be angry at Sharon; if my life had gone the way I'd hoped, I would be moving out, too.

Christmas Eve came at the end of my schedule's first week, and unbeknownst to Paul, I hadn't booked it. Or Christmas Day. I was all for mental health, but there was something to be said for learning the fine art of enjoying one's own company instead of merely tolerating it, and that is what I intended to do. No parties, no families, no Baby Jesus. I deserved a chance to loll in bed, order in, and watch videos. I had even saved a Judith Krantz book, spunky heroine guaranteed. I looked forward to her succeeding against all odds. I planned to take notes.

Christmas Eve day, I left the office and walked all the way home, feeling remarkably serene. The traffic jam in front of Rockefeller Center was reassuringly familiar; at Lord & Taylor, there were still kids on line, bundled up, watching the carousels in the windows. Down toward the Village, families loaded their cars for trips out of town, and I managed to take none of it personally. I had my own treats to look forward to.

Once home, I poured myself a Scotch and settled into bed, flipping channels. The Yule log. I was not nearly drunk enough for that. I kept going until I found Midnight Mass at the Vatican. Oh! My parents were there! My father knew someone who had gotten them a deal to go to Italy for two weeks, and one of my mother's rat cronies knew someone who had gotten them into Midnight Mass.

For the first time that day, I felt wobbly. These holidays were downright subversive, lying in wait for the tiniest crack in my Up with People mind-set. Yes, I had taken charge and defined my own good time, but in this moment, I felt completely out of sync with the norm, that my selected activities were the wrong ones. All these years later and here I was, still alone with my book on Christmas, while other people joined together, celebrating.

Don't do this, Sandra, I warned myself. Think of a year from now. Your life will be totally different. Think of a month from now. Yeah? What then? Well, it would be January. An automatic improvement on December.

I studied the TV screen. There were lengthy close-ups of frescoes and crucifixes and the Pope in his white robes, but none of the audience. Still, I kept watching. There were two people there in that other time zone, looking up at that soaring architecture, who knew my middle name and where the scars from my chicken pox were. That was about the closest I could come to feeling connected to anyone.

My holiday celebration could wait. I moved my pillow nearer to the set and fell asleep.

Christmas Day was better. *All About Eve* and *The Philadelphia Story*, punctuated by naps. An entire package of Stella D'oro Swiss Fudge Cookies devoured, and a Chinese feast delivered to my door. I found myself grinning at regular intervals. Pure sloth.

Then I was back on my Paul schedule, with a Boxing Day cocktail party at Pimm's parents' house. It was lovely, an urban version of my suburban fantasy, with passed hors d'oeuvres, a catered coulibiac of salmon, and a rare, imported Russian vodka. The parents' friends and the children's friends all mingled. There were worn leather chairs in the den, Bing Crosby sang on the stereo, and snow fell gently outside the window. Neither Pascal nor Coco came—he was in London; she was, indeed, in Anguilla. Hard-to-get could wait.

Pimm's boyfriend, Chris, stood up on a footstool and announced that they were engaged. Everyone applauded and cheered, and Pimm cried while her mother blinded her with a flash camera. I spent the rest of the party consoling Pimm's sister, Breezy, whose boyfriend had dumped her on Christmas Eve. She had expected a ring; he had expected her to realize that he was too young to get married. And now, not only did she not have a date for New Year's but she would have to be her sister's maid of honor without any prospects of her own. Had I ever heard of a crueler breakup?, she demanded, blowing her nose. I lit a cigarette and assured her I had not.

The next morning, the phone rang.

"Sandy? Did I wake you?" Susie Schein asked, not even trying to mask her disgust. I saw from the bedside clock that it was 11:27. So what? I was on vacation.

"No, that's okay," I said, pulling myself up. "Is something wrong?"

"Well," she said urgently, "we have a real problem."

"How can we have a real problem when the magazine's closed?"

"I got a call this morning from Kathy Sinclair," she said. "She can't do the Mexico piece. She has a terrible flu and a 104-degree temperature."

That *was* a real problem. Kathy Sinclair was one of our most dependable writers, and she could be sent anywhere at a moment's notice. She would willingly hang around a film set for days, waiting until a star was ready to see her, because she'd sleep with the rest of the cast in the meantime—and save the star for last. The stories she wrote for the magazine were good, but the stories she told about sex with the stars were great.

Kathy had agreed to go to the Acapulco set of a new action movie this week to interview Idina Lhasa, the leading lady already being touted as next summer's It girl, for a major fashion spread.

"Well, we can wait till Lhasa's back from the shoot and have Kathy do it then," I said.

Susie cleared her throat. I could tell that she had planned this next part and that I wasn't going to like it.

"I want you to go," she said.

"*What?*" I almost shouted.

"Sandy, listen," Susie said. "Idina Lhasa is eighteen years old. What kind of preparation do you need? Get a description of the set and her costumes and ask her an hour's worth of questions, most of which her manager will answer anyway. End of story."

"Is this really necessary?" I asked.

"Of course it is," she snapped. "They're only at this location until the end of the weekend and I don't want to lose it. You know that. You're the one who told *me*."

True enough. "Are you sure there's no one else?"

"Everyone else is gone for the holiday," Susie said.

I thought quickly. Why was I fighting her? Would it kill me to go to Acapulco? I thought of the Judith Krantz book. *That* girl would go in a heartbeat, probably fall in love the minute she stepped on the plane. What was *wrong* with me? This was an adventure, it was exciting. To hell with the chafing dish. Bring on the maracas.

"Okay, Susie. I'll go."

"Great." She had already arranged for a messenger to pick up Kathy Sinclair's ticket and bring it to my apartment, along with press clips on the film. What a bitch. She knew all along she would get me to go. I was to leave at seven the following morning and could come back whenever I was done. It was an open ticket.

"Obviously, you'll be done by Monday, when the office re-opens," she added.

"Obviously," I answered dryly. We certainly wouldn't want to have any *fun*.

"Listen, Sandy," Susie said, mustering an ounce of sincerity. "Thank you. I appreciate it."

Well, that was a first. I got out of bed and headed to the shower, peeling off layers of flannel. I glimpsed my white body in the mirror and cringed. I would go to Acapulco, but my bathing suit was staying home.

Apparently no one in the Mexican government has given any consideration to its highway system, I thought as the car jostled over potholes that made New York's look amateur. Groups of men huddled on the roadside every hundred yards or so, watching the cars go by. A few called out curses. Mattresses, bedsprings, and gasoline cans all lay in piles near where the men stood. As we got closer to town, the roads smoothed out and the men disappeared, the sense of menace with them.

We passed Las Brisas, the famous resort, which looked pretty from the outside, and went on to the high-rise hotel where I was booked.

"You can drink the water on the premises," the woman at the front desk advised me, unprompted, "but if you drink it when you leave the hotel, you take your own responsibility."

Take it where?, I wondered, following the porter and my bag up to a thoroughly nondescript room. I called over to the film set and found the publicist, who said I could meet Idina for dinner that evening at six, with her manager. The following day they would be on location, where I could gather my descriptions. So, she suggested, why didn't I take this afternoon off and just lie by the pool?

I could see why Kathy Sinclair was so amenable to these assignments. But even she would have had a hard time dragging out this trip. Idina Lhasa was no star. She was a beautiful hiccup in time who would make this movie and disappear. Then every ten years or so, *People* magazine would track her down for a "Where are they now?" story. She would still have a pretty face, even though (tsk, tsk) she had let her figure go. She would also have had a few husbands, bastards all, and a few children who had taught her the meaning of life. But at this moment, with her figure and face about to be featured on screens around the world, nothing was more important than discovering whether it was papaya or mango she preferred for her breakfast, or how she drank ten glasses of water a day—but only water from a spring in the west of Samoa.

I walked through the airy lobby, dotted with palm trees, and headed out toward the pool. Most people had escaped the midday sun, though one hardy couple lay on chaise longues drinking tequila sunrises and slathering each other with suntan lotion. I went to the café and found a table, but no waiter appeared, and when a mariachi band arrived to sing "Feliz Navidad," I fled.

From the dark cool of my room I ordered a chef's salad (the only thing Mexican on the menu was salsa and chips). After lunch I fell promptly asleep, waking in time to shower before dinner. I looked at myself in the mirror a good, long while before finally smacking both sides of my face. "Be where you are," I said out loud. "Have an experience. Get on with it."

It was nearing six o'clock now, so I finished drying my hair, got together a notebook and some pens, reviewed the list of questions I had made on the plane, and presented myself in the lobby on time.

No one was there. After a few minutes, the concierge approached me. "Señorita Berlin?" he said. "Señorita Lhasa is running late. Won't you have a seat in the bar and wait for her?"

I sat and sipped a glass of white wine, and was surprised to find that I felt genuinely relaxed. The early-evening light was a soft slate blue, and everyone around me looked tanned and rested. I made the wine last—I did have to work, after all.

The concierge appeared again. "Señorita Lhasa wonders if you might meet her at Las Brisas, where she is staying," he said. "She is so tired from the shooting, it would be easier for her."

What a pain in the ass she was turning out to be. I smiled; by all means.

I got into a cab and within minutes was sitting at an outdoor bar at Las Brisas, watching the breeze make ripples in the pool. This time I sipped club soda while a concierge was dispatched to ask my indulgence in waiting. At eight-thirty, Idina Lhasa finally appeared, with her manager. Idina was an absolute knockout, with dark hair, limpid eyes, full lips, and the type of body that makes people want to sculpt or paint—voluptuous, not vulgar. She wore a white Lycra halter dress that would have revealed the tiniest imperfection, had there been one. Her skin was tanned, but not too much, and it seemed to have the texture of velvet. Compared to this girl, Carla Jones was a beauty-pageant wannabe.

At dinner, Idina answered her questions dutifully with, as Susie had predicted, regular prompting from her manager, a frumpy middle-aged woman. This girl seemed to be her most successful client, to whom she was obviously hanging on for dear life. She had that hounded look of someone who has struggled and scraped and discovered, now that she had hit the big time, that it was too big for her. She was behaving badly—snapping her fingers for the waiter and talking too loudly—but Idina didn't seem to notice. She said her piece like a well-rehearsed schoolgirl: She was so very lucky to have won this role. The producers were like parents to her. Yes, her leading man was so handsome, so sexy. She was thrilled.

After fifteen minutes I had what I needed, so I began making up more questions, which Idina politely answered. I liked this. You could ask anything and the person was obliged to respond. I immediately knew when she was lying: She would unknowingly reveal herself by turning to her manager, who would look down and nudge her under the table to reassure her. From these exchanges I was able to surmise that Idina had never graduated from high school, didn't know who or where her father was, and was sleeping with one of the guys financing the picture. And although she claimed to have been born and raised in the British West Indies, she seemed to know an awful lot about Worcester, Massachusetts.

But the truth wasn't the point, after all. The point was that Idina Lhasa would look drop-dead fabulous in next summer's fashions, and when the film opened she would be an instant icon for men, a pyre of hopelessness for women.

By nine-fifteen she began yawning. "Idina has an early call," the manager proclaimed as if on cue. We stood and shook hands, but as Idina turned to waft her way to bed, a group of people appeared, including Charles Buckley, the star of the movie. An Englishman and, reputedly, a fine stage actor, he had had a few roles in British films, but this was his big Hollywood break. I studied him. Tall, thin, angular face. Not an ounce of sex about him.

"Ah, *cara*," he crooned when he saw Idina, taking her hand and kissing it with a flourish. "Oh, Charles," she giggled, leaning on the *r* forever; by the time she was done, he had his arm around her waist and was leading her outside. The manager quickly asserted herself.

"Charles, Idina is in the middle of an interview," she said in her officious tone. "You can't take her out there."

"Oh, really," he said, barely concealing his contempt. He turned to me, taking in my notebook and pen. "Where are you from?" he demanded.

"*Jolie!*" I said.

"Ah." He cupped his hands around Idina's face. "*Jolie, très jolie*," he murmured, kissing her mouth. She didn't resist, but she didn't exactly reciprocate either. Her face stayed absolutely still and expressionless as he buzzed his nose and lips around it.

"Come, *Jolie!*" Charles Buckley barked in my direction. "We are going outside."

I looked at the manager, who now had a sickly smile on her face and her mouth firmly shut, because in addition to Buckley and the crew, one of the producers had arrived and she had lost what little clout she had.

"Cognac!" Charles Buckley commanded, seemingly to no one, and we followed him up a path to a stone terrace and an open evening sky surrounded by the dark outlines of hills. A waiter appeared with a tray of glasses, enough for everyone. I put down my notebook and took one, my eyes adjusting to the light. The lounge furniture was lushly padded, and tiny candles blinked on the tables. The scent of grilled meat was in the air. People talked quietly to one another, while a few of the men ran their eyes over me and bided their time.

Charles Buckley, having finished his cognac in a single gulp, picked up another and suddenly started reciting from *King Lear*. The more he spoke, the louder he got, and he didn't seem to notice when Idina's manager finally spirited her starlet off to bed. I sat and listened to him, his white shirt now open across his bony chest, while I tasted my drink and breathed the air and congratulated myself on being clever enough to have ended up in Acapulco with a movie star.

But the fact was, he was a drunk movie star, and he was slurring. He scoped me sideways every now and then, which left me unfazed, because like most British men he seemed gay to me, whether he actually was or not. American guys have asses that look like asses in their worn-out blue jeans, with their broad backs and sneakers. British guys have asses that look like grapes in those narrow, shiny pants, with their filmy shirts and shoes with lifts. They look like dirty hookers.

Lear was on his fourth cognac—that I counted, at least— when someone started to applaud in the hope of bringing the performance to a close. As the star droned on, the other men invited me to a disco, but I politely demurred and left Mr. Buckley, mid-passage, with the producer, who had switched to beer and was now leaning back dejectedly in his chair, watching everyone else leave. Who says a producer does nothing?

The location was amazing, a house without any external walls that had been built into the side of a mountain. It had its own helipad, an enormous pool, and rooms filled with fancy furniture and chandeliers. A drug dealer owned it, whispered some of the crew. When I asked a production manager about the walls, he admitted that there were temporary ones that could be put up in case of a storm, but that otherwise security was not a problem. The other men laughed. Maybe it was Mafia.

To get details for my story, I spent an hour going through the house, top to bottom. At around eleven, Charles Buckley came out of his trailer, his face pasty in the brilliant sunshine. He looked like hell. There was no sign of Idina, though I saw her costumes being prepared.

At noon, I went back to the hotel and ordered another chef's salad from room service. I had been in Acapulco twenty-four hours, and my work was done. Kathy Sinclair was running a real racket.

I called the airport. There was a plane out at four, and another at seven; neither was filled. I said I'd call back.

I decided to go down to the pool again and find a shady spot to lie in. Looking around, I noticed one of the men from the night before. Clean-cut, attractive. I had assumed that last night's gang were all part of the crew, but since he wasn't on the set, he must have been a civilian. He smiled and waved as he walked toward me.

"Hi," he said. "I think we met last night. I'm Andy."

"I'm Sandy," I said.

Together we said, "We rhyme." And laughed.

"You're writing about Idina, aren't you?" he asked.

I nodded. "Aren't you working on the film?"

"Yes," he said. "I'm the on-site doctor. But this afternoon, I'm off."

"I didn't even know there was a job like that, but I guess it makes sense."

He smiled. "It does. I work with a company that sends doctors to locations in case anything happens. So it's a nice break for me."

He went on about his practice, which was based in Florida, and in no time at all he had segued to insurance, a topic captivating to all doctors.

"Are you here for the week?" he asked.

I found myself shaking my head. "No, just till tomorrow, I think," I said. "Short trip."

He looked disappointed. "Oh, that's too bad," he said. "There are going to be a lot of parties for New Year's. It would be fun if you stayed."

I looked at his hands. Very clean. No wedding band. But what did that mean? He probably had a wife at home who boasted to all her friends about her husband's glamorous job.

"Are you married?" he asked abruptly.

"No," I said, taken aback. "Are you?"

"Well, separated," he said.

"'Well, separated' because you're here and she's there?" I asked lightly, and he actually laughed.

"Something like that." He slipped his sunglasses into his shirt pocket. "So, stay and have some fun with me," he added, leaning in a little closer.

I smiled. For some reason he didn't put me off. Maybe he really was separated. Maybe it didn't matter. Maybe it was entirely possible for me to speak to a man without the specter of the Bloomingdale's china department hovering nearby.

"If you'll come for a drive with me," he said, "I can show you some wonderful places."

I found myself agreeing. Had I lost my mind? One part of me was stamping its foot, warning me off; the other part was sighing with relief, counseling, "It could be worse. He could be a radiologist."

A woman from the hotel staff approached. "Dr. D'Amico?" she said. "There's a phone call for you."

At least he's not a Jewish doctor, I thought as he went inside. Only half a cliché.

Why shouldn't I stay an extra day?, I reasoned, gathering my things together. Eighty degrees and sunny, not to mention all expenses paid—this was certainly an improvement on my Paul schedule. I met Andy in the lobby, where he stood near the desk, waiting. We drove through town and along the water, and then he said he wanted to visit a friend who lived nearby, someone from the film who had rented a house. He pulled into the driveway of a nice-looking split-level—modest, nothing like the film set.

Andy rang the bell, and when no one answered we walked around back and tried the door, which was unlocked. I followed him inside, and he turned and kissed me and I kissed him back as if I had been waiting my entire life for this moment. Here he was, the man of my dreams, a cheating Italian doctor from Florida.

I hardly noticed the interior of the house. It had white walls and expensive-looking framed pictures—but, really, I was sick of noticing things. What did it matter whose house it was? Or how it looked? Why did my life require constant narration?

I felt my shirt going up over my head, and could that possibly have been *my* hand unzipping his pants? You've lost your mind, I thought as we fell onto a bed with a leopard-print spread.

"Um," I began, and "I know," he said, and there was a condom at the ready, and then I forbade myself from thinking and eagerly entered the swirl of sweat and moaning. When I finally noticed shadows in a corner of the room, I looked at my watch. It was after five.

"The crew is having cocktails at the set," he said. "Do you want to come?"

"Sure," I answered, retracing the path from the door to pick up my clothes. We went back to the drug dealer's house, where the day's shooting had ended and people milled around the pool drinking beers and jumping in with all their clothes on. I fell into the scene, enjoying the easy camaraderie offered to anyone on a movie set, chatting and drinking, laughing at stories of Charles Buckley refusing to come out of his trailer because he didn't like the smell of his hair spray.

From there, we moved on as a herd to one of the nearby hotels, where there was a big buffet and more drinking at a poolside bar. This time people took their clothes off before jumping in, but instead of joining them, I took the doctor back to my hotel.

He was on call on the set the next morning and left my room at six. "Come out for lunch today," he said, kissing me goodbye.

"Okay," I answered, marveling at the fact that I had spent the last day having sex with a total stranger and hadn't yet died of syphilis.

But after we had lunch, I decided it was time to leave. It seemed that Mrs. Doctor, who didn't know she was separated, had left a phone message with the happy news that her mother could stay with the kids after all, and she was arriving that very evening to ring in the New Year's weekend. I booked myself onto the four p.m. flight, and Andy very nicely drove me to the airport. He would probably pick her up after he dropped me off.

He asked for my number, for the next time he was in New York. I wrote down the extension of *Jolie!*'s accessories closet and kissed him goodbye. Then I checked my bag, fastened my seat belt, and passed out. The next thing I felt was the bump of wheels as we landed in New York. I started to laugh. I couldn't wait to tell Paul.

#52   The Frog Who Could Fly
by Sandra Berlin

Once there was a young Prince, who played every day by the pond near his castle. It was there he met a frog who he knew was a Girl Frog because she had very long eyelashes and painted her webbed toes pink. The Prince would call out to the Girl Frog every day, and she would leap across the lily pads to sit beside him and tell him stories, for, as an only child, he was a lonely Prince and pined for friends and company. She was lonely too, for the Frog Prince whom she was to wed had recently leapt to another pond—and another and another, though that's another story—and so she sat each day with the young human Prince and told him stories to his heart's content.

One day, though, when the Prince called to the Girl Frog, she did not leap across the lily pads, and he had to search to the far side of the pond to find her. "What's wrong, Girl Frog?" the young Prince asked.

She blinked a large tear, which clung to her eyelashes. "Oh, it's Christmas and my Frog Prince left me," she said. "All my life I looked forward to marrying him and living happily ever after. And now that he's gone, I will have to stay here in this pond forever. And though you are my friend, young Prince, you will soon grow up and leave me too, and here I will sit, alone."

The young Prince considered the Girl Frog's plight and said, "My good friend, I will put a spell upon you so that you will turn into a bird, and you may fly around the world to see what you're missing."

He waved his hand, and the Girl Frog turned into a beautiful white bird who soared through the heavens, straight to the pond where her Frog Prince had fled. "Where is he?" she cried, and the other birds pointed to a locked door that said MEMBERS ONLY. "He's in there," they said. "And he almost never comes out."

Well, the Girl Frog waited a few more days until, finally, she said, "You know, I don't have to do this anymore. I can fly right out of here. I'm not a Girl Frog anymore. I'm now a beautiful white bird."

So she spread her wings and flew to Acapulco and got some sun and then came home to her own pond to report her adventures to the young Prince. But alas! She had been gone so long that the young Prince had grown up and gone away, just as she had known he would.

But he'd left behind a note: "Dear Girl Frog," it read, "I hope you have enjoyed seeing the world and that you've forgotten the foolishness of the Frog Prince. Before I left I renewed the spell, so if you want to remain a beautiful white bird forever, you can. And if you ever get depressed over the holidays, just make a schedule and stick to it."

Well, she never had to. She flew the world over, a beautiful white bird with pink webbed toes (the spell wasn't quite perfect, having been cast long-distance), but rather than moan about it, the bird realized she could swim as well as fly. Now she could go anywhere.

The End

9

I called Paul repeatedly to fill him in on my Mexican romance, but I couldn't seem to reach him. I tried several times over the weekend, but he hadn't returned from seeing Marie. By the time Monday arrived and I had done my due diligence at a New Year's Eve party and a New Year's Day open house and the office had reopened, I still hadn't heard from him.

Susie Schein read my piece on Idina and liked it, though of course she had some notes. I worked on it, flashing back to Dr. D'Amico. It had been so easy! And fun! He had been remarkably good-natured and relaxed, I thought. There seemed to be a lot of those people in the world. People who didn't work seven days a week. People who met for a first date and hadn't booked the honeymoon by dessert. Even back in New York, at the New Year's functions on my Paul schedule, I had a better-than-okay time, talking to guys about any old thing without trying to foresee their genetic possibilities. For the first time in a long time, a new year really felt like one to me.

That Monday morning passed almost in slow motion, the way it often can after a vacation. But right after lunch came a sudden barrage. Mark Lewis's agent called to arrange the long-awaited drinks meeting; a publicist tried cheerily to convince me that each of her three clients was perfect for us; the requisite freelance writer, broke after the holidays, sniffed around for his paycheck. By the time the phone rang a fourth time, I dropped the hello and simply said, "Yes?"

"Well, happy new year to you, too," I heard Paul say.

"Where the hell have you been?" I demanded.

"I was seeing Marie."

"For ten days? I must have called fifty times."

"Sorry, Sandy. It was an action-packed vacation."

"I'll bet it was," I said, leaning over to close my door so that I could light a cigarette. "As a matter of fact," I said smugly, "I had some action of my own."

"Oh?" His voice grew faint.

"I went to Acapulco."

"Really."

"Really. All right, what's going on?"

"What do you mean?"

"You sound deeply bizarre, and I want to know why."

"Well, Sandra, that's actually the reason I'm calling."

"Yeah, so?"

There was silence and a breath.

"So . . ." He paused again, and then, in a rush, he said, "I have AIDS."

My head jerked, as if I'd been hit. "What?" It came out as a whisper.

"I have AIDS," he repeated, this time more clearly.

"Do you mean you're HIV-positive?" I asked, gripping my desk.

"No, it's past HIV-positive. It's full-blown AIDS."

"But, I thought you'd been tested and you were fine."

"Well . . ." His voice trailed off, then came back strong. "I didn't get tested when I said I did. I chickened out. I decided I didn't want to know."

"You lied to me!" I shouted. Now, *there* was a sentence I could hang on to.

"Yeah, I guess I did." He sounded tired yet buoyed, somehow, by that strange surge of energy people get in an emergency. "I just didn't want to know," he said.

"Right." I felt myself grow cold, trying to get logical. "Tell me what happened, how you found out."

"Well," he said, "it was a good indication something was wrong when I passed out at the dinner table on Christmas Eve and Marie had me rushed to the hospital. They did all the blood tests I'd been trying to avoid, but at least it took them until two days after Christmas to tell me the results."

"How is Marie taking it?"

"She's been amazing, actually," he said admiringly. "She's strong as a horse. She says I'm going to beat it and that we'll work together as a family."

"And your dad?"

"Well, he doesn't know yet."

"Excuse me?"

"Marie's going to wait until there's a better time to tell him."

"Romano, does he really not know you're gay?"

"I think, Sandy, that this might have happened because of the drugs," he said. He sounded as if he were choking.

I lit another cigarette and said nothing.

"Look, who knows how this happened?" he sighed. "Yes, I had a lot of unprotected sex, but I did a lot of drugs, too. I used needles, and it could have happened that way."

"Oh, God," I said suddenly. "What about Sally?"

"She knows, and she's being wonderful. She explained to her parents about the drugs and how that was a phase of my life that ended a long time ago."

I stared at the wall, trying to steady myself. I focused in hard, on the detail of the paint, but when I saw that it looked like skin I turned away.

"Is she at risk?" I finally asked.

"She took the test, and she's negative."

"Did you tell your boss?"

"Yeah, I had to. He's being great."

"Paul?" My voice cracked.

"Don't, Sandra, please," he said thickly. "Everything will be fine. There are medical breakthroughs every day, and I have this terrific doctor at Cedars-Sinai who everyone goes to. It will all be fine."

"I want to see you," I said.

"Give me some time," he answered. "I don't think I'm up to you yet."

I half smiled. "I often feel that way myself."

"I've got to go," he said. "I have a meeting."

"Paul," I began, but he cut me off. "Gotta go," he said, and the phone clicked.

This is truly not happening, I thought as I stood and mechanically started stashing papers in different piles. I switched off my computer and grabbed my bag and walked to the elevators. Another editor looked quizzically in my direction, but I turned my back on her and gulped air and jabbed the elevator button. Let them fire me. I would go to California and stay there.

At that point, AIDS was a death sentence. There was no cure, no agreed-upon treatment, and everyone was convinced that the only way you got it (unless you were hemophiliac) was by doing something wrong. That meant promiscuous gay sex or drug use. Very few women had it then, and very few kids. When Paul and I were still at Yale, in 1982, a directing student showed us a purple bruise on his hip; it had just appeared and he was losing weight and none of the doctors at the health service could figure out what was wrong. Six months later he was dead.

By 1988 everyone knew that the purple bruise was Kaposi's sarcoma, everyone knew that when an obituary said a single man died of pneumonia he had really died of AIDS, and everyone knew that there was no cure. No one talked about managing the illness and living with it. Some people still thought it could be spread by mosquitoes.

Once outside, I gulped the freezing air and walked up Madison Avenue, past the shops, past the dwindling throngs of bargain hunters still looking for post-Christmas sales. The acrid smoke of overheated chestnuts burned the back of my throat, and I crossed over to Fifth and reversed direction, walking downtown. I wasn't sure where to go or what to do. Who could I call? Who could help me?

I stood on a corner, waiting for the light to change, and caught the eye of a German shepherd on a leash beside me. We looked at each other for a long moment before he jumped up and licked my face, making a crying sound. His owner pulled him away.

I kept moving, feeling the dog's saliva dry on my jaw, and for a while I followed the back that was directly ahead of me, a man in a black coat. I used him as a guide, to keep me upright, on the sidewalk, moving forward. When I got to St. Patrick's Cathedral, I walked up the steps and through the door. It was dark inside, a comforting darkness, and I walked into the warmth of the sanctuary, where people in front of me dipped their fingers in holy water and crossed themselves and moved silently down the rows.

I walked down the center aisle. No one looked up; people were either lost in thought or lost in prayer. One woman clutched a blue tissue in her fist. I slid down a row and sat on the bench, drawing my coat close. I looked up, up at the majesty of the building, the awesome beauty that man could make to offer God, and I listened as the organ played and the chords struck the room around me. I bent my head as if to weep, and prayed.

10

It was one of life's little ironies, I thought, that I would be meeting Mark Lewis—who was ten minutes late and counting—at the same table at Café 43 where Carla Jones and I had, months ago, attempted female bonding. I would have asked the waiter to move me, but no other table was free.

I studied the Cruvinet list. They had the same Edna Valley Chardonnay Carla had ordered—she probably knew it because Bucky had learned it in his wine course. It was funny, I thought idly, fooling with the corners of my starched napkin, how so few people ever have an independent thought. Someone you know tells you something he knows and then you walk around saying it as if you knew it all along. Bucky, I realized too late, didn't have an original thought in his head. The wine was what someone else drank. The vacation was where a buddy had been. The restaurant of choice was a place the boss loved. Why had I never understood that before?

"Um, hi. Sandra Berlin?"

I started. "Yes," I said, rising. "Mark Lewis?"

"Yes. Hello."

He sat down and put his hand to his tie. "Do you mind?" he

asked, beginning to loosen it. His face was flushed, and he was short of breath, as if he had run an obstacle course to get here.

"No, that's fine, of course not," I said.

He pulled the tie off and stuffed it into his jacket pocket.

"I guess we've sort of met before," I said, smiling. "Sorry about that."

He smiled, too. "No problem," he said. "Um, I don't like those kinds of parties, either."

"I'll drink to that," I answered, handing him the Cruvinet list. He lowered his eyes and studied it.

I studied him. Mark Lewis was of medium height, in his mid-thirties, with thinning hair and enormous slate-blue eyes that dominated his face and seemed surprised, somehow. He was preppy-dressed, with a navy blazer, khakis, and a striped shirt, open now at the neck. He looked like the kindly, somewhat absentminded faculty adviser to a boys'-school newspaper. Smart and in charge, but young and hip enough to get the joke. I guess he looked the same as at the party, though he was tan now. I probably couldn't have picked him out of a lineup, since his only identifiable feature was starting his sentences with "Um." For a writer known for his definitive opinions, that was a curious habit. Maybe he wasn't such a tough guy off the page.

The waiter arrived to take the order, and Mark looked at me. "I'll have the Edna Valley Chardonnay," I said authoritatively.

He turned back to the list. "I'm not familiar with the Havens Merlot," he said. "Is it good?"

The waiter sparked to life. "Terrific!" he exclaimed, and pointed out one or two others, and Mark asked questions and they had the kind of conversation Bucky used to have about this one tasting like berries or that one being famous for its smoky undertones. Mark leaned back in his chair and listened intently, cocking his head and running his index finger back and forth over his lips as if someone were imparting the secrets of the universe and he was pondering what to do with them. Which spurred the waiter to even greater heights, until finally I said, "Forget the Edna Valley. I'll try the Havens."

Mark looked startled. He seemed to have forgotten I was there.

"I think I'll have the Rutherford Hill Merlot," he said, and I gasped. He looked at me. "Is something wrong?"

"No, fine, it's fine," I answered. Bucky loved Rutherford Hill Merlot. It never occurred to me that anyone else in the world even knew about it, much less drank it. "I like it a lot."

"Well, then we can trade tastes," he said amiably, and we smiled at each other, and I felt something give in my stomach, in that place under my ribs where I had been feeling punched all this time. Whatever it was had released, and I breathed freely, at last. He wasn't scary at all. I was beginning to understand why people had agents.

When the waiter left, Mark looked at me full in the face, and seemed not to be in motion for the first time since he arrived. His expression was expectant, almost optimistic, as if he were convinced that I would tell him the most enchanting story and he couldn't wait to hear it. I stared. I didn't know what I could possibly say to satisfy that expression, no matter how nice he seemed. Also, he was such an incredible writer with such an impressive vocabulary—"um"s aside—that surely everything I said would be grammatically incorrect and instantly alert him to the fact that I should be nowhere near his copy.

So much for breathing freely. I froze. I looked down, I looked up. I started to swallow, thought it sounded too noisy, stopped, and figured I was going to choke. Then I felt light-headed and thought I might have a full-scale panic attack right there at the table. All within about ten seconds. This was really Miss Belladonna's fault. If she had met him, why hadn't she called him herself? Because she would never let herself be refused, that's why. That was Susie's job. And Susie knew better than anyone that I was only a glorified assistant with a fancy title and no power. *She* should have had this meeting, even if it meant forgoing the opportunity to torture me once Mark decided to pass on *Jolie!* and make his extra money elsewhere. Well, you know what? Fuck her. I wouldn't give her the satisfaction.

I took a deep, stabilizing breath and dug my fingernails into my palms. "Tell me what you'd like to write for us," I said, hoping I sounded briskly professional.

"I'm not sure," he parried. "Tell me what you have in mind."

Where was that wine? My jaw seemed wired shut.

"Well, we've heard you're from Chicago, and we thought you might want to write about that, give sort of an insider's view into your hometown."

Should I have said "sort of"? That wasn't terribly precise. And was it "view into" or "view of"?

But he was already shaking his head. "I know what you want," he said, "but as I think my agent told you, I'm going through a divorce, and my wife, who's also from Chicago, is threatening to move back there with our son, and both our families are there, and it's not a good time for me to be writing about it now just for fun."

I was torn between the relief of knowing he should have said "for me to write about it now" and the surprise of learning he had a son.

"How old is he?" I asked.

"Almost two," he said. I must have looked shocked, because he flushed and added hurriedly, "I know, it's the old story, really. My ex-wife thought a baby would help the marriage, but obviously, it didn't turn out that way."

"I guess not." I wasn't sure how to respond. I certainly couldn't lay claim to an old story any more original. I remembered that Peter Darby had told him about my broken engagement.

The shared realization of being felled by such desperately ordinary circumstances sent us both into an extended silence in which the mood palpably dipped. Glasses in hand, we were, I sensed, in imminent danger of sliding into a bar scene straight out of a Eugene O'Neill play. Any second now, someone would say "pipe dream" and all would be lost.

But something caught Mark's eye, and he sat straight up. "Do you recognize the man who just came in?" he asked. I followed his gaze and saw Irving Aronburg, a big-deal gallery owner who was always being photographed for gossip columns with Hollywood stars who were buying his artists' work.

"Yes," I replied. "Do you know him?"

"Since I was twelve years old," he answered. "My father's a lawyer who did a lot of work for him when Aronburg was just starting out, and I used to hang around his gallery whenever I came to New York. He was never particularly nice to me—he thought I was a strange kid, because I cared so much about painting—and here it is all these years later and I'm writing about most of his shows."

I suddenly remembered reading about this somewhere. "Didn't you just have a big fight with him?" I asked.

Mark nodded. "He banned me from the gallery during Francis Sydney's first show because he said I would never be able to appreciate the work—I was too intellectual to respond to it viscerally."

"So what happened?"

His grin was devilish. "I went to the opening anyway. It was packed. Irving had so many models there, and so many of his garment-district friends trying to pick them up, that I walked in wearing a hat and a different pair of glasses and passed literally in front of him without being recognized. Then I wrote a column about it for *Art and Our Times*. He went insane."

"I guess you didn't like the work."

The devilish grin had gotten even wider. "I loved it," he said, laughing now. "That was the best part. Sydney was terrific. And once he read my piece and heard the story about Irving banning me, he threw a fit and threatened to switch galleries."

What a troublemaker he was. And fearless. I admired that. Everyone I knew, certainly at the magazine, was dying to be liked, a commodity I'd come to consider overrated, because what it ends up meaning is that you're never allowed to say no. But what was inviting about Mark Lewis was that he wasn't desperate for approval but he wasn't a snob either. I could tell that if he hadn't genuinely admired the work he would have said so, but the fact that he was able to dupe Irving Aronburg *and* boost the career of a new artist was even better. He might love art, but he loved a good story too.

"Mark?" Irving Aronburg was standing at the table. He was about seventy, bald and round and wearing large black-framed glasses that someone must have told him made a striking statement, when in fact they made him look like a very fat bug. Like so many men of his generation, he had managed to parlay his lack of polish into a tough-guy business stance, fancying himself a frontiersman of sorts—from Brooklyn.

Mark had stood and was shaking Aronburg's hand. "Irving, nice to see you," he said, turning toward me. "Sandra Berlin, Irving Aronburg."

I stood as well, and he scoped me, head to toe. It was one leer away from vaudeville.

"Well, Mark, I see that life is treating you well," Aronburg said, as if delivering a proclamation. He had apparently decided to let bygones be bygones and was quite pleased with himself for confronting the enemy head-on. "How are the folks?"

"Great, Irving, thanks. Nice to see you." Mark turned to sit down, but Irving Aronburg was persistent. "You were in to see the new work, I hear," he said, and Mark nodded. "Fascinating talent, you know, really something special." Mark nodded again. I could see he was an expert at letting people hang themselves, giving away nothing, no matter how long they talked. Irving Aronburg babbled a moment or two more until I said, "Nice to meet you," and turned my back, signaling the end of the interlude. Mark shot me a grateful glance as we sat back down.

"Let me guess," I said. "You hated it."

He started to laugh.

"I'll never tell," I said, laughing, too.

He looked at me with admiration, a look I returned. He was ballsy without being bratty, an interesting guy who was also a grown-up. He had an ease with himself I hadn't seen in anyone I had dated, including Bucky. No cheap bravado (Roy Toner), no arrogance (Dr. Barad), no flop sweat (Michael Victor). Just those huge eyes, that expectant look, and unabashed curiosity. About everything. Including me, I noticed.

"Okay, back to the serious business of *Jolie!*" I said briskly. "If we can't send you to Chicago, is there somewhere else you're passionate about? A city, an island, a house, a street, someplace that has special meaning for you?"

He looked off, considering. Finally, his eyes lit. "Well, you know, when I was a kid and came to New York with my parents, there were some days that my mother would take me on the train to Philadelphia for a side trip, which I loved—the train and the town. I haven't been there in a while, but the Museum of Art has a nice collection, and there's the Barnes."

"Yes," I said. "But I got the impression from your agent that you don't want to write too much about art so that you won't make *Art and Our Times* angry."

He nodded. "Um, that's true. But there's so much else going on in that town. Philly cheese steaks on South Street, and those great shops on Walnut Street."

I could see from his enthusiasm that it would be a perfect story. To hell with Susie Schein.

After I promised to call Victoria Segal to work out all the details, he handed me his wineglass for a taste. I took a sip and nodded. "Great," I said. Handing it back, I saw I'd left a lipstick print. "Oh, sorry," I muttered, rubbing it with my thumb and leaving a cloudy blotch instead.

"It's fine, it doesn't matter," he insisted, taking a sip from my glass. "Mm, wonderful, that's wonderful," he murmured. "Wow." I waited for the berry undertone sermon, but instead, he pulled a pad and pen from his jacket pocket. "I'm just going to write it down, to remind myself to try and get some."

The waiter returned. Mark said, "I'd like to look at the menu again, so we can taste some more." He hesitated, then looked at me. "Unless you'd like to stay with what you have."

"No," I agreed, shaking my head, practically giving myself whiplash. "Let's try more."

Another thing I liked was that even though people feared Mark because of his power and opinions, he was the only man I had ever met who wasn't pretending he knew everything. He was coming right out and saying, "I *don't* know everything, so teach me." It was entirely unmale, and entirely appealing.

We moved on to a pair of California Zinfandels, and Mark talked about how terrific American wines were becoming, and how much fun it used to be to drive through France and Italy to eat and to drink wine, but France had changed and was too commercialized, and so many of the great old places were gone now. I nodded, in a way I hoped was knowingly, because I had never been to France or Italy and had no idea what he was talking about. But I sure wanted to.

When he began discussing the Louvre, though, I had to admit I had never been. He didn't seem horrified in the least, but suddenly I felt the need to explain my lack of art education.

"This probably sounds dumb," I said haltingly, "but in second grade I read this story about a master artist and his apprentice. And the master knew that the apprentice would be a great artist one day because he could draw a perfect circle, and that was the only way anyone could be a great artist. So, for years after that, I would try to draw a perfect circle—which, needless to say, I never could do. And I figured that if I couldn't do the most basic thing to become an artist, that art just wasn't for me."

"But the most basic is almost always what's the most difficult," Mark said. "You have to draw before you can do abstraction. Still, you don't have to do either to feel what an artist is trying to say and be moved by it."

"I guess so. It's always been easier for me to stick to words."

So we talked about books and magazines and writers we liked and why, and it began to feel that we had started this conversation years ago, fallen out of touch, and were eager to resume. He was a natural teacher, sharing information without the slightest condescension, yet the pace and range of subjects came fast and furious, and I could see he was capable of losing all patience if someone committed the mortal sin of missing a beat.

The waiter brought more wine, and we traded more tastes, and Mark talked about Philadelphia and his mother, who was a painter, and about growing up in Chicago and how much he loved the architecture there, but also how he could never live anywhere but New York because it was always changing and so much was going on. "There's always sumpin' happening," he said, and I started to smile.

"What?" he asked.

"You said 'sumpin' instead of 'something,'" I said.

"I did?" he asked. "I guess it's a Midwesternism."

"No, it's not," I replied. "It's a Zinfandelism." He laughed, and so did I.

"Listen, I'm starving," he said. "Do you want to go somewhere and get some dinner?"

I looked at my watch. It was nine o'clock. We had been there for almost three hours.

"Sure," I said. "We could just eat here, though."

"No." He stood up. "I'd like to get some air, walk a little."

We strolled through Times Square. At a red light, Mark

stepped close to me to let another couple pass. He smelled good, like clean laundry. He wasn't much taller than me, and with his tie off and his collar unbuttoned, I could see the base of his throat just above the collarbone. It seemed kissable, suddenly.

Forget it, Sandra, I thought as we crossed the street. He had put his hand near my elbow to guide me, a slightly protective, almost Old World gesture, which only made me want to lean in farther.

Not tonight, I told myself, shifting my bag to the shoulder between us, reestablishing my distance. This is the Big Writer you are going to snare for *Jolie!* and cover yourself with glory. But just the proximity to this interesting, good-smelling, attractive man — who, by the way, was not even my type because he wasn't tall enough and wasn't muscly enough and (mercy!) seemed actually smarter than me — was making me reel. Too bad, I told myself sternly. You are not on a date. No matter how much you want to be.

Well, that was something, wasn't it? All these months of involuntary dating, and when I actually wanted to be on one, I couldn't be. Talk about karma.

He pointed out building after building, describing the way things used to look and what had changed. "When I was a kid, I only wanted to come to Times Square," he said. "I used to see pictures of it in books and read about it in stories and it seemed so romantic to me. On one trip, we stayed at the old Astor Hotel. It was right over there." He gestured toward Shubert Alley, deserted now, during showtime. It looked like a stage set, empty and shining with light, the dark sky hanging above. The neighborhood seemed suspended, waiting for its next wave of people. Soon it would be intermission, but at that moment, it felt as if we were in New York alone.

"Do you like Orso?" he asked, and, Roy Toner flashbacks aside, I said yes. We walked into an almost empty restaurant that wouldn't fill until the curtain came down, and we drank more wine, this time from carafes, and ate spaghetti. I found myself telling him about Green Hills and Bucky. I wondered if I should get so personal, but he was so easy to talk to. He listened carefully, and his big eyes got even bigger at certain parts ("That's *awful!*" he exclaimed about the moment at the museum), and even though I knew that his response was sincere, I could also see that he appreciated the elements of the story itself, just the way I would. So I got caught up in all the details, watching him anticipate each new twist and turn until I had wrung every bit for all it was worth.

As I talked, I realized that the words were no longer painful. I had repeated them so often, they had taken on the patina of prayer, almost comforting in their drone. And as I listened to myself now, I heard that this story was only a story—with a beginning, a middle, and an end. I felt a twinge at that. An end. My life with Bucky was over.

"Can I drop you off?" Mark asked when we left the restaurant, near midnight. "Where do you live?"

"Down in the Village," I said. "And you?"

"On the Upper West Side."

"Well, I guess not, then."

"It's a nice night," he said tentatively. "I think I'll walk."

"I'll walk with you." I didn't want the conversation to end.

"Great." He seemed glad. We started up Eighth Avenue.

"How long were you married?" I asked.

"Six years," he said.

"What does your ex-wife do?"

"She's a tax lawyer."

I laughed. "No, really."

He looked surprised. "She is."

"I thought you'd be married to an artist, or an architect, or someone who loves the things you love," I said. I *had* thought that? When?

He smiled sourly. "I thought I needed some balance in my life," he explained. "I guess that wasn't too smart."

"Even smart people aren't smart about these things," I said understandingly. I kept talking—chattering, really, as if I'd just been released from a vow of silence. "You know, when I was about eight years old, I would watch my mother cooking," I said. "She would stand at the counter in the kitchen, making, say, hamburger patties, and she would smack them into shape in this rhythm she had and put them on the broiler pan and then she would wash her hands. And when she stood at the sink, she would look out the window and get this faraway expression and sigh, and I would say, 'Mom, what's wrong?' And she would say, 'Nothing.' And I would say, 'No, I can see there's something wrong.' And she would say, 'You're too young to understand.' Well, I think I understand."

He nodded, and suddenly I felt a pang. What was I *doing*? Running off at the mouth about my mother's hamburgers and the meaning of life to *Mark Lewis*, whom I was supposed to be convincing to work with me. And that was *after* telling him the tawdry tale of my romantic travails. I needed to shut up and preserve at least a shred of the illusion that I was a professional.

"Listen," I said, "I think I'm going to peel off now and get a cab. It's pretty late."

"Oh." He seemed disappointed. I wondered if he could tell that I was, too.

"I am wearing heels, after all," I pointed out. He looked at my legs, and I saw him have his own version of me appraising his throat.

"I thought you might want to come up, for a cup of tea, maybe," he said. What a lame line. Just because it worked—I was dying to—didn't make it any better. But I was not going to jeopardize my career and sleep with this man, however much I was tempted.

"Thank you," I said. "I'd love to sometime, just not tonight. I'll call Victoria, and when you figure out your schedule, let me know, and we'll look forward to the piece whenever you can do it." I extended my hand. "Thank you for dinner. It was wonderful meeting you."

"You, too," he said, and shook my hand, engulfing it in a cushy sort of way.

I waved down a cab. "Good night," I called.

"Good night," he answered, and as the cab drove off, I turned and saw him alone on the corner, watching me go. His pants were too long. He had his newspaper tucked under one arm. He took off his glasses and rubbed his eyes with the hand that held them, and looked so sad standing there—forlorn, really—that I was surprised to realize, for the first time in such a very long time, I felt completely at peace.

Susie Schein was in my doorway before I even took off my coat. "I have to talk to you," she said, parking herself in the chair opposite my desk.

"Good morning, Susie, lovely day," I said, going around to the other side. "Can I get some coffee first?"

"Mark Lewis's agent was on the phone with me first thing this morning," she said. Oh, no. My throat closed. He hated me. The hamburgers did me in.

I took a breath. "What's the matter?" I asked, as calmly as possible. "He doesn't want to do the piece?"

"Yes, he does want to do it, but he's being a real prima donna about it, which is why Victoria Segal called me instead of you. The fee is high, which we expected, but he's also decided he has to stay at the Rittenhouse, which I guess we can do on a corporate rate."

"So what's the problem?"

"Well, he seems very specific about what he wants to write, and I can just see us paying him a fortune for a piece that is so much about him that we can't use it as a travel piece." She paused, but I could tell there was more coming. "You know that our travel writers automatically do the information guide to go with their essay. Well, he refuses to do it. He's much too important to be bothered, it seems, with having to compile a comprehensive list of addresses and phone numbers."

I almost laughed. "Did you really expect Mark Lewis to go tracking down the addresses of local lamp stores?" I asked. "I mean, really, Susie, *anyone* can do that."

She looked at me. "That's what I said. And he asked if *you* could do it."

I sat down—or, more precisely, thudded down. "What?" I suddenly understood why he was taking the assignment.

"I think it's not a bad idea, actually," she continued. "You can go down there and check out some places that the girls in fashion and home design know about. But more important, I want you to keep an eye on Lewis. I get the idea that he's going to take our money to write a quickie story while he's really doing research on something more important for *Art and Our Times*."

I tried to catch my breath. Sending assistants along on photo shoots was regularly done because most of the major photographers demanded them, the way rock stars did; apparently they were unable to do their job without an audience. In features, though, things didn't work that way. And besides, I was an editor now. Or at least I liked to pretend I was.

I considered suggesting that a real assistant go—we had plenty—but none had been working more than a few months. Also, I knew that Susie was suspicious enough of Mark that she wanted to send someone who had something to lose if she neglected to discover him sneaking in bootleg research on *Jolie!*'s dime. There was also the Miss Belladonna factor. Our editor in chief would seem to forget all about something like this, and then just when you thought you were safe, she'd corner you in the elevator, asking, "Why isn't Mark Lewis in the magazine yet?"

Susie felt my hesitation. "I know that you can do most of this by phone," she said. "But I also thought we should do something extra, like a shopping guide to South Street and the Reading Terminal Market. The more we have, the better—especially if Lewis's piece is so cerebral that we have to rescue it with service elements. You don't have to stay the whole weekend, obviously, though you will have to at least give up a Saturday." She tightened her mouth. "Is that a problem for you?"

I tried not to break into a big, goofy smile. A sleep-over date in Philadelphia with a guy who liked me so much he *asked* for me to come? To hell with the cup of tea. This was living.

I shook my head. "No, that's fine, actually. As long as you can do something for me."

"What?" she asked peevishly. This part of the dialogue had not been in her copy of the script.

"My best friend from school has been diagnosed with AIDS," I said. Her eyebrows shot up. "He lives in L.A., and I want to see him. Can I assume that the working weekend entitles me to a day off?"

For the first time ever, the flush passed her jawline. "Is he hospitalized?" she asked.

"No," I said. "But I want to be there before he is."

She glared at me. I had her, and she knew it. "Sure," she said, between clenched teeth, getting up to leave. "But by the way," she added, "*You* don't have to stay at the Rittenhouse. *You* can stay someplace a little less *cher,* if you stay at all."

"Fine, Susie, great," I said. I didn't care if I stayed in a broom closet. She was pissed, I was going to L.A. *and* I was going to Philadelphia with a good-smelling man and his kissable throat.

11

As it happened, I cashed in on Susie's favor before Mark's trip could be scheduled. Between his work and his son, he was booked for another six weeks, and I didn't want to wait that long to see Paul. I picked the first Friday in March and flew to L.A. Paul promised to meet me, but when I landed, he wasn't there. I called his house from a pay phone. No answer. I went to baggage claim and got my suitcase, then returned to the gate. He was standing with his back to me. I charged.

"You're late," I announced.

He turned. His skin had a greenish cast, and he seemed dazed. I caught myself. He's sick, Sandra, I told myself sternly. Go easy.

"What's the matter?" I asked softly.

"I'm not sure where I parked," he said.

I put down my bag. "Paul, are you all right?" He looked at me as if seeing me for the first time. "Sandy." He looked frightened. "I'm not sure where I parked."

"That's okay," I said. "We'll find it." I took his arm. "Do you want to sit a minute first, and think?"

He pulled his arm away and started walking. "I need to find the car," he said.

I picked up my bag and followed him. "Did you just park it?" I asked. He nodded. Silently, we headed for the garage.

"It's still Walt, right?"

He nodded again.

"It's okay. We'll find him," I said as steadily as I could. "Do you think it was the A section? Or the B section?"

"B!" he shouted. "It's B."

"Okay, great." We walked to B, up one row and down the next. He never looked at me. I prattled on about the airplane food, so truly terrible, and how nice it felt to be carrying my coat, not wearing it, because it was so warm out, but he didn't seem to hear. As we made our way up and down each side of every level, it eventually became clear that Walt was not parked in B.

He stopped suddenly and announced, "I have to call Sally and tell her we're late."

"Are we meeting Sally?" I asked.

He nodded. "Um, Sandy, I meant to tell you this before. I'm living with Sally now."

I put down my bag. "You are?"

He nodded again.

"Then where am I staying?" I asked.

"Sally's," he said. "She has an extra room."

"Is that okay with her? She's never even met me." He was still nodding, walking off toward a stairwell in search of a phone. I waited awhile, counting Mercedes convertibles, till he came back, smiling.

"I parked in A," he said with relief. "Sally told me to park in A, and that's where I parked, because it would be faster."

"Great," I said. As we headed to A, I tried not to listen to the pounding of my heart or to feel the handle of the bag cutting my hand, and I tried not to turn and run and get on the next flight home. It had barely been two months since Paul told me he had AIDS, and since then we'd talked as often as we always did.

Whenever I asked how he was, he either said "Fine" or changed the subject. I had no idea things had gotten this bad.

We walked up and down A. "Walt!" he cried with relief, and he opened the doors and we sank into the low bucket seats. Paul leaned his head back and let out his breath, wiped away the large beads of sweat at his temples, underneath his baseball cap. He turned the key in the ignition, and when he pressed his foot onto the accelerator I could see the spindle of his leg through his corduroy pants.

"It's cold out tonight, isn't it?" he asked.

"What? Oh, yeah, I guess it is. Listen, should we get some dinner?"

He looked at me as if I were crazy. "I already told you we're going to the Ivy for dinner," he said. "Sally's meeting us there."

"Right," I said. "I forgot." He pulled onto the street, out of the airport, and when I asked him how work was, he got so confused that he missed the light where he was supposed to turn, and cursed me.

I apologized and managed to keep quiet until we had safely arrived at the white picket fence outside the restaurant. A valet took the keys, and we went inside. Paul looked around anxiously until a short woman with clipped, dark hair approached us.

"Sandy, I'm so glad to meet you," she said warmly, holding out her hand. "I'm Sally."

She looked nothing like her picture, but then again the picture Paul had shown me was years old. The bun was gone, she was thin now, and her short hair was stylish. But it was her eyes that shocked me. Big, chocolate-brown, and ready to cry, just like Paul's. The two of them looked related.

"It was really important to Paul that he pick you up himself," Sally said hurriedly as he excused himself to go to the bathroom and we made our way to the table. "He hasn't been doing too well, but when I suggested that I go, or that we go together, he refused. I hope it wasn't too much of a shock for you."

"No, no," I said. The last time I had seen Paul, he was standing lookout on the garbage run to Murray Hill. Everything had changed.

"He has good days and bad days," Sally continued. "The agency has been wonderful, and even though he still has his assistant, he hasn't been going to the office much. It's hard to predict what the days will be like. The doctor said we should expect that, but it's been really difficult to deal with."

I was just ordering a drink as Paul came back. "I love this place," he said, looking at the menu.

"Good," I answered. "You should eat something. You're a bone."

He looked at me across the table. "And you should eat a salad," he said sharply. "You are not a bone."

Sally looked alarmed, but Paul and I laughed, so she laughed, too. She seemed to be a good sport, actually.

When the drinks came, Paul raised his glass of Perrier. "To my fiancée," he said, beaming at Sally.

"To mine," she answered. I lifted my own glass and offered a loud "Congratulations!" while trying to nudge Paul under the table without breaking his leg, but he ignored me.

"When are you getting married?" I asked tentatively. I was starting to feel a pronounced sense of doom. "Soon," she said blithely. "We're planning to do it in Venice. Or Rome."

"Or Paris," Paul said. "We're going to book the Vienna Boys' Choir to sing at the cathedral." His eyes gleamed with sincerity and delusion.

"Really? I had no idea you could even do that." When his expression didn't change, I quickly added, "How fantastic!"

Sally, seemingly overcome, dabbed at her eyes with her fingertips and, excusing herself, went to the ladies' room for a tissue. She looked meaningfully at Paul as she left, but he seemed to ignore her.

"What are you *doing*?" I whispered across the table.

"What do you mean?" He looked himself again, at his most innocent.

"You're sick, you're getting married in a foreign country, and not only that, but you're booking a wedding night full of *tricks*? Does this girl not realize that you don't give a shit about the way the Vienna Boys *sing*?"

He laughed. That was something, at least.

"Sandy, she's been an angel to me, and I adore her," he said. "She always wanted to get married. What harm does it do?"

"What do her parents think?"

"They know that I once had a drug problem. But they'd like us to be married too."

Sally's return put an end to that conversation, so we ordered and ate and discussed only the safest of subjects. Sally talked a lot about her new job, as a fact checker for *Beverly Hills* magazine.

Paul's grilled tuna had to be sent back twice because it wasn't cooked enough for him. He wouldn't eat even a piece of bread while he waited, and by the time the tuna came back, he took it to go, since without the necessary padding on his behind, he was increasingly uncomfortable sitting on the hard chair. The cars were brought to the front, and Paul and I followed Sally back to her place.

"So, Sally checks facts for a living, eh?" I asked sharply. The words hung in the car.

"Don't do this," he said wearily.

"Why shouldn't I? And when did you start living together, without even telling me?"

"A few weeks ago, I guess."

"And why were you wearing a baseball cap in the restaurant?"

"Bad hair day. Listen, Sandra." He pulled his car into a driveway, right behind Sally's. She stood there, waiting. "I am not up to this," he said. "Get it?" He looked angry and hurt. Well, that made two of us. What the hell was going on here? This was my seriously ill gay best friend, planning to marry his girlfriend in

Venice while being serenaded by the Vienna Boys' Choir. I needed a new playbook. I opened the car door and got out, and Sally led me inside.

The apartment was huge: living room, kitchen, dining room, three bedrooms. This was not, I was certain, being paid for with a magazine salary, but with Sally's father's ice-cream fortune. Sally showed me to my bedroom, next to the one she used as an office. Paul headed toward the master bedroom down the hall, dragging his feet on the carpet.

"Good night!" I called after him with a pronounced tone of aggrievement. I mean, really. He was *engaged*, for Christ's sake, and he was going to bed instead of talking to me about it?

I heard his softer, exhausted response through the closed door. "Good night."

Sally bustled into my room with fresh towels and an alarm clock. "I'm so glad you came, Sandy," she said, squeezing my arm. "You mean so much to Paul."

I thanked her and said good night. This girl was getting on my nerves. She was like a hostess welcoming me to my own friend.

That's not fair, Sandra, I thought, getting into bed. You're just overtired. And overwhelmed. Go to sleep. Things will be better tomorrow.

Mornings in Los Angeles, when they're sunny, make you believe you'll live forever. The colors are so bright, so vivid, you see why someone had to invent Technicolor, just to avoid being out-classed by his own backyard.

Sally was up and in the kitchen, setting out fresh-squeezed orange juice and a big basket of muffins. A pot of coffee was ready, and a pitcher of milk and a sugar bowl sat beside it.

"Good morning," I said.

"Good morning," she called, closing the refrigerator door. "Did you sleep well?"

"I did. Did you?"

"Yes, actually. And it was a good night for Paul, too. He slept right through."

"Doesn't he usually?"

"No, he doesn't," Paul said, walking into the kitchen. He was dressed in a white sweat suit that normally would have set off his dark coloring, but now only heightened his pallor.

"Do you like it?" He preened and giggled. He seemed in high spirits.

"Very pure. Good thing you don't have to worry about white making you look fat."

Sally smiled. "Paul and I are going for our morning walk," she said brightly. "Would you like to come?"

"No," I said. "I'm going to have my morning sit-on-my-behind. But thanks."

Paul sipped some juice. "So, Sandy, later you and I will go out to lunch," he said, "and then we'll go shopping, and then hang out here for a while. Tonight we have reservations for dinner at this Italian place we really like, but first there's an AIDS service at the Catholic church we go to, which should be great, 'cause there's a priest there who's been terrific to me."

I nodded. "Sounds good."

They turned to go. Even for sweatpants, the pants hung on Paul. I looked closer and saw that there was a tiny red dot on them, directly in the middle of the seat. I won't say anything, I decided, turning to the newspaper. It would ruin his day if he thought his white outfit wasn't pristine.

I read for a while, then looked around the kitchen. Cheery, checkered tablecloth, blond wood cabinets, ladybug magnets on the refrigerator door. But on top of the refrigerator, things were not so cozy. I got up for a closer look. Boxes with Japanese labels sat on top of boxes with French labels. "*Attention!*" one warned, and even with my crummy French I could figure out that it was some sort of medicine, medicine that apparently hadn't been approved here yet. I reached up toward the boxes, then pulled my hand back. This was not my house.

The front door slammed. "Paul?" I called out. He ran past me into the bedroom, slamming that door too, but not before I could see a slash of red across his white behind.

Sally came in more quietly.

"He's bleeding?" I asked, trying not to sound as frightened as I felt.

She nodded. "It happens," she said evenly, putting down her keys. "He'll be okay. He just didn't want anyone else to see it." She went to the coffeepot and poured some into a mug.

"Sally, listen," I said. "It was right after New Year's that Paul told me he was sick. Since then I've had perfectly normal conversations with him. What's going on? How can this be happening so fast?"

She sighed. "He waited too long to be tested," she said, sitting down at the table. "He knew something was wrong, but he didn't want to know what, so by the time he finally had no choice, the illness had progressed to the point where now it only seems to gain momentum."

"I know he's taking AZT, but what about those drugs?" I pointed to the top of the refrigerator.

She shrugged. "They cost a fortune. But the doctors say they're worth a try, because at this point, anything is worth a try."

"Are they what's making him lose his memory?"

"They might be. Or it might just be dementia. It's hard to know for sure."

"Are they the reason he's losing his hair?"

She looked startled.

Now I shrugged. "Let's just say I've never known Paul to wear a baseball cap to dinner. Especially someplace like the Ivy."

The bedroom door opened. Paul emerged newly showered, wearing navy sweatpants and a T-shirt. "Let's go shopping," he said tensely, walking into the kitchen.

I looked at him. "Why don't you sit a minute? We have the whole day."

His face was set. "No. I want to go now."

"Okay." I got up and turned to Sally. "Can we get you anything?"

"No, thanks." She smiled contentedly, as if she were on a sun-dappled porch somewhere. I wondered what kind of pills *she* was taking.

Paul drove—well, I noticed—to a nearby mall, where we wandered aimlessly.

"What do you need?" he finally asked.

"I don't know. Nothing, I guess."

"Why are you the only girl in America who needs nothing? What about dates? Don't you need clothes for that?"

"Well, not exactly."

"What does that mean?"

I told him about my trip to Mexico and the delightful Dr. D'Amico and how I no longer felt that I needed to rush down the nearest aisle and cook lasagna. That I had decided to smell the roses and invest in lingerie. Then I told him about my drinks date with Mark Lewis that had lasted till midnight.

"So?" Paul asked. "Are we seeing him?"

"Not really. It's all about work, for now at least. But he did ask for me to help out on a piece he's writing in Philadelphia. So I'm going there with him."

"Oh, I love that!" Paul exclaimed. "A first-date field trip!"

"It's not—"

But he was off, pulling me toward the nearest store with that mad-shopper look in his eye, the boundless exhilaration that would lead to the inevitable crash of the credit-card statement. There was no stopping him now.

"I love that you're dating again! You have to look *wonderful!*" he exclaimed, charging through the store's front door, thumbing through a rack of impossibly expensive leather jackets—like I would ever wear one—while I walked to the opposite side of the store.

Now that I stopped to think about it, why *hadn't* I heard from Mark? We had that great night, but afterward he never called—his agent did. He knew I was going to Philadelphia—at his request—but still, nothing. He's dating like crazy, I remembered Peter Darby saying. Well, what was Dr. D'Amico? An interview?

Paul came bounding toward me. "How about this?" he asked mischievously, holding up a silver bikini.

I turned my back. He was not going to rest until I bought something, so after careful consideration of every item in the store, I finally settled on a leather pocketbook, a plain black rectangle.

"You're a thrill a minute, Sandra," Paul said, shaking his head.

"Why? It's real leather—unlike the plastic thing I have now—I can use it with or without the strap, and it's well made, so it'll last a long time," I answered practically.

His mouth turned down; he clearly did not want to think in terms of time.

"Okay, wait, you're right," I said hurriedly. "I need something more fun." I went to a rack that held a black Lycra dress with a strappy top. "I'll try this on," I said. It wasn't too trashy, actually. It looked like something a cocktail waitress would wear to a funeral.

Wow, I said to the dressing room mirror. Suddenly I had cleavage. The thing was like an Ace bandage, pushing everything around in just the right way. Unprompted, I wouldn't have tried it on in a million years.

"Well, what do you think?" I asked, stepping out of the dressing room.

Paul clapped his hands and hooted. "*Very* Ava Gardner," he said approvingly. "Vampy, not trampy."

"Sold," I said. "To the woman going to Philadelphia on a date that's not a date with a guy who hasn't called her in three weeks."

"He'll call you when he sees you in that," Paul said as I went to take it off.

"Okay," I said as we left the store, "now that I've bought something, why don't we get some lunch?" Paul insisted he wasn't hungry. We continued strolling through the mall, but the dress had satisfied him and he had lost the spark to shop. After a while, we headed back to Sally's. When we pulled into the driveway, I jumped out and turned to find him still sitting in his seat.

"What are you doing?" I asked.

He looked at me, seething with resentment. "I can't move as fast as you," he snapped.

"Sorry." I knew that, of course. I had just become lulled—had wanted to be lulled—by his seeming normalcy these past few hours. I didn't want to treat him like an invalid. He was fine. We were fine.

Once inside I headed to the fridge, found a drawer full of cold cuts, and made sandwiches, which Paul refused to eat. Sally and I had lunch in front of the TV; the only choices seemed to be horror movies or sports. We settled on a horse race, but Paul was oblivious. He was writing something on a pad, something he seemed to be hiding.

"Romano, what are you doing?" I finally asked.

"You'll see later," he said. I looked at Sally, who just shrugged.

"And it's Mix and Match taking the lead!" the announcer screamed.

"Honestly, where do they get these names from?" I asked. "None of them makes any sense."

"I think they do, at least to the people who name them," Sally said. She turned to Paul. "If you were a horse, what would your name be?"

"I don't know, Sally. But I know yours."

"What?" she asked, a little anxiously.

He smiled tenderly. "Good as Gold."

I nodded. "That's perfect," I said. She glowed.

He looked at me.

"Yeah, go right ahead," I said. "Tell me what *my* name would be."

"Sandra, I have no energy for this," he said.

"Okay, let me help you. Relentless Bitch?"

He looked at me seriously. "No," he said finally. "I think it would be Wish List. Or Three Wishes."

"What do you mean?" I asked, puzzled.

He sighed. "Well, I think you tend to look at the people you love and see them the way you want them to be, rather than the way they are. So, Wish List. Or you think that when something bad happens, it can be solved by magic, or should be, because you said so—instead of opening your eyes and seeing that, sometimes, what's in front of you just can't be fixed. So, Three Wishes." He took a breath. "Or if you don't like those, there's always Rose-Colored Glasses."

I felt stung. What provoked that? I saw Paul flush, as if he had said too much. "Well, thanks for the character sketch," I said as Sally got up and went into the kitchen with an armful of dishes. Smart move, I thought, turning back to the television. Because if I was Rose-Colored Glasses, she must be Rose-Colored Cataracts.

When it was time for the church service, Sally insisted on driving us in her car. Paul was beautifully dressed, in pleated black wool pants and a crisp white shirt, but I could see that though his belt was pulled to its last notch, the pants were still loose around his waist.

The church was ultramodern, and the crowd was large. Paul sat between us, and as we settled ourselves into the pew, he turned to me and smiled, really smiled, for the first time all weekend. I loved his smile, genuinely sunny, with its tang of impishness.

The service began, and as I usually do when services begin, I stopped listening and looked around at the congregation, none of whom seemed to be obviously sick. Soon, though, I couldn't help but notice that Paul had become agitated. He was crossing and uncrossing his arms and legs, and his skin had gone that greenish shade again. Sally reached for his hand, but he pulled away. She was distraught, too, I saw.

"We must work together," the priest was intoning. "For the sick among us need our help as their days grow shorter and their journey to God reaches its end. When that day comes, they will be blessed with release from their greatest suffering."

Paul jerked to his feet, tears in his eyes, and started pushing his way blindly down the row. Sally threw me an imploring look, and I got up and followed them out. The priest raised his voice even louder as we left, until I felt it booming through the microphone. "And God, who loves His children, will welcome them—"

As we tumbled out the front door, Sally managed to grab hold of Paul's arm. "Paul, I'm sorry, I'm so sorry," she was saying in a pleading tone.

"Fuck this, get away from me!" he shouted, lurching toward the parking lot.

"Wait a minute, what's going on?" I asked.

Sally turned. "It was a substitute priest," she said. "We thought it would be our regular priest, the one we like so much. This one only talked about death." She looked at me, confused. "Didn't you hear him?"

Before I could answer, Paul started slamming his fist against the locked car door. "I want to get out of here!" he yelled. I climbed quickly into the backseat while Paul got in front with Sally. "I want to go home!" he chanted. "I want to go home!"

Sally looked at me in the rearview mirror. "I guess we're not going out to dinner, Sandy, is that okay?" she asked calmly.

"Yes, it's fine," I said.

Paul was rocking in his seat and moaning now. "I want to go home."

"We're almost there, Paul, we're almost there," I said consolingly, but he didn't seem to hear me. We made it back to the apartment in record time. Sally put her arm around his waist and helped him up the stairs. Once inside, she eased him onto the living room couch.

"I'm cold," he began to repeat, just as obsessively as before. "I'm cold."

Sally was already on her way into the bedroom, and returned with a pile of blankets. "Paul, you know the best thing for this is a hot shower," she reminded him, starting to wrap the blankets around him one at a time.

"No," he muttered. "I can't take my clothes off, I'm cold, too cold." And then his body started to convulse. I stood, rooted, watching him jerk wildly, and for the briefest moment he saw me staring at him and threw up his arms and covered himself with one of the blankets. Moaning and sobbing, he shot back and forth while Sally tried in vain to put her arms around him and quiet him. It went on like that for a while, until he ran out of energy and she managed to encircle him in her embrace. He wept brokenheartedly while she made low, soothing noises and rubbed his arms and his back to warm him, his face and body hidden, until, finally, he was still.

Sally got up. "I'm going to get the shower going," she said to Paul. "And we'll take you inside with all the blankets on so you won't get cold, and you can get right into the hot water and you'll feel so much better, okay?" From underneath the blanket he whimpered his assent.

I followed Sally into the bathroom. "Does he need to go to the hospital?" I asked.

"They'll only send him home," she said wearily. "Sometimes he becomes frightened and then hysterical, and then he gets freezing cold and can't stop shivering, but there's nothing they can do about it."

The room was filling with steam. She smiled unconvincingly. "He'll be okay."

I turned and went back to the living room. Paul was still under the blanket. I reached out my hand to touch what I could see was his arm. He growled and pulled away.

Sally came back in. "Sandy, he's embarrassed," she whispered. "He didn't want you to see him this way."

I didn't want to see him this way, either. I thought I knew about AIDS. I knew it made people die. But I knew nothing until I saw this happening in front of me. Not just the convulsion—a violent cry from his crashing immune system—but his complete and ongoing absence of hunger. Failure to thrive, they called that in infants. That's what he had. He wasn't looking forward. He was stalled, frozen with panic and illness and shame. How had this happened? And why? He was twenty-eight years old.

"I'm going inside to change now," I said loudly. "Since we're not going out to dinner and we get to stay home, I'm just going to put on my nightgown."

I could hear thumping and shuffling behind me as Sally got Paul to stand and start moving toward the bathroom. When she returned, she gathered up the sweat-drenched blankets and loaded them into the wash.

"How about a drink?" I offered, following her, and Sally grinned good-naturedly. "Absolutely," she said. Between the two of us, a bottle of white wine disappeared while Paul was still in the shower. The way I looked at this girl had changed significantly during the last hour. She was, I now realized, some fearsome combination of nurse and girlfriend, sister and pal, who put every ounce of energy into sustaining Paul. But as much as I loved him, I wondered what he had done to inspire such devotion. From the little I knew of their relationship, it was years of broken dates, broken promises, endless procrastination. And still, here she was, giving it her all. Did she *know* about Paul? Could she, really, and keep doing this?

"I think I'll make some dinner," she said, draining her glass of wine.

"Forget dinner, we can order in," I suggested, but she was already taking out a pot to boil water for pasta. I watched her busy herself, not knowing what else to say. Nothing mattered to her but the life of the moment, in which she was living her marriage to Paul Romano. Because this was it. The dinner she was cooking, the church services and the car rides, this was the marriage, the time she would look back on later and say "I remember."

My marriage to Bucky, blessed with vitality and hope, had been Green Hills and Amherst. This girl had to pay a terrible price for her fantasy, because she hadn't signed on for the promise of three kids and a chafing dish. It was this: the aborted walks, the multiple showers, the priest beckoning from behind the lectern.

Her time was now.

My time with Paul Romano had passed, I realized. I belonged to another era, another part of his life, when he was younger and healthy and had the world by the balls and wanted a pal with whom to exult in it. He loved me, and I loved him, but the person huddled under that blanket was no longer mine. I would have taken him in the same way Sally had, tried to nurse him, tried to heal him, but I knew he would never let me. That, to him, would be a defeat. I sat at the table, watching Sally make pasta, and drank.

"Sally?" I spoke her name almost without knowing it. She turned and looked at me. "Sally, do you, I mean, in terms of Paul . . ." I stopped.

Her face darkened slightly, and she put down her bowl. "Yes," she said, locking her eyes with mine across the room. "I know."

And then I dropped my gaze, because for her to admit this, to say she knew that Paul was gay, was incredibly difficult. Almost every woman falls in love with a gay man at some point; I'm not sure I've known one who hasn't. But the ugly part of that particular love affair is that the man does not desire you and never will. Nothing is worse for a woman, living in the culture that *Jolie!* magazine and all the others perpetrate. She knows she's too fat. She knows she's too soft. She knows that her clothes are knockoffs and that her hair will never obey. And her worst fears are realized when the man she chooses, the one who looks into her soul and loves what he sees, never wants her physically.

The awful paradox is that for as many assholes as a woman can sleep with in a lifetime—an infinite amount, apparently—the ones who want to sleep with you, who grab you and hold you as a woman, who respond to you without thinking—even if they're not capable of thinking—well, that's also the way women need to be loved. The soul touch over coffee is swell, bursting with promise. The wardrobe advice is even better. But when it gets down to basics, it's a man's hands on you, in all his clumsy grasping, *wanting* you—that is the part of being a woman that can't be satisfied otherwise. And to look another woman in the eye and acknowledge that you have agreed to live without that is an empty moment.

"Okay," I muttered, embarrassed, looking away.

Paul reappeared, wearing a robe and his baseball cap. He was pale and drawn, and his hands trembled while he tightened the sash around his waist.

"Well, you look bright and shiny," I said gamely. "You smell good, too."

"Thanks," he said. "That was more showers in a day than I ever intended. But I guess God will love me better clean."

"Sure He will. And He'll love you even more if you take Him shopping. I'll bet He's never had anyone who could truly explain the benefits of an Armani cut."

Paul smiled. "Especially being surrounded by nuns."

I laughed. Paul had always hated the nuns who had punished him, seemingly constantly, as he grew up.

"Here we go," Sally said, bringing the pasta to the table. We sat down and ate. Paul finished a whole plate.

"That's so good," I said. "Do you want some more?"

"No, I've had enough." He headed into the living room. "Let's watch some TV."

"I'll be right there," I said, turning to Sally, who was clearing the plates. "Let me help you," I offered, opening the dishwasher. She set the dishes on the counter. "Sally." I took her arm. "Are you all right?"

Tears glimmered in her eyes. "Yes," she said. "It's just so scary when it happens."

"I know," I said, hugging her awkwardly. Here was someone whom I hadn't liked on principle because I thought she couldn't face the truth in her life, and I hadn't liked her double because I couldn't face the truth in mine, and now she and I seemed to be sharing every intimate secret in the world and we had only met each other yesterday.

"Why don't you let me clean up?" I said. "Just sit down and watch some TV."

"Actually, I think I'm ready for bed," she said. "Thank you, Sandy. I . . . I'm glad you're here."

"Me too."

When I was done, I joined Paul on the couch. Sally came in dressed for bed, kissed him on the cheek, and said good night. He put his feet up on the coffee table.

"Are you warm enough?" I asked.

"Well, maybe," he said.

I got a puffy down comforter from a pile of bedding in the hallway and folded it around him like a sleeping bag, covering his legs.

"That's good," he said gratefully. He had a crossword puzzle on his lap. I sat down next to him and snuggled under part of the covers. "Share?" I asked.

He smiled. "Of course."

He flipped on the TV with the remote. It was almost time for *Saturday Night Live*.

I reached for his hand, the part that wasn't holding the pen.

"Hey, Romano," I said softly. "Good to see you."

He put the pen down and smiled his sweet smile. "Hey, Sandra," he said.

The show started, and the announcer said, "Ladies and gentlemen, your host, Bruce Willis!"

We watched as Willis walked through the door and took his place center stage. Paul turned to me questioningly.

"Who is that?" he asked.

I started to laugh, then stopped. "What?" I pulled my head back and looked at him. His expression was blank.

"Who is he?" he asked.

"Well, I think he's an actor," I said, linking my arm through his and pulling him closer to me. "But we'll find out."

12

It had been two hours, I realized, that we were sitting there, watching Susie Schein and Miss Belladonna pace The Wall and shoot questions at each other. One would stop to pull off a fashion layout, switching its place with another. Every so often, they would turn and aim themselves at the editors skulking behind the conference table, demanding to know whether this or that story had to run right *now*. The sales department hadn't sold enough ads, it seemed, which Susie and Miss Belladonna took as a criticism of the editorial content (it probably was), so some of this month's pieces would have to go.

Finally, Miss Belladonna, mouth set in a crimson line, ordered all the pieces pulled down and laid out "the old-fashioned way," on the floor. The assistants scurried to reassemble the layouts, starting at one end of the hallway, in front of Miss Belladonna's cream-colored enclave, and stretching them all the way down to the other end, home to Susie's book-infested hovel. Then they walked, Miss Belladonna leading the way in her stiletto heels, Susie plodding behind in her glove-leather loafers that gapped with every step. The rest of us stayed fixed in the doorway, watching.

Somehow, gazing down upon the magazine seemed to energize Miss Belladonna. She pointed a snakeskin toe, approvingly, at one layout, scraping the next aside like gum.

"Does it really matter whether the bathing suits come first or the evening dresses do?" I asked under my breath.

Buffy Parks glared at me. "Of course it does," she said in her lockjaw sneer. Ever since Mimi Dawson was fired and I'd had to surrender my borrowed Cartier watch to Buffy, she and I had avoided each other. The previous week, though, we'd been thrown together at a cocktail party the magazine had given for Gloria Gaspard, the socialite wife of Scott Gaspard, the movie star. It was one of those pointless parties—someone had interviewed her in the current issue for all of four paragraphs—but the promotions department went at it full throttle, calling all the gossip columns, and the promotions director met with all kinds of caterers in search of "substantial hors d'oeuvres." Even Miss Belladonna laughed at that one.

Anyway, at the Gaspard apartment—Mr. Gaspard, notorious for falling in love whenever he was working, was nowhere in sight—I found myself face-to-face with Buffy in the middle of the crowded library. We had no choice but to speak.

How were things?, I asked politely. Oh, she began, launching into what sounded like a well-rehearsed bit, she was looking to leave Darien and move into Manhattan, but she just couldn't decide which neighborhood would "send the right message" to the fashion industry.

"What's the message?" I asked, trying to keep the contempt out of my voice.

"You know: stylish, hip, now. The Upper East Side is out because it's too establishment. The Upper West Side is too, you know, intellectual. Chelsea is a possibility, I guess. Where do *you* live?" she asked, pointedly.

"West Village," I said tentatively.

"Yes, that's good for features," she decreed. "Lots of poets and writers."

I smiled brightly. "Absolutely. Right before he died, Dylan Thomas collapsed in front of the White Horse Tavern, just a few blocks from my apartment."

I could see her trying to remember if she had read about that on Page Six—but that was the moment when the bookshelves upstaged her. I had noticed, as Buffy spoke, that the great classics of literature that filled this library were all beautifully bound, in maroon and navy leather, with identical gold lettering. I wondered if they were first editions, and marveled that they were the same size and shape. But upon closer inspection, I saw that they weren't books at all. Each shelf was filled with leather-bound carvings of books, and at either end of the shelves, if you looked very closely, you could see where they hooked into the bookcase. Upon even closer inspection, on top of the "books" was finely grooved wood, made to look like pages.

"What's wrong?" Buffy asked, sensing that she had somehow lost my attention.

"Oh, nothing, I just got distracted, thinking about Dylan Thomas," I said. "A tragedy, don't you think?" I started moving away, having spotted Pascal. I threw him an exuberant wave that confused him mightily, because I saw Pascal every day and was never happy to see him. But when I clued him into the bookshelves, our bond was sealed. We were both people who sought salvation in books, and he was as horrified as I was.

It was justice of a sort to forever associate Buffy with that event, I thought now, as she tossed her limp hair in dismissal of my foolish question about the layouts. We continued to huddle in the conference room doorway, watching Miss Belladonna examine the same six pictures over and over. I was irritated and exhausted and sighed loudly to prove it.

"It's the *pacing* of the magazine, you know, that determines whether the reader keeps reading," Buffy said. She dropped her voice low, as if she was sharing a secret.

"The reader doesn't read a photo layout," I said.

She thought about that a minute.

"Why don't *you* just tell them which layout should come first?" I suggested. "They could use the help."

"Yeah, like I might ever do that," she said snippily.

Susie Schein lifted her head and stared at the cluster of us. "Give us a minute, will you?" she barked. Everyone scattered, mincing down the hallway in both directions, careful not to tread upon the shots of Jolie straddling a motorcycle in two scanty strips of spandex that would set the beloved reader back at least a hundred bucks.

Back in my office, I closed the door and lit a cigarette. It was close to spring now, and the trees were starting to turn a soft green in the yard next to St. Patrick's, which I could just see if I leaned over far enough.

Paul.

For the millionth time, I thought of Paul.

I had been home for a week and still couldn't get the visit out of my mind. On that Sunday morning, just before I left, I had walked into the kitchen to find Paul in his robe, drinking coffee, his baseball cap on the table beside him. When he saw me, he fumbled for it, jamming it onto his head, which, I saw, was covered only in sparse hairs and baby fuzz.

"You don't have to put your hat on," I said quietly.

"I don't want you remembering me looking like a rat's ass," he mumbled.

"What are you talking about?" I said. "I'll be back soon, in a few weeks. Don't say things like that." He smiled faintly, as if I had already left, and turned away, to his paper.

Sally drove me to the airport, and as I was getting out of the car she handed me a package. "Paul said to give this to you before you got on the plane," she said. "It's a book."

Once in my coach seat, I unwrapped the package: *Kate Vaiden*, by Reynolds Price. The dust jacket was dark and pictured a white horse in the woods with a man nearby, reflected in a pond, a double image. I opened the book and found an inscription Paul had written in his spidery hand, "To Sandra, There are few things in my life I have loved more than this book. There are few people I have loved more than you. You lighten my soul and make my heart dance. Love, Paul."

I felt a chill. That's what he had been working on when Sally and I were watching the horse race. I turned the next page and saw the opening line of the novel: "The best thing about my life up to here is, nobody believes it." I put the book back in my bag, unwilling to read it.

Once I was home, though, I carried it with me everywhere, to work and back again. I wanted to save it, to hoard it. I wanted, ten or thirty years from now, to sit down and read it and feel that Paul was right there with me, sharing his own special message, new, as if he'd just thought of it. I wanted it to last. I wanted him to live.

The week before the Philadelphia trip, I spent hours doing research. I hardly needed to, but anything was better than going home. Sharon had moved out amid rainstorms of tears when her mother's accountant located a one-bedroom apartment on the Upper West Side that qualified as a good investment. Unlike our building, this new one didn't have a doorman, and Sharon refused to give her mother a key. That was progress in itself. She seemed finally ready to move on, to find the man who would be her husband. She knew she would meet him soon, because that's what all the books said. That if you cared enough about yourself, felt good enough to feel you deserved only good things—like leaving your pitiful friend in your pitiful share so you could use the bathroom whenever you wanted—then you were ready. She had also dumped the mute. Entitled girls were entitled to conversation, at the very least.

After Sharon left, I decided to keep my spot on the living room floor, despite her urging me to move into the bedroom. I just didn't like the idea of closing the door and not knowing what was going on outside. I put an ad in *The Village Voice*, like everyone did who was looking for a roommate, and found one just in time to pay May's rent.

Mary Ann White looked like her name. She must have been six feet tall, with stringy blond hair—a total jock who worked in advertising. No, she didn't know Bucky, had never heard of him, in fact. When she came home at night, she would change out of her tie blouses, put on her sneakers, and run, miles at a time. Then she would bring home from the salad bar on the corner a plastic container filled with chickpeas and cottage cheese that smelled like an old refrigerator, and she would eat it while drinking two of the most enormous beers I had ever seen, straight from the bottle. She declined to sit at the table, the way Sharon and I had, but took the food into her room and ate it in front of her own TV. The fact that we weren't friends and had been thrown together by financial need only was lost on neither of us. In her first week in residence, we hadn't said more than five sentences to each other.

The Wednesday evening before my Philadelphia trip, I came home around seven-thirty, just in time to watch the plastic container make its entrance. I took my place at the table, alone, with a bowl of reheated vegetable fried rice, but I just couldn't eat it. The trip was worrying me, and my stomach was killing me. I'd been drinking from a Pepto-Bismol bottle all day.

I started flipping through the file, then put it down. Okay. The problem was that Mark and I were taking this trip for work and one of us was confusing it with romance. Which one of us would that be? After all, if he had been dying to see me socially, he would have called. And he hadn't. Fine. We would be friends. Or professional acquaintances. Or whatever. But no wish lists here. I would deal with this head-on. I picked up the phone and dialed. He answered on the first ring.

"Mark? Hi. It's Sandra Berlin." My mouth felt dry. I hadn't thought he would actually be home. "I'm just calling to touch base before the weekend, to find out what you're planning, so I can work around you."

"I'm glad you called," he said easily. "I've been so over-whelmed these past few weeks with other deadlines, I have to admit that I hadn't focused on this. Um, that's what I'm doing tonight, though. Sitting here surrounded by all things Philadelphia."

"That makes two of us," I said. "Does it make sense to go through some of it now?"

We did. Naturally, I had overprepared. Everything he wanted was much more manageable than anything I had imagined.

He talked about some of the artists' exhibitions at the Museum of Art that had interested him, and mentioned, in passing, an exhibit at MOCA in Los Angeles. I had wanted to see it when I'd visited Paul, but obviously, I hadn't managed it.

"You know, I was just out there and I missed it," I said. "I was visiting a close friend who was too sick to go."

"What's wrong?" he asked.

"AIDS," I said.

"I'm sorry," he said, as if I'd told him someone had died. Covering the art world, I imagined, put him in close proximity to a number of people with AIDS. He seemed to know the implications better than I did. He asked a few questions, and I told him everything, the whole story, all in a flood. I hadn't realized that I didn't have someone to talk to about this; normally, that person would have been Paul. When I stopped to look at my watch, I realized we had been on the phone for more than an hour.

"Listen, you'd better get off and concentrate on Philadelphia," I said. "Sorry we got off on such a lengthy tangent."

"Don't worry, I was glad to talk about it," he said. Somewhere in the last hour I had lost track of the idea of being professional and found myself hoping he might offer that cup of tea again. Hopping a cab to the Upper West Side seemed a suddenly appealing notion.

"Are you just going to stay in and work now?" I asked. "I mean, have you had dinner yet?" My voice seemed shrill, even to me.

"I had a sandwich earlier," he said. "So I think I'll just sit here and finish things up."

His tone seemed distant now. We arranged to meet at Penn Station Friday morning and rang off. "Think work," I kept repeating, as I drank some more Pepto-Bismol and went to bed.

Friday morning at a quarter to nine, I saw Mark standing underneath the big board with the scheduling information on it, his bag at his feet, reading the papers. My stomach pinched—yet again—and I willed myself to remain composed.

"Good morning." I was as chipper as possible, clutching my coffee and my garment bag.

He seemed to brighten. "Good morning," he said. "Do you need help with that?"

"No, I'm fine. Thanks." It was just too early in the day to be this nervous. I still felt awkward about our conversation the other night. I knew I'd sounded pushy about dinner. I hadn't meant to, but once we'd started talking about Paul, and he was so comforting—well, I got knocked off course. I did not intend to make that mistake again.

The panels on the board started flipping, directing us to Track 9. "Well, how many other assignments do you get where someone goes with you to catalog Amish apple butter?" I said. "I know this must seem silly."

"Not at all," he said as we walked toward the stairway. "My agent told me all about Susie Schein and her rules. I gather that in the world of women's magazines she's a notorious horror. I'm surprised you've lasted as long as you have."

"Me too."

When we reached the train, I took an involuntary step backward. "If you want to get some work done," I suggested, "I'll meet up with you there."

"No, don't be silly," he said. "Let's sit together. The trip isn't long, and I was just going to read some papers. Unless, of course, you want to sit alone."

"No. Fine. Great." For heaven's sake! New rule: All business with members of the opposite sex whom you are secretly dying to sleep with should be conducted only at night, when you're awake and have a fighting chance at forming actual sentences.

He put my garment bag in the overhead rack, we sat down, and he handed me some of his newspapers. His eyes were really shockingly blue, I thought as the train emerged into daylight and the sun hit them. He was wearing a pale blue shirt and navy jacket—which probably helped the effect, I reminded myself—along with beige khakis and loafers. He was excited, I saw, to be taking this trip. He had dressed up. Just do your job and everything else will take care of itself, I cautioned myself, turning my attention to the *Daily News*. Try to relax.

The newspapers didn't last long. Mark started chatting about how much he loved trains, and how often he used to take them when he was growing up. After a while, he pulled out a piece of white paper that had "Itinerary" typed across the top. "Here's what I have," he said, "if it's okay with you." Everything we had agreed on was there: the museums, the Liberty Bell, the Mint, and Benjamin Franklin's house.

"I also made a dinner reservation tonight at Le Bec-Fin," he said. I nodded and said nothing. "Well, can you come with me?" he asked, flushing.

I felt myself flush, too. "Oh, no, sure," I said, stumbling over my words. "I've heard it's great. I'd love to."

Maybe he hadn't been put off by the phone conversation after all. As the train slowed on its approach to the Thirtieth Street Station and the conductor called out "Philadelphia," the excitement of what might prove to be a genuinely fun weekend caught me and buoyed me up. Okay, so it was work. But it was also fun. And I felt as if I hadn't had any fun in a long time. I was ready.

Mark stood and reached to the rack for my bag. I looked up as he handed it to me and saw him blanch, his mouth opening, and for a second I thought he might be having a heart attack. Or maybe I was. He was streaked in Pepto-Bismol.

Long banners of it splashed down the front of his pale blue shirt and onto the lapels of his navy jacket, puddling in the folds of his beige pants. My mouth opened too, in what I hoped was a silent scream, and I looked at the bag, firmly zippered and completely saturated. The family-size bottle must not have been closed, I realized. And here was Mark Lewis, the most famous art writer in America, marinating in my stomach medicine.

"I'm sorry" was the best I could do.

"What is it?" he asked, stunned.

"Pepto-Bismol. I had a stomachache, and I guess I didn't close the bottle all the way and it leaked. Oh, my God, I am so sorry."

Other people walked past us with their own bags, looking suitably aghast at the pink ooze that was now dripping onto the floor. I stepped off the train, holding the bag away from me, following Mark, who trudged on ahead. As we emerged into the station's main room, he turned, but before he could speak, my adrenaline kicked in. "I can fix this," I blurted. "I really can, if you'll give me a chance. But we need to go to the hotel first."

He looked down at himself, miserable. He seemed truly shocked, not that I could blame him. If the roles had been reversed and *my* clothes had been doused with a thick pink liquid associated with diarrhea, murder wouldn't have been good enough.

"Why don't you go to the men's room and see if any of it comes off," I urged, "and I'll get on the taxi line." I walked away before he could protest, and he followed my suggestion as if anesthetized.

I took my place on line and tried not to hyperventilate. This was a bona fide disaster. "Pay attention and fix this," I told myself sternly. As I inched toward the head of the line, I saw him walk slowly out of the station doors, dazed, holding his bag in front of him like armor.

I forced a big smile. "You can't see a thing!" I said too loudly — and falsely. He'd gotten a little carried away and now looked as if he'd showered with his clothes on.

He stepped into the line behind me. "Rittenhouse Hotel," I told the dispatcher, and we were off.

The ride was silent—none of the "Ooh"s and "Ah"s and "I remember when"s I had anticipated. He stared out his window with great concentration, and I imagined he must be cursing the day he'd agreed to this trip. As we pulled up to the hotel, I opened the cab door before the doorman could do it for me. "You pay the fare and I'll find the concierge," I said to Mark decisively. "Meet me inside."

I bolted to the front desk and cornered the concierge, a young man with a kind expression. "Listen," I said. "I'm in terrible trouble. I'm traveling with my boss, and the absolute worst thing just happened, which is that I had a bottle of Pepto-Bismol that opened in my bag and it poured all over him. Now his clothes are ruined, and I'm going to get fired unless I can fix it."

The concierge nodded sympathetically and tried not to smile. "We have a dry-cleaning service," he said. "We can send everything out this afternoon and have it returned by four."

I thought I might cry. "Thank you," I gushed as Mark walked in the door.

"Everything's fine," I proclaimed as the concierge scrutinized the pink-stained wretch before him. "They can send your jacket and pants out to be cleaned, and they'll be back this afternoon. No problem."

Mark looked at the concierge and asked, "Do they do shirts?"

"They can try" was the answer, though now that he'd assessed the damage, the concierge looked doubtful.

"Sure they can," I said peremptorily. "Listen, why don't you go upstairs and change? You don't need a jacket for this afternoon anyway, and we can have an early lunch and see what there is to see. By the time we're done, the clothes will be back and perfect." I was practically pushing him toward the elevator. The bellhop picked up Mark's bags, and he turned and followed.

"I'll be waiting right down here," I said brightly as Mark disappeared into the elevator. "Take your time." I turned back to the concierge. "The shirt's ruined, right?" I asked.

He half smiled. "It doesn't look good," he said tactfully.

"Okay, where can I buy men's shirts?" I asked. "After four, when we know for sure."

"Hecht's is open late," he said, writing down the address and phone number.

"You may have saved my job," I said, and he finally gave me a full smile, which I gratefully returned. To hell with Mark Lewis. I would move to Philadelphia and marry the concierge.

"What about *your* clothes?" he asked, and I stopped, surprised that I hadn't considered them myself. I unzipped the bag and found everything inside untouched. The only thing in the outside pocket had been the Pepto-Bismol.

The concierge then called the bellhop to show me to my own room—in a burst of inspiration, the *Jolie!* travel office had figured out the two-for-the-price-of-one strategy—which was better than I expected, considering the rate. I hung up my clothes, threw the garment bag into the bathtub, and raced back to the lobby, hoping to arrive ahead of Mark. I would buy him a whole new wardrobe if I had to, I thought, noting my shiny nose in the reflection off the elevator door. I dug around my purse for my compact, which I found just as the doors opened and Mark stood before me, watching me slap powder onto my face. He was wearing fresh khakis and a striped shirt and seemed to have recovered his equanimity enough to find the sight of my on-the-fly makeup job most entertaining.

"You know, I have another pair of pants and another shirt I can make do with," he said. "I should have realized that. I guess I wasn't thinking clearly."

"Listen," I said, taking his elbow. "I want to apologize to you. It goes without saying that the magazine will pay your cleaning expenses. And if you need to replace any of the clothes, we'll pay for that, too."

"Really, it's okay," he said mildly as we started out the door. "How about that lunch?"

Thank you, God, he had forgiven me. I realized I was starving. I had scared myself so far past the diarrhea stage, nothing could faze me now.

"Let's get some cheese steaks," he said.

"Sure," I answered gamely. "Sounds great." I'd rather die, I thought. I imagined they must be made with the crappiest meat and Cheez Whiz, and I figured I would just spit mine into my napkin when he wasn't looking.

We hailed a cab and headed to Jim's Steaks. On the way, his speech restored, Mark pointed out buildings, and seemed to have a story about each one. At the restaurant, we took our loaded trays to the upstairs dining room, settling near a window overlooking South Street. I folded half the sandwich, trying not to look at it, and took a bite. It was good. Actually, it was great (provolone, hold the Cheez Whiz). I ate it in what seemed like four bites, demolishing a bag of potato chips for good measure. Well, tough. Talk about a stressful morning!

After lunch, we did all the tourist things—the Liberty Bell,

Independence Hall, Benjamin Franklin's house. I felt like a kid, except this time there was no teacher on the field trip, just the cute boy you had the crush on—all for yourself. We visited Christ Church cemetery, where Benjamin Franklin was buried; one of my guidebooks said it was good luck to drop a penny on Franklin's flat gravestone, as long as it landed heads up. I told this to Mark.

He fished in his pocket for change, pulling out a penny.

"You do it," he said, handing it to me.

"No, you," I insisted, waving it away.

"My only wish is that your bottle's empty on the train ride home," he said slyly. I laughed, and his eyes looked sparkly because now we had a joke together.

We ended up walking along Walnut Street, in the fancy part of town, chatting away. Suddenly, we stopped. In front of us was a window filled with Pepto-Bismol. This optician's shop, for some bizarre reason, had intermingled their display of eyeglass frames with blow-up plastic bottles of Pepto-Bismol, boxes of Pepto-Bismol tablets, and even real bottles of the stuff. We stood there, stunned, until we both burst out laughing. I could hardly catch my breath.

"What does it mean?" I asked.

Mark gasped, "I don't know."

The woman inside, behind the counter, looked out at us, puzzled, which made us laugh even harder. I wiped my eyes finally and saw that it was nearly four-thirty. I sobered up fast.

"Let's get back and check on your dry cleaning," I said.

We walked the short distance to Rittenhouse Square, a beautiful park ringed with hotels and elegant old apartment buildings. In the aftermath of our outburst, Mark Lewis seemed happy and relaxed. I could think only about his shirt.

One look at my fiancé the concierge's face, and I knew that all was lost. He presented the shirt on a hanger, perfectly pressed, with the streaks of Pepto-Bismol embossed into the fabric for all eternity. The jacket and beige pants, incredibly, were perfect. But Mark's spirits seemed to plummet. "It's no problem," I said forcefully. "We'll just run down to Hecht's and buy another shirt."

"No," he said. "It's not worth it. I have this shirt and the other one. I can do without it."

"Absolutely not," I insisted. "But, listen, I'm sure you're tired, so why don't you go upstairs and rest, and I'll run over and pick it up myself. No big deal. Just tell me what size you are."

He looked bemused. "You don't mind?" he asked.

"Not at all," I said. At that point, I would have *made* him a shirt.

"Okay," he answered. "A sixteen-inch neck and thirty-three-inch sleeves."

"Fine, I'll drop it off for you. What time's dinner?" One thing I had learned in my day with Mark was that momentum was everything. As long as you had him going, going, going, he was easy as pie. It was when he stopped that the trouble started.

"The nine o'clock seating," he said.

"Then I'll meet you in the lobby about eight forty-five. Okay?"

He seemed tickled that someone was shopping for him and tickled that we had a date. "Okay," he said. "And thanks."

I sank into the backseat of a cab and headed to Hecht's. I was completely exhausted, but all in all, I was damned lucky and I knew it. Mark didn't have to stay, and he didn't have to be so nice about it either. I would buy him the best shirt in the store.

I liked being in a men's department again, I realized, noting the handsome marble columns. Men's clothes were so simple, somehow. I saw the right pile and headed toward it. Light blue, light blue, I thought, sifting through a number of picked-over candidates. There was only one, and it had some sort of crest embroidered on it, though low enough on the body so that no one would see it.

I dropped off the shirt at the hotel's front desk and asked to have a bellhop deliver it; I could just see myself knocking on

Mark's door and him answering in his underwear—the perfect ending to the perfect day. I headed to my own room—on a different floor, mercifully—and stuffed my garment bag, still splotched pink and hardened now, into the trash. I'd bought a new one at Hecht's.

I ran the shower for the longest time, letting it beat on the back of my neck. Drying off, I surveyed my clothes. Le Bec-Fin was the fanciest restaurant in town, but I'd been so set on this being business that everything I'd brought seemed too corporate. I had resolutely left in my closet the dress I'd bought with Paul.

Finally I settled on a plain black shift, without its matching jacket, black pumps, and pearl earrings. Simple and elegant, I thought, looking in the mirror. Nothing beat diarrhea for a flat stomach.

Promptly at 8:45 I was in the lobby, where Mark was waiting, wearing his new shirt. He playfully lifted his blazer to show me the insignia. "It fits perfectly," he said.

"Hallelujah. Now, if you drop anything on it tonight, you're on your own."

"Fair enough."

At the restaurant, the captain bowed and scraped and led us into a womb of luxury, all flowers and fabric and crystal chandeliers. The luscious scents from the kitchen mingled with perfume and Scotch, the way my mother's mink coat used to smell when she came home from a party. I sailed through the dining room wearing my half an outfit boldly (it was Philadelphia, after all, who was going to see me?), high on my relief at how the day had turned out.

We were seated at a corner table laden with china and silver. "Champagne?" the maître d' asked, and before I could say no, a flute was placed before me, and it was the first Champagne I had ever tasted that wasn't too sweet. My neck loosened and I leaned back in my chair, feeling expensive.

We ordered a procession of wonderful food: asparagus and

foie gras and scallops and lamb, accompanied by equally fabulous wines, white and red, and all the while, Mark talked and told stories, interesting stories. About a book he had thought of writing and hadn't. About growing up in Chicago, and how he had learned about art from his mother and how his father had never cared for it. His father was a tax lawyer, too, it turned out—not to mention the former employer of his almost-ex-daughter-in-law. I tried to hide my surprise. With all the women hanging around museums sporting sketch pads and plunging necklines, Mark had to go to a law firm to find one?

His parents had divorced when he was five. In his second marriage, Mark's father had three more sons in rapid succession, all of whom eventually became tax lawyers and joined the family business, shunning the oddball art writer. The three half brothers had played football for the same high school where Mark had edited the newspaper. He wasn't particularly good at sports, he said, an admission delivered with such a miserable face that I could well believe he was a disaster at them. It was a vulnerable, un-macho thing to say, and it made me warm to him even more than I already had. What a treat not to sit down to dinner with someone whose idea of conversation was reporting his bench-press weight.

"So this is like a big club, this law firm where everyone works except you," I said. "That sounds complicated."

"And my stepbrothers . . . I mean my half brothers," he said, "all love skiing, too. They went together every vacation they could."

"Did you go with them?" I asked.

He smiled wryly. "Jews don't ski," he said. "My brothers to the contrary."

I almost choked. "You're *Jewish*?" I sputtered. Somehow the possibility had never occurred to me. I figured if I liked him, he couldn't possibly be.

"Well, yes," he answered matter-of-factly.

"But I saw your credit card at Orso and it said Mark Lewis, Jr. Jews don't have juniors."

"Well, Jews in my family do," he said, amused. "They came here from Germany before the Civil War. My family thinks they're just as Episcopalian as their Lake Shore Drive neighbors."

"Very fancy, Lake Shore Drive," I said.

"Everyone has to pay taxes," he said, and winked.

This was fun. I kept asking questions, and he kept answering them. He had gone to Yale, where he started an arts magazine. He had always loved journalism and art, and a professor had convinced him he could combine those interests by writing. I learned that he liked his stepmother fine, and his stepfather, too—when he saw him. Mark's stepdad was the CEO of a big pharmaceutical company that had major plants in Asia. His father, by comparison, was a pillar of the local community who sat on numerous committees and seemed to know by osmosis when any traffic light on Michigan Avenue wasn't working. He split his time between the office and his club across the street. Mark's mother was his favorite, warm and supportive. Besides being a painter, she was a docent at the Art Institute.

Before I knew it, it was time for dessert. Mark ordered a mocha meringue, and even though I wasn't hungry anymore, I asked for the tarte tatin, which was exquisite. As was Mark's meringue, apparently, because after a single bite he closed his eyes in bliss. "Taste this," he said, and it was indeed delicious. He took another bite, and his eyes brimmed with tears, which quickly spilled over.

"What's wrong?" I asked, taken aback.

"It's such a Proustian taste for me," he explained, wiping his face with his napkin. "My grandmother used to get a cake like this for my birthday when I was growing up, and I haven't tasted anything like it in years. I thought it was a taste I would never have again." He snuffled a little into the napkin, then smiled. "Sorry about that," he said. "I guess I didn't realize how close to the surface some of this stuff is."

"Like what?" I asked, and just as I had told him everything about Bucky that had come into my head, so he told me his stories, about feeling ostracized from his father and brothers and wanting only to leave Chicago. By the time he was in eighth grade, his mother had gotten him a part-time job at the Art Institute organizing slides, and in his free moments he had had the run of the place. It felt like home, he said.

He visited his father every weekend and was forced into the touch football games, but no matter how often Mark tried to talk to his dad about art, the discussion invariably turned back to traffic lights.

Now, with his own divorce, Mark said, he was determined not to repeat his family's mistakes, and he was committed to having a better relationship with his son than he had had with either his father or his stepfather. But if his ex-wife really carried through on her threat to move back to Chicago, Mark said, he didn't know what else to do except maybe move back as well, so he could see his son, Benjamin, grow up.

"Do you really think you'll have to do that?" I asked, feeling my chest tighten.

He shrugged. "I hope not."

It was after eleven when we left the restaurant, and we walked back up Walnut Street toward the Rittenhouse. He stayed closer to me than he had during the day, and though we didn't touch, I could feel he wanted to. It was like being fifteen again and back at the movies when the guy was about to put his arm around you, all awkward and eager and worried.

Once we were inside the lobby he turned to me. "Want to get a nightcap?" he asked, trying to sound casual.

"Well, it's pretty late," I hedged. "Why don't you give me a call tomorrow, when you're done with the museums?" Our plan was to split up during the day so that I could finish my information guide.

"Okay," he said as we headed through the lobby. "Are you sure about the nightcap?"

I nodded. As we got into the elevator, I instinctively reached toward the lapels of his jacket as I started to explain *why* I couldn't have a drink with him, and he kissed me. His mouth was soft, and his kiss was small and tentative, the next few less so.

The doors opened, and we somehow moved into the hallway, mid-kiss. I pulled my head back. "I can't do this," I said, but when he kissed me again, I let him. It was just too good. Somehow we had ended up in front of his door, and he fumbled for his key.

"Listen," I said, pulling myself out of his embrace. "I really *want* to do this, but I really *can't*."

"Why?" He put his hands on my hips to propel me forward.

"Because my job this weekend is to make sure that you write this piece."

"Don't worry about the piece," he said. Now he was kissing my neck.

"Easy for you to say. Listen," I said, moving my body away from his while holding on to his forearms. "I was thrilled that you still wanted to have dinner with me after everything that happened today. But even though you're doing this piece for extra money and something of a lark, this is actually the high point of my job. So if I go inside with you now, and if for some reason the piece doesn't work out, I'll spend forever thinking it was somehow my fault. You can understand that, can't you?"

"No," he said.

I started to laugh. "Still a guy under all that artistic stuff, huh?" I said.

He smiled. Sort of.

"After this piece is turned in, I demand a rain check," I said, letting go of his arms. "Okay?"

"We'll see," he said, opening the door.

"Playing hard-to-get, now?"

"Aren't you?"

"Yes, I guess I am." I stepped back. "I really did have a wonderful time," I said softly. "Thank you."

He nodded. "Good night, Sandy," he said, shutting the door gently. I stood there a moment, disappointed. I had loved finding that feeling again, the kiss that disconnects you from the world, where you drop and soar and somehow land in just the right place. I was sorry to let it go.

Once I was back in my room, I kicked off my shoes and let out my breath. I really did like this guy. But nightcaps were out of the question. If Susie Schein even suspected that I was down here kissing the help, she'd kill me. I unzipped my dress and couldn't help but giggle. That was half the fun.

I got up early the next morning and made my rounds to the Reading Terminal Market, which was gigantic, and to the stores on South Street and beyond. I was the picture of efficiency; all I could focus on was being finished by the time Mark was, and seeing him again for dinner. By midafternoon I was finally done, though I'd forgotten to double-check some addresses. I went into a bookstore and found a Philadelphia travel guide and, after I'd copied down the information I needed, leafed through the section about the Old City, where we'd been yesterday. Then I noticed it: "Betsy Ross House." I had studiously ignored the fact that I was in the city containing the Ross family shrine, but now, with time on my hands, I thought I should just go ahead and do it, get it out of my system once and for all.

I read the description: "Upholsterer and seamstress Betsy Ross lived either in this house or in the one that stood in the courtyard next door. Though she was long believed to have designed the American flag, this claim has now been disproved. (Meager—not firm—evidence does indicate that she sewed a flag for the early federal government.) Ross, who lived from 1752 to 1836 and was married three times and widowed twice, is buried in the courtyard."

What? She lived in this house *or* the one next door? She was *believed* to have designed the American flag, but the only evidence shows she sewed *a* flag?

So this was Bucky's illustrious ancestor. A big fat fake. Who says there's nothing to genetics?

I went outside and hailed a cab. "Two thirty-nine Arch Street," I said.

"What's that?" the driver asked.

"The Betsy Ross House," I said impatiently. "Ever hear of it?"

"Yeah, but I've never been there."

"Really? That's rather incredible, isn't it, considering the fact that Philadelphia is not terribly large and is usually overrun with tourists?" He looked at me blankly in the rearview mirror. Why was I haranguing an innocent cabdriver when what I really wanted was to harangue the entire Ross family?

The cab pulled up to a tiny, well-kept house. "Well, this is it," I said loudly. "What do you think?"

He looked out the window. "Never been here," he repeated.

I gave him his fare and got out. A group of children was going in ahead of me, and I paced back and forth outside to keep some distance, until a guard started eyeing me suspiciously. I walked in and found the first sign.

"Welcome Is Thee," it read. Oh, brother. "My name is Betsy Claypoole, but thee may know me as Betsy Ross, the name I had long ago. Times were hard then. We were at war with Great Britain, my husband John had died, and I was but 24 years of age. I sewed curtains for windows and beds, but during the war I had to find other work to make a living."

I didn't even want to know what a bed curtain was. I moved on to a dining room setup.

"This parlor, most of all, brings back memories. In early 1777 it was here I met the gentleman from Congress who came to me to make a flag. The design, I understand, was done by Mr. Hopkins."

Oh, really?

"With these hands I cut and sewed a flag with 13 five-point stars and 13 stripes. On June 14 this became our flag, and on July 4 the warships then in port delivered 13-gun salutes and flew the colors I had made."

I turned toward a curio cabinet in the corner, which held a thick book labeled CLAYPOOLE FAMILY BIBLE. The sign said that it had been presented to the house by Betsy Ross's descendants: Catherine B. Swift and Mrs. T. Jones, of Richmond, Ind., and John Balderston, of Beverly Hills, Ca.

Wait a minute! No John Buckingham Ross, Sr., of Green Hills, N.Y.?

Two of the girls in the children's group pushed past me. "It seems to me," one said, "that the guy who designed the flag should be as famous as the girl who sewed it." Well, it seemed that way to me, too.

A sign outside the window, in the alley, caught my eye. "For many years, even after I passed away, the story of the first flag was kept within my family. In 1870 my grandson Will, thinking to do me honor, saw fit to tell the world how I had made the flag. He added to my tale a touch or two of fancy, and I became a famous figure."

A touch or two of fancy? Her descendants were as counterfeit as their ancestor, a composite woman who sewed a composite flag designed by someone else, living in a composite house typical of the period.

I walked out onto the street, dazed, and lit a cigarette. Fake. It was all fake—the historical figure, the lineage, the promises, the illusion, the hope. What wasn't fake? The sex and the ice cream.

What do I care?, I asked myself. I wasn't marrying Bucky. I

hadn't seen or spoken to him in almost a year. Why did it still bother me so?

I just hated the lie. Because I had jumped so high and so far to believe it. Because I had labored to satisfy some mythical standard of perfection—me, with my lack of manual dexterity, who could hardly thread a needle. And because I had yearned to belong, to be right, the right people, without even trying. That's what it was about: to wake up in the morning and be where you were supposed to be. No striving. No wishing. *There.*

It was all so pointless. Look at the Rosses. Where were they? The father with his cocktails, the mother with her afghans. Were they in any more of a "right place" than I was? Was their prized son—who wrecked my life, Carla Jones's life, Beth Brewer's life, and now that decorator, Wendy's, life—was he in a "right place"?

It's over, I thought. It doesn't matter. You've learned from it. Learned what? Not to trust men with blue eyes, for one thing.

Well, not so fast. Mark Lewis was different, certainly. I had loved our dinner at Le Bec-Fin and had been thinking all day about where he'd invite me that night. Someplace casual, probably Italian. Get the full range of experience. And perhaps, afterward, I would even reconsider that nightcap.

Back at the Rittenhouse, I looked for my concierge, but he had been replaced by a woman who returned my questioning glance with a blank stare. I went up to my room—it was after five by then—and found a note, written on hotel stationery. It was from Mark—he had slipped it under the door, but when?

Hi, Sandy—

I ran into some friends at the museum and we've decided to meet for dinner tonight. Also, with your indulgence, I'm thinking I'll skip brunch tomorrow and take a morning train.

Let's talk early in the week. Thanks again for the shirt!

Mark

Oh.

I sat on the edge of the bed. It seemed to be time to go home.

#70   *Me Times Three*
by Sandra Berlin

In the palace of a King toiled a young female servant whose father lay dying on his bed. He turned to his only child, and she leaned in close to hear his final words.

"My dear daughter," he said, "I have kept this ring of your mother's since she died giving birth to you. It is an enchanted ring, given to her by a troll who loved her. She wanted you to have it when you grew up, and made me promise I would save the wishes for you. The ring entitles you to three, and all you need do is put it on your finger when you make your wish and it will instantly come true.

"But remember," the old man continued, "you must not treat this gift lightly, for once your three wishes are up, you will never get any more."

"Oh, but Father," the young woman cried, "during all these years, we could have used these wishes so many times! We could have wished to be free of servitude, we could have wished your illness to be cured, we could have wished that a prince would marry me and take care of us both forever."

The old man smiled. "No, my dear," he said. "You must not use wishes merely to get what you want in your life. You must save them for emergencies, and by your own toil you shall earn the things that make a happy life." Then he died.

The young woman took the ring from her father's palm and slipped it into her apron pocket. She thought of all the wishes she would like to make: to never have to work another day, to never have to date another servant with dirty fingernails, for the Prince to fall madly in love with her so she would be protected forever.

But she remembered her father's words and kept the ring inside her pocket. When she grew very sick herself, she did not wish to be well. When the Prince walked close by her side one day, she did not wish him smitten. She waited.

In fact, she waited so long that years passed. Still she worked in the King's palace, and still she pined for the Prince. Wishes filled her head, but she was so afraid to waste them that she started to be afraid even to *think* of them.

Finally, one day, an affirmative-action notice for palace employees was posted, and the female servants were advised that they could meet personally with the Prince to see if they qualified to be his Princess. It was a very rare offer, indeed, and the servants primped for weeks.

Well, the young woman knew that this was her chance to use her first wish. Still, she appeared for her meeting in a highly agitated condition; she had spent so long silently wishing that she had long ago stopped speaking. She was no longer used to social interaction. She walked toward the Prince and curtsied low. "Your Highness," she murmured.

"Please rise, my lady," he said gallantly, and she did, though when she looked up into his handsome face, she panicked. She grasped one of her hands in the other, feeling for her enchanted ring, but when she found it, she could not bring herself to use the wish, so used was she to hoarding them.

"You goose, you must wish now!" she told herself, but her eyes only widened, and her smile stuck upon her face, and when the Prince spoke kindly to her, she could only nod and bow her head again. Then she turned and left the room. Once the door had closed behind her, she fell to the stone floor, exhausted by the strain.

"Oh, how I wish to become wise," she said without thinking. "I wish I was worthy of becoming a Princess. But most of all, I wish I *never* had any wishes."

After she spoke, she looked down at her hand with horror. Any time that she had said a wish out loud before, the ring had stayed inside her pocket. But there it was, right on her finger. Her foolishness made her weep.

But wait, she thought. I wished to be wise. I wished to be worthy of becoming a Princess. Those were good wishes. But then she realized that because of her last wish, she could never know if either of her first wishes had come true.

The End

13

Four weeks later, it was Sally who picked me up at the airport. I had lied to Susie Schein that Friday morning, just before I left for the airport, claiming stomach flu. Since my last visit, Paul had been hospitalized and lost more weight. A big problem, Sally said, was a lesion on the roof of his mouth, which made eating painful. I wanted to say that he was probably glad to have a lesion where no one could see it, but this was not the kind of comment Sally would appreciate.

She looked remarkably well, I thought. Tired, certainly, but her eyes were luminous. She was going to Mass every day and she was praying with Paul at home. Prayer seemed to have given her peace—one that I envied, actually. A lifetime spent corralled behind screens in the women's section of the synagogue while the men ran the service had never provided quite the same glow.

My mother knew how much Paul loved her potato pancakes and had made a ton of them. Like most people at that time, including me, she didn't understand much about AIDS, but as a mother she understood the concept of a child starving to death, which is essentially what he was doing. She bought a pound of smoked salmon, which he also loved, and packed everything in a cooler for me to take to Los Angeles, where she was convinced they had no food at all.

I explained this to Sally as I stowed the cooler into the back-seat of the car. "It will be wonderful if he can eat that," she said, smiling generously. "We've been trying to keep him drinking this milk shake the doctor told us to make, and he's been doing well with it, but only in very, very small amounts."

I looked at her. "How small?"

"A shot glass full," she said.

"You're kidding, right?"

"No." She kept driving. "Sandy, I want to try to prepare you for what's been happening," she said. "Paul has deteriorated very quickly. Since you were here last, he's lost more than twenty pounds."

"I figured as much," I said. "But he can still eat and gain it back."

"Also, he's been, well, a little more difficult."

"Meaning what?" I asked. Most of the times I had called during the past weeks, he had been either in the hospital or sleeping; we hadn't spoken much. He had called me once, at about two a.m. New York time, convinced that I had stood him up for drinks at the Mondrian Hotel and furious because he said there was something important we needed to discuss. He was so insistent and I was so asleep, I thought for a moment that he might be right. I even thought I was in L.A. and confused by the time change, which is why I'd missed the drink. But then I heard Sally in the background asking who was on the phone. "There, do you see what I mean?" he whispered urgently. "They're all against me." He hung up without saying goodbye.

"A certain amount of dementia has set in," Sally said, her eyes still on the road. "And he's taken to spending lots of money."

"How? On what? He seems to have been barely conscious anytime I've called."

"When I've gone out, to church or to the grocery, he's gotten on the phone and ordered things with his credit card. Last week, he sent himself five hundred dollars' worth of flowers."

"He did?" Fucking Romano. Maybe he thought he was Judy Garland.

Her voice remained calm. "Then, because he knows he needs to eat more, he called a local bookstore and had three hundred dollars' worth of cookbooks sent over. Anyway, you'll see how the situation has changed. It was a very big deal for him to get out of bed and get dressed tonight, but he insisted on it because you're coming. He can't go to his AA meetings anymore, so his group comes to the house instead."

I didn't know how to respond. The gravity of what she was saying didn't fit the congenial tone with which she was saying it.

"Sally, are you getting enough help?" I asked.

"I am."

"Does that mean you're seeing a shrink, I hope?"

She nodded again. "How about you?" she asked.

"Well, I've been thinking about it. I certainly could use one. The closest I've come is going to one of those support groups, for caregivers."

She looked at me questioningly and I felt myself blush. "I mean, I know I haven't been *the* caregiver—or any sort of caregiver, I guess, because I'm so far away—but I wanted to try to understand more about what was going on with him, or at least with people who are in his situation. And yours."

"How was it?" She seemed curious.

"All right, I guess. I'm not sure it was terribly scientific. There was a lot of crying, but not a lot of information. The woman who leads these sessions, Bebe Stewart, is a concerned socialite trying to do the right thing, and she means well. If nothing else, I think everyone likes the idea that a rich person keeps hanging around this crummy building in Chelsea, listening to their problems."

Sally smiled. "I've read about her. But you shouldn't be so hard on yourself, Sandy," she said. "You're doing the very best you can, being so far away." She seemed to want to say more, but she kept driving silently.

"What, Sally? What is it?" I finally asked. These people with manners just wore me out.

She took a breath. "Well, I've been wondering if you've gotten tested," she said, eyes focused on the road.

"For AIDS, you mean?"

She nodded, saying nothing.

"Why would you even ask me that?"

"Well, you know why." Her cheeks flushed. "Because of your relationship with Paul."

We were stopped at a red light, in front of a strip mall. "Sally, why don't you pull in here so I can get some cigarettes," I said, and she obligingly turned into the lot. When I got back into the car, I opened a window in deference to her pained expression and lit one. She turned the key in the ignition.

"No, wait," I said. She faced me, pale and grave, as if she were holding her breath. "Sally, we have to talk about this. I want you to understand something: I have never slept with Paul. Ever."

She stared at me with a mixture of confusion and suspicion.

"Did Paul tell you we had?" I asked.

"Well, yes," she managed.

I gasped. I could just imagine him doing it, too, giving her his innocent look, inventing me as competition. Anything but the truth.

"Sally, do you know that up until last year I'd had the same boyfriend since high school?"

She pulled a tissue from her purse. She was just too young a woman to be so quick on the draw with a tissue, I thought.

"I did know about that," she said, "but I thought it was the same kind of situation that Paul was in with me. That you two had known each other forever, but then you went away to school and met Paul and realized how you both were really soul mates, so you weren't sure if you were going back to your boyfriend, just like Paul wasn't sure he would come back to me." The hand holding the tissue trembled.

"Sally, I met Paul on the first day of school and we have been close friends ever since, but we have *never* been romantically involved."

The tears slid down her face. At last, so much of this baffling situation made sense to me. Her formality, her excessively polite approach to every little thing. She thought I was the other woman. She believed that if Paul didn't marry her, it would be because of me. That was mean. And even though Paul was not a mean person, he had kept her hanging all this time, convinced her to put me up in her home, serve me coffee as if she were my maid, and all the while she was fearing I might steal the love of her life. I felt a twinge. No, Sandra, not mean. Weak. Like Bucky.

"He told Marie the same thing—about you, I mean," Sally was saying, fumbling for another tissue.

"*What?*" I yelled. A little boy walking through the parking lot with a Good Humor in his hand looked at me, eyes wide. He reached for his mother's skirt. "Fucking Romano," I said wearily after the boy was out of sight.

Sally looked startled a moment, then smiled. "I think you're telling the truth," she offered shyly.

"Sally, listen," I said, turning to face her. "I don't really know you, and I've never met Marie. But I am telling you this: The only thing I know about Paul's family, apart from the fact that they are exceedingly wealthy, is that Marie is in love with you, and Paul grew up knowing that if he married you, he would make his mother the happiest woman in the world."

Sally sighed, running her thumb around the rim of the steering wheel. She seemed to think for a moment, hard. Then she put the car into reverse, and pulled out into the traffic.

A few stoplights later, I realized we were headed back in the direction of the airport. "Where are we going?" I asked.

"I want to show you something," she said. "It won't take long."

We drove for a while, and Sally made a number of turns until we were on a residential street lined with tiny houses, kids playing on the front lawns. I had the uneasy feeling that she had decided not to believe me about Paul and was now going to slit my throat and bury me in her housekeeper's backyard.

A few blocks later, she pulled up to a house on the corner and stopped the car. The house was neat and trim, part brick, part clapboard, with an aluminum screen door and a postage-stamp-size lawn. WELCOME, the mailbox read.

"Okay, I give up," I said impatiently. "Who lives here?"

"Paul," she said, studying my face. "Or at least he did growing up. But his parents still live here."

She could have shot me and it would have had the same effect. I stared at her, then back at the house, as if it might be different this time.

"Sandy, Paul's parents are not wealthy and they never have been. Mr. Romano is a foreman in a processed-food factory."

That couldn't be right. I lit another cigarette, trying to absorb it all. "His father made a fortune importing Genoa salami. Paul told me—"

She shook her head. "No. The factory where he works manufactures salami, among other things." She sighed. "The truth is that a lot of Paul's money came from Dennis."

I blinked, trying to catch up. Dennis, the soul mate, the one who'd run back to Australia after Paul betrayed him.

"Paul met Dennis his first year in college, and Dennis just took over his life, paid for everything," Sally went on. "The clothes, the car. He took Paul to Europe and bought him that gold Rolex. That's why you wouldn't necessarily have known that he didn't come from money."

"Wait," I said, but she interrupted me.

"Yes, I knew about Dennis, and I've already told you I knew about the rest of it, or as much as I wanted to know," she said. "I love Paul. I have loved him ever since I met him at a church dance when we were fifteen, and I knew I would never be with anybody else."

"But—"

"It never mattered," she said so unwaveringly that the words in my mouth died out. "Actually, Dennis called last week," she continued. "After he heard that Paul was sick."

"Is Dennis?"

"I don't know. Anyway, that happened to be a good day for Paul, so they were able to really talk. It was helpful for both of them."

I felt a flush of shame at how steadfastly I clung to my rules about life. No matter how many I amassed, no matter how crisply I organized them—love, real love, contagious and messy, vanquished them all.

I looked over at the Romanos' front stoop, on which there sat a wooden bucket of blooming red geraniums. "You know," I said slowly, "in some odd way, this doesn't change a thing for me. I can believe that Paul started here, learned to love the theater here. He wrote his drama-school admission essay on that moment in the dark before the show starts, when you anticipate magic and it comes on schedule, like fireworks or birthday candles. It's also why clothes and all that *stuff* always mattered to him. Costumes. His daily transformation. But he's always still Paul. Ready to find the next thing." I reached for one of her tissues. "At least that's how I see it. I'm not sure I'd be feeling quite so expansive if I were you right about now, I must say."

I mean, really. Paul, it turned out, was as much a liar as Bucky. Only his lies couldn't hurt Sally the way Bucky's hurt me, because Sally knew what she was dealing with. Unlike me, when Paul had named me Three Wishes, Sally *had* opened her eyes and seen what was in front of her—and she had chosen to love him anyway. My eyes had been perennially closed. Until Carla Jones came upon me with a crowbar.

But Paul had also lied to me, I realized, sitting there, blowing smoke toward the front lawn, expecting to see a face appear from behind the drawn curtains. I felt thrown now but, truth be told, not all that much. I *knew* who Paul was, pedigree aside. This scenario actually made perfect sense to me. I remembered our trip to Buccellati. Would a rich person ever have done that?

"It's just hopes and dreams, that's all, about who Paul wants to be," Sally said firmly. She ran a hand through her hair, and I could see that the terrible tension she had been carrying was gone. "He does love you, Sandy," she said. "That part is true. I know, because I feel it from him. Without a doubt."

"It's mutual," I said. "I just can't believe I've known him for so long and he didn't tell me. That he wouldn't trust me to accept him for who he is."

She smiled gently. "That's not who he *wanted* to be," she said. "Paul always had an idea of how his life should go, and if something didn't fit, he just pretended it was gone. That's all."

And he had the nerve to call *me* Three Wishes. He was the original Cinderella, pushing his luck to the last stroke of midnight, and even though he had the sense to flee before whichever Prince saw the truth, he just refused to see it, even back home with the mice and the pumpkins. I remembered how he danced at the opening-night parties at Yale, flinging me around the floor as if he were trying to win a race, pushing and pulling and willing the music to last. When it stopped, he simply picked up and went elsewhere. There was never a morning after with Paul; it was always the morning before.

I watched Sally fiddle with her key ring, her eyes downcast. I realized then that, truth aside, it had been to Sally's advantage to keep Marie believing I was competition. The story would be better that way. When Marie's friends from church discovered that her son was dying from AIDS, he could be the victim of intra-venous drugs, nothing else, with an extra girlfriend from back east to prove it.

The closeness I had felt to Sally, seeing Paul's house with her, was tempered now. So much was happening between us that it far surpassed "I like you, you like me." We were not friends, Sally and I. The only thing we had in common was Paul. And it seemed that all either one of us could look forward to now was more of these conversations—either stilted and painful, or all in a rush—in which I would wish I could be talking to him, instead, and so would she.

She started the car. "He's waiting, we'd better go," Sally said, her calm, official tone reinstated. "Also," she added, "just so you're aware, it's my birthday soon, and I heard Paul on the phone with a friend of ours who has a van, and he wants to surprise me by going shopping and getting me a gift. He wants to do it tomor-row, while you're here."

"Sure," I said.

"I won't let on that I know what you're doing when you leave. But, Sandy"—she looked over at me—"the reason for the van is that you're going to have to take him in a wheelchair."

I crossed my arms over my chest and looked out the window. Paul's illness was the first time in my life I had faced a situation where being smart didn't help, being responsible didn't help, even being nice didn't help. There was nothing I could do to stop it or to fix it. What about all those books about people who have incredible wills to live? People who surmount any obstacle and survive just to stay with the ones they love? Maybe Paul wasn't try-ing hard enough.

I dropped that notion the minute I entered the apartment. Even after Sally's careful preparation, I was completely taken aback. Paul was sitting up on the couch, dressed in a white pressed shirt and black pants. He was skeletal, and his skin had turned a mottled grayish-green. But it was the force of his anger that stunned me. He had seen all the same movies I had but discovered that his will to live meant nothing. Rage shot from his eyes, smacking me from across the room. All that seemed left of his face was his suddenly gigantic yellow teeth, which his lips barely covered. He seethed now like a grotesque monster in a fairy tale. The spell that had been cast on him could never be reversed.

Anything I had planned to say evaporated. For once, my mouth failed me. "Hey," I tried cheerily, and he glared, silent. He kept his eyes on me as Sally eased him into a reclining position. "That was so good that you were able to sit up for Sandy," she said, as if he were a two-year-old. "Wasn't that good, Sandy?"

I didn't answer, but went instead to the coffee table next to the couch and sat on it, close to him, near his head. "Hey," I said again, softly, and this time he cried, throwing his arm over his face for protection. But there was no violence or fury in his sobs, no throbbing or shaking. They were silent. He had been defeated.

I started telling him all about the potato pancakes and the smoked salmon, and my new awful roommate with the white face and white hair, and how Susie Schein was as terrible as always, and anything else that came into my head, while Sally sat in an easy chair across the room. There were piles of books all over, all about coping with illness or pain, about how to say goodbye. Most had bookmarks in them. Sally saw me scanning them. "We read aloud sometimes," she explained. "It helps."

Finally, Paul lowered his arm and looked into my eyes. "I have to go to bed," he said, and I got out of the way while Sally helped him stand. The walk to the bedroom took longer than it had last time, and I followed behind, watching how his feet barely left the ground, how he hung on to her.

The bedroom was a shambles; countless medicine bottles overflowing the night tables or lying on the light blue carpet, which was dotted with shit stains. Once he was perched on the edge of the bed, Paul motioned Sally away. "I *must* go shopping tomorrow," he whispered to me, taking tenuous hold of my wrist with two fingertips, as if I were the one who was sick and he didn't want to get too close. But he was adamant that I understand the importance of his mission. "It's going to be Sally's birthday. And I might not be here."

"I understand," I assured him. "I'll come with you."

And just as it seemed he would lose his balance, Sally reappeared and moved him back against a pile of pillows, then scooped up his legs and brought them around. When his feet touched the covers, he winced and cursed, and she apologized, again and again.

I walked out into the hallway as she began to undress him. "I'm going to bed, I'll see you tomorrow," I called out, heading for the guest room.

"Don't you want dinner?" Sally called after me. No, I insisted, I was just too tired. I needed to be alone now, to think about everything she had told me, and what it meant. I closed the door behind me and reached into my bag for the two squashed tuna fish sandwiches I had taken from my mother's care package. I much preferred this solitary meal to the awkward marathon of small talk that would inevitably follow the greater revelations of the day.

And there had been so many. I sat on the pink carpet, leaning my head back against the flowered bedspread. First off, Paul had lied to me. So why wasn't I angry? From the beginning, he and I had intuited the nasty little secret we shared: We both wanted to belong—and didn't. So why shouldn't he lie? I lied to him every time I lied to myself, about my perfect life shimmering on the Green Hills horizon.

His anger now stunned me, though. The depth of it. I had always thought that when people were dying they tended toward the reflective, the philosophical. But that was usually in the movies, I supposed now, someone propped up against the pillows, looking pale yet radiant.

I rubbed the knots in my neck. I wished the caregiver support group had been more helpful. I had gone twice, the honorable Bebe Stewart presiding. She was certainly an unlikely sight, standing in a room full of metal chairs and dirty linoleum. She was tall and thin, and teased clouds of gray hair framed her milk-white face, flawless even in fluorescent light. She wore a baby-lotion-pink Chanel suit with matching slingbacks, and a load of Bulgari jewelry sat, perfectly balanced, around her neckline. If this woman didn't have the answers to life, no one did.

"For any newcomers," she had said in a voice that was unexpectedly kind, "this is a group that gathers twice a week and is meant to give support to all of us who are living with people who are living with AIDS or HIV. We spend so much of our time ministering to the needs of others that we sometimes forget that our own batteries need to be recharged, too. We have to take good care of ourselves, remember, or else the person who is relying on us will be let down."

An older woman raised her hand. "My son has AIDS," she said. "And I can't get him to eat. I can't get him to take his medicine. I can't even get him to see the doctor. He doesn't listen to me. And he's shopping all the time. He's having trouble sleeping, so he's spent every day for a week at Macy's, looking at mattresses. I'm telling you, Mrs. Stewart, there's nothing wrong with the mattress he has. And we can't afford a new one." She started to cry. "I just don't know what to do."

I thought now of Paul sending himself flowers. Five hundred dollars' worth.

Bebe Stewart had an answer. "One of the things that's so hard for us to understand when we're living with this disease every day is the idea of denial," she said. "It may seem incredible to you that your son won't take his medicine or see his doctor, but to him, it's perfectly logical. If you put yourself in his place, you can see how scared he is, how powerless he feels. Denial sometimes is nothing more for an ill person than a vacation. It's a way of saying, 'No, I'm not sick. This is not happening to me.'"

More people spoke, people for whom life was dreadful, filled with the sordid sights and rotten smells I knew Sally had to endure each day. By the end of the second session, I felt ashamed for even thinking that I needed support. For what? Existential despair? I didn't belong there with those people pushed to strength's end. My suffering was borne at a clean distance, at the end of a phone line, within the confines of a long weekend. I felt ashamed that I had come at all.

I felt ashamed now, because even though I was *here*, sitting on the rug right down the hall from the friend I loved, there was nothing I could do that would ease his pain, increase his appetite, reduce his despair. I had no experience of living without hope. It had always seemed to me that if you worked harder and behaved better, there was a chance you could turn things around.

It was dark out now. The low sounds of a television traveled down the hall. I climbed underneath the flowered bedspread and fell asleep.

The following morning, Paul lay on the couch and I sat in front of him with a plate of potato pancakes. He inhaled deeply, a look of pure pleasure on his face. He took a bite and seemed in ecstasy. My spirits soared. "I knew these would make you happy," I exulted, and he nodded, but his chewing slowed and he held the food in his mouth awhile until, finally, he turned his head and spit it out.

"Too hard to chew?" I asked.

"Yeah."

"Let me see."

He looked surprised. "I want to see what it looks like," I said. "Sally told me you had a lesion on the roof of your mouth, and I knew no matter how bad it was, you were thrilled it wasn't on your face." He smiled and leaned his head back, opening his mouth as if he were at the dentist. The lesion looked like a huge scab. Then he reached down and tugged at his pant leg: Silently, he lifted it and showed me another sore, on his shin.

"Potato pancakes for breakfast?" Sally's cheery voice bounced off the kitchen tiles as she came in with the papers and fresh orange juice.

"Yes, they're great, have some," I called. She and I ate a few, and then she got up to make Paul's milk shake.

"I'll do it," I said, following her. "Just show me how."

I put everything in the blender—sneaking in more nutrition powder than Sally had measured—and poured some of the mixture into a shot glass. Paul drank it in small sips until it was finished.

"Great!" I enthused. "How about another?"

He looked up at me, spent, with a pleading expression, but he didn't speak.

"Maybe later," I said, feeling ashamed. There must be no greater affront to a sick, weak person than a healthy person's pushy vitality.

Paul and Sally's friend Phil arrived, as scheduled, and there were loud explanations of going out for a drive as Sally busied herself cleaning up the kitchen. "See you all later," she called.

Once the three of us were in Phil's van, Paul seemed infused with energy. "This is a total surprise, and no one is allowed to tell her," he ordered.

Phil nodded. He was a slight, blond guy, who Sally had said was part of Paul's AA group. "Where to?" he asked Paul.

"Saks," Paul said authoritatively.

"What are you thinking of buying?" I asked.

"Antique jewelry," Paul said.

"They have that at Saks?"

He nodded. "A great selection."

When we arrived at the Beverly Hills store, Phil got out of the van, set up the wheelchair, and moved Paul into it seemingly without effort, covering his lap with a blanket. "It's air-conditioned pretty good in there, buddy," he explained.

Paul nodded and said, "I think only Sandra should come in with me. We won't be long."

Phil looked surprised, but he agreed. "I'll be here," he said, climbing back into the van.

I wheeled Paul toward the entrance. "What was that about?" I asked.

"He's in my AA group, and I don't want him to know how much money I have. He works for a housepainter."

"Okay." I concentrated on maneuvering the chair, stopping once to fix Paul's blanket, which had slipped. I looked at him, sitting up, expectant, the old shopping gleam in his eye. He caught me looking, and we grinned. I pushed him forward and stopped in the doorway, framed between the shimmering California heat and the blast of refrigerated air. And in that instant I realized— too late—that this was his prized theater moment in reverse; the anticipation of magic had gone perilously wrong somehow, the lights had come up on disaster. Every person in the store stopped, a tableau set against gleaming marble and shining glass cases. Each turned to stare at the shrunken green man in the wheelchair at what seemed exactly the same moment. I couldn't see Paul's face then, only the golden faces before us, shining with lipstick and glossy hair. In that split second it was as if a secret alarm had gone off, and now the only thing anyone could do was agilely shift their aerobicized bodies clear of the disease rolling willfully into their midst.

Almost as quickly as it had stopped, the chatter began again. I pushed the chair forward, and every head turned away, and we were alone, cast adrift among the Gucci bags.

"Do you know where the jewelry is?" I asked Paul, but he shook his head. And when I asked a saleswoman, she answered without looking at either me or at Paul. I followed the woman's directions, wheeling Paul to a counter that said ESTATE JEWELRY, and we looked through the glass together. "See anything you like?" I asked, but he was indecisive. He wanted to see the pieces up close. But the counter was deserted, and I couldn't find anyone to help us. Paul knew exactly what was going on. A few months ago, these same people would have taken one look at his handsome, chiseled face and fought one another for the chance to help him.

I left him there, and finally, three counters away, in costume jewelry, I noticed a saleswoman, her back turned to me, who was busily opening and closing drawers.

"Excuse me," I said, walking up to her. "Excuse me," I repeated loudly, in my most forbidding New York tone of terror.

"Oh, yes?" Her voice cracked as she turned, showing me a forced smile.

"I need some help with the estate jewelry."

"I'm afraid that's not my department," she said, walking out from behind the counter in an attempt to flee.

"Can you make it your department?" I asked curtly.

"Well, now, it's not that easy. I don't have the key," she answered.

"Who has it?"

"The woman who's on break." She was literally walking backward.

"Okay, fine," I said, smiling a dangerous smile. "Here's what's going to happen now. You may not realize it, but you see my friend there, in the chair? Well, did you know that he's a Calvin Klein model? Yes, you recognize him now, I can tell you do. So either you find the woman on break and get the key, or he is going to get up and model a rackful of clothing for your clientele."

Her eyes were wide with horror, and I felt a strange rush of elation. I had finally found something I could do, even if it was only terrorizing this idiot saleswoman whose love handles were ruining the line of her knit Adolfo suit. Bebe Stewart would be thoroughly appalled — on all counts.

"Now," I said loudly. She stood, motionless.

I lowered my voice. "He has the same right to be in this store as any other customer. And unless you want to be named in a major discrimination suit" — I glared at her name tag — "*Sherrie*, I suggest you find the key."

That did it. She began walking backward again, as if I might mow her down with a rifle if she turned her back. She had covered a few feet when, with astonishing peripheral vision, she spotted another saleswoman. "Grace! Grace!" she implored, and the woman came over. Before they had a moment for any private conference, I walked forward.

"Thank you, Grace," I said. "I hear you have the key for estate jewelry." She smiled and said yes though Sherrie was making hideous faces, warning her not to get involved.

But Grace didn't notice until it was too late. To her credit, though, she unlocked the case and, in her most professional manner, asked what the gentleman was interested in seeing. Paul picked out a few pieces, which she placed on a velvet tray for closer inspection, but she never once looked at him and, though she continued to question the gentleman, directed all of her conversation to me.

"Paul, do you like any of these?" I asked, but he shook his head, frustrated. "It's no good," he said too loudly, as if he were someone's deaf grandfather. He was right. It was second-rate, gaudy stuff.

"We'll try somewhere else," I said.

Grace put the jewelry back in the case, and I turned toward her. "Thank you for your help," I said. She smiled feebly toward

my elbow, apparently exhausted by the terrible effort of not looking at Paul, and I got behind his chair and wheeled him back to
the parking lot. He was crestfallen.

"What am I going to do now?" he asked repeatedly. Phil
swung around with the van as soon as he saw us and got Paul back
inside. With great effort, Paul recalled a marketplace—something like a bazaar—where he'd once seen something beautiful, and with Phil's help we found it. All three of us went in this
time, Paul's financial security concerns apparently forgotten. We
stopped at the first counter we saw, and the salesman could not
have been nicer. He removed every tray from the case, and Paul
immediately sensed the change in atmosphere and enjoyed himself now, very lord of the manor, holding up pieces of crystal and
marcasite and inquiring after prices.

"Phil, I think we should take a look around while Paul shops,"
I suggested, and Paul shot me a grateful glance. By the time we
returned from a leisurely tour of the stalls, his purchase was
wrapped in pink tissue paper, though the clerk was nice enough
to undo it and show us an exquisite scrolled necklace that looked
like an heirloom from the heroine of a Victorian novel. Under-
stated, yet intricate. Beautiful.

"You have the greatest taste," I said as, flushed with victory,
Paul got back into the van. After we drove a few blocks, I thought
I recognized the neighborhood and asked, "Are we near Nate 'n
Al?"—the one good delicatessen in Los Angeles. "Maybe we can
get some chicken soup."

But Paul's mood had abruptly changed. "We have to go
home," he said dourly. Neither Phil nor I asked why, just rolled
down the windows.

When we reached the apartment, Sally disappeared into the
shower with Paul, and though Phil stayed awhile, we didn't have
much to say to each other. Before he left, he helped Sally bring
Paul out to sit on the couch, newly bathed and changed. Sally
had a jar of Nivea cream with her.

"Paul's feet hurt, and sometimes massage helps," she said to me. "Do you want to do it while I make some lunch?"

"Sure," I said, looking at his swollen feet. "Just tell me where it hurts so I don't go there."

"It hurts everywhere," he said. "Don't press hard."

I started slowly and, after he made a face or two, adjusted the pressure to a version of what we used to do in camp: "Tickle My Back." One girl would lie on her bed, facedown, and someone else would make feathery circles along her skin, and then they would switch. I was relieved to see Paul actually smile at my efforts and relax back onto the pillows. Even his color seemed better now.

At lunch he drank two shot glasses of his milk shake and ate a piece of smoked salmon, which Sally cut into tiny pieces so he was able to slide them past the roof of his mouth with minimal pain. He seemed elated, and so was I.

I was so eager to grab any moment in which I could see my friend, still in there, however diminished, that I declared, "I'm cooking dinner tonight." They both looked at me. "I'll make chicken breasts and pasta for Sally and me, and for Paul, I'll do what my mom did when I had my tonsils out, and put the chicken in the blender with some applesauce. It's incredibly good."

He agreed, and Sally looked relieved to relinquish a chore, though she insisted on doing the shopping, saying she'd been cooped up inside all day. After she left, I sat at the end of the couch and offered to do Paul's feet again, but he said no. I could see that there was something on his mind, but after living with Sally, he seemed to have learned her reticence for initiating a difficult conversation.

Maybe she had told him about bringing me to his house and telling me the truth, and he wanted to explain. He would know how I'd take being lied to.

"Sandy, there's something I have to tell you," he said at last.

"Okay," I said.

"Remember that weekend when we were in Palm Springs?"

I nodded.

"And we were looking at Bob Hope's house with the ceiling that slid open so that his family could sit in their living room and look at the stars?"

"Yes, I remember," I said.

He took a breath. "That wasn't his house."

"It wasn't?"

"No. I mean, I knew Bob Hope lived in Palm Springs, and I had heard something about a sliding roof, but I honestly didn't know if that was his house or not."

He looked scared. I squeezed his hand as gently as I could. "That's okay, Paul," I said. "We both wanted it to be his house, and we wanted his roof to slide open. So it did."

"Yes." He smiled sweetly, gratefully, then turned his head and fell fast asleep.

And that was enough.

I got back to New York on Sunday night and was relieved to find that my roommate was not in residence. I went through the mail and checked my phone messages. Incredibly, Susie Schein hadn't called. But Mark had.

He had handed in his piece earlier in the week and—big surprise—it was great. I had made very few suggestions, the main one being that he needed to draw more of an emotional connection between his activities today and how he remembered them from his childhood, and he took the criticism remarkably well. I also shook up the order of events so that it wasn't completely chronological, and suggested he add a joke or two in the midst of the arty stuff (completely selfish, I assured him, so I didn't fall asleep). He returned it promptly and called to thank me. I thought the piece the best we'd ever recieved, and I had passed it along to Susie without a second thought. Mistake.

"Um, hi, Sandy, it's Mark," the voice on the machine said haltingly. "I have to admit I was surprised when Victoria got a call from Susie Schein saying she had problems with the piece, especially after you and I edited it and everything seemed okay. I wanted to touch base with you first, because Victoria is thinking of yanking it and taking it elsewhere, since the changes Susie wants don't make any sense. But I felt badly, since you gave me so much help, and I wanted you to know what was going on. Sorry to leave this for you at home, but I was told you were out sick, so maybe if you feel better by Monday you can give me a call and tell me what's happening. Thanks."

I would seem to be the last one who knew what was happening, I thought, dumping the contents of my bag into the hamper. How dare Susie do this behind my back and then expect me to fix it? I sighed. Well, what else was new?

I wasn't actually surprised that Mark had called again; he'd called plenty since Philadelphia. Neither of us had mentioned how the weekend had ended, but he seemed to be having second thoughts about it.

As had I. A veritable epiphany, in fact, once I'd managed to get up off that hotel room bed: No more men.

They simply were not worth the trouble. There wasn't one alive who merited the time and energy he demanded—even one who knew everything about art and seemed to know everything about kissing—so I was going to get on with my life solo. And if I made it to forty and felt I absolutely had to have a child, I would adopt a perfectly behaved Asian orphan who would grow up to be Midori. I would travel the world listening to her play, applauding her genius, and eating everything in sight. I would be enormously fat and wear silk muumuus. Bliss.

But wouldn't you know it? They had radar, all men did, and

no sooner had I made this decision than Mark started calling me in earnest. He had a question about the piece, or he wanted to check a fact with me (one he could have easily checked elsewhere). I wondered about his sudden exit, but until the piece had gotten by Susie, I couldn't ask. So I was polite and professional, and one night, when he wanted to know if I felt like grabbing dinner, I thanked him but said I was deluged with copy.

On the other hand, Sandra, I reasoned now, what *is* the shelf life of this big epiphany? It had been great for the train ride home from Philadelphia, but enough already. All along, you kept saying that when the work was done you'd see him. So what are you going to do now? Punish him for taking you at your word and finishing the piece without you? The Midori track was fine in theory, but did I really want to become one of those self-sabotaging women who live in New York, who get chance after chance to find happiness and then, if the chance isn't six feet tall or didn't pull up in a Rolls, dismiss it? You're just too young to turn into such a pathetic type, I decided. You wanted to have dinner with Mark? Well, you're in luck. He wants to have dinner with you, too. I would call him tomorrow.

When the phone rang a few minutes later, I jumped. I was certain it was Susie Schein, tracking me down to dump the Mark problem back into my lap so I could placate the understandably irate Victoria Segal. But I was the one who was irate: The fact that Susie had gone ahead and called Mark's agent without even waiting to discuss the piece with me remained unacceptable.

The hell with her, I decided after the third ring. It was still Sunday; tomorrow was soon enough for this nonsense. I let the machine pick up, increasing the volume so I could hear the onslaught.

"Hey."

I stiffened. It was Bucky.

"Sandy, are you there? Sanny?"

It felt as if he was in the room with me. I stepped away from the machine.

"Sandra, listen, I have to see you," he said, his voice low, urgent. "I know you haven't heard from me, but I want you to know that I have not stopped loving you for one minute. I miss you so, Sanny, I can't believe how much. Call me as soon as you get this."

He hung up.

14

I most certainly did not call Bucky. Nor did I sleep that night for more than five minutes at a time, expecting the phone to ring again at any moment—which it did, finally, at 7:15 in the morning.

"Sorry I missed you, Sanny, I'll get you later, at the office." His tone was cheery, casual, as if we had just spoken and he'd forgotten to tell me to pick up some milk.

I left the apartment early and, on the subway to work, reviewed the draft of Mark's piece, trying unsuccessfully to spot problems. His tight, well-written sentences built a narrative that was exactly what had been assigned: revisiting a special place from childhood and reassessing it through grown-up eyes. Susie's change of heart in this instance surpassed her usual capriciousness—it was bile, pure and simple. And for what? I couldn't see how she could execute her customary torture with someone of Mark Lewis's stature, or why she would bother trying. This was a real writer, whose income and résumé did not depend on the whims of *Jolie!*

But when I got to the office, steeled for the big showdown, Susie's door was shut, and much of the staff was gathered in a cluster near the coffee machine. I headed for Pimm, my usual contact in an office crisis.

"Marti Lyons quit," she said, seeming as befuddled as everyone else. That was news. Marti was considered the top beauty writer in women's magazines. It was no small achievement to be able to write six witty paragraphs about eyeliners, making each one sound like a brand-new adventure and a surefire way to change your life. And the manufacturers appreciated her efforts. She was forever being flown to places like St. Barth for weekend junkets, so she could better appreciate the newest shades of blush by the light of an island sunrise. Because she kept so many advertisers happy, Marti was one of the best-paid staff writers at *Jolie!*

As everyone buzzed about the news, Pascal came in. Flummoxed not to find Pimm or Coco in their office to receive him as usual, he peevishly inquired as to what was going on. "Marti Lyons quit," Pimm repeated. Pascal half shrugged and quickly retreated to his desk to call Papa in unanticipated privacy.

"Would Coco know why?" I asked Pimm.

"Coco only knows the frog gossip," she said.

"Where is she, by the way?" I asked.

Pimm leaned in close to whisper. "She went to London for the weekend with a Brit she met at Nell's," she said. "He's in some sort of bank training program, and he was going home for a house party—and a fox hunt, I think. Coco thought that sounded like incredible fun."

I rolled my eyes. "Can she even ride?" I asked.

"Does it matter?" Pimm answered. "Anyway, she's called in sick," Pimm said, "and Susie can't know. She won't be back till tomorrow."

Just then, Buffy Parks appeared, poured herself a cup of coffee, and stowed a container of tuna salad in the fridge. She listened to the twittering and, flipping her hair assertively, announced, "I know why she's leaving," which prompted a wave of noise before everyone fell silent, mouths open, waiting. She preened at the attention.

"Well, all I can say is that over the past few weeks, Marti Lyons has been seen being just a bit too chummy with . . . Norma Wilder!"

Hoots and hollers were followed quickly by shushing. Of course, Susie's love affair with Norma Wilder, the editor with whom she frequented the downtown clubs, was openly speculated about in the office, and every once in a while a blind item in a gossip column appeared that seemed to be about Norma Wilder, mentioning "the other woman" with the dead giveaway of "nondescript." But maybe Norma Wilder had finally figured out that she too was entitled to some color in her life.

And Marti Lyons was color—funny and smart. I knew that she was gay because, unlike Susie, she was open about it. I remember one rainy afternoon when we were supposed to be closing the magazine and were sitting around talking instead. Marti admitted she was lonely and wanted a girlfriend and had decided to join the health club around the corner to get in shape. She looked fine to me, but she was embarrassed, she said, about taking her clothes off in the locker room.

"Don't worry about it," I said. "No one will look at you twice."

"I know," she said morosely, and we both started to laugh. It hadn't occurred to me that the one place I could escape sexual scrutiny would be the opposite for her.

"Anyway," Buffy Parks went on importantly, "I heard that Susie found out about it and told Marti that if she didn't stay away from Norma she would be fired, and Marti said her private life was private and she would quit first. So she did."

"Who saw them where together?" I asked.

Buffy gave me her customary disgusted look. "Pandora's Box, where do you think?" she said, naming a lesbian bar.

"Did *you* see them there?" I asked innocently.

Buffy turned red. "Of course not," she squealed. "I've never been there. What do you think I am, a dyke?"

"Not until it's fashionable," I said.

Everyone laughed, and Buffy turned on her heel and stalked off.

"She's being extra-obnoxious even for Buffy, isn't she?" I asked. One of the assistants nodded. "She's been interviewing at *Glamour* for a big fashion job, and it's between her and another girl," she said. "Miss Belladonna killed both her shoots in last month's issue, and she's furious."

I took my coffee and went back to my office. Turnover was typical at magazines, I knew. Every once in a while there would be a mass exodus, but usually it would be connected to a change at the top—a new editor bringing in her own people. *Jolie!*, though, had taken on an air of desolation. Its novelty had worn off. Enemies had been made, too: designers who felt snubbed, writers who were treated badly. I knew now that if Buffy Parks ever did go to *Glamour* and anyone there wanted to hire me, she would assure them I was awful.

"Sandy, Susie wants to see you," her assistant announced, suddenly at my door. I stood, Mark's copy in hand, ignoring my ringing phone. On my way out, I asked someone else's assistant to pick up my calls. Ever since I'd moved into my own office, I'd been promised help that had never materialized. I would gladly have given up the whole promotion charade and moved back in with Pimm, Coco, and Pascal—just for the company—but Miss Belladonna had hired someone to track down food stories and she had taken my desk. She was an older woman who spent most of her time on the phone cooing to the French pastry chef she was sleeping with—he was featured in the June issue—when she wasn't making appointments for manicures. Pimm and Coco made fun of her airs, while Pascal tuned her out altogether. He seemed increasingly disenchanted with the *Jolie!* financial-aid plan for starving novelists.

The assistant who agreed to give me a hand had worked briefly for Susie—which authorized her as an expert in human misery. "After being out Friday, I'll be swamped today," I told her. "And the truth is, I've got an old boyfriend on my trail at exactly the wrong moment and I need to duck his calls." She smiled and nodded. After Susie, I was a picnic.

Unfortunately, none were in store for me. I entered Susie's office and noticed that her face was even grayer than usual. Marti Lyons, I had heard, had stormed out of Susie's office and left the building. I knew not to mention it.

"The Mark Lewis piece is a problem," Susie said peremptorily. "There's not enough about art in it."

I tried to regroup. Of all the complaints I had anticipated, "not enough about art" had not been one of them. "But, Susie, you said the whole point was for him to revisit a special place from childhood and see it through adult eyes," I protested.

Her mouth set. "It seems to me, after reading it, that here we are paying a fortune, bowing down to this man's every desire, and the fact that he's the top art writer in the country should mean that we at least get *part* of what we're paying for."

"But that wasn't the assignment," I persisted. "You knew this wasn't going to be a piece about art."

"Well, maybe it wasn't then, but it's going to be now. Or at least half and half. How will it look for us to have Mark Lewis in the magazine writing about cheese steaks instead of art? We'll look like suckers." Her eyes narrowed. "Weren't you supposed to have been monitoring him?"

"Yes. Except I was monitoring him on the old assignment."

She said nothing. I knew it was pointless to argue logically, so I changed tactics. "I think if we push him on this, he'll withdraw the piece," I said.

"Why should he? We've done everything he wanted. Now he needs to do what we want." I knew from her tone that Miss Belladonna had lost interest in the outcome; three months later, the dinner-party hostess had fallen off her radar screen. So Susie could be as stubborn as a splinter, unmovable. She was going to fight to the death over this newly invented aberration, though it was thoroughly unnecessary and could only further harm the reputation of *Jolie!* among anyone who considered writing for it.

I excused myself from Susie's office, skipped the agent, and called Mark directly. "Here's what's happening," I said, explaining everything. I reiterated that I thought he'd done a great job, and that I found him thoroughly cooperative in whatever editing I'd asked him to do. I apologized for having wasted his time. I told him that if he wanted to pull the piece, I felt confident that the magazine would pay him the full fee, anyway, to avoid hard feelings, but of course, that would be between his agent and Susie.

He couldn't have been nicer. He completely understood. And he wondered if I was free for dinner.

"Well, I guess I can . . ." I stopped.

"Never mind," he said, his voice hardening.

"No, I'm sorry, that came out wrong. Let me explain something to you. I wasn't out sick on Friday. I was back in L.A., seeing Paul."

"How is he?"

"Awful. He's going to die." I tried not to start crying. "So, anyway, it does seem as if this piece is *finally* over, and yes, I would like to have dinner with you. We've already had two great ones, aside from the fact that you dumped me in Philadelphia—"

He cut me off. "Is *that* why you're angry with me?"

I was taken aback. "What do you mean?"

"Well, I knew you were angry about something—I could tell by your tone these last few weeks—but I couldn't figure out what I'd done to offend you. The reason I didn't ask you to come to dinner that night was because the friends I ran into are a couple who are still close to my ex-wife. They're art people; I should have figured they'd be there to see that new exhibit. Anyway, we'd been meaning to get together and sit down to talk, and when we saw each other, we figured we'd just do it then. I mean, it was not a conversation I could have had with you there."

"Fair enough. And what about the early train back?"

He was quiet a moment. Oh, God. Who was I to grill him this way?

"Um, you made yourself clear about the nightcap and all the rest of it," he said. "So I thought it was best for us to see each other again in New York. If that's something you still want to do."

I felt my face burn. "Yes, of course it is. Look, I . . . I'm sorry," I said, lighting a cigarette without even bothering to get up and close the door. "I've just been crazy lately, with everything that's happening. I apologize. I do." I attempted a lighter tone. "Though I may never forgive you for depriving me of brunch."

He sounded mollified, somewhat. "I can live with that. So, are we having this damn dinner or not?"

I smiled. "Yes, we are. I'd love to."

"Good," he said firmly. "Are you free Wednesday or Thursday?"

We agreed on Wednesday and decided to go back to Orso for spaghetti. "Listen, I apologize again about the piece," I said.

"It's fine with me," he answered, "though I can't be held accountable for Victoria Segal."

We said goodbye, and when I put the phone down, I felt swamped with relief—and anxiety. He was such a nice man, honest, straightforward. I had absolutely no experience with someone like that. I would have paid a million dollars for the chance to talk to Paul about it.

The assistant who was helping me tapped cautiously on the door frame, waving her hand at the smoke. "What are you doing?" she whispered loudly, and I snapped to and tamped out the cigarette. I looked at the pile of pink message slips she handed me. Two were from Bucky.

I set them aside and phoned Victoria Segal, who, naturally, pitched a fit, insisting that the full fee be paid since her client had satisfied the terms of the agreement. She seemed taken aback when I agreed, admitting that Susie had changed her mind only in retrospect. "She can do that with everyone else," Victoria declared, "but not with my client."

"You certainly don't need my advice," I said, "but the piece is ready to run, and you can sell it anywhere."

"I know my options, thank you," she said, and hung up.

The phone rang again, and though I was sure it was Bucky, I decided to pick up. The hell with it, I thought. Time to deal and move forward.

It was, in fact, Sally.

"He's back in the hospital," she said, sounding uncharacteristically grim. "He started having trouble breathing last night."

"Cedars-Sinai?" I asked.

"No," she said. "Saint Joseph's."

"A Catholic hospital? You know how much Paul hates nuns."

"I do," she said evenly. "But he seems to feel differently now. This is his choice to be there, not mine. Let's face it, medical care isn't the issue now. Comfort is. And at this point, he finds the nuns comforting. He wants them to pray for him."

She promised to call back after more tests were done and Paul had settled in. We hung up, and I tried to make sense out of it. Paul Romano, who had spent his entire life rebelling against every religious and social convention he could find, had *chosen* to die with the nuns? It was the damnedest thing.

I needed to get out of the office. I walked up Fifth Avenue, passing St. Patrick's. Not today. I kept going, to the Doubleday bookstore a few blocks up. I strode through the aisles, toward the back. "Do you have any books on quilting?" I asked a saleswoman, who directed me to a shelf full.

I read along the spines. My friend was going to die, and I needed to be prepared. I would make him a quilt that would take its place with the thousands of others—all those lives, raucous and daring, now silently arranged in a grid of neat, homey squares. It seemed like the last thing any one of them would have wanted, but the only thing anyone left could think to do.

I found a book that looked right for a beginner and bought it. I would study it later.

Back in the office, Susie Schein was agitatedly pacing the hallway. "They pulled the piece!" she exclaimed angrily. "Did you know about this?"

"No, Susie, but I can't say I'm surprised. What did you think they were going to do?"

"Rewrite it!" she said.

"He fulfilled the assignment, and you changed it after the fact. There was no reason for him to rewrite it."

"Is that what you told him? And his agent? Are you playing both sides against the middle here?"

"There is no middle here," I shouted, a rush of fury pushing up behind my eyes. "The middle moves anywhere it wants to on any given day. I knew from the beginning you couldn't get away with this crap with someone like Mark Lewis, but you wouldn't listen. I don't know what the point was of even hiring him. That piece was never going to run in this magazine—no matter how many fucking boutiques you sent me to."

I became aware that I was screaming—and cursing—at my boss in a public space where everyone was listening, even though they were all pretending to be diligently doing something else. I turned around, went into my office, and slammed the door the way I used to when I was thirteen and fighting with my mother over how long I'd been on the phone. I tried steadying myself, but I was shaking with rage. It was a serious error, I knew, to lose my temper and challenge Susie on a day when her authority had been all but demolished by Marti Lyons. I took a few deep breaths, wondering if she was going to charge in behind me. She didn't.

I paced awhile—picking dead leaves off the plant Coco and Pimm had given me, which I never remembered to water—and finally sat down in my chair. I sorted through my messages and threw the ones from Bucky into the trash. This was not the moment to reminisce about days gone by with the ex–love of my life. I needed to focus on right now. The only hope I had of still being employed by six o'clock was to concentrate on things I could actually fix—even if they were only articles, no matter what Susie had done to them. I put on my glasses, closed my mouth, and got to work.

For the rest of the day, Susie remained scarily silent. I edited pieces and sent them to her electronically, and she accepted them all, without any questions. Maybe I should have screamed a long time ago, I thought in the moments when I wasn't braced, waiting for the knock on the door with my marching orders. But none came. Finally, around eight-thirty, I packed my bag. Susie had gone; her door was closed. I tried calling Sally, but got the machine. Then I called Saint Joseph's hospital in L.A. and asked for Paul, but they said the phone in his room had not been turned on.

He couldn't have died, could he? I worried, waiting for the elevator. Sally would surely have called me. I hated being so far away, not knowing what was happening next.

As I entered the lobby, I saw that the front entrance was closed for the night, so I headed toward the back. There, stationed at the revolving doors, stood Bucky, looking hugely pleased at the shock that must have registered on my face. But his expression changed quickly to concern.

"Sanny, what's wrong?" he asked, and his voice was so gentle and he seemed so familiar that I suddenly couldn't remember whether the last time I had seen him was a year ago or yesterday. I looked up at his face and felt mine crumple.

"Hey," he said softly, gathering me up, and I dropped my bag and sobbed—about everything: Paul dying, Susie plotting to fire me, my willful misreading of Mark's behavior. I felt Bucky's arms surround me, and as I breathed in the scent of his shirt, every awful thing he had ever done disappeared. He hugged me and held me close, and it felt as if my bones had melted and the only reason I was even standing was because of him.

I don't know how long we stayed there, him hushing me and rocking me as I wailed mightily on. Finally, finally, I pulled my head back and looked into his eyes.

"Paul is dying," I said.

He inhaled sharply, genuinely shocked.

"He has AIDS," I continued, and he seemed to have the briefest moment of recognition—Paul was gay, so of course he had AIDS, he had brought that on himself—and that's when I pulled away and leaned over to grab my bag to try to find a tissue—which, of course, I didn't have.

"Here," he said, offering me a handkerchief. I took it—when did he start using handkerchiefs?, I wondered, that was something my father did—and I blew my nose and wiped my eyes and realized that I had imprinted three black mascara smudges on Bucky's white shirt collar.

I started to laugh, and pulled him to the lobby mirror to show him the damage.

"Some things never change," he said comfortingly, and he put his arm around my shoulders and walked me onto the street. I felt cocooned in a dream.

Once outside, the air snapped me to. It was, technically, spring, but it was still cold, not unlike the night at the Met—could it be?—a year ago. In the harsh white light of the street-lamp, I looked up at Bucky's face. He was the same, but different. Balder, for starters. And was that silver now in his blond hair? He resembled his father more and more. He also seemed to have lost the bulk of his muscles, as if he'd forsaken his heavy-duty weight lifting for aerobics. The collar of his shirt looked loose.

"Bucky." Saying his name out loud seemed to help focus me. "What are you doing here?"

"Well, it seems I arrived in the nick of time," he said pleasantly. When I didn't respond, he kept going. "I need to talk to you, Sandra, and I thought this might be the best way to make that happen."

I felt confused—old, suddenly. Nothing was working the way it should. This was a man who had really, really done me wrong. Why was I so glad to see him?

"I'd like us to sit and talk awhile," he said. "Can you come with me now? Or do you have plans?" He was suddenly solicitous.

"No, I have no plans tonight."

He hailed a cab and directed the driver to the Landmark Tavern, way over on the West Side. It was a place we had always liked, especially as a refuge on cold nights. And this one qualified.

We sat at a table in the back room, and I ordered a double Scotch and soda. Bucky's blue eyes were still vivid, I thought, though different from Mark's, which were darker, graver somehow.

He ordered a beer. "Tell me about Paul," he said, and I did, the story of these last months pouring out. I told him about Paul's parents' house and his father's real job, and nothing was more gratifying than seeing Bucky's jaw drop and his eyes widen, and it was like a hundred dinners we had had together when I told him stories and he listened with every fiber. Or seemed to. He asked about Sally, and about Dennis, who I was amazed to discover he remembered, and I don't know how long we kept at it, but we both had two drinks and finished our burgers by the time we were done.

"Listen," I said eventually, "I'm sorry. All I've done is talk about Paul, and me. I know you wanted to talk, too. Is it about your getting married? Because I heard that. Congratulations."

"Well," he said, shifting in his seat, "that's one of the reasons I'm here tonight, Sandra. The engagement is off. I realized that I was too much on the rebound to have gotten involved again so quickly. And I've thought a lot about how much I hurt you, and I was hoping that I could make it up to you somehow."

"What did you have in mind?" I asked, only half joking.

"Well, how about giving me another chance? Can you have dinner with me this weekend?"

I sat there, dazed, contemplating his eager smile. He was undoubtedly up to no good. But the odd thing was, I didn't seem to care. It was almost as if I were watching him on a TV screen—someone who looked like him and sounded like him, but I couldn't be sure it *was* him. But none of that mattered as much as how I felt right at that moment—so purged, so *heard* in telling my story about Paul to someone who had known him as long as I had.

And I realized that I was no different from anyone else I knew who had lost a mate—or a soul mate—and talked about it too much, whether it was my grandmother or a friend my own age. They could talk endlessly, charming themselves backward in time, igniting themselves with the hope of resurrection. It was porn for the mourning, I thought. Nothing was as captivating as the sound of my own voice, rising and falling with the most insignificant memories, painting myself in the center of the picture with the man about to get away.

And somehow, saying it all to the man who *did* get away made it all the more meaningful. Because *look*: After all my suffering, my longing, he had come back, just as I was losing Paul. In the nick of time, he had said.

"Yes," I told him, "I can have dinner this weekend."

After that tumultuous Monday, things quieted down. Marti Lyons packed up and left, trailed by a blind item in the gossip columns: "Which powerful downtown editor got a little too distracted with the beauty biz for her paramour's own good? The poor thing is now out of a job." The poor thing had actually been hired by *Vogue*, posthaste.

Susie Schein grudgingly paid Mark's agent the full fee, and he left a message saying that they had placed the piece in *Condé Nast Traveler*, which had outbid *Manhattan Week*, a new, hip competitor to *New York* magazine. And *Glamour* had passed on Buffy Parks, I heard, so my potential career there was safe.

I had my usual amount of copy to edit, plus some of Marti's writing to do, a task at which I proved hopeless. Since my piece about Idina Lhasa in Acapulco, I had written more, but beauty copy was something else again. I just couldn't get it up for the glories of peach, unless it was in a pie, and everything I tried was rejected by Miss Belladonna as too flat. Instead, I was put in charge of editing the freelance writers who'd been called in until a replacement for Marti was found.

Surprisingly, Susie Schein never mentioned my blowup in the hallway. She stayed sequestered in her office, interviewing beauty writers. I told her about Mark selling his piece, and she nodded casually, as if it meant nothing to her—and in fact, it probably didn't. She was already on to a new selection for her Genius-of-the-Month Club, a pseudo-intellectual discount-department-store heiress who had begun attending editorial meetings, name-dropping her lunch companions, and promising long pieces, one of which she actually wrote. When it was cut down to little more than a caption, there wasn't a peep out of her.

On Wednesday, Sally called to say that the doctors had ordered more tests. She would let me know the results as soon as she did.

That night, I met Mark at Orso, as planned.

"How are you?" he asked enthusiastically as I approached the table.

I launched into my story about Paul, replete with minute detail, and though he listened and asked all the right questions,

he eventually changed the subject to other things: new assignments he was working on, books he was reading, friends who had
called and what their news had been.

I sipped my wine and nodded and laughed in all the right
places and felt as if he were on the same TV screen Bucky had
been on the other night. Who was this man, exactly? I seemed to
have trouble placing him, even in these familiar surroundings,
even when I looked into his bright, soulful eyes. The connection
seemed gone.

There were silences between us, even though people from
other tables stopped by to talk. Mark seemed diverted enough not
to notice that I wasn't exactly as engaged as I'd been in
Philadelphia.

But after the decaf cappuccino was served, he turned toward
me. "Are you still mad at me?" he asked.

"No, not at all," I said, squeezing his arm as reassuringly as I
could. "I'm just distracted, by Paul and everything. You can
understand that, can't you?"

He said yes and smiled gamely, but I could see that he was disappointed. And even though all I needed to do was just focus a
minute, ask him a question, any question, I somehow couldn't.
Without the added impetus of being Mark's editor, I somehow
couldn't force myself to concentrate. Truth be told, the only
thing I *could* focus on, God help me, was the idea of seeing Bucky
again.

Mark and I were out on the street before I stopped to realize
that maybe I'd blown it, that I might never see this man again. He
walked me toward the corner and raised his hand for a cab, and I
looked at his kissable throat, fully exposed above his open shirt,
and I felt a twinge, but from a great distance. It was as if I were getting my tonsils out again, and the doctor was saying, "Count backward from a hundred," and I was in on the joke about how life
would just fade and I'd be back when the bad part was over.

I thought about explaining things to him, about how Paul was dying so Bucky had returned, about how important it was that I be with him now because I had *missed* him. It was like a sign, I wanted to say, that in my hour of greatest need, the man I loved had come back to me.

A cab pulled up, and Mark opened the door for me. I turned to thank him, but his face seemed closed. I got into the backseat with that feeling you have when you know you've done something wrong and feel awful about it, because you never meant to. But I couldn't change it now.

The feeling lasted for the next few blocks, but then I brightened. Saturday was only three days away.

By Friday, Paul was back at Sally's. "He's breathing fine again, and there was nothing more they could do for him at the hospital," she explained. "He wanted to be home."

"Can I talk to him?" I asked. Whenever I had asked in the last week, he hadn't been awake.

"Well, you can try," she said, "but he may not answer, Sandy. He hasn't spoken in days, really."

"Okay."

I heard some fumbling and Sally saying, "This is Sandy, she wants to say hello. Go ahead," and I could hear the receiver being placed near Paul's ear.

"Paul, it's Sandy, how are you doing?" I trilled. Nothing. I listened for his breathing, but all I could hear was Sally moving the phone around, trying to find a good position. "I just wanted you to know that I miss you and I'm thinking about you," I continued.

Silence on the other end.

I stopped. This was too awful.

Sally came back on the line. "I'm sorry, Sandy," she said. "I thought he was awake, but I guess he's not."

"That's okay," I answered. "Thanks, anyway. Will you let me know what happens next?" As I asked the question, I wished I could take it back.

There was only one thing that was going to happen next.

Six o'clock Saturday evening, Bucky picked me up in a car with a driver. He had refused to tell me where we were going. It was all a surprise.

"Where are we off to so early?" I asked, stretching my legs out in the plush backseat.

"Well, first we're having drinks with the Dickinsons," he said.

"We are?" I asked, feeling a scintilla of alarm. "Don't you think that's odd, considering the circumstances?"

I hadn't seen Arthur and Nancy Dickinson—Bucky's uber-WASP Fifth Avenue friends—in I couldn't remember how long. But I wondered why they weren't away for the weekend, off to their mammoth family-money house in Oyster Bay. I had seen the house once; they were both descended from the right people, and the walls were covered with the kinds of portraits you see in museums, of inbred Colonials with pink-lidded eyes and narrow nostrils, holding a fan or pointing a buckled toe. I could never figure out who her right people were, but one of his was John Dickinson, a Pennsylvania signer of the Declaration of Independence, but also a British loyalist who was one of the last holdouts against forming the United States, preferring a reconciliation with the crown instead.

In spite of his ancestors, Arthur Dickinson, who did the same kind of work as Bucky, was a down-to-earth guy. I had always liked him. I remembered Nancy's obsession with the Junior League and hoped we could find something else to talk about.

"Not so odd," Bucky said as the car made its way uptown. "They haven't seen you in ages, and I told them how important it is that we try to be friends and how badly I felt about what happened between us. Arthur's given me endless shit about it." He smiled. "He thinks I'm awash in youthful indiscretions."

"How F. Scott Fitzgerald," I said distractedly as Macy's flew by my window. Was I doing the right thing, here? I hadn't seen Bucky in a year, and the first thing he wanted to do was have drinks with people I hardly knew?

"What's after cocktails?" I asked.

"We're having dinner someplace you love," he said cheerfully. "You're going to be very, very happy."

In the elevator on the way up to the Dickinsons' apartment, I leaned into Bucky's outstretched arm and fit perfectly underneath, as I always had. Bucky was a touchstone for me. It was important to have a touchstone, now more than ever. I started feeling better. This could be fun.

"Welcome," Arthur exclaimed, waiting at the open door. He shook Bucky's hand heartily, then mine.

"Hello there," said Nancy, coming up behind him. She was wearing a kilt and penny loafers. "Nice to see you, Sandy." I felt immediately overdressed in a black sweater and pants with gold jewelry. Not to mention makeup.

"What are you drinking?" Arthur boomed.

"Scotch and soda," I said obligingly.

"And you, Buck? A beer, as usual?"

"Great, Arthur, thanks."

Nancy led us into the den, and we sat amid the city branch of ancestors. "I just love *Jolie!*," she exclaimed as the boys began to talk sports, and I knew I was trapped. She especially loved the home-design section, mentioning it at least three times before jumping up suddenly and disappearing. "I forgot the hors d'oeuvres," she said, returning after a while with a dish of peanuts and plate of cheese cubes with toothpicks in them.

"Salud," Arthur said loudly.

"Cheers," I answered, swigging my drink. Bucky raised his glass, but didn't look at me.

"So, Sandy, we haven't seen you in so long," Nancy cooed. "Tell me what you've been up to. But first tell me if you've given any more thought to joining the Junior League."

Great. I took a breath. "Well, you know, Nancy, I've been so busy," I started.

"But that's true of everyone in the organization," she said quickly. "Most of the women have careers, but they still remember how important it is to volunteer and give of their time to help the less fortunate."

I glanced at Bucky, deep into basketball scores with Arthur. My eye darted around, trying to find something else, anything else, to talk about. I spotted something in the dining room, through the open entryway.

"Nancy, I promise to think about it, but first you must tell me about those fabulous wall coverings." She turned reverently toward the walls covered in blue-and-white-striped silk, like pajamas.

"Boys, boys," Nancy trumpeted, and Bucky and Arthur fell silent. "Sandy was just complimenting me on the wonderful wall coverings. Isn't that something?"

"Let me give you the grand tour," Arthur said, coming to pull me out of a chintz cushion on the couch into which I had sunk past dignity. "We've freshened things up around here recently."

I followed him. "Be careful of that umbrella stand," he cautioned, steering me away from the front door. "It's an antique." Well, that's smart, I thought, looking at the unusable copper receptacle. It was peculiar that they hadn't replaced the worn carpeting around it. Nor had they done anything about the water stains in the corner of the ceiling.

Arthur was especially proud of the living room, which was indeed pretty and looked like every other living room I'd ever seen on the Upper East Side: flowered fabrics, patterned rugs, fat pillows, silver picture frames, knickknacks, and sculpted china dogs guarding the nonworking fireplace.

I spotted a bathroom. "Excuse me, won't you?" I asked Arthur, who genially withdrew. I closed the door behind me with relief. I didn't think I could stand another second of this. Yes, that *was* an enchanting silver cigarette case on that end table! But what was it doing in a house where no one smoked?

I put on some more lipstick, even though Nancy wasn't wearing any. I hoped we weren't going to stay for another drink. Between the Junior League and the upholstery, I'd need coffee instead.

When I opened the door to start back, I got completely turned around and headed the wrong way down the hall. I ended up near the kitchen, where the swinging service door was propped open with a phone book. I heard furious whispering.

Suddenly I was spying. But on whom? It was Nancy, mostly, berating someone—it must have been Arthur. But no, that was Bucky who answered. How odd. Could the two of them have something going on that Arthur didn't know about? I leaned forward, straining to hear.

And I heard. I most definitely heard. I fell back against the wall and stayed there for what seemed a very long time. Then there were footsteps. It was Arthur, coming to fetch me.

I sat back in my chair, sipping the excellent Burgundy that Bucky had ordered, holding the glass in both hands. I looked out the window at the blinking city lights as he talked about the land upstate he was planning to buy. In horse country.

"You don't ride," I said, but he didn't seem to hear me. Had I said it out loud, I wondered, or only thought it? I couldn't tell.

A knock came on the door. "May I clear this for you?" the waiter asked. We made way for him, moving our chairs so that he could roll the table through.

We were in a room on the twentieth floor of the Essex House hotel, which is where Bucky had arranged for our dinner to be served. The Essex House was a place we had gone, over the years, for birthdays, anniversaries, and other special occasions. In the mornings we would have room-service breakfast in front of the picture window overlooking Central Park. We hadn't tried dinner before. It was a first.

Once the table was gone, we sat back down to finish the wine. I sneaked a look at my watch. Without the burble of romance to act as a filler, conversation had proved something of a chore. I did talk about Paul, but soon realized that after my exhaustive mono-logue of the other night, there wasn't much fresh material. It went without saying that Bucky hadn't read a book since *Ancient Evenings*—and the only topics he seemed to warm to all night were real estate values and Range Rover prices. Well, that wasn't entirely true. He still liked the Judds.

"I have something for you," he announced, presenting me with a large brown envelope. I opened it and found pictures of Paul from when we were in school, some from New Haven, some from New York.

"I always meant to give these to you but never remembered," Bucky said. "I thought you'd like to have them now."

"Yes," I managed. There was one of the two of us together, at a party, laughing uproariously, heads back, mouths open. His arms were wrapped around my waist. It was *Paul*. My Paul. The young and healthy and beautiful Paul whom I hadn't seen in such a very long time.

"They're just wonderful," I said, blowing my nose. "You were always such a great photographer. Thank you."

After I put them away, we sat silently for a while. "Tell me what you're thinking about," he said finally. "Is it the pictures?"

I put down the wine. "Sort of. I guess I realized something tonight that I'd never understood before."

He straightened himself in his chair, prepared for praise. "And?" he asked.

"I realized that after all the years we spent together, I never really knew you."

His face fell. "What do you mean?"

"Well, I just can't figure how you can be the person who takes these beautiful pictures of Paul, and be the same person who did what you did tonight."

"What do you mean?" He held his arms out, indicating the room, the dinner, the view.

"No, not this, Bucky. I was talking about the Dickinsons."

"What?" He kept up his innocent outrage.

"I heard you in the kitchen with Nancy tonight," I said, watching his mouth open and his eyes pop. "So I know that you are, in fact, still very much engaged to Wendy. And that the reason for the little cocktail party tonight was to convince me to promote Wendy's work, including the Dickinsons' apartment, in the hallowed pages of *Jolie!* magazine."

His face had gone ashen. "Sandy, it's not what you think," he began.

Another lie. But the amazing thing was that I didn't care. I had no rage left. No anger, just a sort of consolation: I didn't have to do this anymore. This whole world of Bucky's—from the country clubs to the Betsy Ross House—was all based on lies. I had found them so mysterious, so beguiling, for so long. I had never perceived them as lies—only myths, traditions.

But now, suddenly, there they were, heaped in a spindly pile, like kindling. The spell was broken.

I thought of Mark Lewis then and felt a pang about our last dinner at Orso. The man must have thought I'd lost my mind. Which I had. I would fix that immediately, first thing tomorrow. There was a whole other world out there. It was time for me to join it, once and for all.

I stood.

"Wait, Sanny, I can explain," Bucky said hurriedly.

I looked at his imploring face. "No, let me," I said. "You didn't really lie about Wendy, because even though you're still engaged, the truth is you may marry her, you may not. You will marry someone eventually, but in the meantime it would make you feel better, more certain, to see me again. I'm a touchstone. You can decide all the other stuff later."

His face stained red.

"The decorating thing is a separate issue," I went on. "That was Nancy's idea. And you went along with it because you knew it would never happen, but they all would think you were a hero for trying, and when it fell through it would be all my fault."

"No—"

"Yes. And none of it matters, Bucky. Truly. Forget it. Though I do appreciate the pictures." I walked to the door.

"Sanny, please," he wheedled, rushing toward me, pushing aside the chairs. "You were so right about the touchstone part. I don't want to let you go yet, Sanny. I can't. As long as I have you, I have the best part of myself, the part that you see I can be someday. When you look at me, even now, I still feel that I might find it. Remember?"

He fixed his eyes on mine. I looked into them, that dizzying sky-blue heaven I had spent so long trying to infiltrate. This was Bucky, my Bucky. I held his gaze, too, as if it were the final shot of a favorite old movie I was not quite ready to turn off, and I barely noticed that he was unbuttoning his shirt, unzipping his pants, peeling off his underwear, until he stood there in front of me, nude, with a hard-on. He grabbed me, grinding himself against me.

"I need you, Sandra, I need you so much," he crooned into my hair, his hands clutching at me. "Please. Please stay here with me."

I stood for a moment, feeling him against me, but when he pushed his mouth onto mine, it was as if I had been slapped. This was no movie. Yanking myself out of his grasp, I threw the door open and ran down the long, silent hallway. I heard the door slamming shut as I hit the elevator button three, four, five times.

Suddenly the door opened and he came running down the hall, naked. Ah. The grand statement of passion.

I watched him start toward me as the door closed, then locked, behind him. He turned toward it, startled, then looked back at me. He clearly hadn't thought this through. I shrugged as the elevator arrived.

"Hold that elevator!" he yelled, returning to his door, frantically grasping the immovable doorknob.

"Sandy, wait!" he called, running down the hall.

"Going down," I called back.

"No, Sandy, come on. I mean, I'm really locked out. You have to help me here." His eyes were wild. "Please."

"Okay, calm down," I said. "I'll go to the desk and bring back the extra key. Don't worry."

"Hurry up," he said as the doors closed.

In the lobby I walked past the front desk and signaled the doorman. "Taxi, please," I said, and rode off into the night.

15

#77   *The Crippling Slipper*
by Sandra Berlin

The maiden had traveled long and far on her journey, and she was very tired. She stopped beside a stream to drink and rest. A frog jumped up on a stone beside her.

"Dear maiden, you look so tired from your trip," he said. "Where are you headed?"

"I'm going to the Emerald City to see the Wizard," she said. "I'm hoping he will grant me three wishes."

"What do you wish for, fair maiden?" the frog inquired.

"I wish for a loving husband. I wish to live happily ever after. And I wish for three more wishes."

"Why is that?" the frog asked.

"So I may always have whatever I need," she answered. She leaned down and looked at him more closely. "Listen, if you're enchanted, I have no problem kissing you so that you turn back into a handsome prince. Then we could live happily ever after together."

The frog laughed. "You have much to learn, maiden,"

he said. "I am not a prince. But I will travel with you, to see that you get to your destination safely."

And the maiden and the frog ventured down the road for quite some distance until they came upon a small village on the outskirts of the Emerald City suburbs.

"You know, Frog," the maiden said, "I must trade in these shoes for a much nicer pair, if I'm to appear before the Wizard. These are too worn from the road."

"Well, here, look at this," the frog said, showing her a flyer. "Prince seeks SWF for bride. If glass slipper fits, my 401(K) is yours. Call 1-800-SAVE ME for appointment."

"Hmmm," the maiden mused. "The only problem is, I have no address here."

"I know what to do," the frog said. "Let's go to the shoemaker so he can make you a new pair of traveling shoes, just in case you end up needing them. But in the meantime, call in and give the shoemaker's address as your own. That way, the Prince can meet you there."

So the pair set off to the shoemaker, who was a very nice man who sat at his desk reading books when he wasn't working.

"Excuse us, sir," the frog said. "We are sorry to interrupt your studies, but this maiden needs a pair of shoes in case the glass slipper does not fit."

The shoemaker stood up and shook hands, and his eyes were very blue. "May I offer you some wine?" he asked, pouring some Havens Merlot all around. He then measured the maiden's foot.

"Kind sir," she said, "I would not want to trouble you to make me the shoes if I'm lucky enough to fit the glass slipper. Would you let us wait here until the prince comes, and then, if it doesn't work out, you can make the shoes afterward?"

"But of course," the shoemaker said solicitously, and he returned to his books while the frog and the maiden waited for the prince to appear. Which he did, a few days later.

"Here he comes," the villagers said in awe as they watched the white horse pull up in front of the shoemaker's house. The prince alighted, wearing Weejuns, plaid pants, and a Lacoste polo shirt with a grinning alligator at its heart.

"Your Highness," the maiden said, bowing low before him.

"Hey," he answered, getting down on one knee. "Your legs aren't bad. Let's check out your feet."

But first, the maiden looked at the glass slipper. "Wait. I'm having second thoughts," she said, holding the shoe up to the light. It was glass on the outside and glass on the inside, and it had no give at all. Now that she stopped to look at them, she realized these shoes would cripple her. You couldn't go anywhere in them. You would have to stay in the very same spot for the rest of your life.

"I'm sorry, Your Highness, but I don't wear glass," she said finally.

"Okay," the prince said, turning toward his briefcase. "How about black peau de soie pumps? I have another fiancée with the same problem."

The maiden considered. "You know, I love peau de soie, but I need shoes that are sturdier, that will take me farther on my journey—especially if you have another fiancée."

"May I offer a suggestion?" the shoemaker asked. "I can make you some sensible shoes, crafted from fine leather, with low heels and excellent support. They may not be as magical as the glass slipper or as sophisticated as the peau de soie pump, but they will feel good and last a lifetime."

The maiden looked at the frog questioningly. "You

don't need my advice," he said. "You always pick things like that anyway. You've never been fun to shop with."

"Paul, is that you?" the maiden asked, looking again at the frog. "I should have known."

The frog sighed. "I haven't been myself lately, Sandra," he said. "But I gave you my word that I would stay on this journey with you, and I have."

The maiden turned to the shoemaker. "Please make me your shoes," she said, and, bowing, he returned to his workshop. She turned back to the prince. "No hard feelings, I hope," she said as he remounted his horse.

"Not at all," he said magnanimously. "Actually, I have my hands full. You'd be amazed at how many women fit either this shoe or the pump." And off he galloped into the sunset.

"Well, fair maiden," the frog asked, "are you disappointed now that you've lost your prince and your three wishes?"

"Well, sort of," she said. "But we still haven't made it to the Wizard. I think I'll wait and see what happens next."

The shoemaker appeared then with the maiden's new shoes. She tried them on, and they fit like magic! They were beautiful, they were comfortable, they made her feel as if she were walking on air. "Oh, dear sir, I can't thank you enough," she said. "How much do they cost?"

"Well, fair maiden," the shoemaker said, "I thought I would ask for the privilege of your being my bride, which is all the payment I require. Just the pleasure of your company, day in and day out."

The maiden considered. "Okay, I get it," she said. "The shoes fit like magic, so that means every time I put them on I get three wishes, right?"

The shoemaker shook his head. "No. They are only shoes. They don't come with wishes. Actually, after you've worn them another hour or so, you may feel some tightness in the toe or the heel. You need to break them in gradually."

The maiden crossed her arms. "So what is it you're offering me exactly? A lifetime as a shoemaker's wife, no access to wishes, and a bunch of books for entertainment?"

The shoemaker nodded. "Yes, fair maiden, I'm afraid so. You know, I've been married once before. And I would say that beyond a pair of shoes with good support, there aren't many guarantees in a marriage. Though you can certainly wish all you want."

"Well, harumph!" said the maiden. She had waited her whole life to say that. "Can you believe the nerve of this guy, Frog?"

But the frog did not answer, nor was he anywhere in sight.

"Frog, where are you?" the maiden called. "My journey to the Emerald City is still in progress, and you promised to stay with me until its end."

She looked everywhere, but still could not find the frog. Finally, she saw a note on a stone next to a nearby stream.

"Fair maiden," it said. "Sorry I couldn't make it to the Emerald City. But wherever your journey should lead, always remember my money's on you. Gone dancin'— The Frog."

She walked slowly back to the shoemaker's house.

"Have you made a decision?" he asked.

"No," the maiden said. "I'm actually not sure what to do now. I think I'll continue on my road in my new shoes and see what life is like without waiting for wishes."

The shoemaker brightened. "Sometimes it can be lovely," he confided. "So many things—the sun in the sky, the flowers in the field, the bread in the oven—are so beautiful that they are like wishes already come true."

"I'll try and remember that," the maiden said, stepping forward to shake his hand. "And please don't think I'm a deadbeat. I'm broke now, but I shall repay you, no matter how long it takes."

"No rush," the shoemaker said. "After that peau de soie craze, I'm set for life."

And the maiden bade him farewell as she started walking toward the road. When she turned to wave goodbye, the shoemaker pointed to the door of his house.

"I usually leave this open for my son, Benjamin," he said. "But I will leave it open for you now, too. When your journey is finished, you will be welcome here."

"But will we live happily ever after?" she asked.

"I can't say for sure," the shoemaker answered. "But the frog said his money was on you, which means you'll figure out the right thing to do—probably sooner rather than later. In the meantime, take this. It may come in handy once you get to the Emerald City."

He handed her a card that read: "Storytellers Anonymous. Twelve steps to realizing that 'happily ever after' is a pat tag line with no lasting emotional resonance."

"Thank you," she said. "Even though I have a master's degree, there are definitely holes in my education. And I think this one may be the biggest."

This time, when she set out on the road, she did not look back. She kept the note from the frog close to her heart, and she walked and she searched and she looked and she dreamed, and while she debated the validity of "happily ever after" as both a literary and lifestyle device, she thought every day about the open door at the shoemaker's house. And still, she moved on.

The End

16

Sunday, I waited until noon before calling Mark. The machine picked up.

"Mark, this is Sandy," I said. "I realize that I was certifiably insane the other night, and I hope you'll let me make amends. If you're free this week, I'd love to cook dinner for you. I do have this sort of spooky roommate, but she tends to stay in her room, so if you're willing to venture to the wilds of the Village, I'd love to have you. Talk to you soon, I hope."

By four o'clock he hadn't called. By five, I was deep in my closet, vacuuming behind the shoes. By seven, I was pouring myself a drink to calm down, though I did allow myself a toast and a giggle at how I had ended my evening the night before.

At nine-thirty the phone rang.

"Sandy?" It was Mark, thank you, God.

"Yes, it's me, second only to Sylvia Plath in mental stability. Listen, I have got to apologize to you. I was awful the other night. I should have called the very next day, but, well, I've had a few things to work out and I seem to have made quite a mess doing it. But hopefully, it's one I can fix. I so want to."

"You were awful!" he exclaimed. I could hear the smile in his voice. "It was like that scene in *The Manchurian Candidate* with all the hypnotized garden-party ladies. I wanted to shake you, but I don't know you well enough."

"Well, can we rectify that situation, please?" I asked. "At least let me cook dinner, for starters."

"That sounds great," he said, "though I could live without the roommate. How about this? Why don't you cook at my apartment? Then we won't have a problem."

I can't say I blamed him. By this point, we were both headed for the Blue Balls Hall of Fame.

We decided on Wednesday. He would order the meat from his butcher, and then we would rendezvous at Fairway, which was right near his apartment, and choose things together like salad and cheese. "I have plenty of wine," he said.

I laughed. "All stocked up on Havens Merlot?"

"Absolutely."

For the next two days, time seemed to drag itself on purpose. I checked the tabloids, hoping to read NUDE DERANGED MAN NABBED AT ESSEX HOUSE, but there was nothing. He didn't call, either. I told Pimm and Coco over lunch what had happened, and we all just howled with laughter. "Next!" Coco declared.

On Wednesday, I got to Fairway first. Or thought I did. "Sandy?" I heard Mark's voice behind me. He was holding a head of Boston lettuce. I looked into his welcoming blue eyes and thought that maybe up until now someone had been holding me prisoner. Would Midori respect you in the morning if you shut a man like this out of your life?, I asked myself.

We stood on line at the cheese counter and talked about how both our days had been, and nothing felt cozier than walking next to this man toting a can of walnut oil and a basketful of vegetables up and down the aisles. The idea of going home with him seemed completely natural.

We walked to his apartment, talking nonstop. As we entered

the lobby, I saw the doorman take me in with great interest, hurrying to the elevator to press the right button.

Inside the apartment, the paint still smelled new, and a beautiful Oriental rug covered the living room floor (he must have just bought it, I figured; the edges didn't lay flat yet). All the walls had bookshelves on them, half-filled, and boxes of more books were piled everywhere. He led me through the tiny dining room, with its handsome wooden farmhouse table and chairs, into the kitchen, where, after he poured us some wine, he encouraged me to sit while he made the salad. I watched him, and we talked in a rush, as if we hadn't seen each other in a year—though it had barely been a week.

I offered to season the roast beef, but he insisted on doing it himself. "I thought I was cooking you dinner," I said.

"All it needs is some salt and pepper and it will take care of itself," he answered, putting it in the oven.

I looked at the garlic and the bay leaves I had bought. "Are you sure?" I asked, but he was already making the dressing.

"Just keep talking to me," he said, so I did, and we were through the wine in no time.

"Why don't we open a second bottle?" I asked.

He seemed momentarily startled. "You know, my ex-wife never liked drinking wine, and if we didn't finish a bottle she thought it was a terrible waste to leave it—"

"Well, the good news is she's gone now," I said. "And I'll bet there won't be leftovers."

He opened the next bottle, and I came over with my glass so that he could pour me more. He kissed me, and we left the glasses and the salad dressing where they were, making our way through the living room, where I saw cans of Play-Doh and a box of Pampers, on into the bedroom. At last! The kissable throat was mine, and nothing in the world was going to stop me now. We both seemed torn between rushing and savoring, so we did both.

Sometime later, we lay in his bed just grinning at each other.

"The roast beef!" I yelled, abruptly sitting up, and we charged into the kitchen, which was filled with smoke. Mark pulled the pan out of the oven and dumped it in the sink, and we opened all the windows. I started to open the door to the service entrance until I realized that neither one of us had any clothes on.

"The only problem now, of course, is that I'm starving to death," I said, pulling on his discarded shirt while surveying the soaked piece of char.

"Well, we do have salad and cheese," he said.

I hunted through his cabinets. "How about some tuna fish sandwiches?"

"Great," he said, while I pulled out a bowl.

"See, this extra wine came in handy," I said, "and look at all the air it's had." I poured us both some, and this time I made him sit down and talk to me while I toasted the bread and found some pickle chips in the fridge.

We ate and we drank and we kissed and we talked, and I hadn't felt as *right* anywhere in the longest time. And when we were done, we went back to the bedroom, where I traced the outline of his lips with my fingers and listened to the jazz he was playing and thought that I might never go to the office again. Or anywhere else, for that matter. I would stay right here, in this bed. Forever.

It was getting light outside when I fell asleep, and when I woke up I heard Mark padding across the thick carpet toward the kitchen. Soon I smelled coffee, and I was so glad to be here, to wake up someplace where I didn't belong—and belong.

"Good morning," he said, coming back into the room, looking happy and a little bit shy.

"Good morning," I said, feeling pretty much the same way. I got up, got dressed, and thought about leaving and going back to my apartment to change—not only were my clothes wrecked, but they smelled like burned meat. But the music was back on, and the coffee was ready, and the papers had come, so I said the hell with the clothes and stayed as long as I could.

When it was finally time to go, we kissed goodbye, and he hugged me and I hugged him back, and when I pulled away, after the longest time, I realized that whether he was holding me in Philadelphia or all through last night, he never let go first, I did.

"I am sorry to say that Susie Schein awaits," I said, gathering my bag.

"Will you call me later?" he asked.

"Of course," I said.

I swept past the doorman in the lobby, a different one this morning. He took in my wrinkled clothes and tossed hair and, standing at attention, touched the brim of his cap.

"Good morning, lady," he said energetically. "Have a wonderful day."

"Thank you," I answered. "I think I will."

I was almost surprised to find the office the same as when I'd left it the day before. I felt so different, so transported, I was sure that the rest of the world had transported along with me. Well, two things had happened, it turned out: The assistant who'd been helping me had quit, and the new beauty writer had started, an elfin little thing with severely plucked eyebrows whose jokes made no sense to me at all. Susie was ecstatic.

I fought against calling Mark all day, saving it as a treat for the late afternoon. When the phone rang around five, though, I was convinced it was him. I picked up the phone, breathless, eager to hear his voice. "Hello?"

"Sandy, it's Sally." Her tone was somber.

My stomach clenched with fear. I hadn't heard from her in days. "What's happening?"

"Well, Sandy, I want to tell you that Paul passed away this afternoon." Her voice was gentle, a bit formal.

I found it hard to catch my breath.

"When?"

"About an hour ago. His parents were here with him, and so was I. He had really been failing these past few days, he was on oxygen almost all the time, and finally, this morning, we went back to the hospital. He was awake for a while, and I sat with him and told him it was okay to let go. That he had fought as hard as he could, and we all loved him so much, and we really wanted him to go now, to find his peace. He died a few hours later."

"Sally, I'm so sorry. You have done the most amazing job of taking care of him. Without you, he would never have lasted this long, or been as happy as he was."

"Thank you," she said. Her voice was soft and I could hear her tears.

We sat a moment, stunned by the words on both ends, having dreaded their coming for so long. They seemed both expected and strange.

"When is the funeral?" I asked.

"Sunday afternoon," she said. "At five. That will give people time to fly in. You should let me know when you'll get here and I'll have Phil pick you up at the airport. I wish I had room for you to stay in my apartment, but with so much family here, I can't. There are some nice hotels nearby, though, and—"

"Sally, wait. I mean, I have to think about it. It's just. I . . . I didn't believe this would really happen."

"I know," she said.

And she did. That one moment may have been the closest we'd been all through Paul's illness. We had each kept praying that the illegal pills or the empathetic priest or the tooth fairy would step in and save him. We were neither one of us prepared for this moment.

"How's Marie?" I asked.

"Okay, considering. She's very strong."

"And his dad?"

"Not so good."

I didn't ask how much he knew. It didn't seem to matter.

"I have to think awhile, Sally. Let me call you back. But if there's anything you need, just call me. Okay?"

I put the phone down. I couldn't seem to feel anything. I tried to think about Paul, what it had been like before he died, how he looked and how he felt. But my mind wouldn't let me. I tried picturing the funeral instead. It would be at the church we had been to together, what seemed like a hundred years ago. I would finally meet Marie, who would sob and glare in her toeless shoes. And all the other agents, who'd sent get-well flowers and muffins, would be there, air-kissing each other on their way out to dinner with clients. Why waste the night?

No, I decided. I didn't think I could stand one minute of it. I would not go, after all. The only person I wanted to see wouldn't be there. He was gone.

I went home that night and got right into bed. Mark called, at one point, sounding tentative. I had completely forgotten about him. Though he tried to keep his voice casual, I could tell he was worried—was he crazy, or had we not had the most wonderful night together? In the midst of sobbing I told him what had happened, and he offered to come right over. I thanked him but said no. I needed to be alone. He said he understood, that I should call when I was ready. I thought it best not to mention I might never be.

The following week, I got to the office early each day, earlier than Susie. I read someplace that people who are trying to overcome addictions are often assigned chores in order to help them center themselves, to prove that they can do simple things, like make the bed or take out the garbage. That strategy made sense, too, I thought, for people who were grieving. I thought about Paul as often as I tried not to think about him. He was everywhere.

Sally called. The funeral Mass was perfect, she said. There were tons of flowers, but mine—long-stemmed peach-colored roses, Paul's favorite—were especially beautiful. The church was packed, and the service was moving. Paul would have been pleased.

I found that hard to believe, but then again, maybe it was true. Sally had said he was genuinely at peace when he died, surrounded by the nuns who had nursed him and the priest who had administered the last rites. In the end, his searching had led him back to exactly who he was when he started. That is who he had chosen to be.

Wednesday afternoon, I got a call from Peter Garber, the very young, very hot editor of *Manhattan Week*, whom everyone had been writing about recently. He told me how much he had liked Mark's Philadelphia piece and wanted it for his travel issue, but that he couldn't afford to outbid Condé Nast. "I found it to be extremely well edited, and Mark said that was your doing," he said.

"Well, when you're editing someone like Mark Lewis, it's hard to look bad," I answered, flattered that someone like Peter Garber thought I had done a good job.

"That may be, but I was wondering if you'd like to come in and talk. We have a few positions to fill here. I thought you might be interested."

Might be? "That sounds great, I'd love to," I said as sedately as I could, arranging a time the following week, my heart thumping wildly. Could it one day be possible to live life without Susie Schein?

I wanted to thank Mark. We hadn't spoken in almost a week,

though I had left him a message one afternoon when I knew he was out seeing his son, saying I would call soon. He was in Chicago now, trying to bring his divorce settlement to an end. I called his hotel and left a message, and he called back later that night, when I was already in bed, reading magazines. "It's so good to hear from you," I exclaimed. "I wanted to call you again today, but I didn't want to bother you."

"Bother me," he said. "I'm seeing too much of my parents and my almost-ex-wife, closing down the apartment we kept here and deciding who gets the Baccarat Champagne flutes. I'd give anything to be back in New York."

"Why would she want Champagne flutes if she doesn't like to drink?" I asked.

"It's not that logical."

"Are you going to let her have them?"

"I'm not sure."

"You know, a friend of mine who's a divorce lawyer once told me that most people don't want half the things they ask for — they just don't want the other person to have them."

"Now she's definitely not getting them." He laughed. "Tell me about New York. Tell me how you've been feeling. Tell me everything."

I did. We talked for almost two hours, much of it about Paul. At one point, he put me on hold to order room service. I had helped him choose his dinner (Caesar salad; sirloin, rare), and I told him I'd never had a Caesar salad. "I don't like the idea of it," I said. "Raw eggs and anchovies. How could that be good?"

"You should try it," he said. "I think you'd like it."

"Yick." I poured a drink, and we resumed our conversation until, finally, it was midnight.

"Can I call you again tomorrow?" he asked.

"You'd better," I said, then hung up feeling excited, as if I'd just seen both him and Paul. It took me a while to quiet down and fall asleep.

True to his word, he called the next day, and the day after that and the day after that. One night he asked what I was eating.

I was mortified. "How did you know I was eating?"

"I can hear you. What is it?"

I decided to tell the truth. "Heinz beans out of the can," I said. "Still want to talk to me?"

He laughed. "That's disgusting. Why don't you heat them up?"

"I was too hungry."

Then he told me that he had discovered this great method of microwaving bacon, which I thought was more disgusting than eating beans from a can, so we were even.

These conversations were lifesavers. I must have reached for the phone to call Paul fifty times a day, and whenever I was in my Rolodex and passed by his card, I touched it, looked at it, and left it in its place. If I left it there long enough, maybe he'd come back. Sally called a few times, but past "hello" there wasn't much to say. I never felt I was getting through to her, never puncturing her polite veneer. One of the things I had discussed with Mark was how badly I felt about Sally. She had willingly paid every debt that Paul had incurred—and they were sizable, from the flowers to the drugs. She had replaced her rugs and was repainting her apartment. But she had no one to share it with. I so hoped that she would meet someone, soon, who could make her happy without exacting such a terrible price. I wished I could be more of a comfort to her. And I secretly wished that she could be more of a comfort to me.

The meeting with Peter Garber went well. He seemed to be about my age, and he was small, scarcely taller than me. He was teenybopper cute, with long hair flopping into his eyes and a big, guffawing laugh that never managed to detract from how piercingly intelligent his questions were. He asked a lot of them, and seemed riveted by my every answer. He was the kind of editor who made you want to get it right, be smart, have a good idea. Unlike Susie, he seemed decisive, determined, and unafraid.

He asked me to prepare some story ideas, and we arranged another meeting for the following week. "Do you have any clips from the writing you've done?" he asked as I was getting ready to go.

"Um, sure," I said hesitantly. I handed him the Nazi hunter piece and the Idina Lhasa interview.

"That's all you've written?" he asked.

I flushed, embarrassed. "Well, no, I've written a ton of kids' stories, sort of fairy tales, but nothing you'd want to see."

"You're wrong. I would want to see them," he said. "Bring them with you."

I nodded, trying to figure how much typing and copying it would take for me to get them together. More important, I needed to focus on the story ideas.

"I'll be interested to see what you come up with," Mark said when we spoke that night, and after we finished talking I stayed up until I had twenty ideas on paper. The next morning, I still liked ten of them. I loved the way it felt to experiment, to try anything. It was the opposite of what I'd been told to do at *Jolie!*, where each feature was prescribed at a certain length for a certain reason, and where the photo was the real draw of any feature, be it fashion or celebrity. I liked the prospect of a place that was about words first.

I decided not to tell Mark my ideas until after the meeting, and he agreed. "Your ideas are your currency," he said. "You have the skills to do the line-editing part of the job, but ideas in magazines are the most important thing. This is next week?"

"Yes. Will you be back by then?" I asked.

"Probably not," he said. "It's taking longer than I thought. Which is bad news, because I'm going to have to move out of the hotel and into my mother's apartment. I can't ask the magazine to keep paying for it. I've done plenty of work while I'm here, but it wouldn't be right."

"What's taking so long? You're not moving back there after all, are you?" I felt strangled, just saying the words. I had conveniently forgotten that possibility.

"Divorces usually do take so long, but when you're divorcing a tax lawyer and her former boss is your father, they take even longer," he said. "But no, I'm not moving back here, thank God. The good news is that she's decided to stay in New York. She doesn't want to live here with her parents butting into her life any more than I want mine hanging over me. So, all things considered, it's going well. I think if I can last another week or so, I'll be back and done with it for good."

I was more relieved than I expected to be. I knew that just because he was getting divorced didn't mean he was necessarily ready to fall madly in love with me, either. Or vice versa. But I liked him. I really did. And maybe my mother would turn out to be right: Maybe I would get involved and it wouldn't last forever. Maybe it would be a month. Or a year. Was that so terrible? It was like the perfect circle in the second-grade story. Because I couldn't make one, I shut out an entire art form. Was I going to do the same thing with men? Certainly, no one was going to appear at my door vacuum-packed with a lifetime warranty.

But still. What if he betrayed me?

What if he didn't?

By the following week, my ideas list had grown to twenty-five. I knew it was overkill, but I couldn't help myself. I met Peter Garber at the *Manhattan Week* office, which was filled with people my age running around in jeans, holding huge cups of coffee as if they were pulling all-nighters for finals. Everyone seemed to be the tiniest bit scared of him, and he seemed to enjoy that the tiniest bit, too. Observing only a few of his conversations with staff members before we left for lunch, I could see that blood was also spilt here, but the denouement was different than at *Jolie!* At the end of the drama, there was actually something to read.

We sat in the restaurant eating omelets, and he listened carefully to each idea. He nodded a lot. He asked questions. As I was getting up to leave, he asked me for my clips. I half-winced, and handed over a folder that included ten fairy tales. He told me he'd call. I left feeling doubtful and hopeful in equal measure.

That night, I told Mark everything. I started at the beginning of the meeting and the top of the list and went through every detail.

"Great," he repeated throughout the story. "That's great." We spoke about some ideas at length, and he told me about his own experiences working with Peter at other magazines, before *Manhattan Week*. I got lots of details. By the time Peter called back the next day, I felt as if I had known him forever.

He said that though he had initially intended to offer me the job of Arts Editor, my experience at *Jolie!* hadn't sufficiently prepared me for the responsibility of putting out a weekly. Would I accept an associate editor position instead?

I didn't feel disappointed at all. I liked that he told me what he thought, without dressing it up. I told him I would love to come—as long as it didn't mean taking a cut in pay. It didn't. I got a slight raise. Not enough to get rid of my lovely roommate, but better than nothing. I decided I would rather be paid badly in a place where I could learn than stay in a place where all I could do was fight. And lose.

"I also liked your fairy tales," he said, much to my surprise. "I was thinking that we could use them in some way to comment about New York. As an occasional column sort of thing."

"Really?" I couldn't believe it. A high school conception of a suburban mom's pastime had turned into an actual career? Life was too funny. "Sure," I said. "We'll figure it out."

As soon as I hung up, I went straight to Susie's office.

"Can I talk to you?" I asked from the doorway.

She squinted at me from her computer.

"Can't it wait?" she asked impatiently.

"No," I said.

She seemed taken aback. I came in, closed the door behind me, and sat down. The slightest bit of alarm registered on her face, but she folded her arms in front of her and stiffened against the back of her chair.

"*Manhattan Week* has offered me a job, and I've decided to take it."

She stared, her chin jutting out against me.

"I feel it's time for me to be exposed to a world other than women's magazines," I went on. "It's been a great experience, but—"

"Fine." Her tone was flat.

"Of course I'll give you two weeks' notice," I said hurriedly. "Or three, if you need it. I don't want to leave you in the lurch closing next month's issue."

She focused her eyes on mine. They were as dead as her voice. "In my experience," she said, "I have found that giving too much notice is never a good idea. Your heart won't be in it, and neither will ours. What's today? Tuesday? Why don't we say Friday is your last day and leave it at that? That way you can turn your full attention where you want it to be."

I knew perfectly well that she was trying to belittle me and my position by showing me that even with three days' notice she could close the new issue all by herself, and that nothing I could contribute would be of any importance. But all I felt was relief.

I nodded. "You're right," I said. "Thanks for being so understanding."

She looked surprised. All she'd had to say was "thank you" and use me to finish the next issue the right way, and she would have preserved one shred of dignity for each of us. Fuck her.

"I'll speak to payroll and call the writers and let them know they'll be working directly with you," I said. Her face was alarmingly white. "Should I see Miss Belladonna, or will you let her know?"

"I'll speak to her," she said quickly.

"I'm sure you will," I said sharply.

She looked up at me as I stood, but said nothing. Her face had the same hardened expression as when Mark had pulled his piece.

"Thank you, Susie," I said. "I know this launch hasn't been easy, but I appreciate having been part of it."

She nodded, saying nothing.

I turned and left. Back in my office, I started to pack.

Mark was as excited as I was. "This will be so great for you," he said. He praised Peter Garber to the heavens, praised the magazine, praised what a great town New York was and how many story ideas it held. He was coming home the following Friday. And to celebrate my new job, he said, he'd like to take me out to dinner. Had I ever been to the Trustees Dining Room at the Metropolitan Museum of Art?

No, I hadn't.

I'd love it, he assured me. We'd meet at the main entrance and go from there. But, he added, we would speak before then. Many times.

The day I left *Jolie!* was hard. Neither Miss Belladonna nor Susie bothered to say goodbye. But after lunch, the assistants came in to give me a scarf they had pitched in for, and they all gave me their phone numbers, in case something opened up at the new place. I promised I would call.

I actually went to the fashion closet to see if I could find Buffy Parks, maybe give her a big wet kiss to remember me by, but she was in Cabo San Lucas on a shoot. She had dysentery, one of the girls told me with a giggle. Too bad.

Pimm and Coco and Pascal took me for drinks to the King Cole Bar at the St. Regis Hotel. After two martinis Pascal left, kissing the air near both my cheeks. Pimm teared up behind her Coke-bottle glasses but pulled it together—she was off for yet another wedding-dress fitting.

I looked at Coco. "So?" I asked. "Who's the gentleman du jour?"

"Remember the banker from Nell's?" she asked. "He's going back to London for good, so we're meeting tonight for a goodbye drink. Oh, look. That's him now."

I turned and saw a tall, pasty-faced boy in an expensive suit, holding a cigarette between his third and fourth fingers. When I said hi, he barely acknowledged me, and I could see Coco, lips parted, leaning across the table, offering her cleavage by way of greeting. I waved goodbye, and she winked. I knew I would see her again soon. She was going to be my roommate at Pimm's Southampton wedding.

I walked down Fifth Avenue, past *Jolie!*'s building. It was late enough for the front entrance to be closed, so I went to the side, stepping in to see if the night doorman was there. He looked up from his newspaper, and when he saw it was me, he waved. I thought about telling him that this was it, that my first job in New York was over and I wouldn't be coming here anymore. But I liked the idea of him expecting me, wondering where that girl was, the one who always worked late, with the odd assortment of fellows coming and going at the side entrance.

"'Night," he called out. "Have a good weekend now."

My eyes filled. "Thank you," I said, waving back. "You too."

From the moment I walked into *Manhattan Week*, it felt like an adrenaline shot. The pace of a weekly was lightning-fast, and the volume of mail alone required two assistants just to open it. I learned the computer system, went to meetings, made calls. We agreed to start my column in the fall so that I could get my bearings as an editor first.

I was never tired. Some days I thought I might fly out the window. My ideas were good. My contacts were good. I even looked good, I thought one day in the ladies' room. I wasn't so fat after all. I had somehow come to embrace the lesson that Paul had learned at the end, however reluctantly, however incomplete: Be who you are. It seemed so easy, so obvious. Not to mention the fact that I was incredibly good at it. Better, as a matter of fact, than anyone else.

The Friday of my first week was one of those days in May that can be surprisingly, blazingly hot—so much so that the fun goes out of it. The air-conditioning in the office wasn't quite working, and though I thought about going home and showering before dinner, I just didn't have the time. Rather than arrive at the museum sweaty from the subway, though, I splurged and took a cab. Traffic was horrible, as usual, and we crawled up Madison Avenue, missing every light. At least the cab was cool. I worried about being late, but more than that I worried about the copy I was editing. I had a printout on my lap and kept reviewing it. This piece wouldn't run until the following week's issue, but it was my first one, and I wanted it to be great.

I glanced out the window. I had loved the boutiques on Madison since I was a little girl. I used to look in every window and pick out one outfit, then go on to the next. It was something I would still do now, but I turned back to the copy, checking it again.

I looked at my watch: 7:20. Where were we? Seventy-fourth Street. Close, but . . . I looked to my left. Good Lord, it was Bucky and a girl I assumed must be Wendy. He looked totally bizarre. His posture was ramrod straight, as if he'd joined the military. He was expensively dressed—Armani, probably—a dark jacket and a light blue shirt, tailored pants. She was pretty—no Carla Jones, more cheerleader pretty—but the odd thing was that she seemed to have a collapsible neck. She would talk, and her head would bob up and down, keeping time. She went on animatedly, bouncing alongside him, though he seemed to only half listen, the way adults do when a child tells them a dream.

They walked along, and I saw that they were holding hands. Well, not exactly. They had hooked their pinkies together, and I would have bet that the gesture was one of those dating things that happens to people when some detail takes over and becomes a cutesy fetish. *Our* thing.

I watched them go by, swinging their entwined pinkies, and I kept on watching until the cab moved forward. They certainly were adorable, but from where I sat, only one thing seemed clear: He couldn't even give her his whole hand.

Mark was waiting at the entrance to the museum. He looked good—rested and, best of all, excited to see me.

"Hi," I called. As I got closer, I felt a wave of nerves, and then neither of us seemed to know what to do. We bumped cheeks and turned at the same time and started to walk.

"I don't even know where I'm going," I admitted, and he led me through the Egyptians to a back elevator that took us to the Trustees Dining Room. It was pretty in a formal, modern sort of way, and you could see where the sun had just set through the vast expanse of windows.

We ordered cocktails, and toasted my new job and his new divorce, and finally, we both relaxed and talked as effortlessly as we had on the phone. The time just went, and suddenly a man appeared at our table along with the coffee.

"Mr. Lewis, welcome," he said. "When you're finished with

dinner, perhaps you and your guest"—he nodded politely at me—"would like to see our visiting Corot exhibition. The museum, of course, is closed, but if I could escort you, it would be my pleasure."

"Thanks so much, we'd love that," he said, looking over for my assent. I nodded happily, noticing how easily he'd said "we."

After coffee came brandy, and by the time the man reappeared to guide us, I felt as if I were floating. Listening to the sounds of our footsteps echoing through an empty hall, I could hardly believe what had happened the last time I was here. These were not the angry clacks of heels, just three people in no great rush, stopping to look at the beautiful sights. It sounded friendly—homey, almost. A vacuum cleaner buzzed in the background.

"Here you are, sir," the man said, turning to go. "I'll return in a few minutes."

Mark thanked him and stepped close to a painting of a very blue sky with a rounded woman lolling on a hillside, and he turned to me, because I hung back.

"I have to tell you again, I don't know very much about art," I began, and he held out his hand and I reached toward his open palm, broad and warm, and he clasped my hand and drew me closer. He talked about the expression of peace on the woman's face, which I suddenly felt mirrored my own. I could be painted now, I thought, as he reached his arm around me, cradling my shoulders—though I would have to admit I knew nothing about lolling. But as I settled further into the curve of his arm and pondered the sweeping blue of the sky, that didn't bother me much.

I could learn.

A NOTE ABOUT THE AUTHOR

Alex Witchel, a Style reporter for the *New York Times*, is the author of *Girls Only: Sleepovers, Squabbles, Tuna Fish and Other Facts of Family Life*. She lives in New York City with her husband, Frank Rich.